ALSO AVAILABLE FROM TITAN BOOKS

Heat Wave
Naked Heat
Heat Rises
Frozen Heat

Storm Front
A Brewing Storm (eBook)
A Raging Storm (eBook)
A Bloody Storm (eBook)

DEADLY HEAT

RICHARD CASTLE

TITAN BOOKS

NIKKI HEAT: DEADLY HEAT
Print edition ISBN: 9781781167724
E-book edition ISBN: 9781781167717

Published by Titan Books
A division of Titan Publishing Group Ltd.
144 Southwark Street, London SE1 0UP

First edition April 2014

1 3 5 7 9 10 8 6 4 2

This edition published by arrangement with Hyperion.

A CIP catalogue record for this title is available from the British Library.

Printed and bound by CPI Group (UK) Ltd, Croydon, CR0 4YY

To KB:

May the dance never end
and the music never stop.

ONE

NYPD Homicide detective Nikki Heat double-parked her gray Crown Victoria behind the coroner van and strode toward the pizza joint where a body waited. A uniform in short sleeves finger-looped the caution tape for her to duck under, and when she straightened up on the other side, Heat stopped, letting her gaze fall down Broadway. At that moment, twenty blocks south, her boyfriend, Jameson Rook, was taking bows at a Times Square press event to celebrate publication of his big new article. An article so big the publisher had made it the cover story to launch the magazine's Web site. Heat should have been happy. Instead she felt gut-ripped. Because his big article was about her.

She took one step to go inside, but only one. That corpse wasn't going anywhere, and Heat needed a moment to curse herself for helping Rook write it.

A few weeks before, when she gave him her blessing to chronicle her investigation into the murder of her mom, it had seemed like a good idea. Well, maybe not a good idea, just a prudent one. Heat's dramatic capture of the surprise killer after more than a decade became hot news, and Rook put it bluntly: Somebody would write this story. Would she prefer a

Pulitzer Prize–winning journalist or some tabloid hack?

Rook's interviews were intense and took both days of a weekend. With his digital recorder as sentry, Heat started with Thanksgiving eve, 1999. She and her mom were about to bake pies, and Nikki called her from the spice aisle of the supermarket, only to hear her mother get stabbed to death over the phone while she ran home, frantic and helpless. She told Rook about changing her college major from theater to criminal justice so she could become a cop instead of the actress she'd dreamed of becoming. "Murder," she said, "changes everything."

Heat shared with him her frustration in the quest for justice during the decade that followed. And her shock a month ago when a break came and a suitcase that had been stolen from her mother's apartment the night of her murder turned up at one of Nikki's crime scenes—with a woman's body inside it. The path to solve the fresh homicide of the lady in the luggage put Heat on an unexpected journey into her mother's hidden past. The trail led to Paris, where Nikki was stunned to learn that Cynthia Heat had been a spy for the CIA. Instead of the piano tutor she pretended to be, her mom had used music instruction as a cover to gain access to spy on the homes of diplomats and industrialists.

Nikki learned all this at the deathbed of her mother's old CIA controller, Tyler Wynn. But, spies being spies, the old man had only faked his death to throw her off. Nikki discovered this the hard way when her mom's mentor showed up, gun in hand, to relieve her of the secret, incriminating documents Cynthia Heat had died over. Why? Because

Cynthia Heat had discovered that her trusted friend, Tyler Wynn, was a traitor.

During the interview, Nikki confessed she didn't have to imagine her mother's sense of betrayal. She had felt it herself when her college boyfriend, Petar, stepped out of the shadows beside Wynn, holding his own gun on her. And, more deeply, as the old spy slipped away with the pouch of damning evidence and a final instruction to Nikki's ex, to kill her—just as Petar had killed her mother.

At that point, Rook had paused his Olympus recorder to change batteries, but really to allow Nikki to gather herself emotionally. When they resumed, she admitted that, in her heart, she'd always assumed once she captured her mom's murderer, the wound could finally scar over. Instead, everything tore open and bled. The pain didn't lessen, it seared. Yes, she managed to arrest Petar, but the mastermind who called the shots had escaped and gone off the grid. And Petar would be no help tracking him. Not after one of Wynn's other accomplices brazenly poisoned his jail cell dinner.

Heat opened up to Rook with an intimacy she couldn't have imagined a year ago when she got saddled with the celebrity journalist for a research ride-along. Pre-Rook, Nikki had always believed that there were two pairs of natural enemies in this world—cops and robbers, and cops and writers. That belief softened in last summer's heat wave, when they ended up falling in love working their first case. Softened, maybe, but even as lovers, cops and writers would never have it easy. And this relationship constantly tested them.

The first test had come last autumn when the product of

Rook's homicide squad ride-along got published as a national magazine cover story, and Nikki's face stared out at her from newsstands for a month. That attention made her uncomfortable. And seeing her personal experiences turned into prose gave Nikki an unsettling feeling about her role as Rook's muse. Was this life they were living theirs, or just source material?

And now with his new article about to hit the Internet with a splash, what were once mere misgivings about going public had erupted into full-blown anxiety. This time it wasn't about fearing the glare of personal publicity, but her worry that it would harm her active investigation. Because for Detective Heat, this case didn't have loose ends; they were live wires, and Nikki saw publicity as the enemy of justice. And at that moment, a mile away in Times Square, the genie was about to come out of the bottle.

Nikki was glad she'd at least held one big secret back. Something so explosive, she hadn't even told Rook.

"Coming in?" Detective Ochoa jarred her back to the present. He stood holding the glass door of Domingo's Famous open for her. Heat hesitated, then let go of her preoccupation and crossed the threshold.

"Got one for the books here," said Ochoa's partner, Sean Raley. The pair of detectives, nicknamed Roach, a mash-up of their names, led Heat past the empty Formica tables that would have been filled for lunch in a few hours if it hadn't been for the murder. When they got to the kitchen, Raley said, "You ready for a first?" He put his gloved hand on the topmost door of the pizza oven and drew it down to reveal the victim. Or what remained of him.

He—it looked like a he—had been shoved in there on his side, bent to fit, and baked. Nikki looked at Raley then Ochoa then back to the corpse. The oven still gave off a hint of warmth, and the body in it resembled a mummy. He had been clothed when he went in. Remnants of scorched fabric dangled off his arms and legs, and shrouded patches of the torso like a disintegrated quilt.

Raley's look of dark amusement faded and he stepped to her. Ochoa joined him, studying her. "You gonna be sick?"

"No, I'm fine." She busied herself gloving up with a pair of blue disposables, then added, "I just forgot something." Nikki said it dismissively, like it was no big deal. But to her, it was. What she had forgotten was her ritual. The small personal ceremony she went through on arrival at every homicide scene. To pause silently a few seconds before going in, to honor the life of the victim she was about to meet. It was a ritual born of empathy. A rite as common as grace before a meal. And today, for the first time ever—Nikki Heat had forgotten to do it.

The slip bothered her, yet maybe it was inevitable. Lately, working routine homicides had become a distraction that kept her from focusing fully on her bigger case. Of course she couldn't share that with anyone on her squad, but she did complain to Rook how hard it was to try to close a chapter when people kept opening others. He reminded her of the words of John Lennon: "Life is what happens to you while you are busy making other plans."

"My problem," she'd said, "is that death happens."

"Kitchen crew found him, when they opened for lunch prep," began Raley.

Ochoa picked right up. "They thought it was hinky that the oven felt warm. They popped the oven door and found our crispy critter." Roach exchanged self-satisfied grins.

"You do know that just because Rook isn't here, you don't have to guest-host." She held her palms to the oven. It felt warm but not hot. "Did they turn it off?"

"Negative," said Raley. "Cook said it was off when they came in."

"Any idea who our vic is?" she asked, peering inside the oven. The heat damage would make him hard to recognize.

Ochoa flipped to his notes. "We assume the victim to be one Roy Conklin."

The medical examiner, Lauren Parry, rose up from her lab kit. "But that's a guess until we can run dental records and DNA."

"An educated guess," said Ochoa. Heat read the gentle tease of Dr. Parry, his not-so-secret girlfriend. "We did find a wallet." He indicated the stainless steel prep table and the evidence bag on it holding the disfigured leather block and a buckled New York State license.

"And the weird gets weirder," said Raley, taking a Mini Maglite from his vest pocket and focusing it on the corpse. Heat moved closer, and Raley said, "Weird enough?"

Nikki nodded. "Weirdest." Around the victim's neck hung the laminated ID of Roy Conklin, New York City Department of Health and Mental Hygiene.

Ochoa moved beside her. "We already put in a call to

DHMH. Ready for this? The body in that oven is a restaurant health inspector."

"That's definitely a violation." All heads turned toward the familiar voice. And the wisecrack. Jameson Rook strolled in, a vision to Nikki in his perfectly cut navy Boss suit and a purple and white spread-collared shirt—plus the charcoal and purple tie she'd chosen for him. "This joint will have a Grade-B in the window by tonight, you watch."

Heat came up beside him. "Not that I don't appreciate your help, but what happened? Don't tell me you got bored by your big red-carpet event."

"Not at all. I was going to stay for the after-crowd handshakes, but then Raley texted me about this. And thank God he did. Why hang around for another grip-and-grin when you've got a chance to see . . ." He peered in the oven. "Hot damn. An alien from Area 51."

Roach appreciated the gallows humor. Lauren Parry, not so much. "What's that on your shoulder, glitter?" said the ME. "Out, before you contaminate my area."

Rook grinned. "If I had a nickel for every time I've heard that." But he stepped out to the dining room and left his coat on the back of a chair. He returned just as a pair of techs from OCME were removing the body from the oven. Ochoa handed him a pair of blue nitrile gloves to put on.

"Check out this badge," said Raley. Heat got on one knee beside him for a closer look. Conklin's ID badge and its lanyard showed absolutely no signs of scorching or melting.

Rook knelt with them. "This means whoever killed him must have waited for the oven to cool down or come back later and put this around his neck." Nikki turned and gave him a look. "Hey, not fair. That's your wild conjecture face. Don't tell me you're also going to bust my balls for a timely summary of facts."

Ochoa, who was standing at the oven, said, "Detective?" Heat stood and followed the beam of his flashlight. In the back corner of the oven, where it had been blocked from view by the body, sat a folded coat. Just like the badge and lanyard, it showed no signs of scorching. Detective Ochoa used a long-handled pizza paddle to shovel it up. When he slid it forward to them, nobody spoke. They just stared at the coat and what was on top of it: a neat coil of red string and a dead rat.

Detective Feller had completed his interviews with the cook and the busboy by the time Heat, Rook, Raley, and Ochoa emerged from the kitchen. "Their stories square up," he reported. "They served their last pies at midnight, tore down, closed up at one a.m., came back at nine, and found the vic." He flipped through pages of notes. "No unusual activity in the days prior, no sign of burglary or forced entry. They do have a closed-circuit camera system, but it died last week. No beefs with customers or vendors. As for the health inspector, Conklin's name or photo didn't ring a bell with either one. I held back the info about where you found the ID, of course, but when I asked, generally, if they touched or tampered with the body, it was a double no."

Heat said, "Soon as we rustle up some better head shots from family or DHMH, have them take a look. Meanwhile, go ahead and kick them loose."

Determining exact time and cause of death would be tricky, since a baked corpse corrupted cellular structures and body temps. So while Heat left her BFF the medical examiner to take the body to 30th Street for its postmortem, she plotted the immediate moves for her crew. Ochoa would deploy a team of uniformed officers to canvass the neighborhood with cell-capture copies of Conklin's ID photo. Once the unis got launched, Ochoa would go to Conklin's home to notify family and see what could be learned there. Raley would do his usual spot check for area security cameras that might have caught something. Heat put Detective Feller on a trip to the Health Department to get the victim's employment records and to interview his supervisor about his case work and office relationships. As for Rook, he offered to be an extra brain at the squad briefing, and Nikki couldn't resist saying, "You flatter yourself, but sure."

When the two of them stepped out of Domingo's Famous, Rook wagged his head in disdain at the gathering of onlookers behind the yellow tape. "You know, Nikki, I can't get over the looky-loos who hang out for whatever macabre thrill they get out of watching a body bag loaded into a van. More like looky-loozahs."

A voice called out from the crowd. "Jameson? Jameson Rook?" They stopped. "Here, over here!" The waving arm belonged to a big-haired young woman in black leather pants and what could charitably be described as fuck-me heels. She pushed to the front of the rubberneckers and pressed the fullness of her leopard-print vest against the yellow tape. "Could I get a picture with you? . . . Please?"

Sheepish, Rook muttered to Nikki, "It occurs to me that, after my Times Square thing, I may have Tweeted that this is where I was going . . ."

"Make it quick." And as Rook headed over to the woman, Nikki added, "You do know this is why Matt Lauer Purells."

Heat waited in the undercover car while Rook posed with not just the one fan, but each of three additional babes who materialized from the crowd. At least he wasn't signing their breasts this time.

She made a quick e-mail check. "Yesss," she said aloud to the empty car when she saw one from a private investigator she'd been waiting to hear back from. "You about done?" she said as Rook got in the passenger seat.

"The photo was just the beginning. She wanted me to Tweet the picture myself and add *hashtag-ruggedlyhandsome*." He put his head back on the headrest and said, "Apparently, I'm trending as we speak."

Nikki started the car. "Remember Joe Flynn?"

Rook sat upright. "That PI. The one who has the hots for you?—No."

"Well, that PI did me a favor and dug through his archives and found some old surveillance photos of my mom. He wants to have lunch."

"I thought you called a squad meeting in an hour about Krusty the Corpse." And then he added solemnly, "May he rest in peace."

Heat drummed her fingertips on the steering wheel, once again feeling the conflict of the daily homicide grind. She did some quick calculations. "We'll tell him it has to be a quick bite."

"OK," said Rook with a side glance at the crime scene. "But no pizza. Just sayin'."

Since Heat and Rook didn't have time to be trapped in a restaurant for two hours of small talk and dessert-tray recitations, Joe Flynn had arranged for a deli buffet in the conference room of Quantum Recovery, his elite investigation service headquartered atop the exclusive Sole Building. He had brought in a charcuterie platter from Citarella stacked with Parma ham, roast beef, Jarlsberg, Muenster, as well as rustic mustards and herbed mayo. They declined the microbrews poking out of tubs of shaved ice and opted for the Saratoga springwater, which their host poured for them.

"You've come a long way from your roots, Joe," said Rook, who munched a cornichon, standing at the huge window looking out over Midtown Manhattan.

"You mean from staking out adulterers at hot sheet motels for a three-hundred-dollar per diem?" He joined Rook and admired the spring day with him. "I'd say fine art recovery has made life a little easier. Plus I don't feel like I need a shower after I cash the check."

Before Joe Flynn climbed to elite ranks and the express elevators that came with them, Nikki's mom had been the subject of one of his adultery investigations—commissioned by Nikki's dad. Worried about Cynthia Heat's increasingly secretive life, her husband hired Flynn in 1999 because he suspected his wife was having an affair. Flynn never found evidence of infidelity, but he did have stakeout photographs of Nikki's mom which could be useful now in her search for Tyler Wynn.

Just as Nikki sidled up beside them, unable to resist the view of the Empire State Building and, in the distance, between skyscrapers, a sliver of Staten Island, Rook got a cell phone call and excused himself to take it. As soon as the door closed, Joe Flynn said, "Lucky man." Nikki turned to find him staring at her like a beaming hopeful on *Antiques Roadshow* awaiting the appraiser's verdict. Nikki wished her phone would ring, too. Instead she switched topics.

"I appreciate you digging for those photos."

"Oh, right." Flynn produced a thumb drive from his pocket and rolled it on the fingers of one hand, not teasing but not yet giving it to her, either. "I looked for the man and woman whose pics you texted me last week," he said, referring to the images she'd sent of Wynn and his accomplice, Salena Kaye. "Didn't see them in here." And then he grinned at her again, adding, "Your mother was a beautiful woman."

"She was."

"Just like her daughter."

"Thank you," she said as neutrally as possible.

He finally read the signs and handed over the memory key. "May I ask who they are? The pair you're looking for?"

"Sorry, I'd like to, but it's a confidential police matter."

"Can't blame me for asking. Curiosity comes with the job description, right? Can't switch it off."

Oh, did Nikki hear that.

Heat hoped to find more in those photos than something

to spark leads on Tyler Wynn and Salena Kaye. She also sought a clue to solve her big secret.

A few weeks ago, Nikki had stumbled upon a series of strange pencil notations her mother had left embedded in her sheet music. She believed it was a coded message. The dots, lines, and squiggles followed no pattern she recognized. Nikki had Googled Morse code, Egyptian hieroglyphs, the Mayan alphabet, even urban street graffiti, all to no avail. To satisfy her police objectivity, she'd even researched to determine if the symbols were simply shorthand for how to play the music. All she found was another dead end.

She needed help to crack it, but, acutely mindful of its sensitivity—this code could be why Tyler Wynn had her mother killed—Heat knew she had to keep it secret. Absolutely secret. She weighed the notion of telling Rook about it, knowing Mr. Conspiracy would throw his body, soul, and hyperactive imagination into breaking that code. But Nikki decided to hold on to it herself, for now. This wasn't just a secret.

This secret was deadly.

After their meeting at Quantum Recovery, Heat signed her and Rook out at the lobby security desk. She took a step toward the Avenue of the Americas exit but sensed Rook lagging. "Change of plan," he said. "That call? Jeanne Callow, you know, my agent?"

"Gym rat, too much makeup, Jeanne the Machine, that Jeanne Callow?"

He smiled at her snarkiness and continued, "The same.

Anyway, I'm going to hoof it to her office on Fifth so we can plan publicity for the new article."

A familiar claw dug into Nikki's diaphragm, but she smiled and said, "No problem."

"Catch up with you at your place tonight?"

"Sure. We can go over these pictures?"

"Um, yuh. We can do that."

Heat drove back to the precinct alone, reaffirming her instinct to withhold the code from Rook.

Nikki shot a tense look from her desk across the bull pen and once again felt torn between her big case and another homicide. The team of detectives she'd called in on the Conklin murder sat cooling their heels because she was late for her own meeting. Desperately trying to get a lead on Tyler Wynn, Heat had thought she could squeeze in this call before the squad briefing but found herself stalled by a gatekeeper. "This is my fourth attempt to reach Mr. Kuzbari," she said, trying not to let her anger seep through. "Is he aware this is an official inquiry from the New York Police Department?"

Fariq Kuzbari, security attaché to the Syrian Mission to the UN, had been one of her mom's piano tutoring clients. Heat had tried to interview him weeks ago, but he and his armed goons rebuffed her. She wasn't about to give up. A man the likes of Fariq Kuzbari could well shed some light on a spook colleague the likes of Tyler Wynn.

"Mr. Kuzbari is out of the country for an indefinite

period. Would you like to leave another message?"

What Nikki would have liked to do was throttle her desktop with the phone and shout something very undiplomatic. She counted a silent three and said, "Yes, please."

Heat hung up and caught a few antsy glances from her squad. On her way to the front of the room, she started wording her apology for keeping them waiting, but by the time she reached the whiteboard and turned to face them, the homicide squad leader had decided her call and the delay were police business. Screw John Lennon, she thought. Then Detective Heat dove right in.

"OK, so we're looking at Roy Conklin, male, age forty-two . . ." Heat began, running down the basics from the crime scene. After placing on the board blowups of the victim's ID photo and a color head shot cropped from the Health Department Web site, she continued. "Now, there are a few wrinkles in this death, to say the least. Beginning with the condition and placement of the body. A pizza oven is not involved in your everyday homicide."

Detective Rhymer raised a hand. "Do we know yet whether he was killed in the oven, or if it was used just to dispose of the body?"

"Good question," said Heat. "OCME is still testing to determine both cause and time of death."

Detective Ochoa said, "We did get word from the ME that traces of chloroform were found on the front of the victim's jacket." Heat whipped her head his direction. She hadn't known that. Her mind shot back to a missed call from Lauren Parry while she was in the thick of it with the Syrian

Mission. The medical examiner's boyfriend gave Nikki a small nod. Ochoa had her back.

"So . . ." Nikki picked up her rundown quickly, "it's possible Mr. Conklin was either chemically subdued at the crime scene, or else beforehand, and transported. Until we know COD, we won't know if he went in the oven alive or dead. If he was alive, we can only pray he was totally unconscious from the chloroform." The room stilled as the cops contemplated Roy Conklin's last moments.

She resumed. "The other wrinkles are the unburned items on and near the body." She recited each as she posted Forensic photos on the board: "The lanyard and ID around his neck; his folded jacket; and the coil of red string with the dead—unbaked—rat beside it. At the very least, this bizarre MO suggests kinkiness, revenge, or a message killing. Let's not forget, he was a restaurant health inspector, not only killed in a restaurant—potentially by one of its pieces of equipment. The placement of the rat plus the preservation of his DHMH badge mean something. Exactly what, we need to find out."

Ochoa reported that the unis had come up zero on neighborhood eyewits. And his visit to Conklin's apartment revealed no signs of struggle, burglary, or anything. The building super said Conklin's wife was away on a business trip, and the super gave him a cell number. Raley had found a half dozen surveillance cams in the area and was poised to begin his video surfing. Feller, back from the Department of Health and Mental Hygiene, had spoken to Conklin's supervisor, who characterized him as a model employee, using terms like "motivated" and "dedicated" and calling him "one of those rare types who lived the job and never went off the clock."

"Nonetheless, we have to see what else he was about," said Heat. She assigned Rhymer to run his bank records to look for irregularities, with an eye toward bribes, big vacations, or living beyond his means. She put Feller on digging deeper with his coworkers and to see if there were any complaints about him from the places he inspected. "Rales, along with your surveillance screening, you and Miguel pair up and hit the restaurants and bars on Conklin's roster. Listen to what they say about habits, vices, enemies—you know the drill. I'll put in a call to the wife and try to meet her in the morning."

Afterward, at her desk, Nikki studied the slip of paper with the name Olivia Conklin on it and the 917 number under it. She put her hand on the phone, but before she lifted it off the cradle, she paused. Just ten seconds. To honor the body. Ten seconds, that's all.

When she came into her apartment, she found Rook twisting the wire cage off the bottle of Louis Roederer that *First Press* had sent him to commemorate his role in launching their Web site. "The amazing day I've had, Nik, what I really want to do, is saber this thing off. I've always wanted to try that. You wouldn't, by chance, have a saber, would you?"

As he filled their flutes, Nikki said, "You never told me about your ceremony. I only saw the glitter on your shoulder."

"I confess it was fun. Of course, I pretended it was a pain

in the ass, but truly? It was so cool. We were all behind this rope line on the sidewalk right there on Broadway, across from *GMA*. Me, the mayor, Green Day, the magazine suits . . ."

"Wait a minute. Green Day was there?"

"Well, not all of them. Only Billie Joe Armstrong. *American Idiot* opens this week at the St. James, and he had his PR haftas to hafta do, also. Anyway, the moment comes, the editor in chief, Elisabeth Dyssegaard, gives me my intro. The cameras are flashing and/or rolling, and I press this huge red button."

"Like for dropping the New Year's Eve ball?"

"Mm . . . More like the That Was Easy button. But the whole deal was about me making the 'first press' of the button that posted the first article on *FirstPress.com*."

"Clever."

He raised his glass. "Here's to 'Bringing Heat.' " The title of the article brought her a sudden gut twist. But she smiled, rang her glass on his, and sipped the Cristal.

While they ate takeout from SushiSamba, Rook went on about the huge number of hits his article had already gotten on the Web site. He asked her about the pizza murder, and Nikki gave him the bullet points but quickly moved off that topic to vent her frustration at trying to reach Fariq Kuzbari.

"Wanna bet that he actually is out of the country?" Rook said. "My correspondent pals in Egypt and Tunisia tell me things are restless. Kuzbari's probably been called back to Syria because a security pit bull like him has a big to-do list. So many tortures, so little time."

She put down her chopsticks and napkinned her mouth.

"Forget Kuzbari. That still leaves two other persons of interest my mother spied on that I haven't been able to follow up with. One has been out of state competing with his show dogs and the other has stonewalled me through his attorney. God, talk about pit bulls."

"Want to hear a win-win idea? Send that lawyer off to trade places with Kuzbari. While she kicks ass in Syria, you'll have two of your POIs available."

"Glad you think this is funny, Rook." Heat shoved her plate away. "I am merely trying to catch the man who ordered my mother's execution, OK?" He dropped his grin and began to speak, but she rolled over him. "And clearly, since Tyler Wynn also tried to have me killed in that subway tunnel, that old fucker is either still hiding something damaging from the past, or something bad is going on right now. So if you want to treat this like it's all some sort of fodder to amuse you after I've opened my life for your precious article, keep it to yourself."

She left him looking pale at the dining room table and hoped the slam of her bedroom door gave him a coronary. When he came to her ten minutes later, he didn't switch on the light and she didn't bring her face from her pillow. He sat beside her on the bed and spoke softly in the darkness. "Nikki, if I believed for one second that Tyler Wynn was a threat to you, I would drop everything and move heaven and earth to protect you. And find him. But the fact is, Tyler Wynn got everything he wanted in that subway Ghost Station when he got his hands on that pouch you found. Trust me, Wynn's big concern is to disappear and become a ghost himself. Surfacing to do you harm would only expose him to risk. Besides, DHS, the FBI, Interpol, they're are all on this. Let them carry the weight, they're the experts. But I apologize for shooting my mouth off. I don't think this is a joke at all, and I never, ever want to hurt you."

A silent moment passed. She sat up, and in the dim light spilling from the living room, she could see a glistening under one eye. Nikki gently thumbed his tear away and held him. They embraced each other long enough that time evaporated.

At last, when the silence had done its healing, he spoke. "You said fucker. You did. You called Tyler Wynn an old fucker."

"I was upset."

"You never swear. Well, hardly ever."

"I know. Except when we . . ." She let it trail off and felt the heat come to her face. Then the speed of his pulse rose and thrummed against her ear where it rested against the soft of his neck. They turned to face each other without a sign, just the knowing, and kissed. It was a tender one, at first. He tasted her vulnerability, and she his gentle care. But soon, as they shared breath and space, passion filled her. She pushed hard against him. Rook arched toward her, and she clasped both hands on his backside and pulled him closer. Then she traced her fingertips to his lap and felt her palm fill with him. His hand found her and she moaned, then fell back under his body to let his weight find all of her there for him.

Later, after they'd dozed in each other's arms, he left the room, giving her a choice view of his magnificent ass. He returned with two flutes of Cristal, which they sat up and sipped. The bubbles were still tight and the wine rolled clean on her tongue.

They nestled against each other, and Rook said, “I’ve been thinking what hell all this has been for you for ten years.”

“Ten-plus,” she said.

“Know what I can’t wait for? I’m longing for the day when this whole Tyler Wynn case is closed and I can take you away someplace where just the two of us can sit and veg. You know, sleep, make love, sleep, make love . . . Get my theme?”

“It’s a good theme, Rook.”

“The best. Only to be interrupted by kicking back on tropical sand with a rum drink in one hand and a nice Janet Evanovich in the other.”

“Let’s get back to the make love part.”

“Oh, count on that.”

“I me an right now,” she said. And placed their champagne glasses on the nightstand.

Distant thunder awoke Nikki. She made a curtain check and saw by the city lights that the streets and rooftops in Gramercy Park were dry. The low cloud ceiling pinked up with a flash, probably from a bolt way out east over the Island.

On the couch, cross-legged in her robe, with her laptop cradled on her thighs, Nikki clicked on *FirstPress.com*, and her breath caught when she saw her own face staring back at her under the title:

BRINGING HEAT.

The shot was a candid, taken by a photojournalist when she emerged from the precinct after her ordeal in the subway the night she arrested Petar. Her face showed all the fatigue and hardness and gravity she'd borne. Heat never loved pictures of herself, but this was, at least, easier to look at than the posed magazine cover shot they had forced her to take for Rook's first article.

She scanned the piece, not to read it—she had already done that days before—but to absorb the fact of its reality. Some genies come from rubbing lamps, others from uncorking complimentary Cristal. This was out there now, and she only hoped it wouldn't kill her case.

Nikki Heat braced herself for the next round of notoriety. And the mild irritation that Rook had published some little bits of her investigative jargon, like "looking for the *odd sock*" and visiting a crime scene "with *beginner's eyes*." If that was the worst that came from it, she could deal.

The next morning, nursing a brain that had spun its wheels all night, Nikki stopped at her neighborhood Starbucks on her walk to the subway. She never used to bother with movie ticket–priced drinks. Blame Rook. He'd gotten her in the habit. To the point that when he donated an espresso machine to the squad room, she taught herself how to pull a perfect twenty-five-second shot.

When she ordered her usual, she got that unexplainable pleasure from hearing "Grande skim latte, two pumps, sugar-free vanilla for Nikki" called out and then echoed back over the jet *whoosh* of the milk steamer. It's the tiny rituals that let you know God's in his heaven and all is right with the world.

She made a scan of the room and caught a twentysomething guy in a sincere suit staring at her. His gaze darted back to his iPad then back to her. Then he smiled and hoisted his macchiato in a toast. And so it begins, she thought.

The barista called out, "Grande skim latte for Nikki," but when she moved down the counter to get it, Sincere Suit blocked her, holding up his iPad with her face filling it. "Detective Heat, you are awesome." He smiled and his cheeks dimpled.

"Ah, well, thank you." She took a half step, but the beaming fanboy backed up, staying with her.

"I can't believe it's you. I read this article twice last night . . . Holy shit, would you sign my cup?" Inexperienced at this, she agreed, just to move it along. He held out a ballpoint he probably got for his graduation, but before she could take it, a wooden chair tipped over, followed by a chorus of gasps.

Across the room, near the drink pickup, a homeless man writhed and bucked on the floor, his legs kicking wildly against the toppled chair. Stunned customers fled their tables and backed away. "Call 911," Heat said to the barista and raced to the man's side. Just as she knelt, he stopped convulsing and someone behind her screamed. Blood had begun to flow from his mouth and nose. It mixed with the vomit and spilled coffee pooling on the floor beside him. His eyes stilled in a death stare, and a telltale stench arose as his bowels released. Heat pressed his neck and got no pulse. When she withdrew her fingers, his head rolled to the side, and Nikki saw something she had seen only once before in her life, the night Petar had been poisoned in the holding cell.

The dead man's tongue lolled out of his mouth, and it was black.

She looked at the spilled drink on the floor beside him. A grande cup with "Nikki" grease-penciled on the side. She stood to study the crowd. That's when she saw a familiar face on the way out the door.

Salena Kaye made eye contact with Heat and bolted.

TWO

Nikki dashed to the exit, shouting, "Police officer, everyone outside." Few patrons seemed eager to get closer to the corpse, but Heat worried about the poison and wanted to preserve the crime scene for clues. She yanked open the door and called to the barista holding the phone, "Tell 911, officer in pursuit of homicide suspect."

Heat flattened against the wall of the vestibule then goosenecked a peek up the sidewalk to make sure she didn't hustle out into an ambush. There. A flash of Salena Kaye, weaving away through pedestrians. She took off after her.

Kaye never looked back, just kept sprinting with purpose. And speed. Nikki made a quick scope of 23rd, hoping for a blue-and-white. In that split second, she collided with two teenagers backing out of a bodega, laughing at their Twizzler fangs. They all kept their footing, but when Heat cleared the boys, she spotted Salena popping the back door of a taxi.

The cab was too far away to read its plate or medallion number. Heat memorized its missing-a-chunk bumper and the gentlemen's club ad on the roof, hoping to find it again in the sea of rush hour taxis about to swallow it.

She stepped out into the middle of the street, holding her shield out to drivers and signaling them to stop. An off-duty cab blasted its horn and accelerated off. A green Camry screeched to a stop just past her. Nikki rushed up and opened the driver's door. The startled old man looked at her from behind the thick glasses of another decade. "Police emergency. I need your car. Now, please."

Without a word, the slack-jawed senior climbed out. Heat thanked him, got in, saw the tiny old woman looking at her from the passenger seat, and floored it.

"Hold on," said Nikki, taking a sharp left onto First. She'd briefly spotted the XXX from the strip club's rooftop ad and scanned the avenue of cabs ahead of her to find it again. Her passenger said nothing, just clawed the dash with arthritically distorted hands while her seat belt clunked into lock mode. Up ahead, partially blocked from view by an ambulette, Heat picked out the taxi's scarred bumper and then Salena Kaye's face peering out the back window.

Nikki punched it through the red light at 24th, offering calm reassurance. "You don't have to worry, I've done this before." The elderly woman just stared at her, saucer-eyed. But she nodded. The old gal was game. "You have a cell phone?"

"It's a Jitterbug," she said, and held up her bright red phone. "Shall I call 911?"

"Yes, please." Heat tried to sound casual even as she lurched the wheel and mashed the brake. A gnarled forefinger tapped the large, senior-friendly keypad. "Say 'Officer needs assistance.' " While Heat threaded through the uptown rush, keeping pace with the cab, her passenger repeated Nikki's parceled-out messages to the emergency operator, asking her to radio for patrol cars to get ahead of them so they could wedge the suspect in a vise. "You did great." As the woman snapped her Jitterbug closed, Heat threw a protective arm out across her. "Hang on, hang on."

Just beyond Bellevue Hospital, Salena Kaye bailed from her taxi and ran into the ambulance driveway. Heat checked her mirrors, pulled a hard right to the curb, and stopped. "You OK?"

The old lady nodded. "Hot dog."

Detective Heat flew out of the car, sprinting after her suspect.

Nikki eyeballed the row of FDNY ambulances parked at the trauma entrance, looking inside and between them all as she ran, but she couldn't spot Kaye. She jogged deeper into the passageway, slowing to check behind some laundry bins. Then she caught it. A figure going over the wall at the dead end of the lot.

Kaye had taken one of the spine boards stacked beside the ambulances to cover the razor wire. Heat used it, too, pausing at the top to get bearings on the suspect before her drop to the sidewalk. She landed with knees bent to absorb the impact, and tore off up the service road that ran between NYU Medical Center and the FDR.

Ahead stretched a straight line of sidewalk. And a runaway killer.

Salena Kaye had skills. She ran in a random zigzag pattern that made it futile for Heat to shoot from that distance. But her dekes and dodges also slowed her forward progress. Nikki kicked up the sprint until her lungs were seared.

By 30th Street, just past the big white tent housing

remains from the 9/11 attack, Heat knew she had her. Close enough to risk a shot, she drew. "Salena Kaye, freeze or I'll shoot." The suspect stopped, raised both hands, and turned to face her. But then a pair of orderlies from the medical examiner's office stepped out of the rear courtyard for a smoke break. "Get back!" Heat shouted. The man and woman froze, blocking her shot. Kaye sprinted off through traffic, into a parking garage across the street.

Gun out and pointed up at the car park's ceiling of green steel girders, Nikki Heat tiptoed through the shadows, scanning every square inch, listening intently over the thrum of FDR traffic above for any sound that would give away Salena's hiding place. The detective squatted to scout under the cars, with nothing to show for it but a sooty palm. Then she rose up and stood stock still. Just to listen.

She never heard the blow coming. Salena Kaye pounced on top of her, dropping from the steel I-beams of the ceiling, taking her by surprise.

Nikki knew better than to stay down in hand-to-hand combat. She pushed Kaye off and sprang to her feet, bringing her Sig Sauer around toward the woman still on the concrete. But Salena clearly had close-fighting experience. Her right leg scissored up in a blink, and the instep of her foot whacked Nikki's wrist. The impact, square on a nerve, deadened feeling in her hand, and the pistol clattered across the deck and took a bounce off a car tire before it spun to a stop.

Kaye kipped up, quick as a gymnast, and came at Heat with a rapid-fire pair of wrist blows to each side of her head, *boom-boom*. Nikki's vision fogged and her knees jellied. She fought the blackout and recovered to find Salena going for her gun. Heat side-kicked her ribs, and the woman dropped. But then she caught Nikki off guard again with a jujitsu leg lock—a submission hold Heat had practiced herself—but now she was the victim of immobilizing pain as Kaye forced her knee to hyperextend. Unable to move, unable to free herself, she saw the dark form of her Sig Sauer on the cement and reached for it. Kaye pulled her back toward her, but in so doing, she released Nikki's leg just enough for her to wiggle out of the lock. Heat threw herself forward on top of Salena, raining blows to her collarbone and neck. Kaye reacted by kicking both knees upward, somersaulting Heat right over her. Nikki landed hard on her back and lost her breath.

"Hey, what's going on?" shouted the security guard coming out of the kiosk. In the spilt second Salena paused to gauge the threat, Heat rolled for her gun. She scrambled wildly for it, snatching it barrel-first. When she came up in ready-fire, Salena Kaye was long gone.

Heat pursued, hobbling on her sore knee. She jogged through the pain and caught sight of Salena making a right turn toward the river up at 34th Street.

And then Nikki heard the helicopter.

When she reached the intersection, Heat knew it would be close. A hundred yards away, a royal blue Sikorsky S-76 warmed up on the commuter helipad. A side door stood open, and the pilot, in a white short-sleeved shirt with epaulettes, lay on the asphalt beneath Salena Kaye, with both hands to his face and blood streaming through his fingers.

For the second time that morning, Detective Heat drew

her service piece and called a freeze. Kaye probably couldn't hear her over the copter's engine, but she saw Nikki. With a lingering look and a slow turn that spoke of arrogance, she climbed inside the S-76 and closed the door. Seconds later, as Heat reached the tarmac, the chopper lifted up about two feet and then rotated on an axis, its rear rotor spinning within a yard of Nikki, who plunged to the asphalt. Salena Kaye rotated again, brazenly presenting the helicopter's side to Heat long enough to chuck her the finger. Then the chopper slowly drifted out over the East River, churning up a circle of spray.

Heat got on one knee and braced her elbow on the other, taking aim with her Sig Sauer. She figured if she emptied the entire clip into the engine, she could, maybe, bring it down in the drink. She envisioned the shot, and then hesitated.

It occurred to her that there could be an innocent passenger aboard.

Nikki holstered and called for NYPD air support as she watched the Sikorsky become a dot against the morning sun over Brooklyn.

Jameson Rook hurried into the Homicide Squad Room at the Twentieth, strode up to Heat, and locked her in a hug. "My God, are you OK?"

Nikki gave the bull pen a sheepish scan and modeled a quieter voice for him. "I'm fine." They unfolded from their embrace, and he revealed the Starbucks cup in his hand. "Brought you a fresh latte."

"Thanks, I'll wait."

"I'll taste test it for you." He took a sip, made a ceremony of swirling it in his mouth, and swallowed, following the whole thing up with a lip smack and a satisfied "Ah." He held it out and said, "See, it's just fi—" Suddenly his eyes bugged and he made a choking gasp and brought his free hand up to his throat. She stared blankly. He miraculously recovered. "Too soon?"

"Too late." Nikki gestured to the squad room, where a grande cup labeled "Nikki" sat atop every desk. "These idiots beat you to it."

"Half hour ago, homes," said Ochoa as he approached. "Shoulda seen Rhymer after his sip. Opie hit the deck bucking and snorting." He smiled. "That frothing was inspired."

Rook said, "What is it about cop humor? So dark. So inappropriate. So awesome." He had learned from day one of his ride-along with Heat that cops responded differently to sadness and stress than most folks. They hid their emotions in opposites. All this joking, acting out false poisonings, was more than grabass or gallows humor; it carried a message of affection that said, I'm worried you almost got killed. Or, I care. Rook figured it was in the same realm as why the Three Stooges never hugged.

Ochoa wagged his notebook, signaling business. "Just hung up with a detective from the Seventieth over in Flatbush. She's in the ball field where your chopper set down in South Prospect Park. Good thing you held fire. There was a passenger aboard. Some fashion CEO coming in from the Hamptons. He never got a chance to unbuckle his seat belt when they touched down and got skyjacked."

"Technically, if they were on the ground, wouldn't that be 'hijacked'?" asked Rook. He felt their glares. "Please. Proceed."

"The fashionista says Kaye speed-dialed a call while they were still over the river." Detective Ochoa knew better than to drag out suspense and flipped a page to the witness's quote. "She said, 'Dragon, it's me,' then something he couldn't make out that sounded like 'busted play.' Kaye never said anything else, just listened, then hung up. Five minutes later she was booking east across the empty Parade Grounds while he sat there with the rotors still spinning."

Ochoa peeled off to his desk, and Rook said, "I have to shake my head about Salena Kaye. To think of all the time that woman spent in my apartment giving me physical therapy. I have to say—helluva massage." He paused, cheesily relishing something private, then grew serious. "Of course it kinda spoils the mojo, knowing she was really only there to plant listening devices for Tyler Wynn."

Just the sound of his name sent a twinge through Heat. Not just because it reminded her of the betrayal by the man behind her mother's death. The CIA traitor still had some reason to want Nikki dead, and he'd sent his lethal accomplice Salena Kaye to poison her latte. If Nikki could keep herself from getting killed, she might even find out why.

That sunny thought filled her head as she gathered her squad around the Murder Board. "Don't bother sitting," Heat said as she block printed "DRAGON" in all red caps across the top of the display. "We have an apparent code name for Salena Kaye's controller."

"Isn't that Tyler Wynn?" asked Rook.

"We assume, yet never assume. You know that by now." Nikki then turned her attention to Detective Hinesburg. She figured a straightforward task would be Sharon-proof, so she assigned her to run Dragon and any variations through the database at the Real Time Crime Center downtown. "When you're done with that, see if it lights up anything at Homeland, Interpol, or DGSE in Paris." She put Detective Rhymer on checking the cellular carriers to see if they could slurp a number off any towers near the river at the time of Salena Kaye's phone call. Heat bet Kaye had used a burner cell, but she had to be thorough.

Rhymer, as good-natured as his Virginia hometown, smiled and nodded. "Good as done," said Opie.

Next she posted a Google Map enlargement of the Brooklyn neighborhood where the Sikorsky landed. "It's not likely the suspect had time to arrange a pickup. And good luck hailing a cab in an outer borough, right? But look here." Heat pointed to the map. "The Church Avenue subway station is in the direction of her escape. Raley, get on the blower to the MTA. Start pulling security cam video from Church Ave to see if she got on a train and, if so, which direction. Then check pictures from stops along the line to see where she got off."

When she turned from the map, Heat caught Ochoa eye-rolling to his partner. "Problem, gentlemen?"

Ochoa said, "I know, like, Rales is your King of All Surveillance Media, and all that. But we're getting spread a little thin. We still have to get back in the field to brace more of the restaurant owners on Conklin's roster."

"You'll have to juggle both," said Heat. "Like we all do." She didn't need to take it further. Nikki could see the impact on all their faces. Every detective in that room knew their squad leader not only juggled these two cases; she did it while someone was actively out to kill her. She adjourned, continuing to ponder the why of that. Heat didn't have the answer yet, but the attempt on her life that morning told her one thing. Something new was up with whatever conspiracy had led to her mom's murder ten years ago. Otherwise, they wouldn't be working this hard to kill her now.

On the drive with Rook to City Island to interview Roy Conklin's widow, Nikki found her eyes on the mirrors a lot more than usual. When you know a professional wants you in the crosshairs, a little extra vigilance may get you a chance to see the next day.

Heat was at risk, and nobody would have thought less of her if she bunkered up. Captain Irons was so worried about her safety, he'd even offered her administrative leave or vacation time, if she wanted it. Nikki had stomped out that idea on the spot. The cop in her would never hide in the face of personal danger. That was the gig. But she did feel a healthy nerve jangle. Who wouldn't? So Heat did what Heat did best: She compartmentalized. Experience had taught her that the only way to move forward was to cage the beast—put her fear in a box. Because what was the alternative? To close herself inside her apartment? Run and hide?

Not this detective. This detective would bring the fight to them. And check her mirrors.

The phone rang as they crossed the Pelham Bay Bridge,

where the Hutchinson River separated the urban Bronx from the expansive green woods surrounding Turtle Cove. Nikki fished her Jawbone earpiece from the side door pocket and got an earful from her friend Lauren Parry. "Do I need to remind you that I will kill you if you get yourself killed?"

Heat chuckled. "No, you make that pretty clear. Every time."

"See?" Lauren kidded, but sisterly worry came through. "That's why you're still walking God's earth. Because I will come after you."

Admonishment completed, the medical examiner filled in Heat on Roy Conklin's postmortem. "Hard to call it good news," said Lauren, "but Mr. Conklin was deceased before he went into the oven."

Nikki pictured the body. Envisioned the high-temp bake. "So he didn't suffer?"

"Doubtful. Cause of death was a .22 delivered to the base of the skull." Heat answered Rook's inquiring face by miming a finger pistol while the ME added, "Condition of the body and the small caliber hid the GSW from me on-scene. I found the slug when I opened him up. Ballistics has it now."

"What about my poisoning vic from Starbucks?"

"He's next up."

"Be sure to run a cross-check versus whatever killed Petar," said Nikki, mindful of Salena Kaye's earlier poisoning victim.

"Gee, ya think?" said Lauren. "Leave the autopsies to me. You concentrate on staying alive."

Heat and Rook patiently waited out another round of Olivia Conklin's sobs in the living room of the airy, seashore-themed two-bedroom that would never feel the same to her. The apartment, in a complex of neat gray clapboards with bright white trim, sat waterside next to City Island's sailing school in the Bronx. In the distance beyond the balcony, Long Island shimmered under a spring sun. The view back at them from Great Neck might have been Jay Gatsby's when he contemplated the green light shining across the water. But symbols of brightness, beauty, and optimism had no place in that room. It should have been raining.

For Olivia Conklin, still wearing the crumpled business suit after her night flight home from a software training seminar in Orlando, the only solace was that her husband had been shot. When that's the good news, it's all downhill.

Even though Heat despised this part of the job, it was the part she was best at. She connected, having once been in a similar chair filling Kleenex herself. So she navigated the interview gently, yet alert for signs of guilt, lies, and inconsistencies. Unfortunately spouses proved worthy suspects. With delicacy, she probed the marriage, money, vices, mental health, and hints of infidelity.

"Roy only had one mistress," she said. "His job. He was so dedicated. I know some people hear civil servant and think laziness. Not my Roy. He never left his work at the office. He took public health personally. He called them *his* restaurants and never wanted a sickness on his watch."

All this only confirmed the research Heat's team had done so far. Roy Conklin's finances were in line with his pay grade. Roach's restaurant checks revealed a man consistently called tough but fair. Neither his wife nor his colleagues knew him to have any enemies, recent erratic behavior, or new people in his life.

"It just makes no sense," said Olivia Conklin. Then the new widow wailed out the single, heart-crushed word Nikki heard from all grievers after the sudden theft of a life. That word was the beacon that guided Detective Heat in her work: "Why?"

As Heat and Rook walked back to her car, past the tidy row of Sunfish trailered in the sailing school parking lot, Nikki's gaze roamed out to the glistening open water. She imagined the smart pop of Dacron as wind filled her sail and she tacked out into Long Island Sound. Then she pictured Roy Conklin standing right there his last living day and wondered if he'd savored that view or if his heart had felt too heavy with fear or guilt at some horrible secret he kept from his wife—a secret that got him killed and left her asking why. Or, Nikki speculated, did poor Roy never see it coming, either? Then her phone rang and yanked Heat into her other case. Sailing would have to wait. Back to juggling.

The call came from the police in Hastings-on-Hudson, a quaint village about a half hour upriver from New York City. Hastings only employed two detectives in its small department, and Heat maintained regular contact with them, checking for sightings of one of the town's residents she needed to talk to.

Vaja Nikoladze was just one of numerous people Heat

had put feelers out to, all seen as persons of interest because her mother tutored piano in their households prior to her murder. Nikoladze, an internationally renowned biochemist who had defected from the former Soviet Republic of Georgia, had been eliminated as a suspect in her mother's case. But since Tyler Wynn frequently booked her mom's piano jobs as CIA spy dates, Heat wanted to know if the Georgian expat had had any recent contact with the fugitive.

But just like the elusive Syrian UN attaché and the other prominent clients Heat had reached out to, Nikoladze had been unresponsive, leaving Nikki frustrated, waiting weeks for a chance at contact that could bring a break in that case.

She gave Nikoladze the benefit of the doubt. He had been friendly and cooperative when Heat and Rook first visited him three weeks before. But since that time Vaja had been away showing his prized Georgian shepherds at various out-of-state competitions. Now the Hastings detective was calling to alert Nikki that her person of interest had just been spotted back in town. Wrenched but resolute not to let it drop, Heat juggled the Conklin ball up in the air and headed north. As she pulled onto the Saw Mill Parkway, a flicker of anticipation filled her. She knew better than to get ahead of herself, but Nikki dared to hope she might finally be moving forward after almost a month of relentless disappointment.

Forty minutes later, steam cleaning rubber floor mats outside the kennel on his back pasture, Vaja Nikoladze looked up at the undercover police car pulling off the two-lane that ran between his neighborhood's horse pastures and woodlots. Even from a distance, the small man looked surprised when he heard them crunch the pea gravel of his car park. As they made their way across the vast lawn, deep-throated barks echoed inside the long outbuilding before Nikki even spoke. "Afternoon."

Nikoladze didn't reply, but instead pulled a push broom from a bucket of soapy water and power steamed the foam out of the short bristles. The two of them waited, not even trying to engage over the noisy jet spray of the pressurized nozzle. When he had finished, he cut the steam, leaned the broom against the wall, and draped the thick black rubber mats over the decorative railing to drip dry in the sun. Unlike their cordial visit weeks prior, Vaja gave every sign now that he wanted nothing to do with Detective Heat or her ride-along journalist.

"I have a telephone, you know." After more than twenty years in the US, his Georgian accent remained thick and still sounded Russian to Heat's ears.

"We were kind of in the neighborhood," said Rook, earning a glower in return.

"You have come to get more material on me for your next article, Jameson? Maybe not everyone in United States is eager to be so well known, you think of that?" When Rook had accompanied Nikki last time, he and Vaja got along quite well. Nikoladze had offered refreshments, swapped stories, even given an obedience demonstration of his top show dog. Rook's subsequent write-up of the biochemist in his *FirstPress* article had been minimal—a couple of lines at the most—mere connective tissue in the story of Nikki's quest to find a killer. Clearly, Vaja took exception to the limelight.

Heat didn't care. She pushed right back. "We're here to follow up on my official police investigation, Mr. Nikoladze. And the reason I didn't call first is that you have been uncommunicative. I have left you too many unreturned messages and e-mails. So ding dong, comrade."

Rook circled off to sightsee the Palisades, visible above the tree line. Vaja set aside his chores and crossed his arms. "I have some pictures I want you to look at," said Heat.

"Yes, so your unending messages have said. I told you last time, I don't know this Tyler Wynn."

As she swiped each image on her smart phone, Nikki said, "Indulge me. I want you to see Tyler Wynn, and also this woman, Salena Kaye, and this man here, Petar Matic."

He barely looked at them. "I cannot help you."

"Does that mean you don't recognize them or you can't help?"

"Both." He stared at her with resolve mixed with petulance. "I must inform you that I have been told not to speak to you, or risk deportation."

Rook circled back around from his sightseeing and made eye contact with Nikki. Then her brow lowered and she took a step closer to Vaja. "Exactly who told you this, Mr. Nikoladze?"

When she heard the name, Nikki fumed.

"Detective Heat, NYPD." She flashed tin and added, "Special Agent Callan is expecting us." The reception officer at the Department of Homeland Security's New York field office cleared his throat in an exaggerated way that pulled Rook's attention from the ceiling. He'd been counting cameras since they stepped from Varick Street into the lobby of the huge government building.

"Oh, sorry. Jameson Rook, model citizen." He handed over his driver's license and whispered to Nikki, "More cameras than a Best Buy at Christmas. Five bucks says Jack Bauer already knows we're here."

"Elevator on your right," said the receptionist, handing them each photo-capture passes to wear that read "Floor 6." But when they got on the elevator and pushed six, the doors closed, the lights in the car dimmed, and it descended.

After a brief moment of startled disorientation, Rook said, "Black elevator," and began punching the keypad, which did absolutely nothing to stop their downward movement. He gave up and said, "Sweet."

The doors parted in a high-tech subbasement command center. Dozens of plainclothes personnel and military from all branches worked computers and stared at giant LED wall screens. The JumboTrons displayed scores of live security cams and lighted grids, one of which resembled a connect-the-dots of the US Northeast. A waiting pair of agents attired in complementary Joseph A. Banks escorted them along a back wall to a situation room where DHS special agent in charge Bart Callan came around from the head of the empty conference table to meet them at the door.

Last time Heat saw him, it had played like a sixties spy movie. Nikki ate her lunch in solitude on a park bench; Agent Callan materialized out of nowhere and sat beside her to deliver a sales pitch to join his team to help track down Tyler Wynn. She heard him out but declined. Nikki couldn't be certain, but it felt to her like Callan then tried to open the personal flank, sending signals of friendship . . . and perhaps deeper interest. But Heat had a relationship, and more than that, she needed independence from the feds. Her investigative style didn't lend itself to bureaucracy, politics, and red tape. Now, judging from the smile beaming her way as he approached, Special Agent Callan clearly hadn't given up on Nikki.

"Heat, my God, I never thought I'd see you down here." He thrust out a hand, and when Nikki shook, he clasped his other one over hers and held it exactly one second past friendly. Bart Callan's face brightened around a corn-fed smile that made her blush. Then he turned and said, "Hey, Rook, welcome to the bunker."

"Thanks. And so nice to visit you under my own power." Rook still smarted from what he called the Great Homeland Carjacking. A few weeks before, when Heat and Rook returned from Paris, an agent posing as a car service driver had locked the doors and steered their limo into an empty warehouse off the Long Island Expressway, where Agent Callan interrogated them both about their activities overseas.

Now Callan clamped an arm around Rook's shoulders as he led them into the Situation Room. "Come on, you're not going to hold a grudge about our little impromptu chat, are you?"

Suddenly blown away by the high-tech room, with its flight deck–sized mahogany table and imposing array of LED screens, Rook said, "Not if you let me meet Dr. Strangelove."

The earnest agent gave him a puzzled look and turned

quickly back to Nikki. "Sit, sit." He gestured to the leather high-backed chairs, but she stayed on her feet. Callan sniffed trouble. "OK, not sit-sitting . . ."

"You told my witness—a person of interest in my mother's case—that he can't speak to me. I demand to know why you are interfering in my investigation."

Callan tugged the knot in his necktie loose. He already had his coat off, and Heat watched his triceps flex against his shirtsleeves. "Nikki, this should be *our* investigation. All you have to do is come aboard."

"I told you, I want independence, not some federal machine messing with my case."

"Too late," said a woman's voice.

Heat and Rook turned to the door. The woman breezing in carried herself like she was in charge, and knew it. And from Callan's sudden loss of affability, he did, too. Suddenly taut, he said, "Nikki Heat, say hello to—"

But the slender brunette in the tailored black suit jumped in, making her own introduction. "—Agent Yardley Bell, Homeland Security." She gave Heat an appraising look and a strong handshake. Then she turned to Rook, whose face wore an expression Heat had never seen.

"Help me with your name again?" he said, barely able to hide his smile.

And then she said, "Jameson Rook. Holy fuck." The two moved to shake but, halfway, opted for a hug. Then Yardley Bell surprised Nikki—and Rook—by kissing him. Sure, she planted it on his cheek, not his mouth, but—a kiss.

Heat forgot her DHS beef for a moment.

Yardley Bell pulled back, but not far. She still cupped his shoulders with both hands while she laughed and said, "I'm sorry. That wasn't very professional, was it?" Rook just gaped, speechless for a change. Then Callan, Heat, and Rook sat. Agent Bell chose a spot to lean against the wall behind Callan's chair at the head of the long table. Nikki considered the power message that signaled.

"Detective Heat," she began, "I'm visiting from our team in DC. I came up here to liaise with Special Agent Callan on bringing this Tyler Wynn business you stumbled upon to a happy conclusion. I'm aware of your emotional connection to this case, and you have my deep sympathies." She paused only briefly and rolled onward. "However, make no mistake, this is The Big Show, no lone wolves. We have more of a handle on this than you know, and a big-picture strategy that cannot concern you as an outsider. But—if you choose to smarten up and join the team—you may get an answer to your question. What do you say?"

"Agent Bell, is it?" said Heat. "It's a real pleasure to meet you. But I think my visit is about over. Special Agent Callan, thanks for the tour." She rose. Rook hesitated slightly but got to his feet as well.

They were almost out the door when Bell said, "Don't you want to know about Salena Kaye's phone call from the helicopter?" Nikki hated herself for it, but she stopped and turned. A jumbo LED flat-screen on the wall came to life with a series of animated graphs scanning a map of Lower Manhattan and Brooklyn. Yardley Bell moved beside the giant touch screen and swiped the map with her fingertips to magnify detail of the East River. An oblong box of rolling numbers in the upper right corner time-stamped the grid search.

"This was recorded at the time Kaye escaped from you and borrowed the general aviation chopper." She touched an icon on the side of the glass, and bright green crosshairs found the middle of the river and blinked steadily. "This is the perp's cellular signal crossing over toward the Brooklyn Navy Yard at twenty-five MPH." Another light flashed on the screen. "This is the cell tower in Red Hook that picked up the call. The trace, as you can see, is bouncing to about eight cellular repeaters in Queens, Staten Island, back to Brooklyn, and so forth." Bell stepped aside while the lights flashed and pinged around the screen like a second-gen video game, then died. "This indicates four things. It wasn't a burner cell. It was an encrypted cell. And it was a sophisticated digital transmission designed to be untraceable, then implode."

"That's only three things," said Heat.

"Oh, right. Number four. You're over your head. You can join us and have access to resources like this, or stay outside and chase your fucking tail."

At the sound of a hot button getting pressed, Bart Callan got to his feet and injected himself into the conversation. "That's not about you personally." He stood close to Nikki, giving her his most conciliatory smile. For a military type he had true warmth, and it had a calming effect.

Heat held the brake on her anger. "What's it about then?"

"Assets, plain and simple. We have the infrastructure, the

team, and the experience to do this right. What I'd like personally . . . ?" He paused and pressed his palm against his chest. "Is for you to join us and give us the benefit of your insights and, frankly, remarkable skills, Detective Heat."

Callan held her eyes with his, and a small, involuntary flutter rose in Nikki's chest again. She turned to Rook, wondering if he'd read it. Then she looked over at the striking agent across the room, who seemed just to be waiting the whole thing out, and wondered if this was a good agent/bad agent soft sell/hard sell or if Yardley was just a plain asshole. Heat returned Callan's pleasant smile. "This has been very helpful, Bart. I do have to say that I have changed my mind. I came here all pissed off to ask you why you were interfering in my investigation, and now . . ." He looked at her with anticipation. "And now I am telling you to stay the hell out of it."

Callan insisted on riding topside with his two visitors so he could put in his bid for another meeting, giving Nikki time to cool off and reconsider. When Heat and Rook stepped out into the DHS lobby he stayed on the elevator, holding the door open with his hand. "And don't be put off by Agent Bell's brusque style. I went through an adjustment myself. Kinda had to cinch up my jock when she swooped in on my case."

"Aren't you the ranking officer?"

"I am."

Heat said, "Looks more to me like you're working for her, Special Agent. And now you want me to jump into that political dysfunction?"

"Let's be pros. Let's get past the pissing on trees we just saw down there. Agent Bell has an amazing track record in counterintelligence. Just ask your friend here." His reference carried a whiff of animosity that made Rook avert his gaze and threw Nikki off balance as she processed his prior relationship with Yardley. But Nikki regained her footing and pushed back.

"I still want an answer to my question. Vaja Nikoladze."

"OK," said Callan, "I'll give you this one as a gesture of good faith. The Georgian is an informant. We'd like to keep it that way." He cast a buffalo eye at Rook. "I'd go on, but I don't want to be quoted in the media."

Rook said, "Hey, you carjack a journalist and an NYPD detective on the LIE, you're going to buy a paragraph in my article."

Callan didn't respond. He asked Nikki to think it over, then released the door for his descent.

First thing back in the car, Heat said, "OK, spit it out. Who is Yardley Bell?"

"She is a force, isn't she?"

"Rook, she kissed you. Start talking."

"We met in the Caucasus five years ago," he began. "That was when my early reporting on the Chechen rebels began making noise."

"Stick to Yardley Bell, Rook," she said. "I know all about your reporting."

"OK, so I'm in-country, sitting in the café next door to my hostel, tapping a dispatch into my laptop, when this woman sits across from me and introduces herself as a field producer for public radio. She said she'd been reading my stuff and wanted to tag along to do advance work for a documentary. I thought about it and figured, why not?"

"Because she was hot?"

"Because I'm a sucker for *All Things Considered.* And because someone who spoke English—let alone was an American—was something I hadn't encountered in six weeks riding with the rebels." Then he shrugged, admitting, "All right, and she was hot."

"How long until you figured out she was CIA?"

"That night. I woke up and caught her going through my laptop and Moleskines."

"In the middle of the night," said Nikki.

"Yes."

"The first night."

"Let's review. Six weeks, American, hot."

"Got it."

"I had my journalistic ethics, though. I wouldn't travel as cover for a spy. And I sure wasn't going to burn the cred I'd established with the warlords. So I sent her off the next morning—OK, next night—and that was that."

Heat made a turn north along the Hudson and said, "No it's not. Rook, I interrogate liars for a living, don't snow me. Not about this."

"Let me finish. I thought that was that—until six months later when I got kidnapped on a mountain trail by a splinter group that accused me of working for the Russians. They beat the shit out of me for a week in their caves. And guess who found me and led the rescue mission?"

"Susan Stamberg."

"Next best thing. Yardley hung out with me while I recuperated in Athens, and eventually, I moved some of my stuff into a flat she kept in London. You can do the math; it was great fun but it was complicated. She had a job that she couldn't talk about, and I had one that I wouldn't. We shared a place but both traveled." They stopped at a light in Columbus Circle, just a few blocks from the precinct. "I won't lie to you, it was good while it lasted. But it didn't last."

"Conflict of interest?"

"The biggest. I met you." Nikki turned to him, and they stared at each other until a horn honked behind her on the green light. She drove on, and he continued, "That's when I stopped seeing her."

Nikki thought about the intimacy of Yardley's greeting, and her undisguised physicality with Rook, and thought maybe she had a new understanding of Agent Yardley Bell's interest in her case. But the DHS meeting had told her something else more important. If Homeland was pinging Salena Kaye's cell phone calls deep in a Situation Room bunker, something big was definitely going on with Tyler Wynn and his band of conspirators.

Heat double-parked her Crown Vic along with the other police vehicles in front of the precinct on West 82nd. "Wouldn't lock it up," called Ochoa. He and Raley stepped out of the walled parking lot on their way to the Roach Coach. "Got a fresh homicide."

Nikki knew these guys and could read the signs: their impatient eyes, the pace of their strides. Heat's gut told her things were about to get jerked into a new dimension. "What?" was all she said.

"There's string," said Raley.

His partner added, "Looks like we have ourselves a serial killer."

THREE

Against the dimming of the day, the crime scene floods could have been lights from one of Manhattan's ubiquitous movie shoots. But as Heat and Rook rolled south on Riverside Drive, approaching 72nd, there were no box trucks, no RV dressing rooms, no port-a-potties with doors marked "Lucy" and "Desi." When they pulled up, she parked behind the van from the Office of the Chief Medical Examiner. None of this would be make-believe.

Nikki got out and paused in the street before she closed her door. Rook asked her if everything was OK. Detective Heat nodded. This time she took her private interval for the deceased and felt ready. Raley and Ochoa joined up from the Roach Coach, and the four moved on to work.

The first thing Heat did when she recognized the victim was to call for the ranking scene supervisor. Nikki never broke stride, just told the sergeant to order up crowd control immediately. "Press, paparazzi, gawkers—nobody gets near."

"Whoa," said Rook. "It's Maxine Berkowitz."

"None other," said Raley. "Your Channel 3 Doorbuster."

"Gentlemen" was all Heat needed to say. They quieted, stopping in place. She moved forward, using her palm to shield her face from the powerful CSU lights while she made her

Beginner's Eyes tour around the victim. The body of the Channel 3 consumer advocate sat upright on a city bench facing the Eleanor Roosevelt statue in the pedestrian entrance to Riverside Park. Maxine Berkowitz wore a nicer-quality, tan, off-the-rack business suit. Her hair, although heavily sprayed, spiked out at the back where it had been disturbed. Her makeup bore smudges around her lower face and mouth. Both hands rested gently in her lap. To the casual passerby, she could have been any thirtysomething Manhattan professional taking a break to contemplate the memorial to the First Lady of the World. Except this woman had been murdered.

"Asphyxia through strangulation," said Lauren Parry over her clipboard. "That's my prelim, with the usual caveats about letting me run my tests, and yadda, yadda."

Nikki bent forward to examine the pronounced bruise line around the victim's neck. "Not manual."

"I'm betting electrical cord. That contusion is sharply defined. And I see no abrasion or strand pattern like with rope." Heat drew closer and got a sick-sweet whiff. "Chloroform?" The ME nodded. Nikki studied the smear of makeup around the victim's nose and mouth and felt a pang of sadness for the reporter, recalling her own abduction a few months before. She rose up and said, "Show me the string."

The CSU technician's camera flashed one last shot. He picked up the six-inch aluminum ruler he had placed beside the string to illustrate scale and said, "All yours."

It sat atop the victim's purse at the other end of the park bench. Red string, similar to the one left with Conklin's body, had been tied to an equal length of yellow string, then coiled as one and placed on the purse in a figure-eight loop. The gesture, the care, the quietness of the message—whatever it meant—brought a chill to Nikki. Then Rook moved close by and she felt his warmth against her.

"What do you know," he said. "A lemniscate."

"A what?" asked Ochoa.

"Lemniscate. The word for infinity sign."

Raley weighed in. "I thought infinity sign was the word for infinity sign."

"Ah, except that's two words."

Nikki looked at Roach and shook her head. "Writer." Then, she said to Rook, "Where'd you learn that, interviewing Stephen Hawking?"

Rook shrugged. "The truth? Snapple cap."

They worked the scene for over an hour, interviewing the teenage boy who had discovered the corpse while he was walking his neighbor's pug and had asked the deceased for an autograph. He'd seen nobody else around; in fact, the only reason he paid Maxine Berkowitz any attention was that she was the only one there. The canvass of the nearby dog park yielded nothing to go on but did give Dr. Parry time to set up the OCME privacy screens and run a preliminary temperature and lividity field test. She fixed the time of death as noon to 4 p.m. that day.

Forensics called Heat over to the bench. "Found something when we picked up the victim's purse to bag it." With gloved hands, the technician lifted the purse and revealed, underneath it, a small disc. Nikki crouched down beside it for closer examination, to makes sure it was what she thought it was. She frowned and looked up at the tech. "Weird, huh?" he said. "Rollerblade wheel."

Heat tasked her squad to run the usual checks of facing apartment buildings for eyewitnesses—especially anyone who might have registered a Rollerblader—and to scan for security cams. Then she and Rook set out for Channel 3.

WHNY News occupied the bottom two floors of a media complex wedged between Lincoln Center and the West Side Highway. As she waited for security to clear them, Nikki stared across the courtyard at the neighboring studios where her ex-boyfriend, her mother's killer, had worked as a talent booker for a late night talk show. The wave of betrayal washed over her anew and refreshed her anxiety about Tyler Wynn's whereabouts. Heat sealed it off and focused. One murderer at a time, she thought.

The newsroom felt to Heat like her own bull pen, but with higher technology, brighter colors, and better wardrobe. The buzz of preparing for *News 3 @ 10* clicked along with the same measured adrenaline rush of working a murder case on deadline. The pressure and excitement ran in the blood, not in the air. Call it controlled chaos.

The news director, George Putnam, a stocky redhead, was still reeling from the shock of his consumer reporter's murder. Heat walked through a vapor trail of Scotch as she and Rook followed him through a maze of desks. Nikki wondered if the whiskey was Putnam's reaction to the death, or how he managed to mount a nightly newscast in Gotham.

They settled into his office, like Captain Irons's at the Twentieth, a glass box that gave him a view of his world. "This is a big blow to our family," he said. He gestured to the newsroom. "We're all working, but it's hard. We're doing it for Max. She was special, that girl."

The little fans in Heat's bullshit filter started to whir, but she said, "That's admirable." Rook caught her eye and, in the way only lovers can, vibed that his antennae had also risen.

Putnam described Maxine Berkowitz as the perfect marriage of reporter and beat. She'd come to WHNY from Columbus, Ohio, as weekend anchor, but "she never won the focus groups, so instead of releasing her, I got the notion to recycle her as a consumer watchdog. You know, an in-your-face viewer advocate. Somebody who'd walk through walls and bust down doors." He dabbed an eye and said, "She herself came up with the segment title, 'The Doorbuster.' " He went on to describe a team player, beloved by her coworkers.

Not satisfied with the company line George Putnam handed her, Nikki asked to speak with someone who was close to Maxine. The news director hesitated then led her and Rook onto the set, where *News 3*'s hip-hop meteorologist bent over his weather desk. "Oh my God," said Rook, "I can't believe I'm actually meeting Coolio Nimbus."

The young black man straightened up quickly, and short dreads danced on his head. But the signature smile and mischievous eyes of New York's Most Playful Weathercaster were dimmed by sadness. This man looked like he had lost his best friend.

Nimbus walked them to his cubicle just off the set. When

Nikki got there she turned, looking for Rook, but she had lost him along the way. Heat spotted him gawping at his own face with bewildered fascination as it filled a fifty-four-inch LED monitor above the sports desk. By the time he joined her, she had gotten pretty much the same view of Coolio's best friend Max as she'd gotten from the news director, although the weatherman said, "There's some shit maybe you need to know. But I'm not sure I should spill."

"I know this is tough, Mr. Nimbus," said Nikki, "but we need to hear about any possibility if we're going to find your friend's murderer."

A familiar voice interrupted. "Good lord, it's Nikki Heat."

Greer Baxter, the iconic face of WHNY News, towered over them. The veteran news anchor's stiff helmet of blond hair framed her handsome features. The newscaster had several tissues tucked into her blouse collar to keep her neck makeup from rubbing off. Both Heat and Rook rose, but he might as well have been invisible. She clasped Nikki's hand in both of hers and said, "Poor Maxine. Such a tragedy. Such a loss." And then, in a gear shift as smooth as turning the page on the night's top stories, she said, "Now, Nikki Heat, you and I need to have a talk. We need to book your appearance on my little spot."

The spot Greer Baxter humbly referred to, "Greer and Now," was the expanded interview segment that closed out each night's primetime newscast. Baxter had a reputation as a skilled interviewer who scored newsworthy guests. "With all due respect," began Nikki, "I—"

"Ah-ah," said Greer. "I won't take no. We lost one of our

own. If you don't have enough information to go on with me tonight, I understand. But I need you. I'm serious. Call me. Or I'll be calling you, Nikki Heat."

After she moved on, Heat turned her attention back to Coolio Nimbus. "What should I know about Maxine Berkowitz?"

Minutes later, back in the news director's office, George Putnam came around his desk and closed his door. "Coolio told you this?" Heat nodded. He flopped into his executive swivel and rocked back with an exhale, deep in painful thought. Then he came forward, resting rolled-up shirtsleeves on his desk and presenting his block of a freckled face to them. "It's true. Max and I had an affair. It started years ago when I began coaching her for her new role."

"As your mistress?" asked Rook.

"As the best damned consumer advocate in TV," he said. "I had this notion that people could sleep together and still work together." Both Heat and Rook kept eyes front. "I was wrong. I knew too much. Running this newsroom, I had to keep secrets from her. She'd find out, of course, when I'd send a memo to the staff about a change, and she'd get all bent about not being told first. It ate us up." Nikki let the silence do the work. Putnam filled it. "I broke it off a year ago. It ended ugly. But that affair was ancient history. I mean, when a romance is over, it's over. Right?"

Rook turned immediately to Nikki and said, "Yes . . . Absolutely."

Heat said, "Mr. Putnam, I'd like your whereabouts

midday today, please." But even as Heat jotted down his statement, she knew it wasn't him and that getting Putnam's alibi was just a formality.

The real killer was somewhere out there.

Rook made their dinner that night in his loft while they drank unfiltered hefeweizen and Nikki watched across the kitchen counter after her bath. "What magic's happening in that oven of yours, Mr. Jameson?" she said. "Loving the garlic and fresh thyme."

"It's *Good Eats* Forty Cloves and a Chicken." Then Rook held up the cookbook and said, "How weird is this? Alton Brown calls this the perfect make-ahead meal for those pesky serial-homicide weeks, or when you've had a long day chasing Naughty Nurses."

While they ate, they watched *News 3 @ 10.* Of course, the lead story was the strangulation murder of their consumer advocate, Maxine Berkowitz. Greer Baxter's stoic reading was offset by video of WHNY staffers in tears and a live shot from 72nd and Riverside Drive, where the field reporter, standing before a makeshift curbside memorial of candles and flowers, showed the crime scene, which police had cordoned off waiting for a daylight evidence search. The reporter said, "NYPD Captain Wallace Irons is with me. He is commander of the Twentieth Precinct."

"He's also the shortest distance between a body bag and a TV camera," heckled Rook as Wally stepped into the bright lights beside the reporter.

Irons kept his appearance basically ceremonial. When Heat had briefed him a half hour before, she gave him the fundamentals: cause of death, time of death, and how the body had been discovered. He used his airtime as a plea for eyewitnesses to come forward, as she had coached him to do. Nikki had not, however, told Irons about the string. Or that this likely was the work of a serial killer. She would do that first thing in the morning. But for now she held it back simply because she did not trust her commanding officer's big mouth.

After dishes, they uncorked an Haute-Côtes de Nuits then time traveled to 1999. Joe Flynn's surveillance photos of her mother made it an emotional trip for Nikki. The private eye's telescopic lens captured Cynthia Heat just as her daughter remembered her: sleek, elegant, and poised. Nikki's dad had commissioned the tail, suspecting his wife of having an affair, and not without cause. Cindy Heat's moves were all about hiding a secret life—from her husband and from her own kid. Nikki and her father never discussed it. They were each afraid to give it voice, but they both suspected her of hiding something. Both had no idea it was a double life as a CIA operative spying on the families that hired nice Mrs. Heat to tutor piano. Nikki reflected on the irony that a husband's worry about a cheating spouse led him to hire a private investigator whose creeper photos might now give up clues to a rogue ex-CIA conspiracy.

Nikki had loaded the thumb drive Flynn gave her onto Rook's MacBook Pro and, shoulder-to-shoulder, they watched the slide show on its monitor. Once Nikki got past the nostalgia of seeing eleven-year-old images of her mom, she focused on the other faces. Some pictures were peep-shots taken through windows into homes; most were taken on Manhattan sidewalks as the tutor-under-surveillance arrived or departed with binders of sheet music under one arm. Heat recognized the Jamaican, Algernon Barrett, who had been ducking behind his lawyer's skirts to avoid her. One shot captured Cynthia with the brewery tycoon Carey Maggs, sitting on the planter outside his apartment building, laughing at something his little boy must have just said. More pictures of the same ilk flashed by. Vaja Nikoladze's Rudolf Nureyev mop of hair dated the photo of him chatting with Cindy Heat on the gravel drive of his Hastings-on-Hudson property. A Georgian shepherd pup sat obediently by his left leg.

Rook fast-clicked through a series of duplicate shots, but when Nikki said "Whoa," he paused the slide show and they stared at the familiar face of the man in deep conversation with Cindy Heat on a Midtown sidewalk. They didn't know his name, but they would never forget him. He was the doctor who, three weeks prior at a Paris hospital, had helped Tyler Wynn fake his death in front of Heat and Rook. "Holy fuck," said Rook under his breath.

"Curiouser and curiouser," agreed Nikki. "One more picture, let's see it."

Cynthia Heat was not in the next shot, but the French doctor was—in the front seat of a parked car with another man they didn't recognize. Rook said, "Looks like our French doc spent enough time around your mom to earn some photo ops." Nikki jotted down the date and time of the picture so she could call Joe Flynn to ask if he had an ID on either man. When she finished, she found Rook staring at her. "I have an idea you are going to hate."

"You're right," she said, "I hate it." Nikki settled onto the couch in his great room with the million-dollar view of the Tribeca skyline and added, "What world do you live in that you think I could just drop everything and go to Paris?" He brought over the bottle of wine and their glasses, and while he set them on the coffee table, she continued, "If this is some covert plan of yours to whisk me away to safety, it's a debatable strategy, Rook. I can get poisoned at a zinc bar on the Left Bank just as easily as at the Gramercy Starbucks."

"First of all, this isn't some covert plan. It's just something I've been thinking about secretly." He realized what he had just said and held out her wine. "Let me finish. What I mean is that ever since Tyler Wynn escaped, I've been considering a trip back to Paris to see if I can pick up his trail on his old stomping grounds. Maybe even recontact my Russian spook pal, Anatoly. That's not covert; those are just inner thoughts I didn't express."

"Something very new for you," she said as she took a sip of her Burgundy.

"Come on, Nik, now that you've seen that French doctor with your mom in those old pictures, isn't one investigative bone in that body of yours aching to find the connection?"

"Well. I have been thinking the same thing."

"Covertly?"

"Shut up."

"A moment, while I savor this rare tit-for-tat victory." He closed his eyes, smiled, then opened them. "OK. Here's what I want to do. I want to show up at that Paris hospital, surprise Dr. McFrenchie, and see what he knows about Tyler Wynn, then and now."

Nikki sat upright and rested her glass on the coaster. "You know, I'm hating this less."

"So you do see the logic of going?" he asked. When she said she did, he pressed it. "And you'll come?"

"Get real, Rook. I can't get away."

"Not even for a working trip?"

She smoothed his collar then left her hand draped on his chest. "May I point out I have plenty of loose ends I'm working right here, including a fresh trail to Salena Kaye? Not to mention a little thing that's come up called a serial homicide."

"It's always something," he said, kidding, but only sort of.

Nikki nodded to herself, reaching a decision. "You go. But answer this: Are you trying to help me solve the case, or gather more material for your next article?"

Rook said, "That hurts." He stared out the window into the New York night, then said, "But I'll forgive you if we can have make-up sex."

Nikki Heat called her team in for an early start. When the detectives rolled in at 6 a.m., she positioned her computer screen so she could peek at their reactions as each discovered a coffee waiting on his or her desk labeled "Nikki" in grease pencil. "You'd better laugh," she said over their chuckles.

"This prank cost me twenty dollars."

Her cell phone vibed. Rook, texting that he was about to go through TSA screening for his flight to Paris, and before he jetted off, he wanted to let her know how much he enjoyed his wake-up service. Heat had slept deeply after their make-up sex, descending into sweet oblivion folded into his arms. She awoke because of the morning-after soreness from her jujitsu round with Salena Kaye. Since he'd planned to get up at four to make his plane, she decided to be his alarm clock and slid under the sheets. Nikki texted back that she looked forward to his next layover and walked to the front of the squad room, but slowly enough to lose the smirk.

She'd rolled two Murder Boards side by side: one for Roy Conklin and a new one, for Maxine Berkowitz. She briefed the detectives who hadn't been on-scene at Riverside Park on the bullet points of the TV reporter's death. When Ochoa asked about boyfriend troubles, Nikki shared about the bad breakup with the news director and assigned him to check out George Putnam's alibi. "Check his wife's whereabouts, too," said Heat, just in case there was a volatile side of that triangle. "But tread lightly. Let's not rule anything out, but this feels like more than a jealous payback."

That brought her to the connection between the two murders. "We have a unique telltale that indicates a serial killer." She posted blowups of CSU photos of the string found at each crime scene and then picked up her notes. "Forensics burned some midnight oil to get us some data this morning. Both the red and the yellow string are made from a braided polyester widely used for everything from hobbies and crafts, to jewelry making, to yo-yo strings and something called kendama."

Randall Feller raised a finger for attention and said, "That's a Japanese game that uses a wooden spindle with a cup at one end that you use to catch a wooden ball attached to it by a string." He paused only briefly and added, "Don't ask."

"Nice to know when Rook's not here there's somebody to pick up the know-it-all slack," observed Raley.

Since Detective Feller had demonstrated a special interest, Heat assigned him to make checks of area hobby, craft, hardware, and toy stores to see if they had any customers worth checking out. "Detective Rhymer, you assist. I'm sure this string is also available on the Internet. Find out who sells it and contact those sites for customer records."

A civilian aide came in from the front office and handed a message to Heat, who digested it and addressed her crew. "A foot patrol making checks of trash cans discovered a three-foot coaxial cable not far from the Eleanor Roosevelt statue. Forensics has it now. It's only prelim, but there appear to be traces of makeup in the center of the cord." Heat reflected on the tissues she saw protecting Greer Baxter's collar from her TV makeup and said, "That would be consistent with our strangulation."

"What about the Rollerblade wheel?" asked Rhymer.

"Strange, isn't it?" said Heat. "The strings are plenty creepy, but the Rollerblade is weird, too. Forensics says it's a brand-new, standard polyurethane inline skate wheel, no prints, no wear. It's straight from the package." She reflected a moment and said, "Sharon?" Detective Hinesburg sat up like she'd been poked with a stick. "I'd like you to team with

Raley and Ochoa and run the skate wheel."

That evening, when the shift had ended and Heat had the bull pen to herself, she embraced the stillness to contemplate the Murder Boards and let her instincts talk. The case work had not yielded any new clues, and her cop sense told her that the elimination of the few leads they had was not a negative but a means to an end. For instance, both George Putnam and his wife's alibis had been confirmed. Similarly, Roy Conklin continued to check out as a man who was easy to love but difficult to investigate for that very reason.

Nikki sat on her desktop, letting her eyes drift from board to board, letting the known elements speak the mind of a serial killer over the low hum of fluorescent tubes. String. String was the literal common thread. What else? Oddball props. A dead rat. An inline skate wheel. How were they connected? Or were they at all?

Geography. The obvious. Both victims had been found on the Upper West Side, in particular, the Twentieth Precinct—a self-canceling clue because it meant the killer lived or worked there, or else traveled there to kill away from his home base.

Minutes passed, maybe even an hour. When Nikki got into this flow, she not only lost time, she hid from it. She reached for her notebook and wrote one word: "Jobs."

What came to her was more than just that both victims had been either mutilated or killed by an instrument related to their work: the restaurant inspector by an oven; the TV reporter by a coaxial cord, the kind used to connect cable TV. Those similarities were already top-lining the squad conversation.

This was something not as obvious, but close enough. She called Roach, Feller, and Rhymer back to the precinct.

Far from being annoyed at getting boomeranged in, the four detectives gave off the edgy vibe of anticipation, and when Heat began, "It's right in front of us. Both vics were in the business of consumer protection," she saw their eyes come alight. "I want to find out if they knew each other or if they knew someone in common." From there on, the meeting was short. She put Roach on contacting Olivia Conklin, Feller back on his beat at the Health Department, and Rhymer on Maxine Berkowitz's coworkers and friends. "Check e-mails, texts, phone records, everything that leaves a trail," she said, and watched them cancel their evenings and hit the phones with renewed purpose.

Back early the next morning, with little to go on yet much to cover, the day for all of them became the essence of good detective work: drudgery. The hours of phone calls and computer checks got broken up only by meeting up to compare notes after pounding the pavement for face time with shop owners, park nannies, and doormen who'd seen nothing out of the ordinary. The true chore of Nikki's day came when Captain Irons arrived in the late morning, camera-ready with a fresh white uniform shirt in dry cleaner plastic, just in case someone needed a statement. After satisfying himself nobody had tried to kill his lead homicide detective in the last twenty-four hours, he asked for a briefing of both active cases. Wally was more an administrator than a cop, and his eyes glazed over as she filled him in on the details. When she finished, his first question was his go-to:

"How much overtime is this gonna drain from my budget?"

Always prepared for that resistance, Nikki managed to sell the precinct commander on the long-term savings of bringing in more manpower, and came out of his glass office with an OK to bring in one of her favorite detective teams, Malcolm and Reynolds.

Rook checked in from a taxi heading from Charles de Gaulle Airport to his hotel in Paris. It was night there, New York plus six, and he said he'd left word with Anatoly Kijé, his old Russian spy friend, hoping they could meet for a late dinner-slash-debrief.

"You mean the same Anatoly Kijé whose henchmen kidnapped us from Place des Vosges just so he could be sure we weren't being followed?"

"Ah, memories," said Rook. "Don't you wish you'd come?"

"So you know, Rook, I don't consider it a Michelin Tour just because my nose is pushed against one of their radials in the trunk of a car."

They hopped off the line with the promise to catch up later that night so Heat could grab a call from OCME. Lauren Parry's prelim on Maxine Berkowitz bore out the COD as asphyxia by strangulation. "The killer took her from behind with a cord. And Forensics is committing to that coaxial cable found in the park. The makeup residue on the insulation is an exact match to the victim's."

"Save me a call to geekland, Lauren. Any prints on the cable?"

"None," said the ME. "And no sign of struggle. He chloroformed her and strangled her when she was out."

Nikki jotted that down then riffled pages in her spiral until she came to notes on her other case. "OK to switch gears?"

"Detective Heat, you have got more corpses to ask about than anyone I know."

"You should give me a rewards card."

"Cold, girl."

"As ice. What about my poison vic from the Starbucks?"

"Same as what Salena Kaye used to kill Petar. A fast-acting cocktail of strychnine and cyanide, plus a few additives, including a lab-modified derivative of bismuth subsalicylate, which is what turned the tongue black. It's not a poison, it's mainly for show."

"You'll forgive me if I don't applaud."

"Nikki," said Dr. Parry, "this is potent stuff. She knows her chemistry. You watch yourself."

Heat awoke with a start on her couch at six-fifteen the next morning to the Norwegian duo Röyksopp singing "Remind Me"—the ringtone Rook had installed to ID him on her cell. It took Nikki so long to orient herself and find the phone, she was afraid he'd dump to voice mail, but she caught it in time. "You were going to call me last night," she said.

"And *bonjour* to you, too. Things got very busy over here. You won't be sorry." Rook's voice sounded clear, next-room clear. And there was something in it. Exhilaration, maybe.

She moved aside the sheet music she had fallen asleep studying, another futile attempt to break her mother's code. "Tell me." Wired to be a note taker, Heat reached for the pen and spiral pad she kept on her coffee table, clearing the night from her throat.

"I made contact with Anatoly Kijé."

"Did his goons slip a bag over your head and drop you at Deux Magots?"

"Even better. He met me alone on the banks of the Seine. Just me and an old KGB warhorse. Isn't that cool? Like walking into a le Carré novel."

Nikki drew the picture in her mind and smiled. "I'm warming up to this."

"Just wait. First off, Anatoly ID'd the doctor in Joe Flynn's old photos. François Sisson. Turns out Sisson was a real doctor over here until he became one of the operatives in Tyler Wynn's old CIA network. Ready for this? François Sisson turned up on a slab in a Paris morgue the day after helping Wynn play his death scene for us."

"Poison?"

"Let's call it lead poisoning. One slug behind his ear."

"I'm still waiting for the good news," she said. "Sounds to me like you got your George Smiley jollies then hit a dead end."

"In Paris, yes. But things are a bit different down here in Nice."

Heat looked at her watch; it would be just past noon in France. "What the hell are you doing in Nice?"

"Talking to you from my room at the Hotel Negresco. Want to know why? Because I just came from a meeting at a beach club called Castel Plage. It's up the Promenade des Anglais between here and Le Château. By the way, that's French for—"

"Rook, I know what château is French for. Spit it out."

"OK, you ready for this? I just had brunch with none other than your elusive Syrian security attaché, Fariq Kuzbari."

Nikki set her pen down and just listened. Rook explained that, after his meeting by the Seine, he hopped the overnight high-speed train to Nice, where the Syrian security man had agreed to meet him. He dropped his bag at the Negresco and then walked the promenade along the bay to the Castel Plage, where Kuzbari waited for him at a secluded table on the beachside patio. "You know, Fariq's a lot nicer guy when his men aren't holding guns on you."

"Rook."

"Sorry." He paused and, in the background, she heard the outdoor sounds of Nice: seabirds; motor bikes; a cruise ship's horn. She wished she were there. "Kuzbari told me that your mother was not spying on him while she was tutoring his kids."

"And you just believe that?"

"I'm only telling you what the man said, and the man said if anyone would know he was being spied on, it would be he. But Kuzbari did tell me something, and it's big. Remember that week the PI said your mom spent at that conference center in the Berkshires with Kuzbari and his family?"

Nikki remembered it very well from Joe Flynn's 1999 surveillance report. And recently, when the Syrian and his security goons accosted her on the street in SoHo, she made sure to ask him about it. "I remember Kuzbari was more concerned about denying any hanky-panky. What did he tell you?"

"He said he went to the Berkshires for a symposium on

limiting weapons of mass destruction, and that when your mom wasn't giving his kids piano lessons, she was spending an inordinate amount of time with another attendee."

Heat picked up her pen again. "Who?"

"Dr. Ari Weiss."

A jolt of adrenaline shot through Heat. Wide awake now, she paced her living room floor. "Remember that name?" asked Rook. She did. Of course it lived in her notes from a few weeks ago, but like most things she took down, the facts were burnished in her memory, and the movement of pen across paper only helped her memorialize them.

Right before her murder, Ari Weiss had been the houseguest of another prominent family her mother tutored. Nikki had assumed her mom was spying on them, but Rook's information cast things in an entirely different light. It's possible her mother had worked her way into that home so she could snoop on the houseguest, Ari. "This is big," she said.

"Yeah. Just too bad you can't talk to him."

When his name came up three weeks ago, Heat and Rook had discovered that Dr. Ari Weiss had died of a blood disorder. But Nikki felt energized now and wasn't giving up. There still might be a way to get more information about the dead doctor. Even while she paced, she was looking through her notes for the number of the person whose family Ari had stayed with. Maybe he would know if Weiss had any connection to Tyler Wynn or his accomplices. Then, to make sure the sound of her gratitude for the new lead carried across the Atlantic, she repeated, "Hey, Rook? This is very big."

"Thanks. It's kind of a whirlwind. I haven't even been to

bed since I left New York, but I feel so pumped."

"Well ya done good. This Kuzbari stuff is a coup. He's so hard to pin down, how did you manage to make contact?"

"Professional courtesy, I guess. You know, the spy quid pro quo. Like most Mideast governments, Syria's heading for the rocks, and I think he's trying to make nice with our intelligence in case he needs an escape hatch."

Nikki stopped pacing. "Don't you mean Russian intelligence? I thought Kijé set this up." Sounds of traffic and a distinctly European siren rose up and filled Rook's long pause. "Who set this up for you? . . . You there?"

During his hesitation she heard a female voice she recognized in the background. "Rook, come out here and see, it's a car fire."

Heat said, "Really? She's there with you?—in Nice?"

FOUR

Nikki fought the urge to hang up on Rook and instead listened to him squirm. He hemmed. He hawed. He backed. He filled. And then had the nerve at the end of her silence to ask, "Is everything OK?" She told him she had to get to work and left him to hold a dead phone in his stupid hotel room overlooking the stupid Mediterranean. Then she cranked the shower as hot as she could stand it and stood under the jet. "Fucking Nice," she said to the steam. "Fucking stupid."

Shouldering the glass door of the bodega open, Heat burst out onto the sidewalk on Pearl Street ripping at the orange Reese's wrapper with extreme prejudice. She stood by a trash can near the curb, shook one of the two peanut butter cups out, tore away the brown paper enfolding it, and popped the entire disk into her mouth. She closed her eyes and tilted her head to the sky while she chewed, feeling the tiny sharp ridges of the chocolate coating scrape the roof of her mouth while the salty, grainy succulence of the peanut butter center mixed with the melting sugars on her tongue. Bastard, she thought. Stupid boy. Her breath whistled through her nostrils as she munched, eating not for pleasure but as an act of aggression. That part done, she swallowed, feeling the delicious indulgence tamp out the fires of her rage.

She looked at the package. Still one peanut butter cup left. Nikki decided to save it and shoved it in the side pocket of her blazer. She might need it later, if the idiot called again.

Heat elbowed aside her anger at Rook for going to France with his ex-girlfriend and walked on. She had better things to dwell on. For the first time in weeks Nikki felt like she found a real trail that could lead her to Tyler Wynn, and as she strode along, she started rolling everything she knew. If Fariq Kuzbari's version of events were true, was it possible that her mother used the Syrian as cover to get into that symposium in the Berkshires to spy on Ari Weiss? Following that premise, could that be the same reason her mom got herself a tutoring gig later in the home of the brewing magnate Carey Maggs—to keep tabs on Weiss while he stayed with his former Oxford classmate and his family? She hoped to find out in a few minutes when she met with Maggs.

The last time she'd seen the beer tycoon and social activist, Heat was thrashing around looking for clues in her mother's murder. Now she hoped for another crumb—any connection, however slight—that could link Weiss to the fugitive Tyler Wynn and warm up the trail to his capture.

When she reached the cobblestones of the South Street Seaport, Nikki stopped. Survival instinct took over and she made a survey of the area. The pedestrian walks and courtyards were empty. It was way too early for the tourists who would pack the place later. She saw only a soda delivery truck and a solitary cleaner hosing off a café patio. Feeling suddenly alone and exposed, Heat made a back check behind her then scanned the rooftops of the old buildings. Somewhere a killer waited for her. Despite that fact, she pressed on toward the nineteenth-century brick warehouse that housed Brewery Boz. Nikki knew she was a target. She also knew this could be the next stop on the road to staying alive.

At the loading dock behind the microbrewery, Nikki climbed four concrete steps off the alley and heard a high-pitched whine on the other side of a metal door. Carey Maggs had told her to knock loudly so he could hear her over the power tools. She rapped with a key and the whirring stopped. Hinges squeaked, and a filthy man who looked more like a day laborer than a multimillionaire stood grinning. "You still look just like yer mum." That's what he'd told Nikki on her visit three weeks before. He would know. Cynthia Heat had also been his piano tutor in London back in 1976, when Maggs was just a boy.

"I'd say pardon the mess, but you didn't give me much notice, and I'm in the middle of a restoration. Behold, an authentic relic of the London Metropolitan Fire Brigade, circa 1870." Behind him, surrounded by giant stainless steel vats filled with Durdles' Finest lager, stout, and pale ale, stood a vintage fire wagon—a carriage that once got pulled by horses and probably was why London burned.

"Looks new."

"Bloody better. Been slaving on it morning and night to get it ready in time for the march." She gave him a puzzled look and he explained, "The Walk Against Global Oppression.

I committed Brewery Boz as corporate sponsor. What can I say? Bleeding heart, bleeding checkbook." He set aside his electric buffer and followed Heat around as she admired the wagon. Its red paint gleamed from the wax he'd applied, and the copper chimney of the steam pump's giant boiler shined like a mirror. "But I get promo out of it, too." She noticed the gold leaf stencil on the side. " 'Boz Brigade,' " he said, reading with her. "I mean, what better mascot for a Charles Dickens–themed beer than a Victorian artifact like this?"

Niceties having been observed, Detective Heat said, "Let's talk."

The gastropub adjacent to the brewery wouldn't open for hours, but Maggs led her inside to the bar and made them each a latte.

"Delicious," she said. "But latte in a pub?"

"I know, scandalous." Maggs's British accent had a playfully challenging tone that reminded her of someone she couldn't quite place. "But we can be true to our Dickens leitmotif without confining ourselves to blood pudding and spotted dick, right?" Then she put her finger on it. Christopher Hitchens. "Yeah, I get that a lot. He's Portsmouth, not London, but it's the Oxonian thing. We're a bunch of know-it-alls, petrified that we don't."

Since he'd brought up his college, Nikki snagged it. "Oxford is kind of why I'm here," she said. "I need to ask you about your old classmate."

"Ari." He grew serious and slid his coffee aside.

"When we talked a few weeks ago, you said Dr. Weiss was a houseguest of yours around Thanksgiving 1999."

Nikki didn't need to, but she glanced at her notes from the prior interview, a technique that kept interviewees honest. "You said his stay overlapped the week my mother was tutoring your son."

He paused to reflect. "Yes, but as I told you before, I can't believe Ari had anything to do with your mother's murder."

"And—as I told you before, Mr. Maggs—this works better if you simply answer the questions." He nodded. "Can you tell me any of the activities Dr. Weiss was involved in during his visit?"

"Let me think. We're going back over a decade." He wagged his head slightly. "Sorry. I guess mostly sightseeing and clubs, maybe a Broadway show."

"Did he have any diplomatic or foreign service acquaintances in New York?"

Maggs furrowed his brow. "Ari? Doubt it. Ari was a science geek, pretty much just a lab rat. Rarely left the maze, if you know what I mean." That didn't square with what Fariq Kuzbari had said about his attendance at the symposium on WMDs. She made a note and went at it another way. "Was he political? I mean, you donate significant profits from your company to radical organizations like," she referred to notes, "Mercator Watch. What was your nickname for it?"

"GreedPeace," he chuckled, but his eyes flashed with a sudden and visceral anger. "The world is fucked up by top-down greed, Detective. It's why we have so much war. The wealthy use their power against the powerless. It's got to stop. It will stop." He gestured through the showcase window to the copper and stainless vats hulking in his production area. "This beer business is just my springboard. I plan to rival Bill Gates and Warren Buffett in their philanthropy—but in my own way. These days I spend more time with my broker than my brewmeister for one reason: I am completely committed to using my business and investments to create a war chest for peace." He laughed and finger-combed his hair back. "And, yes, I hear the irony. I went to Oxford, you know."

"Didn't any of your political passion rub off on Ari Weiss?"

Maggs came off his mini-tirade and relaxed again. "For Ari, rest his soul, if it wasn't under a microscope, it didn't exist. The only thing radical he gave a rat's arse about was free radicals with unpaired electrons."

"Did Ari ever mention the name Tyler Wynn?"

He thought and said, "Mm, no."

"Does this help?" She tapped her iPhone and brought up Wynn's picture. He shook no. Then she showed Maggs Joe Flynn's old surveillance shot of the two men in the front seat of the parked car. The driver was the French doctor; she didn't know the other. "Do you recognize either of these two men?"

"You're kidding, right?" Maggs pointed to the man on the passenger side. "That's my friend. That's Ari Weiss."

There it was. Carey Maggs had made a connection between Tyler Wynn and Ari Weiss, and the link was the French doctor who helped the CIA man fake his heart attack. But what did it all mean? On the subway uptown, while she scrutinized the lethal potential of everyone who got on and off her car, Nikki tried to do the math and couldn't get there. What she needed was to bounce it off Rook, whose nutty speculation both annoyed her and freed her from linear thinking at the same time.

Rook.

A butterfly rose, stirring dark sediment. She pushed it down and concentrated on the case.

Before she even got to her desk, Detective Heat called across the squad room for Roach to start digging on Weiss. At her computer, she opened the Web page Rook had bookmarked weeks before and reread the obit of Ari Weiss, MD. The brief article said the medical researcher had been a graduate of the Yale School of Medicine and a Rhodes Scholar, which was how he would have met his friend Carey Maggs at Oxford. He had died in 2000 of a rare blood disease called babesiosis. Heat clicked that hyperlink and the Wikipedia page described babesiosis as a malaria-like parasitic disorder. Like Lyme disease, it was generally tick-borne, but it could also come from a contaminated transfusion.

Loose thoughts started to ping, but Heat didn't like hunches. Facts were her friend, and she could have used some. She thought a long moment. Then she steeled herself and picked up the phone.

When Bart Callan answered, he seemed surprisingly cool to her. At prior meetings, including the visit she'd just made to the Department of Homeland Security, the agent had not only pressed her—relentlessly—to join his investigation team, he'd wrapped his outreach in something more. The vibe Heat got was personal. She believed Special Agent

Callan wouldn't have minded getting intimate. So when he said he was kind of busy, Nikki felt taken aback. And what else? Maybe a little disappointed? But then he fell into form. "I'm in the swamp and up to my ass in alligators, but I could meet you later. Want to hook up for a cocktail?"

She said yes. And then felt guilty. And then wondered why.

Heat wanted to meet someplace packed and noisy, but Callan had an interview on the Upper East Side and chose Bemelmans in the Carlyle, to her chagrin, a softly quiet bar with leather upholstery, dreamy lighting, and worst of all, intimacy. She gave him the long arm when they shook and let him take the banquette. Normally she liked a view of the door, but a chair made her feel less trapped. She ordered a wine spritzer, a drink Nikki despised, but she needed a clear head and didn't want to send a false cue with a gateway cocktail. He surprised her, going for a mineral water. His second surprise was getting right to business.

"You'll be happy to know we scored some surveillance pics of Salena Kaye following her escape from that chopper."

"That was quick," she said, remembering the check-in she'd made on her way out of the precinct house, of poor Raley still poring over miles of security video.

"Facial recognition software. I'll zap you copies."

"Great. Where did you pick her up?"

"Coming off the Q train in Coney Island. Speculation is she either operates out of there or had a meet. We're checking car services and other resources we have. If I told you more, I'd have to, well, you know the rest." He smiled and she felt uneasy. After the waiter came with the drinks and left, he said, "Kaye must have put up quite a fight to get away from you."

"Please, I feel guilty enough. My combat skills have gotten a little rusty lately."

"The Navy SEAL?" he asked. "Tragic. His name was Don, right?" God, this guy did his homework. Callan knew her murdered friend Don had been her close-combat sparring partner. Nikki studied the DHS agent, wondering if he also knew that she and Don once had a no-strings sexual relationship. The ex-SEAL used to call himself her trainer with benefits. If Bart Callan knew about that part, he didn't let on. So she couldn't tell if there was deeper meaning when he said, "Listen, if you want a new partner, I love a good workout."

Her gaze left his to dwell on the walls of the bar, which she recognized had been illustrated by the same artist who'd drawn the Madeline books. "I called because I want to hear again about your contact with my mother," she said, glancing back his way, glad now to be on her ground. "A few weeks ago you said something about an informant."

"There's not much more I can tell you."

"Then tell me again."

"I'm not holding back, Detective. Data is sparse." She arched a brow at him, and he said, "But I'll happily go over it again. I was FBI then and was made point liaison with your mother when she reached out to the Bureau to say she knew of a threat to security within our borders. She told me she had been developing an informant within a terror group, and we funded her two hundred grand to bribe her insider in exchange for proof and details of the plot. We gave your mother the money for the transaction the day she was murdered."

Heat had already known that much. But she now wanted to ask some new questions. "Did you know who her informant was?" When the agent shook no, she said, "I believe it was a man name Ari Weiss. Deceased now, so no help. But he was college friends with a Brit living here named Carey Maggs." She searched his face for recognition of either name and got none. "Would it be a pain to ask you to run a check on Maggs for me?"

"You think he might be involved?"

She shrugged. "Doesn't seem to be. But I like both belt and suspenders, you know?" Callan twisted open his gold Cross ballpoint and wrote the name down. When he'd finished, she asked, "What about the two hundred thou? Did it ever surface? I know you guys had to mark the bills."

He wagged his head again. "End of our intel, end of story." Then he added, "Well, it was the end of the trail until you exposed Tyler Wynn. Which is why I am renewing my pitch to you. The memos out of DC call it cooperative interface. Join me, Nikki. I have resources. We'd make a great team." He started to reach a hand across the table, but she casually slid hers onto her lap.

"Thanks, but I do better independently."

He waved his hands back and forth between the two of them. "Then what do you call this?"

"Cooperative interface. And your NYPD appreciates it."

Out on Madison Avenue, she declined his offer of a ride,

even though it would have afforded her a measure of security with Salena Kaye on the hunt for her. The agent said fine, but reminded her that if she ever wanted a sparring partner, he'd be game. From her taxi, Nikki glimpsed him getting into a black Suburban with US government plates, and figured Bart Callan could give her quite a workout.

Detective Heat closed her eyes and ran her math. The equation began with Callan's intel that her mom had been cultivating an informant. He couldn't name the insider, but with the new connection Nikki had drawn from her mother to Ari Weiss as a member of Tyler Wynn's circle, she didn't have to be at a blackboard in *Good Will Hunting* to surmise that Cynthia Heat had not been spying on Dr. Weiss—she was cultivating him as a snitch.

She pulled up his obituary on her iPhone. The date of his passing from a tick-borne illness was January 2, 2000. Only six weeks after her mother's death.

As soon as she locked her apartment door behind her, Heat speed- dialed the home of a judge she'd met at one of Rook's weekly poker games. After Judge Simpson razzed her about giving him a chance to win his money back, Nikki asked him a favor: to write a court order for the exhumation of Ari Weiss.

Röyksopp startled her from the computer screen. After Rook's call that morning from Nice, his ringtone, a song from a caveman commercial, seemed newly appropriate to Nikki.

"It's late there. I was afraid you'd be in bed," said Rook.

"I'm going over squad reports on my serial killer."

"I'm in London. Heathrow, actually. Workin' my way back to you, babe." The joker, trying to laugh it off, she thought during the long silence she fed him. "Should be there by sunup, your time. I'm flying Virgin."

"I doubt that." Another dose of awkward pause.

"Nikki, I guess I can see why you got all bent about Yardley, but you're reading way too much into this."

"Am I?"

"Yes." They listened to each other breathe. Then he said, "They're calling my flight."

"How long is it?"

"Let's see, uh . . . a little over seven hours."

"Good," she said. "Use it to work on your empathy."

Detective Heat brought her crew in for another early roll call the next morning. This time, they were joined by Detectives Malcolm and Reynolds, on loan from the major case squad. They were quick studies, so Nikki only needed to use the first ten minutes to recap the two murders and get them up to speed. As she wrapped it up, Sharon Hinesburg slid into the back of the bull pen, the only detective to be tardy.

Traces on the physical evidence from each homicide scene had brought no results after a day and a half of calling and canvassing. The red and yellow string was so common and widely available that screening recent purchases could take weeks, plus it could have been bought months or years ago. Same, too, with the skate wheel.

Malcolm raised a hand. "Let me tell you something." He slouched back in his usual pose and planted one of his work boots on the back of a chair. "Coming in cold? . . . Whenever I come across props like this in a case, it's one of two things. Either there's some sort of personal crap the guy's working out . . ."

"You mean like fetishes?" asked Heat.

"Yeah, or some fucked-up, brain-fried, thumb-sucking obsession like his mommy wouldn't let him have pets or ride a skateboard."

". . . While carrying scissors," added his partner, Reynolds.

"Or second, he's just seeding chaff to mess with our heads." Malcolm brought his cup up to sip. "Who knows?"

"Only the killer," said Heat. "Let's keep on tracing those items, especially the string, which is common to both, but keep digging on the victims. People in their lives, how they spent their last day, and especially—are they somehow connected to each other beyond their job types?"

Detective Raley reported that only one neighborhood camera was pointed at the Maxine Berkowitz crime scene. "It's outside a neighborhood Islamic center on Riverside Drive," he said. "And it's out of order."

Heat logged that in marker on the Berkowitz whiteboard, then tapped the identical notation for the pizza joint cam in the other murder. "Coincidence?" she said. "I would say strange enough to be considered . . ."

"Wait for it," called Feller.

". . . an odd sock," said Nikki, and the room erupted in a chorus of "Yessss!" at the first invocation of Heat's pet investigative phrase on this case. But the rowdiness was quelled when one of the administrative aides brought in the morning papers and held one of the tabloids up to the room. The bold headline screamed: dead tie! Underneath, against a white background, blared a giant photo of two coils of string: one red, one yellow.

Heat dismissed the meeting, and the rest of the squad did exactly what she did: They dove into the *New York Ledger.* "Exclusive," read the subhead, and the byline was Tam Svejda, Senior Metro Reporter for the *Ledger*—whom Heat knew, among other things, to be a lazy journalist prone to easy handouts from "insiders." Detective Hinesburg had whispered confidential material to her before, acting as Captain Irons's mouthpiece—an apt term, considering her sexual relationship with the skipper. To Nikki the article felt warmed over, derivative of old reports already made public. But then there was the leak of the big hold-back: that the two homicides were literally bound together by string, which pointed to a serial killer operating in Manhattan.

"Now, calm down, Detective," said Wally Irons. Heat appeared in his office before he could set down his briefcase. "We were going to release that today anyway."

"But we didn't. Someone leaked it. And whoever it was put our MO hold-back on page one," she said, brandishing the picture of the string.

"First things first," he said, seeming to enjoy this. "Tam Svejda called me for comment, and you can see for yourself, I downplayed the serial killer angle. Here it is." He ran a finger down the column and quoted, "Precinct Commander Captain Wallace Irons cautioned against leaping to conclusions. 'We cannot rule out the possibility that these killings could be the work of separate individuals.'"

"Nobody's going to buy that," said Heat.

"Ah, but it's on the record. I did my part."

Nikki slapped her thigh with the tabloid, wondering how she had gotten so lucky to work under the Iron Man. Detective Ochoa stuck his head in the door.

"Excuse me, Detective? Got a call on your line from a guy who says he's the serial killer."

"See?" Nikki shook the newspaper at Irons. "The bogus calls are starting already."

But then Ochoa said, "Detective Heat? He asked if you liked to roller blade."

Heat tossed the tabloid on a guest chair and rushed out to her desk.

FIVE

"This is Detective Heat."

"Got your attention, did I?" The voice sounded male, but distorted, the way *20/20* electronically disguises voices of mob witnesses and whistle-blowers.

"It's a start," said Nikki. She sat at her desk, and when she swiveled in her chair, she saw that the entire squad had gathered around her. "So. Tell me what you're calling about." There was a loud click and the line went dead. She stared at the phone and had started to tell the others he'd hung up when her line rang. She jumped on it. "Heat."

The distortion made him sound even more chilling. "Do not fuck with me. Pull that casual chatty bullshit again, I'm gone. Got it?"

"Got it."

"I'm going to talk, and you're going to listen." Nikki looked over at Raley where he coordinated the call trace at his desk. "What's this shit in the paper about it could be two people? Do I have to prove it's not?"

"No," she said immediately.

"We'll see. I get to decide that, cover girl." All of her training had taught Heat to remain dispassionate in these kinds of calls. But her heart bumped at the reference to her magazine cover. She tried to bat away the personalization. He had other ideas. "Think you're so smart, Detective Heat? How smart do you feel running around like a rat in a maze? You smell a clue but you can't see it. You need something to unlock that door."

Nikki wanted to keep him talking, not just for the trace but to get a handle on him. "You don't have to make this a contest."

"Sorry." Then he laughed, a digitally altered Darth Vader. "Tell you what, cover girl. Maybe I'll give you a hand on the next one." And then he clicked off again. Heat stood to look over the other detectives at Raley, who shook his head and hung up his phone.

Nikki went into the restroom and splashed water on her face again and again. It just seemed like something to do when all she wanted was to be alone. Drying off, she felt the paper towel tremble in her hands as she took in the magnitude of what had just happened. A challenge had been laid down. An already baffling case had suddenly taken on a new dimension for Heat, who now found herself matching wits against a serial killer, with innocent lives at stake over how good she really was. "Cover girl," she muttered into her hands. Nikki peeled the wet towel off her face, chucked it, and left the room without so much as a glance in the mirror.

When Heat came back into the bull pen, she found another unsettling surprise waiting. "*Je suis retourné!*" Jameson Rook slid off her blotter and stood beside his roll-along bag. Grinning through traveler's stubble, he held his arms open wide as she approached. She wouldn't ice him in public, but the hug Nikki gave him wouldn't exactly have lighted up the

Kiss Cam at the Garden. "Brr," he said in a low tone. Then added, "See, I've been working on my empathy."

"Not the best time, Rook."

"Let me guess." He held up his copy of the *Ledger*. "I saw this in the airport when I got off the plane."

Raley walked by, holding out a transcript of the phone call. She made a no-look snatch as he moved on, distributing it to the squad as they assembled around the Murder Boards. "The serial killer reads the *Ledger*, too, and he just called."

"You spoke to him?"

"I did."

"Then I got back just in time." He breezed past her and took an empty seat with the detectives. Determined to ignore this new distraction, Nikki took her place up front.

"An assignment," said Heat as she surveyed the room. "I need someone out at Reception to monitor incoming calls so if our serial killer tries me again, he gets right through." Her gaze fell on Detective Hinesburg. "Sharon, you're elected."

Hinesburg made the face of snippy annoyance. "Fine. Your party."

"You're right," said Nikki, who waited for Hinesburg to saunter off to the precinct lobby, figuring that if the detective was out of earshot, she couldn't learn anything to leak to the paper. Heat addressed the rest of the group. "Before we begin, has anyone not read this?" She held up her copy of the tabloid.

After a moment of silence Ochoa said, "Want me to ask Detective Hinesburg?"

When the squad's knowing laughter settled, Heat said, "Yeah, I have a feeling Sharon's caught up." She waited out a few more chuckles then brought them to business. "Most of you heard my side of the two calls we just got. And you've all got the transcript. Detective Raley also has dubbed an audio copy off our digital call server. Rales?"

He opened the WAV file on his laptop speakers. At first, Rook and the detectives started to read along. But as the chilling call continued, enticingly sinister because of the digitally futzed voice, they all abandoned their hard copies and leaned forward, staring instead at the computer, as if it were the man himself instead of the playback device for a killer's audio bit stream. When it finished, Detective Raley clicked it off.

Complete silence followed.

Heat broke it by asking, "OK, what did we learn?" She bisected the Maxine Berkowitz Murder Board with a vertical line and began a brainstorm list in the open white space.

"It's him," said Detective Feller. "He worked in the holdbacks that didn't get leaked: the skate reference and the rat in the maze thing? It's him."

"For now, let's say so," Heat agreed, and saw bobbleheads.

"Tech-savvy," said Detective Reynolds. "Not everyone out there knows how to alter his voiceprint like that."

Rook couldn't resist. "There's an app for that?"

"Raley," said Heat. "As my King of All Surveillance Media, find out if there is." Rales nodded and made a note. "What else?"

"Dude's controlling," called out Ochoa.

Heat said, "No kidding," and wrote the trait on the

board. "The way he hung up on the first call to let me know who's boss."

"And the second call," added Rook. "It was all about making his points his way, in his own time, like a billiard champ running the table."

Detective Rhymer said, "I'd put smart up there, too." As Nikki posted that, he continued, "He knew exactly how long to stay on the call to beat the trace, and he also knew how to push your buttons, talking about case frustration . . ."

". . . Calling you a cover girl," said Reynolds. Nikki's eyes went to Rook's and then away.

"I think this guy's beyond smart and controlling," said Malcolm. "I say he's pissed. Check it out." He skim-read from the transcript, " 'Do not fuck with me.' . . . 'I'm going to talk, and you're going to listen.' . . . 'Think you're so smart, Detective Heat?' "

"That's not just pissed," said Raley.

"That's competitive," finished his partner. "Talking about making it a contest, and maybe 'helping you' with the next one."

"That's the biggest clue of all," said Heat. "And the worst." She didn't have to voice it. The caller already had—that there would be a next one.

Later that morning, Roach came to Nikki's desk. "Rook was right," said Detective Ochoa.

"There *is* an app for that." Raley picked up. Across the room at his squatter's desk, Rook overheard and came to join them as the media king briefed Heat. "There's not only an actual app, but we found a slew of consumer software out there for altering voices. All you need is a laptop to change how you sound."

His partner continued, "You can do the Darth Vader like our man, or girls can sound like old ladies, or men can pretend to be women . . ."

Rook jumped in. "That's why I always say . . ."

" 'Check the Adam's apples,' " said Roach in a singsong chorus.

Heat stayed on task. "So this is all widely available?"

"Maybe not as much as skate wheels and string," said Raley, "but close. Plus a hobbyist could probably go to his neighborhood Radio Shack and find all he needed to build his own electronic voice box."

"Then we start calling Radio Shacks." As Nikki said it, she knew—and they knew—it could be tail chasing. The kind of thing she'd put Sharon Hinesburg on. "We have to take every shot."

They split off to work it, and she called after them, "And ask Detective Rhymer to reach out to the app vendors." To Heat's irritation, Rook stayed put. "A little busy," she said, picking up a report.

"Well, when are we going to talk about this? And you know the 'this' I mean."

She gestured to the bull pen with the file. "I doubt the Homicide Squad Room is the optimal place to talk about your romp in the South of France with an old flame."

"No, the Homicide Squad Room is perfect. Because this is murder for me."

"Very glib, Pulitzer Man. We'll definitely talk. But I have enough distraction to deal with right now, and two murders to work."

"Make it three." They turned to Detective Feller as he made his way over from his desk. "Can't be sure it's your boy's doing, but another one just turned up." And just like that, another ball got juggled up in the air.

In the category of extended-stay, hybrid hotel-apartments, the HMS pressed the envelope. The über-hip HMS, acronym for Home Meet Stay, catered more to the actor in town for a movie shoot than the road warrior looking for a plexi cylinder of Cheerios at a breakfast bar. On the way through the dour, mood-lit lobby, Detectives Heat and Feller had to pause while Rook got snagged by an Irish rock legend who was camping there while he scored a Broadway musical. Rook freed himself with a vague promise of cocktails sometime, and they moved on to the crime scene upstairs.

A pair of uniforms stood a little taller when Heat got off the elevator on nine and walked the herringbone carpet toward their posts at an open door. Camera flashes from inside popped against their backs, briefly printing their shadows on the opposite wall.

"African-American male, age sixty to sixty-five," recited the medical examiner on their arrival in the bedroom of the suite. "Photo ID on the deceased indicates he is one Douglas Earl Sandmann." The top mattress had been pushed aside, and Heat and the other two had to move around the bed for a look at the victim, whose body reclined faceup on the box spring.

Feller asked, "Isn't this the exterminator dude from those TV commercials?"

"Oh, my God, it's Bedbug Doug," said Rook, who then recited the deceased's catchphrase, " 'We squash the competition!' "

"Easy, Rook, we get who he is." Nikki turned to her friend Lauren Parry, whom she had been seeing too much of lately for the wrong reasons. "What about COD?"

"Prelim cause of death is asphyxia. But not strangled like Maxine Berkowitz. Mr. Sandmann was suffocated by a mattress."

"Ironic on so many levels," said Rook. "But mainly because Bedbug Doug was killed with a bed."

Heat forgave his irreverence because Rook had made a point. "Just like the restaurant inspector being killed by a pizza oven and a Channel 3 reporter getting strangled by a TV cable."

Detective Feller walked the room, which had not been disturbed, except for the upset bed and bedding. "If he was done here, there's no sign of struggle."

Dr. Parry, waiting out the body temp reading, said, "I picked up chloroform traces here on the front of his coveralls. Forensics roped off some scrape-and-drag depressions in the living room rug. They're testing the fibers for chloroform spills."

Heat turned to the responding officer. "Who found him?"

"Housekeeping. Manager says there's a supermodel coming in to do a calendar shoot, and the maid was checking to make sure the apartment was ready for her."

"So this isn't the victim's room?" asked Heat.

"No, but he does have a bedbug contract with the building."

"So why was he here? Did they call him in to check out the room?"

"Manager says no. He didn't even know the guy was up here."

Nikki sent Feller off to interview the manager more fully, and sent the pair of unis in the hall to knock on some doors to ask if anyone heard or saw anything. Lauren completed her field testing and ballparked the time of death window between midnight and 2 a.m. "Which means," said Rook, "that your serial killer had already murdered him when he called you this morning."

"If this is his work," said Nikki. "We don't know that yet." She crouched down and lifted the dust ruffle with her gloved hand to look under the bed.

Rook scanned the dresser and stuck his head inside the armoire housing the TV. He lifted up the Bible inside the nightstand and said, "Death, where is thy string?"

"Got it," said Lauren Parry. They came to her side, and she indicated about an eighth of an inch of red string, barely noticeable because it was wedged between the victim's shoulder and the box spring.

"OK to move him?" asked Nikki.

The ME said to hang on, called in the crime scene unit photographer to document the string and its position, then gave Heat a nod. She and Rook stood back while Parry and her technician rolled the body on its side. The CSU shooter positioned himself and clicked; his flash strobed at what they found underneath: a length of red string tied to a length of yellow string, tied to a length of purple string. The end of the purple string was knotted through the hole in the head of a futuristic-looking door key.

"I need you, and pronto, Heat," called Captain Irons as she double-timed past his office door toward the squad room. In spite of her low opinion of him, as the skipper, Wally deserved a briefing. So she reversed field and caught him up on the murder of Bedbug Doug. When she'd finished and turned to go, he said, "Not done yet, Detective." Nikki stopped, not having a second to waste, hoping he could make it quick. "Do you know the pressure I'm under? Do you know how many times I get called about bringing this to a resolution?"

"Yes, sir, I can only imagine they're all over you at One PP."

He made a face and shrugged. "No, actually, the commissioner knows we're busting our humps. I'm talking about the media."

"Seriously? This is about media pressure?"

"Listen, Heat, this has been on my mind, so I might as well get it out." He gestured to a chair and they sat. "I know you're spending your time on your other . . . more personal case. But now that we have a serial killer and people are paying attention in the press, you have to stop chasing that dog and put your focus where I need it."

She had been waiting for this shoe to drop. She had

known that her dimwit commander, who'd initially been so alarmed by Nikki's poisoning attempt that he tried to bench her ass, would forget all that. Had known that he'd whimper about her split focus. Had known that because his coconut couldn't hold two thoughts at once, he'd assume nobody else's could. It pissed her off that Irons talked so casually about this "other case" when it was her own mother's murder she was trying to solve. But as Nikki had waited for this inevitable chat to come down, she'd been forming a strategy.

Cement heads like Wally Irons had to be managed, not cornered. Heat needed to set her personal anger aside and be effective, because much more was at stake than justice for her mom. Nikki felt in her bones that something else was coming from this Tyler Wynn conspiracy. Otherwise all this new activity—including the attempt on her life—wouldn't be bubbling up. So instead of outboxing the Iron Man, she'd outsmart him.

"Sir, although my connection to the Tyler Wynn investigation started personally, there is one thing I am dead sure of."

"Which is?"

"That you and I are probably the only two cops in this department smart enough to see that this is all bigger than one homicide." A white lie of flattery couldn't hurt. In fact, it was pathetic to see how Wally lapped it up.

"True . . ." He smiled to himself, then to her. "True."

"And when the handcuffs come out—and they will—who is going to be the hero of this?" She watched his eyes rise to the trophies on his bookcase. "One more thing, sir? What you have so wisely done here is put me on notice not to drop the ball on either of these cases. You have my pledge, Captain. I won't fail you. Just watch."

She held her breath while his brow creases deepened in some version of thought. Then Irons stood and said the magic words. "Just let me know if you get swamped."

"Will do."

"Meantime, the media's storming me with ladders and torches. Can you give me something to tell them?"

"Sure," she said. "You might even want to write this down." She waited for him to uncap a pen with his teeth and turn to a fresh page of his legal pad. " 'No comment.' " And then she left to get to work.

Heat recited a download of the HMS crime scene for the bull pen. When she finished, Detective Rhymer said, "Trying to grab at any connection here. We found that rat with our first vic. Did Bedbug Doug, by chance, also exterminate rats?"

"Bedbug Doug?" asked Ochoa, incredulous.

"No rats, just bedbugs," said Raley, reenacting one of Bedbug Doug's TV commercials.

Rook couldn't resist. "What about ants?"

Raley came right with it. "Nope, just bedbugs."

"Raccoons?"

"Just bedbugs."

"Skunks? Cockroaches? Opossums?"

"Nope, nope, nope. Just bedbugs."

Heat said, "Are you done? Be done."

"Got something," said Detective Malcolm as he and Reynolds rolled chairs over from their shared desk. "A link between our first two victims." The room hushed, and all heads tilted toward them. "Know how in ratings sweeps, TV stations do those shocking exposés about restaurant kitchen gross-outs? I just tracked down an ex–assignment editor at Channel 3. When they bumped Maxine Berkowitz off the anchor desk at WHNY, guess what her first 'Doorbuster' segment was? And who her prime on-camera source was from the Health Department?"

Nobody said it. But Heat took a red marker and drew a line connecting restaurant inspector Roy Conklin and Maxine Berkowitz. She tossed the dry erase pen on the aluminum tray of the whiteboard and said, "Malcolm and Reynolds, you rock."

Feller said, "I wonder if Maxine B. ever did a 'Doorbuster' report on bedbugs or Bedbug Doug. That would connect them."

"We're all connected one way or another," said Rook. "You can trace anyone to anyone in six hops. It's like playing Six Degrees of Marsha Mason."

Detective Rhymer said, "You mean Six Degrees of Kevin Bacon."

Rook said, "Please. I grew up with a mom who's a Broadway diva. In our house, it was always Marsha Mason."

Roach interrupted with a report on the unusual key found under Doug Sandmann's body. Raley posted photos of it as Ochoa recited from his notes. "It's a high-security key. New technology from an Australian company. As you can see from the close-ups, it's futuristic in design. Looks like a *Star Wars* X-Wing fighter and a barracuda made a baby."

Raley picked up from his partner. "According to the

manufacturer's Web site, because of its dual shank and one-of-a-kind cutting, this key would fit only one in about seventeen thousand locks. Here's the good part: Each set is registered. It's the middle of the night in Australia, but hopefully, we can get a line on whose lock this fits, because it could be the next victim's."

"We're also making rounds of local locksmiths who carry the brand," said Detective Ochoa. "It's high-end, so there aren't that many."

"So go to," said Heat, and the squad dispersed. Her excitement at sensing some traction became muted by mistrust. This killer was a gamesman, a manipulator who had already murdered his third victim hours before he called to threaten it. Nikki only hoped they could move fast enough to save his fourth.

Heat's e-mail chimed with a message from Bart Callan: "Ran Carey Maggs, per request. Your instinct right on. Clean returns on all data. PS: If you worked here, you'd be home now! Haha—BC."

As she saved the e-mail, Detectives Raley and Ochoa speed-walked to her desk, both wearing eager faces. Raley said, "The lock manufacturer in Australia has a 24/7 help desk."

Ochoa overlapped, "They tracked the serial number and said the lock and key set is registered through a locksmith on Amsterdam."

"Did you call?"

"No answer," said Roach.

"At a locksmith?" Nikki leaped to her feet. "Amsterdam and what?"

Heat and Rook pulled up behind the Roach Coach five blocks south, at 77th. As they came together on the sidewalk, Ochoa said to them, "Rales and I were just in this neighborhood running a check on that Rollerblade wheel." He indicated the skate shop with a sign that read, "Central Park rentals by the hour or half day."

Nikki's attention went to Windsor's Locks, the storefront next door. Something was definitely off. The window had an "Open" sign, but behind it the shop was dark.

"OK, now this is too weird," said Rook, pointing. "Rats. Check it out. A pet store on one side with rats in the window and a roller skate store on the other?"

The pair of backup blue-and-whites Heat had called for pulled up behind her. Without taking her eyes from the store, she told the unis to cover the back. As the patrol officers deployed, she took the lead toward the glass door, flanked by Raley and Ochoa. They paused. Heat put one hand on the grip of her Sig Sauer. She reached for the door handle with the other.

"Wait," said Ochoa. "You smell that?"

Heat sniffed. "Gas."

SIX

"That smells stronger than just a tiny leak," said Ochoa.

Detective Heat turned immediately to Raley. "Call it in." Then she flashed back to the natural gas explosion she'd investigated in 2006, a suicide that completely leveled a three-story town house. "No sparks," she told him. "Use your phone on the upwind corner. Also, tell those uniforms to come back and start clearing these buildings." She waved a circle over her head to indicate the residences above the shops. "And tell everyone: no smokes, no light switches, no phones."

Ochoa was already on the move, waving people off the sidewalk, when Rook turned to her from peeking in the locksmith's window. "Nikki. Someone's on the floor."

She cupped her hands on the sides of her face to cut the glare and put her nose to the glass. In the back of the narrow store, a pair of man's legs protruded from behind the counter, toes splayed out. Heat ran a quick calculation. The risk of setting off an explosion versus the chance that if that man was alive but suffocating on fumes, she might save him.

Decision time.

"Miguel!" Detective Ochoa turned to her from up the street, where he had corralled some pedestrians. "Man down.

I'm going in." Then she turned back and caught Rook reaching for the door handle. "Whoa, whoa, whoa!" He froze. "If that door has an electric chime or alarm contact, you could blow us to Newark."

Rook withdrew his hand. "What say we avoid that?"

A rapid sidewalk check. Nikki jogged to the corner and grabbed a city trash can. The steel barrel was heavy, and Ochoa met her to lift the other side. "Careful not to scrape the concrete," she said on their way up the sidewalk. "Don't want any sparks."

"On your three," said Ochoa. Litter spilled onto the ground as the two detectives lifted the garbage can sideways with the metal bottom aimed at the glass. Nikki gave a count and they rammed the window. Instead of breaking, though, it spider veined. Heat made another three count, and they hit it again, much harder. This time they not only punched a hole, the entire window shattered, cascading jagged-edged chunks down from above, nearly guillotine-slicing them before crashing to bits on the sidewalk and the floor of the shop. Nikki kicked out the shards on the spiky ledge of the sill, swung one leg inside, then the other.

She ran to the end of the front counter and knelt beside the man, pressing her fingers to his neck. The carotid bumped against her touch. Ochoa joined her. Holding her breath in the toxic air, she nodded to Miguel to indicate the locksmith was still alive. Getting him out would be a challenge. He was short and slender, but unconsciousness had made him dead weight. Heat's aching lungs burned for air, and in the strain of lifting him, she gasped in a breath she instantly regretted.

The rotten eggs smell from the mercaptan in the gas made her throat clutch and her head go light. Nikki lost her grip and the man fell against her. She quickly jammed her thigh under him and stopped the fall. Fighting nausea, she got a better hold and clawed his work shirt. Together she and Ochoa managed to lug him to the window, where the new, sure hands of the arriving FDNY crew took him from them, lifting the victim over the ledge and onto to a gurney, where paramedics took over.

Heat and Ochoa stood bent over on the sidewalk, coughing and gasping. Both took hits off the oxygen they were offered. In the short minutes it took them to recover, New York's Bravest had already killed electrical power to the building, shut off the gas main, and cranked up portable fans to vent the fumes.

Rook gave Heat and Ochoa each a bottle of water, and both chugged. "While you were in there, I went in the pet shop and got everyone out. Ever see *Pee-wee's Big Adventure*? I was this close to running out with two handfuls of snakes."

The paramedics said they had rescued the locksmith just in time. Glen Windsor had stabilized on oxygen, and they were about to transport him to Roosevelt for observation. Heat said she wanted to ask him a few questions first. The paramedic didn't like that, but Nikki promised to keep it brief.

"Thank you," said Windsor looking up from the gurney at Heat and Ochoa. "They said I almost didn't make it." An EMT asked him to keep his oxygen mask on, but he said he was fine, took a hit, and held it resting on his chest.

Nikki saw the tremble in his hand. An ordeal like this

would take its toll on anyone. The locksmith was young, maybe about thirty, but for a small guy built slim like a pro bowler, it must have been extra rough on his body. "Mr. Windsor, we won't keep you, but I'm wondering if you can tell me what happened."

"Shit, you and me both." The pale guy on the stretcher had an affable soft-spokenness that reminded Nikki of Detective Rhymer, in whose mouth profanity sounded quaint instead of offensive. "Sorry," he said. "Another quarter in the swear jar for me." He took one more pull off the O2 mask and continued, "It was a slow day for business. I was sitting, just doing the Angry Birds at the counter. Next thing, I hear something behind me, and before I can turn, this hand comes around over my face. That's all she wrote till I woke up out here."

"Was there a rag in the hand?"

He shrugged. "Sorry, just don't remember."

"Did you smell anything? Something sweet, maybe?"

His face lit up and he nodded. "Now that you say, yeah. Sort of like cleaning fluid or something." Heat whispered an aside to the EMT to have the ER check him for chloroform.

"What time did this happen?"

"Let's see. I was waiting for lunchtime. About noon." Nikki looked up the block at the bank clock. That would have been almost an hour ago. She felt a hot trail going cold by the minute.

"Sorry, Detective Heat," said the paramedic. "You're going to have to continue this later." Heat thanked Glen Windsor for his time as they wheeled him to the back of the ambulance. Then she appointed one of the uniforms to ride with him and stay by his side at the hospital until she got there.

"Got your gas source right here," said the FDNY supervisor when Nikki came back inside Windsor's Locks, using the door this time. He pointed to the open metal hatch on the heating unit embedded flush in the wall of the shop. He had to shout over the din of the ventilator fans. "See here? Pilot's out, the combustion motor's been disconnected, and somebody pulled the stopper plug out of the test feed joint. Nothing to stop the gas and nothing to burn it off, so it just streamed out and filled the room. I don't want to think about what this could have done."

Detectives Feller, Malcolm, and Reynolds arrived to assist them in the search for clues. "And by clues, you mean string, right?" asked Rook. " 'Cause it don't mean a thing if it ain't got that string."

"Let's just strike a match and end this," said Reynolds to Malcolm.

The first wave of the search yielded none of the earmarks of the prior crime scenes. As the fire crew declared the atmosphere safe enough to turn off their fans, Heat stared at the one positioned at the open back exit and asked the supervisor to find out if his men opened the door themselves or found it ajar.

"Found it that way," said the uniform next to her. Officer Strazzullo had been among the patrolmen that Heat sent to cover the alley then called back for the evacuation. "When we accessed the alleyway, the back door to the shop stood open about yay." He sectioned about eighteen inches of air with his hands.

"Dang," said Detective Feller to Heat. "Bet you almost had him, and he booked."

Raley asked her, "You think he could have been in here when we rolled up?"

Heat didn't say anything. Instead, she stepped out the open door to the alley. The rest followed, and when they joined her, Nikki stood beside a Dumpster positioned under the fire escape ladder leading to the roof. "Officer Strazzullo, was this bin here when you arrived?"

"Sorry, I don't recall."

"Can I play out this scenario?" asked Feller. "Our killer's inside when you approach, Detective Heat. You interrupt his job on the locksmith—'Uh-oh!'—and flush him out the back door. He hides behind this Dumpster . . ." The detective acted it out, tracing steps from the back door and hiding behind the bin. "He's here when Strazzullo arrives—this close to a collar—but then the cavalry gets called back out front and he gets away."

"Looks like an escape setup to me," said Ochoa, eyeballing the short distance from the Dumpster lid to the fire escape ladder. "Right after Strazzy got called away to work the evacuation, our boy climbed up on the bin, and poof."

"Could be how he came and went, both," agreed Raley.

Detective Heat boosted herself on top of the bin and ascended the fire escape ladder with teeth clenched. On each rung, she silently voiced anger and frustration at the killer being this close to capture—if he truly had been there.

If.

The others followed her up, and they all walked the roof in a line, searching the flat, grimy surface for anything that told them if.

They found it at the far end of the rooftop. Everyone saw it at the same time. And knew.

One end of a length of red string had been tied to the knob of the door to the access stairs and fluttered in the warm breeze. The string had many colors, following the pattern of the other homicides. Red was tied to yellow. Yellow was fastened to purple. And purple was knotted to a new piece of string, this one green.

Heat had already stationed officers to cover all exits of this building, including the stairwell. Silently, she drew her service piece and held it up at-ready beside the door. All but Rook, who was unarmed, did the same and took tactical positions. She nodded, and Detective Feller yanked the door open. Inside, at the top of the steps, stood Officer Strazzullo and his partner. Everyone holstered.

They looked down at the threshold at a broken piece of cinder block. Feller bent, and when he lifted it, a small piece of paper, slightly larger than a postage stamp, that had been underneath it fluttered off in the wind. Raley chased the scrap across the roof so it wouldn't blow away, and picked it up with his gloves.

Everyone stood around him in a huddle to see it. The paper, about an inch square, was blank on one side and had a color image on the other. It looked as if a small section from a photocopy of an oil painting had been cut with scissors. All it showed was someone's fingers and knuckles.

Detective Raley used his cell phone and captured a decent close-up image of the hand on the little square of paper before they turned it over to Forensics to fingerprint and lab it. Heat tasked Roach with seeing what they could find out about the painting it had been clipped from. "What you found out about the key saved this guy's life. Find out about the painting, maybe we'll capture our killer."

At Roosevelt Hospital, Heat had to hunt for parking because of all the news vans that had gathered outside the entrance to the Emergency Room. Reporters who were staking out positions for their stand-up pieces for that evening's newscasts saw Nikki and called out to her by name, hollering for comment. She kept her eyes front and badged herself and Rook past the officer at the door.

They found Glen Windsor sitting up with his legs dangling over the side of a bed in one of the trauma bays. He sipped apple juice through a straw, and the color had come back to his face. "How are you feeling, Mr. Windsor?" asked Heat.

He smiled and said, "Lucky to be alive." She returned his smile and thought, Buddy, you have no idea. "Thank you again. I've been thinking. How the hell did you know to come help me?"

Heat wasn't sure how much to tell him. On the one hand, he had been the target of a serial killer. But on the other, the press waited, and she wanted to control what got out there. "We smelled gas," she said, truthfully enough.

Windsor said he felt up to it, so she asked him to take her back over his version of the assault. His account from the crime scene held, and when she moved on to inquire about any unusual contacts, activity, or new people in his life, the locksmith reflected then shook no.

Next she showed him a picture of the key she had found with the last victim. He recognized it immediately. "That's a BiLock. Aussie. Very high-security product. They manufacture rim locks, cam locks, deadlocks, mortise locks, padlocks . . ." As he went on and on, Rook caught Nikki's eye and turned slightly away to hide his smile. He had often entertained Heat imitating Bubba Blue, reciting to Forrest Gump all the ways to cook shrimp.

When Windsor finished his list, she said, "BiLock told us this is registered to your business."

"That's right, I sell them. Not many yet but it's a good product."

"What I mean, Mr. Windsor, is that this exact key is registered to your inventory. Did you notice it was missing, and if so, is the lock gone, as well?"

He studied the picture and said, "I didn't know anything was missing." He stood up, suddenly worried about his shop. "I'd like to get back and do an inventory."

"We'll do that and send a detective to help. But I have a few quick things to ask."

He calmed, but she could sense his understandable distraction, so she hurried. What she needed to find out was if he had any connection to the other victims, however slight. She showed him head shots of the three prior victims. Roy Conklin meant nothing; same for Maxine Berkowitz, whom he only recognized as a reporter on TV. But when she flashed the picture of Douglas Sandmann, Windsor's eyes popped and he tapped it with his forefinger. "Hey, I know him. Bedbug Doug."

"From his TV ads?" asked Heat.

"Yeah. But I also did some work for him. About six months ago I upgraded all the locks and alarm keypads at his office over in Queens."

Heat and Rook traded glances, each registering a sudden rush of excitement at the break. Nikki tried to remain casual, masking her hope that the victim she saved could shed light on how an active serial killer was choosing his targets. "Glen, did you spend any time personally with Mr. Sandmann?"

"Most definitely. Doug approved the bid and cut the check when I finished."

"May I ask what you talked about?"

"Prices and my time frame. Pretty much what every prospect talks about."

"Anything else? Take a moment to think."

The locksmith took a sip of his juice and stared into the middle distance, then said, "No, sorry. I pretty much just walked him through the job. Nothing memorable. Nice guy, though. Let me pet his dog."

Rook chimed in. "Did you and Bedbug Doug have any friends in common?"

"No, sir."

"Did anyone arrange the job for you?" asked Heat, following Rook's thread. "Maybe a referral from another customer?"

"I wish. Got that account the usual way. Just me making cold calls. Opening the Yellow Pages and smiling 'n' dialing."

With Nikki's breakthrough hopes dimming, she asked him to keep thinking during the next few days. Heat gave him her business card so he could reach her if any detail, however insignificant, came to him.

Detective Feller called to alert her that he was in an undercover taxi he'd borrowed from his old NYPD unit and was standing by at the hospital's side door. The first thing Heat had done when she saw the media setting up was to arrange a discreet exit for Glen Windsor. But before she and Rook could sneak him out of the ER, Nikki got an unwelcome surprise.

"Here's our man!" called Captain Irons across the triage area. She turned as Wally breezed in along with Detective Hinesburg. As her precinct commander approached, Heat could see he not only had on a freshly pressed uniform shirt but wore a dusting of makeup on his porcine face. Like a moth to light, Irons had found the media and arrived ready for his close-up.

After a round of handshakes, back-claps, and a rousing "Glen, way to stay alive," the Iron Man asked Windsor if he would mind stepping out along with him to meet the press. The locksmith cast an anxious look at Heat, but the captain said, "Don't be nervous. You don't have to say anything, just stand with me, I'll do all the talking."

Heat drew her boss aside. "Cap, I really think this is a

bad idea. We don't want to spike the ball in the killer's face, do we? And I think the less that's public, the better."

"That's what you always think," said Sharon Hinesburg, inviting herself into the conversation. "Our skipper's taking a lot of shit. I say give him a chance to have a moment of victory."

"What victory, Captain?" said Heat, putting her back to Hinesburg. "He's still out there."

"Appreciate your input, Detective. But I am going to step up and let New Yorkers know the Twentieth Precinct is on top of this and saved a life. Excuse us." He left for the main entrance and the news cameras, his arm on the shoulder of Glen Windsor. As they stepped out the sliding glass doors, Detective Hinesburg turned to look back at Heat and winked.

Rook asked Nikki if she was ready to go. But she paused, struck by the recollection that, in this very emergency room, John Lennon had been declared DOA. Heat moved on, busy making other plans.

She came home that night to find Rook sound asleep on her couch and *No Reservations* blasting on the Travel Channel. He startled awake when she muted Anthony Bourdain's tetchy pub crawl through Ireland's politically charged saloons. Rook sat up and massaged his eye sockets with the heels of his hands. The jet lag, he explained, had crept up and walloped him. And with that, he served a natural segue to his French adventure. Nikki didn't seize it.

The awkwardness of dancing around the subject seemed less daunting—and less work—to her than confronting it.

Besides, why dance when you can distract? She began a monologue about work. "Randall Feller texted from the locksmith's shop," she said, putting her backup piece, a Beretta 950 Jetfire, in its cubby on the living room desk. "They located the matching lock for the mystery key in his storeroom, so that's that, as far as some potential vic being caged in a room somewhere." She moved to the kitchen and called from behind the open fridge door, "Forensics came up zip, no usable prints. Nothing in the store, or on the doorknob on the roof, or on the little piece of paper. And get this. In addition to locks, Glen also installs security systems. You think he had even one security cam in his own place? God. He's like the cobbler whose kids go shoeless. I'm having a beer, you want a beer?" She didn't get an answer, so she closed the refrigerator. And found him standing on the other side of the door. Waiting.

"This isn't going to go away," he said.

Nikki considered that a moment. She opened the fridge and got him a Widmer's to go with hers, then they headed back to the couch.

"Answer me this," she said when they sat down. Each tucked a leg under so they could face each other.

"What have I started here?" He chuckled. "Am I going to get interrogated by The Great Interrogator?"

"Your meeting, Rook. What were you hoping for?"

"To clear the air. So I can allay this irrational—totally irrational—jealous vibe I'm getting from you about Yardley Bell. Jesus, I went to France to help you. Why do I feel like I did something wrong?"

"My question—if I may ask it now—is how did Yardley Bell know you were there? And don't tell me it was coincidence. Did using your passport light up her Homeland Security grid, and she followed you across the Atlantic?"

"She suggested we go."

Nikki rocked backward in astonishment. "Oh. Right. Air cleared. Jealousy allayed. Boy, how irrational could I be?"

"See? That's why I didn't tell you. I knew you'd go to the bad place."

"And this doesn't do it?"

"In hindsight, I'll admit I may not have exercised my best judgment."

"What did you exercise?"

"Come on, you know me better than that."

"You, I know. She's another story."

"I told you, Yardley and I are past history."

"To you. But I know her type."

"And what type is that?"

"Obsessive old girlfriends who can't let go. You know what I'm talking about. The ones who drive across the country wearing NASA diapers and have tasers and duct tape in the trunk. Or who write thirty thousand e-mails with veiled threats to rival lovers."

"Yardley sent you an e-mail?"

"No! She doesn't have to. She can hop on a federal Gulfstream to France and rendezvous with you in fucking Nice."

"Where she provided invaluable support setting me up with Fariq Kuzbari. You should be delighted by that."

"Yeah, look at me. Couldn't be happier."

"You were happy when I told you. Until you found out she was there."

"That's the other thing. Rook, I have been on a mission to keep the feds away from me and out of my case. I've dealt with them a hundred times on a hundred other cases. Their so-called resources come with a price tag. I refuse to let them screw it up with their departmental politics or sell me out in the name of diplomatic expediency. I've kept DHS at arm's length," she said, deciding not to bring up Bart Callan. "Now Agent Heartthrob is sticking her nose in it—and using you to do it. Or vice versa, what's the diff?"

Rook tried to slow things. "Hey? Nikki?" He brought his pitch down and rested a hand on her knee. "This is so not you."

All of it, not just the past few days, but eleven years of it boiled over. She despised it whenever her emotions spilled out, but it was too late to stem this tide. In spite of herself, taciturn, compartmentalized, stoic Nikki Heat blurted her raw vulnerability to him. "I feel alone on this. Everything's coming at me at once. I can't do it by myself."

"Then why don't you want help?"

"I do. Just not from everyone. I can't trust everyone."

"What about me? The idiot who jumped in front of a bullet for you. Do you still trust me?"

There it was. The kind of moment an entire life pivots on as surely as the needle of a compass.

Nikki didn't answer yes or no. She did something else. Something bigger than she could ever speak. She showed it. Without a word, she rose from the couch and walked to her mother's piano bench to get the codes.

Rook listened intently as Heat told him everything. About the night three weeks ago when she had finally been able to bring herself to play her mother's piano for the first time since the murder. How she opened the music bench after eleven years and took out the music book, the one she had been taught from as a girl. And how, while playing it, she saw something unusual. Small pencil notations between the notes of the songs. He leaned over the book to examine them, squinting, turning his head, trying to make sense of the marks, and she told him what she believed, and, in doing that, answered his question about trust.

Nikki told Rook she believed that these markings were a secret code left by her mother. And that whatever information the symbols hid was the reason she had been killed. "And because all the signs say whatever conspiracy Tyler Wynn is involved in is heating up, I also believe if the wrong person found out we had this code, we'd both be killed, too."

"Swell," he said with a deadpan. "Thanks a lot for dragging me into this." And then they fell into each other's arms and held tight.

A few seconds passed. With her face still buried into him, Nikki said, "You're dying to get at that, aren't you?"

"It's killing me."

She pulled away and smiled. "All yours."

Rook didn't hesitate. He swung around to face the coffee table and opened the music book, bending closer, turning his head side to side, squinting some more at the pencil marks. While she let the man she trusted with her life study in peace, her gaze went to the silent TV, where a bartender at the Crown Salon in Belfast pulled Tony Bourdain a perfectly murky pint of Guinness. Nikki had made her leap of faith. At least for the moment, she, too, had no reservations.

They sat up most of the night, working together, banging their heads, trying to figure out the code. They switched from hefeweizen to French Roast, but the coffee only made them more alert, not any more enlightened. Heat answered all of Rook's questions but tried to avoid sharing too much of her path; his fertile imagination would do its best work unconstrained.

Even when he signed on the Internet, covering the same ground she had again and again, Nikki didn't warn him off or try to stop him. With his Beginner's Eyes Rook might find something she hadn't, and she didn't want to pollute his fresh thinking.

His quest went beyond her searches of the Egyptians, Mayans, and urban taggers, to the Phoenicians and Druids. Rook even investigated a site devoted to the mutt languages of some TV series called *Firefly*. That was when they knew it had come time to call it a night and start fresh at sunup. "You mean in about forty-five minutes?" she asked.

Immune to the caffeine, Heat fell into the deepest sleep she had enjoyed in ages. Call it the power of sharing her burden. When she awoke, the sheets on Rook's empty side of the bed felt cold to her touch. She pulled on her robe and found him sitting on the bench seat of the bay window, staring down at Gramercy Park, although Nikki couldn't be certain he was actually seeing anything at all except pencil marks on sheet music.

"Now you know where my head's been all these weeks," she said, resting her palms on his shoulders.

"My brain itches." He tilted backward and she kissed the top of his forehead. "You're going to hate me."

"You're giving up?"

"No."

"You don't believe it is a code?"

"I do."

"Then what?"

"I've been thinking."

"Always a source of concern."

"We're not going to crack this on our own. At least not soon enough to do any good. We need an assist." Nikki tensed and withdrew her hands. He turned from the window to face her. "Relax, I'm not talking about going to Yardley Bell. Or Agent Callan."

Old doubts about sharing with Rook began their noxious trickle. "Who then?"

It was only eight in the morning, but when Eugene Summers opened the door to his Chelsea loft, he greeted them looking radiant, groomed, and polished. The professional butler turned reality TV star bowed his silver head and smartly kissed the back of Nikki's extended hand, dismissing her apology about coming by so early and on short notice. "Nonsense. I'm delighted to see you. Plus it got me out of my robe."

"No kidding," said Rook. "You'll have to show me how you get a perfect dimple like that in a necktie."

"Will I?" said Summers. In spite of the fact that Rook was an unabashed fan of the reality star (or maybe because of that), his idol seemed less than thrilled to see him again. But the Maven of Manners, as the network promos and billboards advertised him, shook pleasantly nonetheless and gestured them to the living room, where he had set out warm croissants and jam beside a porcelain coffee service.

Back in the mid-1970s, then-twentysomethings Eugene Summers and Cynthia Heat had operated as spies for Tyler Wynn's CIA operation in Europe. They both had been part of his team, nicknamed the Nanny Network because Wynn's moles gained access to the homes of intelligence targets by working in domestic service. Heat's mom worked undercover as a piano tutor; Eugene, as a butler. That connection was why Rook had proposed that morning's visit to Nikki: to find out if the Nanny Network had a secret code.

Initially she was opposed. Sharing the existence of the code with Rook had been a giant step. Widening the circle of awareness—especially to someone once handled by Tyler Wynn—represented great risk. But Rook's calling out of the truth, that they were stuck, led her to agree. As long as they agreed to back-door the subject and not reveal they were personally in possession of the coded message.

"What brings you here so urgently, Detective?" asked the butler, politely waiting until after he'd poured their coffees and sat. His posture was perfect, and when Rook got appraised by the star's TV trademark Summers Stare, he rose up out of his slouch. And smiled.

She began her lie with "Just routine, really. As you must have heard, Tyler Wynn is still at large. We're just doing our diligence, following up with everyone who knew him."

"I had heard." Summers placed a palm against his top vest button and continued, "And I read the account of your horrible ordeal in Mr. Rook's Web article. Terrifying and heartbreaking." He paused, and she nodded to acknowledge his sympathetic look. "But I honestly don't know if I can be of use. The man certainly hasn't been in contact with me."

"Naturally that's one of my questions," said Heat. "Thank you."

"Good java." Rook set his cup down, sounding as offhanded as possible. "Some of Tyler Wynn's other acquaintances may have received communications from him."

"May have?" Eugene had smarts. They could see the granules of each sentence getting sieved and sorted behind his frameless glasses. "You aren't sure?"

"We're wondering, that's all," said Heat. "As we go through some of the effects of Tyler's accomplices, it occurs to me that there might be messages in code that we would never recognize as such."

"You want to know what you're looking at," said the butler. "For clues."

"Precisely," said Rook.

"Did you ever use a code in Wynn's network?" asked Heat.

Summers shook his head. "The closest we came were the drop boxes I told you about last time. We only put plain messages in them. Handwritten, and certainly not in any code." He grinned. "We were all a bit too rowdy and undisciplined to learn codes, let alone use them."

"What about Tyler Wynn?" she asked. "Did he use a code?"

"That I don't know. You could ask me anything else about Tyler Wynn. I could tell you his favorite wine, where he got his shoes custom made, the shop where he bought his Brie de Meaux. But as far as his means of encrypted communication, I'm sorry."

Nikki stared down at the coffee she'd let grow cold. Just as she put away her notebook, lamenting the trip and the exposure that had come with it, Rook spoke. "Eugene," he began, "something you said just gave me an idea. Tyler Wynn is a man of specific tastes, right?"

"Oh, please, you have no idea how particular."

"If you would indulge me some time, could I take a few hours to pick your brain about some of his habits, his likes and dislikes? It would really help me color my next article about him. You know, the American James Bond with his custom shoes and his personal *fromage*."

"A couple of hours . . . I have an interview with Lara Spencer this morning."

"Great," said Rook. "Then lunch after?" Boxed into the obligation, the famous butler gave Rook his trademark Summers Stare, then said yes.

On the elevator down from his loft, Heat said, "Tell me something, Rook, is everything in my life all about helping you write your next article?"

"That? That's not for any article. Here's what I'm thinking. If I can get a line on a few of Tyler Wynn's personal tastes and buying habits, we might be able to track him down through his purchases."

The doors opened in the lobby and Nikki said, "That's a horrible idea."

"Why?"

"Because I didn't think of it." Then she stepped out ahead of him, hiding her grin.

The bull pen sounded like a telemarketing boiler room when Heat came in from her meeting with Eugene Summers. All the detectives were either working their phones or at the Murder Boards conferring on leads they'd checked out. Except, of course, for Sharon Hinesburg, whom Nikki glimpsed shoe shopping on Zappos before she boss-buttoned the screen to an NYPD internal site.

Raley and Ochoa were saddling up for Sotheby's, to interview a contact that they met last summer when they solved the murder of one of the auction house's art appraisers. Raley said, "If anyone could tell us what oil painting this hand belonged to, she could." That made Heat think of Joe Flynn. A top art recovery specialist like him would also be a great resource. As Roach left, she even scrolled her iPhone for his number. But before she pressed Call, Nikki remembered her last visit to Quantum Recovery, and his needy, longing looks. She put her phone away. Flynn could wait until Sotheby's had a shot.

Heat checked in with the Sixty-first Precinct over in Brooklyn to get an update on their search for Salena Kaye spottings. After getting bounced to three different voice mails, she hung up, called over Sharon Hinesburg, and assigned her to head out to Coney Island and conduct a search herself. “It’s early in the season for tourists, so hit the hotels and, especially, the by-the-week apartments.”

The detective gave Heat an exasperated look. “Shouldn’t I be working the serial killer instead of pounding the pavement on this?”

“Nothing wrong with pounding the pavement.” Nikki couldn’t resist a shot. “I’m sure you’ve got the shoes for it.”

Early in the afternoon, her cell phone vibrated. Greer Baxter of WHNY, by the caller ID. Heat let it dump to voice mail, then listened back. “Detective Heat, Greer Baxter, Channel 3 News. Have you forgotten that I need you on my live segment? We’d love to hear what’s happening with our serial killer.” Then the news anchor paused for effect and added, “Unless, that is, you’re hoarding this story for your boyfriend’s exclusive. Call me.”

Heat felt a brief swell of light-headed rage. At the dig, at the manipulation, at the distraction. She set the phone gently on her desk and rested her eyelids to collect herself. “Detective?” She opened her eyes. Feller stood over her, looking ready to burst. “I got one. I just found the coolest connection between our victims.”

SEVEN

Detective Feller wanted to show, not tell. Nikki followed him to his desk, where he gestured her to sit. "Like you told us to, I've been drilling down on our three victims, searching for anything that ties them together." He reached for the mouse on the desktop and double-clicked. An image loaded on the monitor, of Maxine Berkowitz seated on a kitchen floor in sweats and Uggs, surrounded by puppies. "Been going over all her social media and found this Facebook posting she made three years ago." Nikki's heart grew heavy, as it always did, at the sight of the joyful smile of a murdered young woman beaming at a camera. "Note the beagle pups," said Feller.

"Adorable."

"You'll love them even more when you see this." He opened another window, beside the Berkowitz image. It was an advertisement for Bedbug Doug posed beside Smokey, his bedbug-sniffing beagle. "Apparently beagles are great at finding bedbugs, and exterminators are using them like crazy. Doug even made Smokey his company mascot."

"Yeah, I've seen the ads," said Heat. "So you're telling me your connection is that both victims liked beagles? Kind of thin, Randall."

"Stand by, please." With the eraser end of a pencil he pointed to the litter surrounding Maxine Berkowitz. "Mixed litter, lots of colors. You've got one here that's mottled, these two are lemon and white, and then there's this boy here." He zoomed on the image of one puppy. "This, they call open marked. White coat with tan and black spots. Notice the pattern of these three black spots on his shoulder?" He zoomed on the image of Smokey.

"Identical," she said, more interested now. "Is it the same dog?"

The detective smiled. "You tell me." He moused open a YouTube video. While it loaded, he said, "This was shot a year and a half ago in Danbury, at a canine scent-training academy. Basically, it's Smokey's graduation from bedbug school." Nikki watched the amateur video of Douglas Sandmann climbing a riser to applause as he accepted a diploma, with his beagle matching stride, on heel. After Sandmann took the certificate, there was a jump edit to a video that chilled Nikki. Clearly taken in the parking lot after the ceremony, the camera captured Douglas Sandmann and Maxine Berkowitz kneeling and praising her little guy, Smokey, who licked her face.

Heat gave Feller a nod of appreciation. "Who's a good boy?" he said.

Rook came into the bull pen from his lunch meeting and joined Heat and Feller. Nikki recapped Randall's beagle connection for him then turned to the Murder Boards. "So we already had one connection from Roy Conklin to Maxine Berkowitz. Now we have one from Maxine to Bedbug Doug. We don't know what they mean yet but it's something." She turned to Detective Feller. "What you just did for Maxine? Do it for Douglas Sandmann. And the locksmith, Glen Windsor, too."

"Got it. Anything that connects to the other victims."

"Or helps us learn who his next one might be," she said. As Feller left for his desk, Nikki drew a line in marker from Berkowitz and Sandmann and labeled it "Smokey."

"Nice name for a beagle," said Rook as she capped her dry erase. "Barry Manilow had two beagles. Named them Bagel and Biscuit."

"Fascinating." Heat made her way back to her desk, and he followed along, still talking.

"Speaking of Barry Manilow, I just saw an ad for that sitcom *The Middle*. So funny, Patricia Heaton walks in on her mom dancing to Barry Manilow. Oh. The mom?" he said loudly to the room. "Played by . . . Marsha Mason. Even fewer than six degrees, thank you, thank you very much."

"Rook, maybe you could save the parlor games until we're a little less busy," said Heat. "Like after we finish, I dunno, catching a murderer or two?"

"Well, Detective Heat, as it turns out, I do have something to contribute to the search for one of your suspects, a certain Tyler Wynn." He sat on her desk, as was his habit, and she again had to yank a file out from under one of his cheeks.

"I'm listening."

He unwrapped the elastic band from his black Moleskine. "In spite of his misplaced enmity for me that I just don't get, Eugene Summers gave up some really useful intel on Tyler Wynn at our lunch. He's a perfect source. Summers not only spied for Wynn all those years, he's a butler—a combo of observant plus oriented to detail. The man gave me an incredibly complete list of Tyler's personal buying preferences." Rook opened to a page he had bookmarked with the notebook's black ribbon. "For instance, did you know Wynn wears custom shoes? Six-thousand-dollar bespoke loafers from John Lobb boot maker in Paris."

That got her attention. Not just the self-indulgence; the price served as a red flag for anyone doing a background check on a government employee. Tyler Wynn's treason clearly supported his expensive tastes. He looked up from his notebook. "Maybe it's just I, but if a shoe costs six grand, can it really be called a loafer?"

"Agreed. And superb use of that personal pronoun." She habitually needled Rook for being the writer boy, but seeing him riffling through interview notes, she respected his journalistic chops. All the more, if they led her to capture Wynn. Hell, it might even keep her alive.

"Let's see what else. Outerwear, only Barbour, only from Harrods. Briefcases from Alfred Dunhill, sweaters from Peter Millar, shirts from Haupt of Germany, and athletic socks from South Africa—Balegas, if you must know. His booze habits are also quite particular. His white Burgundy of choice is Domaine Leflaive Puligny-Montrachet. His red is a Mil-Mar Estates Cabernet Sauvignon from Napa. He goes for WhistlePig rye and Vya sweet vermouth. His Irish whiskey brand is Michael Collins."

"What," she said, "Jameson's not good enough for him?"

"Nikki Heat, it's like you're reading my mind."

Personal habits had a way of becoming a trail, and reality TV's premier butler had given them a trove of leads. So much to go on that Heat pulled in Detective Rhymer to pair with Rook and start making contact with the retailers and distributors who supplied Tyler Wynn with his unique brands of consumer products. "Your investigative journalist's gut is doing the job, Rook," she told him. "Now take it to the next step and find out if Uncle Tyler's been buying himself any goodies lately, and where they've been delivered."

"You can't have specific tastes like his and fall completely off the grid."

"Prove it," she said. And he and Rhymer got to work.

Raley called in from the Roach Coach. "Miguel and I are just now wheels-up from Sotheby's on the East Side," he said.

"Do you think they can ID the painting for us?"

"Already have. It took them five seconds. The hand on that slip of paper was clipped from a work by Paul Cézanne. It's called *Boy in a Red Waistcoat*. The appraiser e-mailed me a digital image of the whole painting. I'll forward it to you or you can pull it up online if you don't want to wait."

"Thanks, I will. That was fast, Rales."

"Yeah, well, turns out the painting is not only well known, it's on everyone's radar these days."

"How come?"

"It's hot. It got stolen in 2008 from the . . . hang on, I can't read my own writing. The painting got jacked along with a couple others from the Bührle Collection. That's in Zurich, Switzerland." After a pause he said, "I lose you?"

"No," said Nikki, "I'm with you, just thinking I've got a call to make. Good work."

She hung up, bit the bullet, and dialed Joe Flynn at his Quantum Recovery office. While the phone rang, she Googled the Cezanne and got multiple hits, most two-year-old news items about its theft. "I'm sorry, Mr. Flynn's out of the office," said his assistant. "Would you like to leave a voice mail?"

After the beep, Nikki left word for him to call. Then she checked her notes for his cell number and left a message there, too. When she hung up, she chided herself for not calling him earlier; she could have saved half a day chasing down the painting. It's what happened, she thought, when she let her personal feelings interfere with an investigation. Heat vowed not to let that happen again.

That reaffirmation met a challenge sooner than she'd thought. "Nikki Heat. It's your number one fan," said the caller. At the sound of his voice, her guard went up and she cleared everything else from her mind. Zach "The Hammer" Hamner, senior administrative aide to the NYPD's deputy commissioner for legal matters, never made contact unless he wanted something. And when the man Rook had dubbed the unholy spawn of Rahm Emanuel and Gordon Gekko wanted something, "no" came at your own risk.

"Glad to know my name's still alive at One Police Plaza," she said, keeping her side light; feeling anything but.

"Oh, you know it is," he said cheerfully. Guess Zach could keep the weasel out of his voice as well as Nikki could keep the dread out of hers. "Got your hands full, I know. We're all glad it's you on point with this serial killer. That's from the Commish on down." Zach knew the value of rank dropping.

"We'll get him."

"If anyone can, Heat, it's you. Now . . ." His pause must have lasted five seconds, a deliberate technique to suck in her attention. Superfluous. He had it. "Been getting calls from Greer Baxter over at Channel 3. Media requests usually kick over to Public Information, but Baxter has a relationship with this office, so here I am. You know what this is about."

"I do, Zach. But you must know what it's like running a case like this. If you're doing the investigation properly, the last thing you have time for is media."

"Which is why we're seeing fucking Wally Irons's face on every screen. Listen to me while I count fingers. One: Greer Baxter is a friend of the commissioner. Two: Her newsroom lost one of its own to this creep. Three . . ." He worked another pause. Heat knew what was coming before he said it. "You owe me this."

Nikki sank deeper in a quicksand of gloom. Earlier that year Hamner had championed her to become a captain and the precinct commander of the Twentieth, only to have her embarrass him by publicly rejecting the promotion at the last moment. And just within the past month, she had come back to him for a favor when Captain Irons gave her an unfair medical suspension, citing a phantom concern for her mental state following a shooting. The Hammer got her badge back but warned her his bill would come due.

Today was payday.

"I'll bring you out to Greer's set in two minutes, Detective," said the stage manager, who then left the small room backstage at WHNY. Rook moved over to stand behind Nikki's makeup chair. The mirror framed them both. One of them looked unhappy.

"For somebody who wanted to be an actress once upon a time, I'd think you'd be enjoying this," he said. "People rushing in saying, 'Two minutes, Detective,' 'Bottle of water, Detective?' "

"Touch up your makeup, Detective?" asked the woman who appeared at the door.

"See?" said Rook. "Magical."

"Thanks, I'm still good."

The makeup artist left. Rook asked, "You sure? Almost a million people watch this newscast."

Nikki said, "I just want to get this over with. I don't care how I look."

"Mm, OK . . ."

"What?"

"Forget it," he said. "Well. You've got a little . . . Never mind." Heat sprung out of the chair and moved close to the mirror. She saw nothing of concern except the reflection of him behind her, laughing. When she sat back in the chair, Rook composed himself and said, "Have you decided what you're going to say?"

"Don't you see, that's the whole problem with this. I'm being forced to go on live TV when I can't release anything they don't already have without screwing our case."

The stage manager came back. "We're ready, if you are."

During an arthritis pain commercial, someone clipped a wireless microphone on Nikki's collar and the stage manager showed her to a leather chair that would have been right at home in an airport first class lounge. It angled toward an identical seat in the tiny interview area off to the side of the stage, away from the anchor desk. Three video cameras glided in to block Heat's view of the rest of the studio, which she couldn't see anyway because of the brightness of the lights. "Thank you for coming," came a familiar voice. Then Greer Baxter materialized from inside the glare with an extended hand. Nikki shook it and was about to lie about how it was her pleasure when the anchorwoman sat and said, "Pretend the cameras aren't there; focus on me," and then looked into one of the lenses herself.

"Tonight I go straight to the source about a serial killer. We are live. We are 'Greer and Now.' " A short theme played under animated graphics and a montage of Greer Baxter interviewing Al Sharpton, Daniel Moynihan, Whoopi Goldberg, Sully Sullenberger, Donald Trump, and Alec Baldwin. When the intro finished, the stage manager used his rolled script to point to the middle camera, which Baxter addressed. "She may be New York's most famous cop. Homicide Detective Nikki Heat has been written about in national magazines, received decorations for valor, and has the highest rate of case clearance of any investigator in the NYPD. Welcome, Detective."

"Hello."

"There's a serial killer out there. He's claimed three victims so far. An employee of the Health Department, an insect exterminator, and, tragically, News Channel 3's own Maxine Berkowitz." On the monitor, Nikki saw photos of the victims superimposed behind her and Baxter. "What can you tell us about the case?"

"First of all, I want to express my sorrow to you and your colleagues for your loss, as well as to the families of all the victims. As for the status of the case, there's very little I can contribute beyond what is already known in the media."

"Is that because you haven't made enough progress?"

"To me, there's no such thing as enough progress until a killer is captured and taken off the streets. Obviously we aren't there yet."

"What about some of the things that haven't been reported in the press yet? Is there anything you can share that will make us feel better?"

"Greer, if sharing inside information would help capture this individual, I'd be the first to do it. The fact is that there are some details that only we can know because we don't wish to harm the progress of the case, either by tipping off the suspect or helping create copycat scenarios."

"So that's all you're giving up." Greer leaned forward slightly, a pose of cross-examination. "Not to be rude, but why did you come on if you weren't willing to share more?"

"I think I made it clear in advance I couldn't go beyond what's been released. But if you have any questions, I'll certainly—"

"OK, here's one. We know the killer leaves colored string behind." She held up the cover of the *Ledger*. "According to this, the first two strings were red and yellow. My source tells me that there are additional colors now. Like purple? And green?"

Her source? Nikki wished she had worn more makeup to hide the blush that began filling her cheeks. "Again, I can't comment on that."

"Red, yellow, purple, and green. Sounds like the colors of a rainbow. Let me ask. Have you given this killer a nickname?" Before Heat could respond, she rolled over her. "Know what I would call this killer? The Rainbow Killer." She turned to the camera and repeated for effect, "The Rainbow Killer." Satisfied she may have coined a nickname, Baxter said, "Detective Heat, you're a woman of few words. If you can actually share something with our viewers, I hope you'll come back."

"Most definitely," said Nikki, but thinking, Only in a straitjacket and wheeled in on a dolly.

"This is a first. We have thirty seconds left. Seen any good movies, or can't you talk about that, either?"

"Actually, I haven't," said Nikki. And then she decided to take a leap. "I could talk about another case we are working. We apprehended the killer but are still looking for his accomplices." The stage manager began a ten-second countdown. Heat reached in her blazer pocket and took out a page with double head shots of Tyler Wynn and Salena Kaye and held it to the camera with the red light. "I'd like to invite the public's help, asking if they have seen either of these two. The female was last observed around Coney Island."

"And we're out of time, Detective," said Greer Baxter. "Good luck with that, and good luck apprehending . . . the Rainbow Killer."

In the taxi downtown, Rook said, “Pretty lucky you just happened to have those head shots in your pocket like that.”

“Yeah, said Nikki. “Imagine having them ready to show the very night I was on live television. Couldn’t have planned it any better.”

He gave her hand a squeeze. “Didn’t have to.”

The next morning at the Twentieth, Wally Irons came to Heat’s desk before he even unlocked his office. His doughy complexion was mottled with salmon blotches of agitation. “Happened to catch you with Greer Baxter last night on the ten o’clock news. As your precinct commander, isn’t it proper you clear all media contact through me?”

Heat wanted to laugh in his face. She wanted so badly to be insubordinate and say, You mean, clear it with you, or clear a path to the camera? Or, You mean, clear it with you like Sharon Hinesburg does—on her knees? Instead, Detective Heat maintained her professionalism and told him the truth. “I didn’t want to do the interview. I was directed to by the office of a commissioner at One PP. Would you like to speak to him?”

Irons stood there, vapor-locked, gloriously impotent, and said, “Next time tell me.” And he was gone.

Like clockwork, Detective Hinesburg sauntered in five minutes behind Irons, the interval designed to maintain the fiction that she wasn’t sleeping with the boss. She grumbled about the assignment Heat had given her to canvass Coney Island for Salena Kaye sightings. Nikki named some of the hotels and extended stays she knew of, and Hinesburg reported that she’d come up empty at every one of them. All but certain Sharon was deep-throating insider tips about the serial killer to Greer Baxter, the *Ledger*, and others, Heat isolated her with the task of following up on the calls that were coming in about Tyler Wynn and Salena Kaye after their pictures had been shown on TV. "Fine. Long as I don't have to drive back out to Coney," she said.

A uniform held up a cautionary hand to Nikki on her way back from the precinct kitchen. "Might want to keep some distance. Got a badass here." She relaxed against the wall and turned a spoonful of yogurt upside down on her tongue while a pair of officers wrestled a shackled biker into Interrogation One. Following close behind strode the biker's attorney, Helen Miksit. The sight of the lawyer made Heat wonder which badass the uni had warned her about.

"Counselor, what a pleasant surprise. Business so tough you're defending Sons of Anarchy now?"

Helen Miksit, nicknamed the Bulldog for both her physical appearance and interpersonal skills, reacted sourly to seeing Heat. "More like son of Manhattan's top cosmetic dentist, not that I owe you that explanation. In fact, thought I'd get in and out of here without having to deal with you."

"Do you ever return phone calls, Helen?"

The lawyer paused, annoyed, then shouted through the open door to her client, "I'll be right in. Howard, say nothing. You hear me? Say nothing." Miksit pulled the door closed and turned to the uniform who had warned Nikki. "He have to stand here?" Heat gave the officer a smile and he moved on. "Detective, you're a fucking pest. Two calls a day, sometimes more."

"All I want to do is have a short interview with Mr. Barrett." Algernon Barrett, the self-made millionaire who'd emigrated from Jamaica and made his fortune as the chef-founder of Do the Jerk chicken rubs and spices, had also been one of Nikki's mom's piano clients. "Barrett may be able to help me locate two dangerous suspects I'm tracking down."

"Don't bullshit me, Heat. You remember when I was a DA and we worked together? I kicked cops with weak links like that out of my office on a daily basis so we wouldn't have the judge kick me out of court."

"I'm not any cop, Helen, and I know you remember that." Nikki saw that register with the lawyer and pressed her case. "I want two minutes to show some pictures. Look at the upside. I'll stop calling you."

Helen Miksit pressed her lips together, as close as she ever came to a smile. "Tomorrow." She stepped into Interrogation One. As the door closed, she said from inside, "Call first."

Heat found Rook and Detective Rhymer in the temporary command center they had set up for themselves in the booth Raley used for video screening. The two of them worked phones, calling retailers of the signature goods favored by Tyler Wynn. When Nikki asked how it was going, they looked up at her with the vacant stares of galley oarsmen.

Rook said, "You know, it's funny. A good idea seems so damned invigorating—until you actually have to do the work."

"It's tedious, but we'll get there," said Rhymer, ever Opie in his optimism.

"Let me catch you up," said Rook. He moved to the giant presentation pad he had set up on an aluminum easel—complete with a status grid for each item. "So far, his bespoke shoemaker in Paris says Monsieur Wynn is not due for a new pair for about a year, according to his buying cycle. *C'est dommage.* The Barbour coat department at Harrods is checking with management before they will share customer information."

"I'll call New Scotland Yard, if we need help," said Heat.

Rook's eyes lit up. "Scotland Yard? God, I love this work." As he continued with his list, he explained they were starting with calls to Europe and the US East Coast. They planned to work their way west along with the time zones. California, he observed, was still in bed.

"I should point out one thing before you get in too deep," she said.

"Am I going to hate this?" asked Rook.

"He may be ordering under an alias."

"I do. I do hate that." He turned to Rhymer. "And I was so happy up till Scotland Yard."

On her way out, Heat said, "We've got a couple of Wynn's AKAs in his jacket, but I'd also call your best friend the butler. Find out what other names he might have used." She opened the door and pulled in Raley, whose hand gripped the knob from the hall.

"It's him," he said, nearly breathless. "Your serial killer's on line two."

She raced for her desk and grabbed the line lit by the blinking red dot. "Heat."

"Slow it down, Detective," said the chillingly altered

voice. "I called you, remember?" And then he laughed a joyless laugh. "Rainbow Killer, huh? Kinda like that. Red, yellow, purple, green. Green . . . Wonder who's green. Do you wonder who's green?"

"Let's talk about what's going on here, OK?" She sat down and picked up a pen, just in case. "Who am I talking to?"

"Are you shitting me?"

"I've got to call you something. You know my name. What about you?"

"Sure, OK, how about you call me Fuck You? Because if you think you can work the psych bullshit on me by trying to personalize, that's what I am. I am Fuck You."

"Come on, I was only—"

"Rainbow, then," he said, suddenly pleasant. "Yeah. Call me Rainbow. Fuck You Rainbow." He laughed again and then cut himself off, turning ice-cold. "Think you almost got me yesterday at that fucking locksmith's, huh? Think you're smart?"

"Smart enough," she said, testing him with a bit of defiance.

"Oo, the bitch pushes back." He paused, and she could hear his electronically altered breathing. It sounded like Brillo. "Well, I'll give you that one. Never had a cop this smart." And then he added, "We'll see pretty soon how smart. Think green."

Click. The line went dead.

EIGHT

Of course there was not one detective in that precinct who had not been thinking in colors. Wondering every moment who the other end of that green string connected to—bent on beating the killer there again like they had with the locksmith. The difference this time was that they not only wanted to spare a life, they really wanted this bastard.

"Fuck you, Rainbow," said Randall Feller when the detectives listened back to the recording.

During the playback, Heat circled the only note she had made during the brief conversation: "Nvr hd cp ths smrt." She weighed those words and put in a call to the FBI's National Center for the Analysis of Violent Crime at Quantico, Virginia. Nikki had worked several cases recently where she reached out for a Center assist. Dealing directly with the analyst she had befriended there felt different than the muck and mire she tried to avoid in dealing with the feds. This felt more personal. Her own Bureau boutique, FBI-Lite, she thought, and smiled.

The NCAVC analyst told Heat she had already been briefed on the case, and indeed she knew just about everything, including the colored strings. Heat said, "We've run this string MO through our RTCC data banks, of course, but I want to see if you get any hits on something kind of new." She recapped the call she'd just gotten and could hear a keyboard clacking on the analyst's end of the line as she spoke.

"Detective, can you send me WAV files of both those calls for me to scrub here?"

Nikki told her she'd attach them to an e-mail right after they hung up. "Meantime, there's a marker we haven't run for cross-check yet. You'll hear it yourself at the end of today's recording. He said he'd never had a cop this smart."

"Oh . . ." The analyst felt the gravity of that, same as Heat. "I'll bet you want me to look for intersections of serial homicides involving direct voice contact with law enforcement and get back to you with any hits."

"This is why you do what you do," said Nikki.

"Just helping the good guys, Detective Heat."

At first, Nikki thought it was a hallucination. The stress she'd been under, the crazy hours she'd been keeping, things like that could bring on an episode. She rolled her chair to peek around her computer screen. Across the bull pen, inside Captain Irons's glass fishbowl, it looked from the back like . . . Yes, it really *was* . . . DHS Special Agent Callan shaking hands with Wally. Wally, rising wide-eyed from his desk. Wally, whose jaw had gone slack and whose mouth gaped like an oxygen-starved goldfish, to complete the full aquarium effect of his office. Then both men turned, and the captain's face shaded crimson, as he extended a hand to greet the lovely female guest, Agent Yardley Bell.

Frozen, Heat could only stare back when Irons gestured through the glass wall to the bull pen and the two federal agents turned her way. Nikki watched both of them smile at her. At least Bart Callan's seemed genuine.

A minute later Nikki sat in a guest chair in the fishbowl with Irons standing beside her looking superfluous. "If you need me for anything," said the captain.

"No, just your office will do it." Callan looked around. "Unless you've got some other place we can meet privately."

Wally added, "There's Interrogation, you could use that."

"We're good here," said Yardley Bell. They waited for Irons to read their silence. He gave a two-finger salute and left. Bell closed the door and leaned on it. Callan dragged a guest chair closer to Nikki's and sat.

"Am I becoming old hat?" asked Heat. "Because carjacking me to your warehouse in Queens felt a little more special."

Bell said, "Don't feel ambushed. Agent Callan and I were in the area and thought we'd just drop in."

"Golly." Nikki borrowed her credulous grin from Joey on *Friends*.

"Wanted to ask you about Eugene Summers," said Callan. "You and Jameson Rook spent some time at his apartment in Chelsea, and we were wondering why."

"Are you interrogating me? Seriously?"

"Not at all. This is purely informational. We just like to close all the loops in our investigation." He grinned. "Belt and suspenders." He sounded about as credible as Bell's claim about being in the neighborhood. Clearly, with this effort, they wanted something, and Heat told herself she'd better focus. As a skilled interrogator, she knew she needed to put her head in theirs and be them. What would she be after?

The code.

Could it be they were looking for the code? Or evidence one existed?

"We obviously know Summers was once run by Tyler Wynn," continued Callan.

"So what did you talk about?" asked Bell.

"Did you ask him?" Heat asked.

"Kind of asking you," she replied. Yardley gave Heat a soft stare, but the moment crackled with meaning. About dominance in the interview. And maybe about something else, too.

"Naturally, I wanted to know if Summers had heard from him."

"And?"

"He hadn't."

"And what else?" Bell's gaze didn't waver.

She knew the best strategy was to tell the truth. Since Nikki would never give up the code, she did the next best thing. She told *a* truth. "Tyler Wynn has very specific tastes, and we wanted to get a track on him through his consumer trail. We didn't know how far to trust Summers, so Rook used the cover of picking his brain for a magazine article to get the specifics we needed." Heat stopped there. She'd seen so many people over-talk when they were on thin ice, when the best thing to do is get off it—and fast. She sat back in her chair and let them work.

"So this would be Rook's version, too?" asked Callan.

Nikki shook her head derisively. "Version?" She stood and asked them to follow her.

The pleasure Heat hoped to get out of putting it in the agents' faces by leading them inside Rook's retail tracking center was quickly offset by his reaction to seeing Yardley Bell. And hers to seeing him. Nikki couldn't write a clear caption to their expressions. Was it just the way old lovers looked at each other, or were these the smiles of unfinished business? She stepped right between them and said, "This is the makeshift command post Rook has set up with Detective Rhymer to pick up Wynn's consumer trail."

"Quaint," said Agent Bell.

Heat said to Rook—and pointedly, "I was telling the agents how you and I met with Eugene Summers for the purpose of getting this enterprise going."

"That's right," he said. "And we'll see how polite the Maven of Manners is after he finds out his in-depth interview wasn't for any article." Smart. Even if Rook hadn't picked up on her cautionary note, he knew enough to be circumspect.

Yardley Bell said, "I'd like to see what your process is, Jamie." She turned to the others. "Could you give us a moment?"

Heat didn't like getting split up. Not tactically, not personally. But when Rhymer slid out with his Diet Pepsi and half-eaten club, Callan held the door for Nikki. She hesitated and left, too.

Alone again in the captain's glass house, Heat said, "So,

was divide and conquer part of your drop-in strategy?"

"For the record, it wasn't my idea to come here to brace you."

"Who's running your case, Agent Callan?"

"It gets complicated. It's my office, my control, but Agent Bell packs major Beltway clout. She Bigfoots my whole day whenever she gets a wild hair." He threw his palms open. "And here we are."

"This is why I told you I didn't want to get tangled up inside your little investigative community," she said.

"I want to talk to you some more about that."

"You can save it."

"What if I said I agree with you?" He waited while she had time to absorb that surprise. "That's right. I've been giving it some thought since our cocktails the other night, and I don't think it's a good idea for you to be on this team."

She studied him warily. "Just like that, you change your mind?"

"More like a change of heart." He rolled his chin to the glass like he didn't want an interruption. Or scrutiny, maybe. "Heat, I think I'm feeling a little personal about you, and that wouldn't be good for a close working relationship."

"Right," she said immediately, but then felt at a loss; not prepared for this, not at all.

One teenage summer on Cape Cod she had gotten it in her head to teach herself to windsurf. Starting after breakfast and going until sundown, Nikki's day did not become the blissful, athletic sail she had envisioned. Instead, it devolved into a relentless series of crashes, spills, and wipeouts punctuated by mere seconds of balance until a sudden gust or rogue wave pitched her into another endo. Nikki stared at Bart Callan and wondered how her entire life had become like that day. Of all the curves she'd been thrown lately, of all the complications she had pulling at her, this one could be the most damaging. She sensed jeopardy if she mishandled this.

"I didn't want to say anything about it, but I know you sort of got the vibe," he said, then waited for her to respond. She didn't, so he continued, "I sure got it from you."

And there it was. The second wave, the blindsider. Had she flirted? She sure didn't feel she had. Did she have a few "what if" thoughts? Who didn't? As she regained her center, Heat knew exactly what she had to say. "Bart, you need to know something." She made sure the eye contact left no ambiguity. "I am in a relationship now." She didn't elaborate. Didn't tell him he was a nice guy or anything that might leave a door open or be subject to interpretation. For good measure, she added, "It's important to me."

He nodded and said, "I hear you."

She smiled. "Good."

Then his gaze swept to the hallway where Yardley Bell stood in close conversation with Rook. "But let's keep in touch." He looked back at Nikki and said, "You never know."

As soon as her surprise company departed, Heat jumped back into the pressing business of hunting the serial killer. It wasn't until nine that night, in the back of the town car he had ordered to drive them to his loft, that they were able to connect. "What did you and Agent Yardley talk about?"

"If you're wondering if I mentioned The Thing, I didn't mention The Thing. Give me some credit."

"Maybe some," she said, wrapping it in a tease. "But seriously, you did make a quick pickup of my Eugene Summers meaning."

"Hey, I can be as duplicitous as the best of them. Except with you, of course. With you I am an open book, especially between the covers." He wanted to be playful. Heat wanted to be reassured.

"Then what did you two talk about?"

"Well, per her request, I gave her a quick primer on my Tyler Wynn project."

"How much?" Heat chafed at this interference in her case. Callan called it: Bigfoot.

"Enough to find out I may be chasing my tail. Like you, Yardley pointed out he used numerous aliases, plus the fact that he might be doing his shopping through some third party."

"So that's her contribution? To basically piss on your investigation?"

"No, actually, she was quite helpful. Nikki, she gave me this brilliant new strategy to follow." If Rook had a clue how much his exuberance chapped her, he didn't let on. "Yardley says more and more retailers are using RFID technology."

"Educate me."

"Radio frequency identification. You know how your E-ZPass lifts the gate at a highway toll booth, or a security tag on a leather jacket sets off an alarm in a department store? Those are transponders that emit radio signals. Well, technology has now shrunk them down to chips smaller than a grain of rice, and manufacturers and retailers are planting them in their products for inventory control and consumer research. And how do they do that?" He paused to frame the significance. "They electronically track the chips to see where their products are distributed geographically." He slapped her thigh to punctuate his excitement.

"You're scaring me, Rook, going all geek on me."

"I can't help it. Don't you see? Of course you see. If we find enough products on the Tyler Wynn list that have RFID chips embedded in them, the little transponders could lead us right to his door, no matter what name he used."

Begrudgingly, reservedly, but, in the end, objectively, Heat admitted Yardley Bell's idea had merit. She told Rook she would assign more manpower and resources to the task first thing in the morning.

"And can you call it a task force?"

"No."

"I've always wanted to be on a task force."

"You'll have to save it for that video game you play in your boxers."

He turned away, watching Bryant Park go by his window. "Why do you hurt me?"

Upstairs in Rook's kitchen, he put some flame under a pot of water for angel hair to go with his scampi while she poured the Sancerre. Without naming it, they had taken to eating meals in more since the poisoning attempt. On high alert was not the way either wanted to live, or admit to living. "How you holding up?" he asked.

"Not exactly brain-dead. But I'm working on it."

He lifted his glass. "Here's to the living brain-dead. Makes you almost a zombie." After they toasted, he said, "If you want to kick back and take a shower, I'll keep busy sweating some garlic and sautéing these shrimp."

"You know what I'd really like to do?" she said.

"I do. You want to take another shot at The Thing."

"Rook, we're alone. We can call it the code."

He put on a mock pout. "Oh, you mean the code. I was hoping when you said you wanted another shot at The Thing . . ."

"You disgust me," she said with a laugh.

As she walked to the back hall, he called out, "I hid a copy in my office. It's in the top filing cabinet drawer under 'Nikki's Top Secret Code.' " And then she could hear him laugh.

Wide awake at 4 a.m., Heat eased out of bed, pulled on some gym shorts and a workout top, and slipped out of the room. Minutes later, she walked barefoot across Rook's rooftop and sat on the wall to stare at the city that also didn't sleep much.

The spring thunderstorms forecast for that morning hadn't arrived yet, but ominous clouds rolled in from the west, swallowing the ambient light of New York City and spitting it back the color of spilled blood.

Nikki fought despair. Out there in those concrete canyons a serial killer roamed free. So might the man responsible for her mother's murder. Not to mention his accomplice, who almost killed her. Heat looked all around, felt vulnerable, then told herself she didn't care. She almost believed it.

So far, Heat had managed to rescue one target of the serial killer, but still had no solid leads—nothing she'd call traction. Her quest for Wynn and Kaye remained stalled, with the added attraction of federal meddling: Bart Callan, vigorous, competent, and misguidedly personal; Yardley Bell, disruptive to Nikki's case and threatening to her relationship.

Downstairs in Rook's bed, Heat had tried to clear her mind of these demons. Since she couldn't sleep, she decided to be productive and mentally projected the lines, dots, and squiggles of her mom's code on the pale canvas of the ceiling. The solve still would not come.

So she changed the scenery. Resting a bare heel on the ornate scrollwork of the frieze beneath her, Heat listened to her breathing instead of the taxi horns, night sirens, and the *doop-doop* of garbage trucks at work. She let her eyes gloss over until she no longer saw the iconic Empire State and Chrysler Buildings looming out of the cityscape. Instead, her vision fused with the thin curtain of urban haze in the middle distance. Piano notes from her childhood songbook appeared and merged with the blurred apartment lights in the high-rises before her. Then those strange pencil notations surfaced like watermarks. Nikki could see the characters as clearly as she had on the page where they were written, so embossed were they in her mind's eye.

But whether studied on paper, a ceiling, or the crimson Tribeca skyline, they still told her nothing.

"How long have you been at this?" came the voice behind

her. Nikki had wedged the access door open and didn't hear Rook come out on the roof.

She tilted to her right where dawn tried to muscle through the stubborn sky. "A couple of hours, maybe."

"Not tonight. I mean total." She didn't answer because he knew damned well how long. So he said, "Almost a month, Nikki. It's time."

"No." Heat said it so sharply pigeons flew. Much more measured, she added, "I'm not taking this to Homeland. Or Yardley."

"I agree."

"Then what?"

"You trust me, right?" he asked. "I mean really, really trust me?"

"What."

"I know a guy. A code breaker."

Heat didn't say no this time. She just continued to stare out at the city slowly coming to life. Then she nodded almost imperceptibly and turned to him for the first time as he stood there on the roof. "Rook?"

"Yeah?"

"You're not wearing any clothes."

Rook found Keith Tahoma where he knew he would at seven in the morning. In Union Square playing simultaneous games at a pair of Parks Department chess tables. And winning both.

Nikki watched the skinny old guy in sunglasses, with the George Carlin whiskers and gray ponytail, dancing from game to game, talking smack and busting some blatantly OCD moves. Through a taut smile she muttered to Rook, "Are you kidding me?"

Even though Heat had accepted intellectually that it was time to get some expert help with the code, Rook still had to overcome her emotional reticence. "Look, you said yourself that Wynn may be trying to cover up something imminent." He tapped the copies of the marked-up music they had scanned. "We might be sitting on the answer to that right here. And the longer you delay, the greater the chance you're blowing your shot at stopping whatever conspiracy you believe is heating up. Now, if you want to be all proud and stubborn and bang your head against the wall while time slips away, go ahead. But if you seriously want to crack this, I trust my expert completely."

Rook's expert tore open six packets of sugar, dumped them all at once into his coffee, paddled-stirred the paper cup waving his pipe cleaner arms, and then sipped with a stage wink across the café table at Nikki. "Mr. Tahoma, I hear your grandfather was one of the Navajo code breakers back in World War Two," she said.

"You're a friend of Rook's, you call me Puzzle Man, OK? And yeah, my *shi'nali* was a Windtalker, damn straight." He blew across his coffee and set it down. "He and his unit created codes for the Marines rooted in our Navajo language. Totally skunked the Japanese. Is it in my blood? Duh. I spent the Cold War in the army eating schnitzel and cracking signal traffic out of East Berlin, basically getting medals I can never wear for turning the Soviets into jackasses. The

NSA snatched me up, and next thing, I'm breaking down secret cables about who shot down an airliner over Korea, which tent Gadhafi sleeps in, and who's buying ammo for the Chechen rebels."

"Is that where you and Rook met, Chechnya?"

"Fuck no," he said. "*Star Trek* convention."

Rook gave her a rueful shrug. She asked Tahoma, "I assume you're no longer involved in government work?"

"What gave me away, the shorts and flip-flops?" His high-pitched laugh turned a few heads, then he leaned in to her speaking in a low voice. "I was invited to pursue independent interests when a psychological review suggested I might be borderline." He cocked an eye and grinned, "Like that's a drawback in the spook trade."

In a weird way, his nuttiness made it easier for Nikki to make the leap. An on-the-spot, unscientific gut profile told her that Puzzle Man possessed a genius-level knack that also made him such a social misfit that he survived by operating under strict personal rules. He was a head case who not only broke codes, he lived by one, too.

Plus, Rook had nailed it. The longer she sat on this, the more likely she was to squander the opportunity, either to find Wynn or to head off whatever he was involved with—or both. Time to give Puzzle Man his shot.

Ten minutes later, at the kitchen table of his cluttered shoe-box apartment above the Strand Book Store, where he worked part-time, Keith Tahoma swept aside the draft of the 3-D anacrostic-Sudoku puzzle book he was designing and studied the copies of Heat's coded sheet music. She tried to give him the provenance; that the pencil marks between some of the notes appeared in the songs of Nikki's old piano exercise book, and how her mother, whose handwriting this was, had been killed hiding some unknown secret information from spies. But when she began to speak, Puzzle Man just snapped a finger at her to stop, keeping his eyes riveted to the pages. After a few minutes, he looked up at the two of them and said, "Man, I am impressed. And I've seen them all, Vigenère ciphers, Polybius squares, Trimethius tableaux, Alberti discs, the Cardano grille, Enigma machines, *Kryptos* . . . I've trained in acrophony, redundancy, word breaks, *Edda* symbols. But this. Wow."

"What does it say?" asked Rook.

"Beats the fuck outta me." Heat's chin dropped to her chest. "But dispirit not. Give me some more time to rassle this gator."

At the door on the way out, Rook said good-bye, but Puzzle Man didn't hear. He was already lost in the code.

Nikki's first order of business when she arrived at the Two-Oh was to pull in Malcolm and Reynolds to help Rook and Rhymer set up their RFID track on Tyler Wynn. She knew Captain Irons would pitch a fit when he got a whiff of the redeployment of assets from the serial killer investigation, but the electronic consumer tracking presented the hottest lead in either case, and Detective Heat's training and experience dictated the hot lead was the lead you followed until a hotter one came along.

That happened mid-morning.

Raley and Ochoa came to her desk, each one trying to get there first. "Detectives, you've got those funny looks again," said Heat.

"I know you don't like curse words in the bull pen," said Ochoa, "but see this grin? This definitely is my shit-eater."

Raley said, "We spent all morning over in Long Island City at Bedbug Doug's HQ. You should see the place; it actually has a giant metal sculpture of a bedbug on the roof."

"Anyway," continued his partner, "we went there to go over the victim's accounting books, like you had us do with Conklin."

"And you found a connection to one of the other victims?"

"No," said Ochoa, "but we found something you'd call an Odd Sock. Made us wonder if it might point to a new victim."

"These are copies from Douglas Sandmann's accounts receivable." Raley held up a file. "We found a pattern of him performing bedbug checks in buildings, but getting paid by a third party who has no connection with the buildings Doug inspected."

Ochoa picked up. "So we asked his wife about it, and she says, 'Oh, yeah, Doug made some money on the side from that guy because he could get into buildings and apartments pretending to do his inspections.' "

"But he was really snooping undercover for the guy who paid him. You know, the third party," said Detective Raley.

"And here's what set off the alarm bells in our heads," continued Ochoa. "Know that little hand snipped from the oil painting the serial killer left us? This third party guy is in the art business."

"I assume you got a name," said Heat. Raley opened the file. Nikki reeled when she saw who it was.

By the time Heat, Rook, and the other detectives rolled down to the marina on the Hudson at West 79th Street, Parks Enforcement had already found Joe Flynn's body. It bobbed three feet under the surface of the river, tethered between the marina dock and the fifty-foot ketch he had lived on. They didn't need a coroner to know he was beyond CPR; Flynn's eyes bulged in their sockets, peering skyward through the murky water from a swollen face. His body had bloated with gas, and his skin had changed color to a pallid shade of green.

Distant thunder mixed with the pair of diesel 60s from the harbor unit response boat that slowed up to kill its wake on the other side of the Boat Basin's wave wall. The smooth water in the protected marina broke with the first drops of the approaching storm. Heat got down on one knee. Through the dimpled river surface she could see the wooden handle of a small knife, something a painter would use—perhaps a palette knife—protruding from Joe Flynn's throat. She also noted that his body wore no shoes. He had a sock of a different color on each foot: one light, one dark.

"Boat's clear," said Detective Feller, climbing from belowdecks to the cockpit. "Detective Heat?" The slight waver in Randall's voice made her and all the others turn his way.

Nikki put on her crime scene gloves and climbed aboard.

Wordlessly, Randall Feller stood aside from the hatch to allow her to pass. To preserve fingerprints and DNA, Heat avoided touching the polished brass rail as she descended the teak steps leading below to the main cabin, an opulently appointed space which functioned as the galley and den. Nikki heard footfalls behind her and made room for the other detectives and Rook to come below.

The cabin had sufficient height for them all to stand, and there—right before them, at eye level—an eight-by-ten head shot of Joe Flynn, captured from the Quantum Recovery Web site, dangled from the ceiling. It hung from a row of equal, six-inch lengths of colored string: red, yellow, purple, and green. Colors of the rainbow.

Finally, after a few silent moments of watching the latest victim's photo wave slightly with the rocking of the boat, Heat said, "Do you all see the pattern?"

"Hard to miss," said Ochoa. "Each color of string corresponds to the string found with one of the victims."

"And there's a new string," said Feller, speaking for the first time with a voice that sounded thick in his throat. They all followed him behind the photo. Taped to its back, a new color—orange—was strung like a clothesline to the forward cabin, where its end disappeared around the bulkhead door.

Together, Roach moved to the forward compartment to see if it linked to some clue to the killer's next target. They were only gone a moment.

Both detectives returned looking ashen.

NINE

"I'm ordering protection for you, Heat. Trust me, this asswipe isn't going to get near you." The springs of the executive chair creaked under Captain Irons as he rocked back and crossed his arms in front of his belly. She tried to ignore the fact that his hands could barely meet and he had to be satisfied lacing his fingers.

"I certainly appreciate the support, Cap, but—"

"No buts. I can't have the NYPD's cover girl killed on my watch." So nice to know, she thought, that his concern for her safety was really just the flag Wally wrapped around his worry that her murder could be a career hindrance. Nikki would push back on the round-the-clock detail he had proposed, and win. But even she had to admit how deeply unsettling it had felt to follow the orange string into the forward cabin of that boat and see it link from the latest victim to her own picture. The captain's cover girl ref wasn't lost on her, either. The serial killer's photo of choice was a printout of her cover shot from Rook's *FirstPress.com* article.

"With all due respect, sir, risks like this come with the job. I'm armed, trained, and this guy's worst nightmare. Plus with two big cases in my lap, there's no way I can be hamstrung in my investigations by tripping over a detail of unis or grade-threes who can't keep up." Or worse, Sharon Hinesburg, she thought but had the restraint not to mention.

"Not making me feel any better here, Heat. You've not only got two cases going, but two death threats. I'd say wake up and smell the coffee, but there might be cyanide in it."

"Hilarious, sir."

"You know damn well what I mean."

Since Heat couldn't convince her precinct commander with logic or bravado, she played her ace: fear. "Your call, Captain. Which is why it'll be too bad when the media gets word that you did something to slow me down and impede progress on these cases."

"Who would say something like that?"

She shrugged. "Things get out. You know that."

He paused and signaled his surrender by telling her to watch her ass and to call in backup even if she heard an alley cat screech. Heat left his office feeling relieved. Good thing she didn't tell Irons about the return call she'd just gotten from her NCAVC friend in Quantico. The FBI analyst told Nikki she had gotten two hits when she added the terms "law enforcement outreach" and "electronic voice alteration" to her database search for multiple unsolved homicides. In each case a suspect claiming to be a serial killer had made anonymous contacts with detectives, in Bridgeport, Connecticut, in 2002 and Providence, Rhode Island, in 2007.

Both detectives were dead.

Heat called Helen Miksit to tell her she'd be a half hour late for the appointment she'd made with Algernon Barrett that day. Predictably, the Bulldog bristled, accusing Nikki of playing a mind game to throw her client off balance. "Counselor, if I wanted to play a mind game, I wouldn't have made this courtesy call. I would have left you sitting there wondering where the hell I was."

She needed the extra time to contact the homicide squads in Bridgeport and Providence. Heat could have delegated these checks to her own crew, but that might have raised alarms, and next thing, she'd have been shackled to a protection detail. The detectives in both out-of-state departments recalled the cases clearly and didn't need to research old notes; cop killings never go cold.

The cases in both cities remained unsolved. Referring to the Murder Boards across the bull pen, Detective Heat shared bullet points from her own serial killer, including victims and MOs. None matched hers: no colored strings; no props; no apparent connections between victims. The only similarity was the killer's outreach to the case's lead investigator by phone with the altered voice. When she asked how each detective died, she got one additional similarity. Each one had been shot unexpectedly after being lured into an ambush set up by the killer.

The glorified closet Rook and Detective Raley had commandeered to follow the consumer trail of Tyler Wynn had outgrown itself with the addition of Malcolm and Reynolds to the detail, so the operation moved to more spacious digs in a far corner of the bull pen. The three detectives chattered simultaneously on calls to retail distributors around the country, accumulating tracking data from the RFID chips in the packaging of Wynn's favorite brands. They relayed their findings to Rook, who, between his own calls, pushed colored pins into a tristate map to mark the delivery zones for everything from outerwear to whiskey to sunglasses to artisanal sausages.

"The thing is," said Rook to Nikki as she came over to him, "that we don't know which—if any of these—are products going to Wynn. But the idea is that if enough of these items intersect with his consumer habits, we'll be able to narrow the list when we see a discrete pattern."

"Right, so if only five people are buying, say . . . Barbour coats, Whistlepig rye, and D'Artagnan rabbit-and-ginger sausage, you've, at least, tightened the likely prospects and we can go knocking on doors." She looked at the colored pins on his map and added, "Not seeing much of an overlap yet."

"It's slow going."

"But it feels promising. Keep at it. I'm heading over to interview Joe Flynn's assistant and then on to Algernon Barrett."

"Really."

She didn't like the judgment. "Rook, you know how hard I've been working to brace him."

"I do. It's just . . . first the Tyler Wynn–Salena crew wants you dead. Now the serial killer? Is it really wise for you to be gallivanting around with two killers hunting you?"

If life wasn't shitty enough, Nikki felt him planting the fear seed, and if that took root, she knew she might as well be dead. So she pushed back. "Rook, I refuse to live my life in paranoia. And the only sure way for me to stop them is to get out there and stop them."

"Oh, splendid logic," he said with some bite. "Maybe with any luck they'll both come after you at the same time and you'll be able to duck so they'll kill each other."

Heat interrupted his sarcastic laugh, snatching him by the shirt and drawing him out of earshot of the others. "I will say this once. This is what I do. I multitask. I spin plates. I live in danger. I have to. Why? I'm throwing John Lennon back in your face, Rook. Murders happen while I am making other plans. But I see my plans through. And yes, that includes following up on persons of interest like Algernon Barrett."

On her drive to midtown, Heat calmed herself to the rhythm of her wiper blades in the rain. Rook had hit a hot button but apologized, saying he was freaked about that orange string ending on her picture. Nikki cut him slack for that. In fact, she found herself extra vigilant, scanning windows and rooftops outside the precinct on the walk to her car. Even the thunder cracks made her jumpy. By the time she ascended the elevator to Quantum Recovery's floor, she decided snapping at Rook called for some smoothing over later.

Joe Flynn's assistant sat with the lights off in her dead boss's office. Grim midday sun, filtered through rain clouds, erased the colors from the large-format paintings on his walls. The young woman's eyes were puffy and cried-out. Nikki approached the interview gently, empathically. But her questions about the private investigator's recent activities, behavior, new clients, etc., brought no more light into that room. The PI's schedule had been to-pattern; his attitude remained good-humored; he had no conflicts, disputes, or threats in his life. The only thing out of the ordinary was that Flynn had misplaced his iPad, prized because it was a beta version, a gift from Apple after he recovered a lost prototype. It still hadn't turned up. The assistant said her last communication with Joe Flynn had been when he left the office a few days before. She didn't find it odd that he didn't check in, because he did that sometimes when he was on a case. He called it the romance of chasing international art thieves, and had always surfaced, eventually, with jet lag and cool stories. "Did he say where he was going?"

"Not specifically," said the assistant. "Just to meet someone with information about a stolen painting Joe wanted to recover."

"The Cézanne?" asked Heat. The assistant raised her head up in surprise. Nikki took out her photocopy of *Boy in a Red Waistcoat.*

"How'd you know?"

Randall Feller arrived, and Nikki put him on checking phone logs, e-mail, Internet history, and bank records. He suggested his routine checks could wait, and that he should ride shotgun with Heat to her meeting in the Bronx. The detective didn't take his no easily.

Heat did a little bit of self-talk crossing the Harlem River. Her encounter with Algernon Barrett about a month ago had been contentious and, essentially, nonproductive. Back then, Barrett was a person of interest in her mother's murder hiding behind his lawyer's pantsuit, so Nikki bad-copped him into losing his temper to see what shook loose. Nothing did, so this time—especially since she didn't regard him as a potential murder suspect—she decided to play nice, to be the kinder, gentler cop, and see if that got any more out of him.

The Jamaican had risen from poverty, coming to New York in the early 1990s as an immigrant running illegal horse bets from his sidewalk food cart. His live-in girlfriend, a business major at Fordham, drew up a marketing plan for a company to sell Algernon's Caribbean spice rub recipes, and within two years, Do the Jerk broke the million-dollar profit ceiling and kept climbing. When Heat pressed the button to announce herself at the driveway on an industrial block of 132nd Street, the iron gates that rolled aside led to the headquarters of a food empire built on the lore of a New American's success story.

She found the pair as she had left them a month ago. Except for the clothing, Algernon Barrett and his lawyer might have never departed his office. The jerk spice magnate in the track suit sat behind his desk with a turquoise Yankees cap floating atop his shoulder-length dreadlocks. At a side chair, Helen Miksit acknowledged Heat without standing. Nikki began her charm offensive by leading with a smile and energetic handshakes for both.

"Thank you for making the time. You must be busy. I noticed a lot of people lined up in your parking lot. Are you holding a job fair?"

"You don't have to answer any of that," said the Bulldog.

"Detective Heat, you said you had a few questions about helping you ID suspects. Let's stick to the agenda."

Algernon slid off his Kate Spade Vita sunglasses. "I don't mind. Lets her know I'm not some punk to fuck with, right?" He turned to Nikki. "I'm expanding. The food truck thing is so yesterday, mon. Pop-up stores, that's the thing. I just secured permits to set up surprise locations at all the prime New York spots. No more playing Where's the Jerk? on social media. This week people are going to be seeing my Do the Jerk stores springing up at Grand Central, Empire State Building, Columbus Circle, Union Square, outside all the stadiums." He slipped the Vitas back on. "You want a job?"

"You never know. But congratulations, Mr. Barrett. I'll have to come by."

He stood and opened the desk drawer. "I'll get you a free coupon." He found one and handed it to her, an oversized fake dollar with his picture in the statesman spot. Helen Miksit then suggested the detective move along to business.

"First of all, Mr. Barrett, you are not under any suspicion. I am merely seeking your help because my mother tutored your daughter in piano . . ."

"Ah, sweet lady, that Cynthia."

". . . Thank you. Anyway, I wanted you to think back to that time. May I ask if you ever saw any of these people?" She came to the side of the desk and set out twin head shots of Tyler Wynn, one circa 1999, the other present-day. He studied them at length then shook no. When she placed the photo of Salena Kaye on his blotter, Nikki caught a reaction. "What, Mr. Barrett? You recognize her?"

"No, but I'd sure like to. I'd have a fine time with that." He chuckled salaciously.

"Trust me, you wouldn't." She moved on to her last picture: the surveillance shot of Dr. Ari Weiss and François Sisson, Wynn's Paris doctor, taken as both men talked in the front seat of a parked car.

"I'm sorry," said the Jamaican. "Don't know them, either."

"So we're done," said Miksit, getting to her feet. "And by done, we're done-done, right? My client will be left in peace?"

"Absolutely. But just one more question." Nikki sat. The lawyer sat, too, but not without checking her watch. "Mr. Barrett, would you try to think back? Do you ever recall seeing my mother with anyone, even if it was before or after those piano lessons?"

He tilted his head toward the acoustical tile to ponder, twirling the end of a dread. He began to shake his head but then said, "You know, one time I remember. I remember because, hoo, I got pissed off." Heat gently opened her spiral pad. "I got pissed off because my little Aiesha's lesson got interrupted. See, that day we had our tutoring session in Cynthia's place in Gramercy Park because I had business in Manhattan. Right in the middle of the lesson, buzz-buzz, someone's at her door, and Teacher Heat says, 'pardon me,' and goes into the hallway, leaving my girl to sit there while she argues with someone."

"Did you hear what they were arguing about?" Nikki leaned forward in her chair, full of new anticipation.

Miksit stuck her nose in. "Detective, it was over ten years ago, how would he remember what they were arguing about?"

"Money," said Algernon Barrett. "When somebody talks big money, it's not something you forget."

"What money? How big?" asked Heat. "Can you remember?"

"Not only can I remember how much, I remember what your mom said." Nikki paused her note taking and glued her eyes to him. "Teacher Heat, she say, 'Two hundred thousand dollars is nothing to you people, so get off my back.' "

Barrett had just named the exact amount of FBI seed money Agent Callan gave her mother to bribe her informant. "Did you hear any more of the argument?"

He thought about that and said, "That's all that sticks."

"By any chance, did you happen to see who my mother argued with?"

"Lady, you kidding? Anybody says two hundred long is no biggie to somebody, I'm gonna see who it is." He curled the fingers of one hand to his palm and looked at Nikki through the tunnel he'd made. "I peeped the peep hole in that door." He paused. "Looked like a cop."

Heat had expected that. Just for drill, she asked, "Can you describe him?"

"Him? Wasn't a him, it was a her."

"And she looked like a cop?" Nikki drew a line through Callan's name. "Can you describe her?"

He thought again. "Sorry . . . It's just been too long." He laughed. "And too many spliffs."

His attorney quickly added, "That is a figure of speech, not an admission of guilt."

That evening, Rook's only response to Nikki's conversation with Algernon Barrett, including his plans for jerk chicken pop-up stores, was to say he was starved and insist they dine like human beings. "We can still be dedicated, nay, obsessed investigators and enjoy at least one meal that isn't delivered in a greasy bag with a menu number instead of a food name."

"I don't know," said Heat, "I really enjoy my forty-sixes, hold the elevens."

"They all start tasting like number two to me."

"Appetizing."

"I'll make it up to you." And he did. Just stepping into Bar Boulud, Daniel Boulud's French bistro, across from Lincoln Center, Nikki's guilt about taking some downtime melted away. "Besides," as Rook pointed out, "we can still talk shop, if we keep our voices down." They scored a back table at the far end of the charcuterie, and as she sipped her Sidecar and he his Prohibition Manhattan, Rook observed, "Here's how immersed I am. I look at all the *saucissons* and *fromages* behind that bar, and all I can see are Tyler Wynn's buying habits and how far we have yet to go."

"Nice to get away from the office," she said, rubbing her toe against his leg under the table.

"Actually, it is." He set down his glass and lowered his brow. "I miss the 'us' part of doing this."

"We're working together."

"Yes and no. It feels more to me like parallel play instead of teamwork. You're doing your thing, I'm off doing mine. I miss you. I miss our connection. I want it to be like old times. And by that, I mean a month ago."

"Likewise. But welcome to police work. This is what you do when it all piles on—and why I flared at you earlier today.

I'm sorry. However, the beach and the Janet Evanovich are still out there."

"And the sex."

"Count on that." Both their cell phones were in front of them. She swept them aside with her forearm and patted the tabletop. "Right here. Wanna?"

"Detective, please," he said in mock reproach. "You're a marked woman. Behave."

They ordered the grilled day boat scallops and a Colorado lamb cavatelli. While they shared plates, she recapped her visit to Quantum Recovery. After her rundown, he said, "You know what I can't shake about this Joe Flynn murder?"

"Uh-oh. I know that tone. Do I hear the revving of the conspiracy engine?"

"You hear an inquisitive journalist with an open mind shining light on inescapable considerations. Like how Flynn's murder just created an intersection of the two cases you're working. Like how is it that Rainbow happened to find the link between you and Flynn?"

"Rook, did you seriously just call him Rainbow?"

"Hey, even a serial killer needs a brand. Anyway, my point is that the real connection may not be from Flynn to you, but from you to whatever this Tyler Wynn conspiracy is all about." She smiled dismissively while she chewed a bite of scallop. "Don't scoff, I've thought this through. Tell me it wouldn't suit Tyler Wynn's purposes to see you dead."

"I'm going to ask the waiter if he can go in the kitchen to get some foil to make you a hat. Rook, it's too convoluted. Kill four people just to get to me? Get real."

"Curse you, logic," he said. "Well, at least we discussed it."

"Don't feel too bad. I do agree with one thing. You ask a very smart question: How could Rainbow know Joe Flynn was connected to me?"

"Rainbow," he said. "Catchy."

After their dishes were cleared, she asked Rook if Yardley Bell had ever worked for Bart Callan. When he said he didn't know, she told him about her interview with Algernon Barrett and the argument he said he witnessed with the woman who looked like a cop.

"First of all, is the Jamaican jerk your most reliable witness? And secondly, what would that mean, anyway? Is it your turn under the foil hat?"

They both got a chuckle out of that, but she said, "You never know what something means. You just gather what facts you can and hope they land, eventually."

"Fair enough. Want me to ask her?"

"No."

"Why not?"

"I don't know. Just don't."

He paused and said, "You could ask Agent Callan."

"I don't think so."

"Why not? I know you and Bart are on speaking terms. Didn't you two have cocktails while I was in France?" She eyed him, and he said, "Relax, I didn't go all jealous. People have business meetings all the time over cocktails. Even at hideaway bars at the Carlyle."

Nikki felt annoyed and a bit exposed but smiled and said, "But you didn't go all jealous."

The cell phone in front of him vibrated. The caller ID read, "Yardley Bell." "Perfect," said Heat. "Go ahead, take it."

He picked up the phone but then handed it to her. "These must have gotten mixed up. This is your phone."

When Nikki took it from him, the vibration pulsed all the way to her wrist. She pressed to accept and said, "This is Heat."

"We found him."

Nikki's head swooned. She looked to her martini glass, which was still over half-full, and knew it wasn't the cocktail. "Found whom?" The question sounded dumb to her as the words came out of her mouth—and, damn, sounding dumb to Yardley Bell, of all people—but Nikki sought grounding; she wanted to hear something concrete while she sat there with her vision tunneling and the world slowing down. She wanted to be sure.

Agent Bell said, "We've located Tyler Wynn. How soon can you and your people meet?"

TEN

An adrenaline surge swept through Heat, but she kept her head. Training trumped emotion, and she flipped the switch from exhilaration to logistics. Before she even got up from the table, she speed-dialed the radio dispatcher at the Twentieth and ordered up a blue-and-white to Code Two it to Boulud and meet her at the curb. This would not be the time to look for a cab.

As they rushed to the door, Nikki stayed on her cell to give Dispatch the list of detectives she wanted mustered to the staging area that Homeland Security had already established on the East Side. Heat didn't have to do much thinking. She asked for everyone but Sharon Hinesburg.

At the same time, Rook put in a direct call from his phone to Detective Rhymer, whom he knew was still in the bull pen working their RFID detail. By the time he and Nikki hung up, the cruiser's emergency lights strobed the block and its siren chirped as it cut a U-turn around the median on Broadway to pick them up.

Fewer than two minutes had passed since Bell's call. To Heat, it felt like forever.

DHS had taken over East 57th and Sutton Place, an area that gave them a quiet residential cul-de-sac that terminated at a pocket park bordering the East River. Plenty of room for the Mobile Command Center and absolute control of the zone. Heat and Rook jumped out of the cruiser at the cordon and single-filed between the line of plain-wrap Crown Victorias, Malibus, fire trucks, and ambulances to the white RV, where they found Agents Callan and Bell standing outside its open door. Twenty feet from hello, Yardley Bell spotted them and called, "Sorry to inconvenience your date night with a little law enforcement."

Nikki wanted to smack her. So what if it was only dry cop humor? It might have only been that. It also might have been cheap snarkiness from Rook's ex. For the second time that night, Heat firewalled her feelings and held professional focus. "Agents," she said, "bring me up to speed on the target."

Agent Callan beckoned them inside the RV, the interior of which had been fitted with all the tech essentials to command and communicate during a tactical operation. "Cool," said Rook. "It's like Air Force One's dinghy." He scowled and attempted Harrison Ford. "Get off my RV." Registering their stares, he said, "Proceed."

"To the best of our info," said Callan, "Tyler Wynn has a safe house in a fourth-floor apartment up the block near First Avenue." A junior agent at the console brought up a satellite photo of the neighborhood with resolution unlike anything available on Google Earth. He then touched the screen to zoom in and highlight the building. Callan continued, "Like the rest of this neighborhood, it's mostly over-sixty-fives with money."

"Hide in plain sight," said Heat.

"Exactly."

Then she asked, "What do you mean by your best info? Have you had a sighting or an eyewit?"

"We have not seen the target ourselves, although we now have a surveillance dome over this place." Then the agent went on, "What we did, however, was send in one of our tech units posing as a repair team to service the building's security cameras. Basically, that allowed us to tap their system without sending up any flares, in case the doorman or concierge are getting spiffed by Wynn for warnings." Callan signaled the board operator, and a window of security video rolled and then froze on the image of Tyler Wynn getting off the elevator on the fourth floor, holding a tennis racquet. "Is this your man?"

Heat said, "The time stamp is just after ten this morning. Is this the latest hit?"

"Affirm. We scrubbed video from then until now, all possible exits. Target went in this ayem and hasn't come out."

"How did you find him?" asked Rook.

"All thanks to you," said Agent Bell. Nikki caught the shoulder pat Yardley gave him. And how it lingered and trailed across his back.

"Hey, great, I'll take it, but how?"

"You gave me the idea yesterday of tracking him through his retail purchases. You know, the RFID chips?"

Rook said, "Of course, I know. We are all over that at the precinct."

"And that's adorable," she said, somehow not sounding condescending this time, not to Rook. "But come on, we're in The Bigs. We have the resources. We do this in our sleep. In fact, we did. Our mainframes were humming overnight, and—thanks to your list of Wynn's connoisseur tastes—they spit out critical overlaps to this address. We sent in the geeks to tap the security cams, and by noon, we had him."

"Noon?!" shouted Heat, unable to control the flash bang of rage that had just gone off inside her. "Are you kidding me? You have known this since noon today?" She turned to Rook and saw him fuming, too, which only fueled her anger and resentment. "You walk into my precinct, you essentially hijack my investigation—*plus*, without telling my squad we're wasting our goddamned time, you duplicate our efforts to follow the RFIDs—and now take a bow like we should throw roses and kiss your ass?" She whipped her head to Callan. "Is this what you feds call cooperative interface?"

Before Callan could answer, Bell jumped in. "Detective Heat, give me a fucking break. Is this your first rodeo? The fact that we've known since lunchtime has nothing to do with anything. We needed every bit of that time to set our logistics and bolt this down. He's in there, we are here, and he's not going anywhere. And second?" The agent took a step closer to Nikki, literally and symbolically nudging Callan out of her way. "I got him. He's under the jar. Are you seriously complaining?"

Nikki paused. Her fury cooling to embers, she collected herself and said, "No." And meant it. Interference aside, Yardley Bell had come through. In one day she had accomplished what Nikki had not been able to in a month. The irony for Heat was that she had only told Bell about tracking Wynn's consumer habits as a smoke screen for hiding the code. Yardley had not only run with it, but within hours she'd found the man who ordered her mother's murder. Her feet back under her, Heat looked from Callan back to Bell and said, "How can I help?"

Special Agent Callan stepped forward, as if to remind everyone of the in-charge part of his title. "You can run the capture," he said. When Bell turned to him, about to protest, he continued, "We are already utilizing resources from the Seventeenth Precinct. My decision is that we continue our cooperation with local law enforcement by having Detective Heat lead the takedown. End of conversation."

"Forget it, Rook, you're staying here," called Nikki on her way back from mapping out the plan of attack with the Emergency Services supervisor. Rook stayed on her heels as Heat strode between a dozen heavily armed emergency services unit cops—The NYPD's elite SWAT officers—suited up in black fatigues, ballistic helmets, and Ironclad gloves. The writer stayed close as she walked toward her detectives from the Twentieth, who were pulling on body armor from the trunk of the Roach Coach. "You wanted it to be like old times, Rook, you got it. Stay with the car."

"How's that for a stroll down memory lane?" teased Ochoa.

"More like the boulevard of broken dreams," from Raley.

"Come on, Nikki, I've come so far. Why are you leaving me behind?"

"We've been through this before. You'll be in the way. And it's dangerous."

"Ah, but this time I brought my own protection." He unzipped a gym bag. "I called Rhymer so he'd bring this. Tada." From the bag, he pulled out his own bulletproof vest. One word was stenciled across the chest and back: "Journalist."

"You are kidding," said Heat, as she tightened the Velcro tabs on hers.

Standing at the open trunk of his car, Detective Feller said, "Hey, what are these embroidered things on the front that look like two gold coins?"

"These? Pulitzers." And then he added, "There's room for a few more."

Sharon Hinesburg said, "A bulletproof vest with bling?" They all turned as the detective approached, pulling on her own gear. "You guys forgot to give me the heads-up. Good thing I still had the monitor on at home."

The loose chatter stopped, and the detectives attended their preparations with eyes averted from her. The squad knew the open secret. "Detective Heat, a moment?" Hinesburg beckoned her aside and lowered her voice. "Look. I'm not blind. I'm aware how I get kicked to the curb a lot or get handed the dog assignments. I also know it probably wasn't any accident nobody called me to roll on this." Heat saw tears welling in Sharon's eyes and knew two things: One, Hinesburg was in on the open secret, and two, Nikki didn't have time for this.

She decided to be honest. At least about the latter. "Sharon, this isn't the place."

"I promise I'll have my head in this. You won't be sorry."

Nikki decided these were the last two seconds she could afford on Hinesburg and said, "Get ready."

Numerous high-rise luxury apartments and office towers didn't make Sutton Place the friendliest neighborhood for air support. But as the first phase of her deployment began and her unit moved on foot along East 57th to the front door of the Kluga Building, those same elevated rooftops provided the dome of cover Agent Callan had boasted about. In lieu of a chopper, DHS and NYPD sharpshooters kept vigil on the roofs overhead as Heat's team silently double-timed up the sidewalk. Simultaneously, a contingent from ESU's fabled Hercules Squad mirrored their movement on East 58th to cover the back exit. When she reached her position mid-block, two doors from Wynn's entrance canopy, Nikki hand signaled and her troop stopped, all of them planting their backs against the stone façade of the building to minimize their visibility from overhead windows.

"Heat in position one," she whispered into her shoulder microphone.

"Copy, position one, Heat." Bart Callan's voice came back in her earpiece, from inside the RV. "We have visual of you. Hercules is also confirmed position one."

"We go in one minute, mark."

"Copy the mark," came the voice of the Herc team leader.

Nikki held up a forefinger to the unit and then waited the long minute, trying not to think of this culmination and all it meant to her life. This was the wrong time for emotion. It was time to be thinking of only two things. She summoned them, as she always did, from the Academy. To the little sign posted in every hall, in every classroom, even in the basement shooting range. The sign that saw her through every situation: "Good Cops Are Always Thinking Tactics and Cover."

Above her, behind her, and on the next block stood the best cover available anywhere. In her logistical planning with ESU and the One-Seven's site super, the blueprint review of the building had not only marked tactical access and contingency passages, but had delineated cover within. Each cop had an assignment on entry and had memorized the route to get there—from the elevators to the front desk, the mail room, the private gym, the stairwells, even the trash chute, should Mr. Wynn decide on such an undignified escape. And who knew, from the fourth floor, he might survive the drop. If so, Sharon Hinesburg would be waiting.

Twelve seconds to go. Detective Heat breathed some night air, keyed her mic, and as her last detail before going in, repeated the same thing she had told them back at the staging area. "Watch yourselves, but try to take him alive. I want to know what he is working on."

When her watch zeroed-out the minute, she calmly said, "Green to go."

And they went.

If it weren't for the body armor and 9mm machine guns, it could have been a ballet. Detective Rhymer slid ahead of Heat, as planned, badged the doorman, and stayed under shelter of the canopy with him to make sure no calls got made to the upstairs. The double glass doors auto-opened, and an ESU officer sandbagged them to stay that way. Nikki streamed into the lobby calling out, "NYPD, everyone stop what you're doing. Come out from behind the counter and the office with your hands in plain view, and stand here with Detective Feller." The suited concierge and the day manager did just that, finding spots on the polished marble and wearing expressions of awe and nervousness. "Don't be alarmed," Heat assured them. The dark-suited Hercules Squad pouring in the back entrance and into the stairwells did little to mollify the pair.

The day manager—"Carlotta," according to her brass name tag—asked, "Do you need a key to one of the apartments?"

A voice beside the manager's desk said, "Already got one," and Carlotta's eyes widened when she turned and saw the ESU cop holding the battering ram. But she relaxed when she saw that it hadn't been he who spoke, but Detective Ochoa, coming around the counter holding up a passkey to 4-A that he had pulled from the cubby. Nonetheless, the ESU man and his battering ram got on the elevator with Heat and Roach, as well, just to be sure.

As the doors started to close, Rook skidded into the car, wearing his "Journalist" vest. "Four, please." On the ride up, he ignored Nikki's annoyed glance and said, "I'm selling subscriptions to *Douchebag Monthly*. Have a feeling I've got a live one in 4-A."

"OK, last time, Rook. You have a job. Stay in here and hold the door open."

"Don't you have a sandbag for that?"

"You'll do." Then she brought her Sig Sauer up in a combat stance. The doors parted onto four, and she led her team out into the hall. According to plan, a team from the Hercules Squad had already taken positions at the open door to the stairwell and behind the love seat off the elevator, with assault rifles and machine guns aimed, ready to give cover.

Using only hand signals, they padded lightly up the carpeted hallway to the end unit with "4-A" etched in a pale blue frosted glass square anchored to its outer wall. The muted sounds of music from a radio or MP3 bled from inside. To Heat, it sounded a lot like Billie Holiday singing "Trav'lin' Light." A reminder of listening to American jazz with Rook in Paris wafted over her like a happy scent from another time. She knelt near the doorjamb while the others took their high and low positions; Ochoa, closest to the knob, held the key. Straining to listen through the music, Nikki heard a man singing along.

She knew the voice well. She had heard it, disembodied, on a grainy VHS video shot when she was five years old and played Mozart for him by her mother's side. She had heard it in her waking hours almost every night of the past month instructing her ex-boyfriend to push her in front of the next subway train. Even now, over the thud of her quickened pulse, she could hear it casually tossing off the last words she heard it say as he left her there to die in that subway Ghost Station. That voice on the other side of the door had said, "Shoot her, if you have to."

Heat turned to the group around her. She touched her ear and nodded to indicate she heard Tyler Wynn in there. Nikki then held up three fingers to indicate the coming countdown. Still in a crouch, she rotated up the hall to make sure the

Hercules men and women saw it.

That's when the explosion blasted inside 4-A. The floor shook, pictures fell off the wall, and the concussion knocked Heat on her ass.

Black-gloved hands grabbed Nikki by the back of her vest and jerked her to her feet. A giant of an ESU cop extracted her, yanking her in reverse up the hall, away from the door. He deposited her with Rook outside the elevator and raced back to 4-A, shouldering past Raley and Ochoa, who were clearing the area. In the pandemonium, car alarms sounded and a few frightened tenants opened doors to hollers from Nikki and the others to evacuate immediately, using the stairs. They didn't need a second warning. Heat noticed the elevator doors were closed. She also realized her headpiece had flown out of her ear. She popped it back in to hear frenzied chatter. "Bomb squad on the way up." . . . "Paramedics standing by for all clear from the Code Ten." . . . "Ladder and pumpers rolling up, awaiting clear from the Ten."

Heat keyed her mic to report, "Negative injuries in hallway on four."

"Copy no injuries" came back from Agent Callan.

"ESU evacuating collateral fourth-floor tenants via stairwell; intercept in lobby and remove via rear."

"Lobby has them now," replied Callan. "Assets now clearing floors above and below."

"Reporting positive audio fix on target inside 4-A, no

visual yet." Nikki looked up the hall and continued, "Door still intact."

"Instruct you to hold for bomb clearance."

"Copy. Holding."

Nikki made eye contact with Rook for the first time. "You OK?" he asked.

She nodded. "You?"

The elevator doors parted, and an ESU sergeant in a hooded blast suit clomped out flanked by two Hercules cops. As they passed, Rook said to Heat, "I officially feel like I'm in *Star Wars.*"

Everyone waited in the stairwell while the bomb squad hero opened the door, just in case of a booby trap. "What do you think that was about?" asked Rook. "Did Wynn know we were here? Was he making bombs and screwed up?" When Rook realized he was the only one talking, he stopped. "Shutting up now." He waited.

They all waited. Finally, Heat heard the all clear in her headpiece . . . followed by the call for paramedics to aid a victim.

"He's alive," she said hurling herself back to the hall. On the way to Wynn's door, she keyed her mic. "Let's move on those paramedics—*now.*"

The apartment had two floors. The blueprint she'd committed to memory back at the staging area showed a living room, hall, powder room, kitchen, and dining area downstairs, and two bedrooms and two baths upstairs. Heat hustled in the front door and broke left—the bomb sarge had radioed that the victim was down in the kitchen. Her face plowed through the thin layer of blue smoke suspended in the hall. Nikki hand signaled Raley and Ochoa, who had her back, to clear the closet and powder room as she passed each. Five paces ahead, a stream of bright crimson leaked across the hardwood from a source unseen around the corner in the kitchen.

A surreal view greeted her as she made the turn. The bomb sergeant, still cloaked in his bulky armor suit, knelt on the floor, applying direct pressure to the wound gushing red from Tyler Wynn's neck. Heat made a flash assessment of the damage. All of the old man's wounds were from the torso up on one side of his body, the side that had been exposed to the blast, which she could see—quite graphically—had come from the dining table on the other side of the counter. The eating area had been ripped by the explosion: leather dining chairs shredded; glass from the solarium-style windows gone; vertical blinds—those that remained—wagging back and forth in the breeze, mangled, sawed-off, and powder-charred; the thick glass table shattered into bits. Some of the glass was spread across the floor like fractured bits of ice. The rest of the jagged shards had been broadcast around the place, blending with the shrapnel packed inside the bomb: a mix of screws, nails, and ball bearings that peppered the ceilings and walls.

Wynn had taken the blast while in the kitchen. The granite counter had blocked his lower half from injury; meanwhile, his upper body resembled tartare. Heat knelt beside the man from the bomb squad and reached out to plug another ugly pumper on Wynn's chest. But she had to pull her hand back. Something sharp etched her palm. She lifted the sopping tatter of his shirt and saw the broken blade of a bread knife the concussion had shot out of the wood block on the countertop and into his ribs.

"Heat," he coughed out, making it almost sound like "hee."

"Help's coming. Hang on. Just hang on." She found a dish towel on the floor and made a wad to press around a gash on his forehead. The skin had been so flayed, she could see skull. The chest wound still flowed prolifically, so she carefully fit the bread knife blade between two fingers and applied what pressure she dared around the metal.

"Was it . . . ?" He coughed again.

"Don't try to talk," she said.

"Was it . . . Salena? . . . Did Kaye . . . find me?"

"Breathe. Don't talk. Just breathe and stay with me. Look, here come the paramedics."

In truth, Nikki wanted him to talk. But she wanted him to live first, so he could talk a whole lot. When the EMS crew took over, she stood by, bloody to her elbows and knees, not wanting to leave his side, in case he said anything more. It didn't seem likely. Even without medical training, Heat had been around enough trauma scenes to know from a paramedic's tone of voice, when the medic verbalized vital signs, when things were dire. They were having trouble stabilizing him. The paramedic said, "We gotta transport, and now."

Heat rode down with the gurney and got in the back of the ambulance for the ride. If Tyler Wynn were going to die, she wanted to be there when he did. And, yes, she also wanted to make sure he didn't get away again.

No sooner had the double doors closed than he rolled his head to her. He raised the hand on his good arm, the one without exposed tendons and bone showing, and beckoned her close. She held the rail of the gurney to steady herself and leaned forward inches from his shredded, monster face. "I'm sorry," he said. She could see him whimpering a cry and put a hand on his good wrist. "I loved your mom. I . . ." He choked a sob back and closed his eyes, which made her think he'd died, but then he flashed them open, and they were wild, full of some found strength and determination.

"I sold myself. They made me rich." He sucked in a gulp of air. "But they made me do awful things. So damn sorry. They made me . . ."

"Who?"

"Him!" The old spy coughed the name out on frothy blood: "Dragon."

Heat remembered. The person Salena Kaye had called from the stolen helicopter. "Who is Dragon?" she asked. "Aren't you Dragon?"

He wagged his head vehemently and moaned a no. The effort drained the fight from his eyes and he blinked. Then in a sudden exclamation, he shouted, "Terror!" And then he sucked more air. "Death, mass death here in New York. Worse than . . ." He shuddered down a breath. ". . . Worse than 9/11." He gagged and labored to swallow. "I'm cold."

"My mother found out about it? Is that why you—"

"Yes!" he blurted. "I am so sorry." He sobbed again and said, "She almost stopped them."

"Who did stop them? Nicole?" she asked. It felt logical

that her mom's friend and fellow agent intervened—and then ended up a frozen body in a suitcase.

His head wagged urgently side to side on the sheet. "Nobody stopped them."

"I don't understand. When was it supposed to happen?"

"Not was." His neck wound gurgled and red froth formed around it. Then he grunted out, "*Is!*"

"What is? Tyler, what?"

Nikki had to put her ear to his lips to hear him, his voice had grown so weak. "Mass death. It's coming." She rose up a few inches to see his face, to try to comprehend. And to believe. With a gaze fixed on hers from under flayed eyelids, he nodded with a message of certainty and warning. "You, Nikki. You stop it."

Another shuddering, labored breath. Heat could see him slipping away, and the injustice of his exit enraged her. "Talk. Tell me." She put her face right up to his. "You killed her, you goddamned bastard, and it's not going to be for nothing. Talk. Tell me what's coming. When?" The old man didn't answer. He reached for her cheek, but his hand never got there. It dropped lifelessly to his chest.

The paramedic swept in to try to revive him. For the second time in a month Nikki watched Tyler Wynn paddled by cardiac jolts on his deathbed. And, as before, a shrill flatline tone from the cardiac monitor called it a day.

The difference this time: Tyler Wynn was really dead.

The paramedic switched off the monitor and knuckled the glass behind the front cab. The ambulance driver killed the siren and slowed for the remainder of the trip past

Columbus Circle to the ER. Nikki looked at the old spy's body then out the window as they pulled up to Emergency at Roosevelt Hospital. If Wynn had told her the truth, a terror group was somewhere out there right now—busy making other plans.

ELEVEN

Heat stayed with the body until Lauren Parry arrived to do the preliminary postmortem. The medical examiner had been at *Jersey Boys* when she saw the text alert after the show and responded that she would handle it herself, since she was merely seven blocks from Roosevelt Hospital. But the real reason didn't need to be articulated, the part about knowing the deep significance to her friend, Nikki.

"Dr. Parry, now, you double check to make sure he's dead," said Rook as the ME pulled a surgical gown over her evening dress. "Use a wooden stake if you have to. This one has a nasty habit of coming back from the grave."

While the medical examiner went to work, Heat closed the door to an empty exam room and briefed Agents Callan and Bell on what she had been told on the ambulance ride.

Bart Callan asked the same questions they all had. "Was he specific? Did he say what kind of terror event? Did he say when? Or where? Did he say who was behind it?"

"It's not like I'm holding back," said Heat. "Wynn flatlined before he could give it up."

Rook chimed in, "So annoying. This guy always does

that. Gets you all sucked in and then dies before he finishes the story."

Callan began texting as he spoke. "This just popped to a new level. I'm getting NYPD Counterterror in on this right now."

"Is Tyler Wynn even credible?" asked Agent Bell. "I mean, come on, look at this guy's history."

"Really?!" Heat whipped her head to Yardley. Maybe it was the stress of it all. Or the raggedness of this ending and its denial of closure. But something roared inside Nikki. "Are you really going to stand here and pretend to tell me—tell *me*—about this guy's history?"

Instead of pushing back, Agent Bell gave her a passive stare. Then she broke it off and sauntered to the door, speaking coolly. "Agent Callan, I've got work to do."

When she walked out, Callan said, "Let's take a breath. It's been a crazy day. I'm going to set up a task force debrief down on Varick Street first thing in the morning. I want you there with us."

"You're kidding, right?"

"Come on, don't let some petty friction keep you outside." They both turned and watched Yardley Bell thumbing her BlackBerry outside Triage. "Nikki, I could use you." And then, reading her reaction to the personal tone of his appeal, he added, "Oh, and as far as that other thing I mentioned? That's off the table. This is a new game."

Nikki said, "Thanks, anyway. But I'll be in touch if I learn anything. You do the same."

On their way to the exam bay to check with Lauren

Parry on Wynn's prelim, Rook said, "Nikki, a task force. We could be on an actual task force." When she didn't acknowledge him, he asked, "What was Callan talking about? What other thing?"

"Rook, do you really want to help me?"

"Name it."

"Blow that off, OK?" Then she tugged a Velcro strap loose from his body armor. "And lose the stupid vest."

Heat never went home. She kissed a reluctant Rook good night, caught a radio car uptown to West 82nd, and napped on the cracked leather couch in the bull pen break room. After a brief but deep slumber, she made some coffee and drank it sitting in her rolling desk chair in front of the Murder Boards. Her grogginess actually helped her think. Before the snooze, her brain had been a primate house at the zoo, chattering with details; rowdy thoughts slinging on ropes and jumping from high to low. The solitude of the bull pen helped Nikki shoo the monkeys. By the time Raley, Ochoa, Rook, and the others gathered for their early roll call, she had some new ideas to share with her crew. One of them felt big.

"Tyler Wynn is dead," she began, then had to pause when Detective Hinesburg thought it would be cute to applaud. She did so alone, then stopped in the nakedness of silence and stares. Heat continued, "This time, it's verified, but we are far from resolved. In fact, a dying declaration he made to me not only leaves this case open, it kicks off a new phase that's going to require doubling our efforts."

While they stirred their first cups and bit off bagels, they also made notes as Heat recited the last words of the dead spy. "As frustrating as it is to get left with more questions than answers, at least he gave us something. It's up to us to turn that into enough." Preemptively, she voiced the questions she knew they were asking—the same ones Bart Callan had asked her in the ER a few hours before—the same ones she had been asking herself all night. They were already numbered on the whiteboard behind her: (1) What kind of terror event? (2) When? (3) Where? (4) Who is behind it?

"Let's start with what we know, starting with where." She block-printed the initials "NY" beside number three. "Pretty general, but it's a start. As for the type of event, calling it bigger than 9/11 and involving mass death broadens the scope beyond shooters, a car bomb, or the like, although nothing can be ruled out. I have a notion here that I'll come back to." She made eye contact with Rook, who smiled slightly, knowing she was percolating something.

"Who's behind it? Who knows? I've already briefed the counterterrorism unit, which tracks foreign and domestic groups. They are on it, but we can't kid ourselves. We have our work cut out for us there." She capped the marker.

"You didn't address when," said Rhymer.

"And that is the part that scares me. Let me share some thinking I've been doing." She came around to sit on a table in front of the boards and dangle her legs, looking to each of them as they looked back in rapt attention. "It's safe to assume the death of my mother came as a result of her uncovering two deadly things: the existence of some terror plot, and Tyler Wynn's involvement as a traitor to the CIA." She paused to allow the predicate sink in. "Although she was killed, my mother's efforts must have been disruptive because it appears she turned a mole in the terror group, a biochemist, who himself died suddenly weeks later. We're awaiting a new autopsy on him, but I'm working from the assumption of an execution. Everyone on board the ride so far?" They assented. She slid off the table and walked to the front of the room. "So this plot got derailed for years. We don't know why or how."

Rook said, "Maybe Ari Weiss's death put a freeze on things. He was definitely a key man if he's having secret meetings in cars with Tyler Wynn's cronies like we saw in that PI's picture. That happened a lot in revolutionary groups I've covered. One of the leaders dies or goes to prison, and they have to shut down to regroup or re-recruit."

"Quite possible. Especially if it's a small terror group, infighting and membership changes can knock them off balance." Heat saw Ochoa's hand. "Miguel?"

"So can scrutiny. I saw it tons when I worked gangs and rackets. You bring some surveillance, do a little nosing around, the bad guys go into sleep mode."

"Yes." Nikki pointed at the detective with fervor. "That's exactly where I am going. I know we've all worked this together, but indulge me while I bullet-point: My mother's killed, but she has a close friend and fellow CIA agent named Nicole Bernardin."

"The frozen lady in the suitcase," said Raley.

Nikki relived the successive shocks: being on Columbus Avenue that day, thinking she was investigating a routine homicide, a body in a suitcase; then reeling when she recognized the suitcase as one that had been stolen from her mother's apartment the night she was killed; then feeling stunned again when the victim turned out to be her mother's best friend . . . and CIA spy partner.

"That's correct. Like my mom, Nicole Bernardin was part of Tyler Wynn's network. And something that Nicole had discovered got her killed, too. Also by Tyler Wynn. But recently. After a decade-plus gap."

Heat walked back behind the table and picked up a manila folder. "Let's look at some highlights from Nicole Bernardin's case file. First, residue found on her body came from a potent medical lab solvent. Next, we never got a tox report on Nicole because Salena Kaye—Tyler Wynn's accomplice—sabotaged her toxicology lab test. And before the medical examiner could rerun the test, some mystery person ordered Nicole Bernardin's cremation."

Nikki looked up as she turned the page. She had their total focus. "Wynn had another accomplice. A crooked cop named Carter Damon. When we located Damon's van, Forensics not only found a blood match to Nicole Bernardin, they also found traces of the same lab cleaning solvent." She paused, marking her place in the folder with a finger.

"I've been thinking a lot about a murderer cleaning a dead body with lab solvents. Why? To clean what? And going to such lengths as to sabotage a toxicity test. Then destroy the body so no test can ever be run. Why would somebody do all that?" She scanned the room, seeing everyone's eyes locked on hers. "It suddenly dawned on me that Nicole Bernardin must have come in physical contact with something while she was investigating Tyler Wynn's secret activities. And I can only think of one reason to erase all traces of it so rigorously."

She closed the file and turned to the whiteboard. She had just uncapped her marker when she sensed the group behind her back drawing the same conclusion she had. Somebody—it sounded like Roach—muttered a long "Fuuuck."

And then she caps-printed her hypothesis beside "Type of Event" in a single, horrifying word: BIOTERROR.

When she turned from the board, Captain Irons spoke from where he stood at the back of the room. "Heat? A moment?"

The precinct commander closed the door when she stepped into his office, but he didn't bother to waddle around behind his desk, so neither of them sat, which suited Nikki's preference for a drive-by meeting. "Good briefing," he said. "I was a fly on the wall for most of it."

"Yes, sir, I noticed."

"Be nice to get a heads-up next time, so I don't have to be lucky."

"Absolutely," she lied.

Thinking that was that, she took a step to go, but he said, "Tough going on Tyler Wynn. You got your man, but he still left a bucket of worms to claw through. However, on the sunny side, now that that's closed, I can have you full-time on Rainbow."

"That's far from closed, Captain. You were at my debrief. It's a bioterror case now."

"Which DHS is running. Got to tell you, Detective, if Rainbow was tying colored strings to my picture, I'd be all over it."

"Sir, let me reassure you, I am capable of handling both."

His ears reddened and plum blotches mottled his cheeks. "I am anything but reassured. Now, you may have all the big magazines and primo TV interview shows courting you, but this is still my precinct. And my order is, you got Wynn, this now goes to the feds. If not, well, I suspended you once before. Do we need to revisit?"

Heat flopped at her desk, barely containing her temper. Strictly speaking, Wally Irons stood on solid ground. The scale of her case had escalated beyond a murder. The skipper's demand that she attend to the police work of his precinct—of the homicide squad she led—made sense. But Nikki didn't want to make sense; she wanted to see it through. Thousands of lives in New York City were at stake. Heat asked herself which motivated her more, her obligation to stop the terrorists or the responsibility she felt to finish her mother's work?

She decided they were one and the same, then went to her desk to make the call she didn't want to make.

"Nikki Heat, I couldn't be more pleased," said Bart Callan. "On behalf of DHS, I am so glad you decided to join us after all."

"Well, you sure put the home in Homeland, Special Agent Callan." Nikki hoped using his title would quell the effusiveness before things got out of hand.

"Whatever I can do," he said. And then Heat told him what that was.

Soon Nikki heard the muted phone ring across the bull pen and watched through the glass of the precinct commander's office as the federal card got played. Wally Irons nodded like a dashboard doggy to his caller, but he didn't appear happy. That was all right by her. She'd try to be happy enough for both of them.

An hour later, Detective Heat stood before a joint Bioterrorism Task Force in the basement bunker of the United States Department of Homeland Security, six reinforced floors under Varick Street in Lower Manhattan. Facing a mixed conference table of military, police, and intel officers, including Callan and Bell, she briefed them on her path into the investigation, via an eleven-year-old cold case, and the developments of the prior month that led her to Tyler Wynn's dying declaration on his last ambulance ride.

It all lived in her head, so she spoke without notes, fundamentally repeating the download she had given the squad that morning up at the Twentieth. She didn't use a whiteboard, and felt a bit startled when her peripheral vision caught the large LED screen behind her filling with text as she spoke. One of the secretaries in the back of the room was keying in an instant PowerPoint of her report. Resources, she thought. This is what they mean by resources.

The group questioned her afterward, mainly for details she had decided to spare them, and she answered everything candidly, holding only one thing back: the code.

When Nikki sat, Cooper McMains, the commander of the NYPD counterterrorism unit, said he bought the logic of her clue construction that pointed to a bioterror event. The rest agreed. Without any dissent beyond the prudent caution to keep open minds for other possibilities, gears shifted to practicalities. Special Agent in Charge Callan reclaimed the lectern and outlined the basics. "Top priority, we need to know the what, when, and where of this strike. I'll ask all of you to ramp up your eyes and ears with informants and to re-scrub all your data with this threat in mind. Obviously, we want hard focus on State's designated groups on the Foreign Terrorist Organizations list, starting with al-Qaeda and all its cousins, plus Hezbollah, Mujahideen, FARC, Shining Path, and so forth."

"What about the domestic watch list?" asked a brown-suited man with an academic's goatee and bow tie.

"Wouldn't rule it out. Especially if there's some new alliance we don't know about that's forming, but Tyler Wynn's CIA background tugs my sleeve to foreign. However . . ." He pointed a finger for emphasis and added, "Let's not neglect the splinter cells. We've all seen how a pair of foreign exchange students with a chemistry set and a list from the hardware store can be a threat."

"That's a wide spectrum," said the prof.

"Then we'd better be good," he said. "And quick."

As the Situation Room emptied, Heat met up with Callan at the door and said, "Now that we're agreed on bioterror, there's a thread I'd like to follow, and I'm telling you in advance because, as you'll recall, it was an issue before. Vaja Nikoladze."

"Forget Nikoladze, Detective," said Yardley Bell, shouldering her way into the conversation. "He's a nonstarter."

Nikki's expression appealed to Callan to intercede, but

he seemed cowed by the other agent, so she engaged her. "Not to me, he isn't. Let me count them off for you, Agent Bell." Heat held her gaze and numbered with her fingers. "Nikoladze is a top biochemist. He's a foreign national, a defector from the former Soviet Republic of Georgia."

"Do you think I need a primer on Vaja Nikoladze?"

"And," continued Heat, undeterred, "he was being spied on by my mother."

"Here's all you need to know about Nikoladze," said Agent Bell. "He's been a credible and productive informant in our system for years. Plus, our biochemist is in a disarmament think tank that promotes the demilitarization of science. If anything, your mom was using Vaja as an expert source."

"You were the FBI liaison with my mother back then," said Nikki to Callan. "Was that the relationship?"

"I honestly couldn't tell you one way or the other."

"Then I want to find out."

"No, you want to be right and me to be wrong," Yardley said. "Stop wasting time."

Bell stalked out of the room. Callan said, "Heat, maybe there are more productive lines of investigation to focus on."

"Sounds like an order." The DHS man didn't answer, except to smile. Nikki said, "Silly me. Here I was afraid if I joined your team I'd find it full of infighting and dysfunction."

Captain Irons made a show of turning his back on Heat to stare out at 82nd Street when she returned from the DHS meeting. Somehow, she'd be able to live with that. She got to her desk, woke up her monitor, and began clearing accumulated e-mails. There were a few progress updates from the squad on the serial killer, but most of her inbox brimmed with statements taken throughout the five boroughs from Rainbow pretenders. Nikki concentrated on the reports from her own detectives while she stirred the strawberry compote from the side cup into her two-percent yogurt.

"I had a real lunch," said Rook as he sauntered over. She moved some files from her desktop before he could sit on them—and just in time. "No yogurt on the fly for this man."

Roach came over, passing a basketball, a long-standing brainstorming habit of theirs. Ochoa said, "Writer Boy's been a sulky boy."

Rook ignored them and went on about his lunch. "I took myself for a chilled seafood salad over at Ocean Grill on Columbus."

Raley caught Ochoa's pass. "He's all bent because you went to the DHS deal without telling him."

"A white tablecloth and real silverware." He leaned toward her. "Excuse me, is that plastic spoon cracked?"

"Rook," she said, "are you really bugged?"

"No, why should I be bugged?"

"Trust me, we had to listen to him. He's bugged," said Rales, who then passed the ball to Rook, who flinched instead of catching it.

While Ochoa shagged the ball from under a desk, Rook blurted, "All right, I didn't go to Ocean Grill. I lost my appetite. A task force, Nikki. How could you go to the DHS Task Force without me?"

"Because it's restricted."

"Like that's ever stopped me." From anyone else, it would have seemed like an empty boast.

Detective Ochoa said, "My partner and I have been tossing around the idea of this van, the one that had Nicole Bernardin's blood and traces of lab cleaning solution in it. No sit-down lunch for us, either."

"What did you come up with?"

"OK, follow this," said Raley. "Let's suppose, like you said at the briefing, that Nicole Bernardin picked up some sort of biological toxin on herself while she was checking out whatever Tyler Wynn was into. Whoever caught her snooping around and killed her must have worried her body might register telltale contamination."

Ochoa picked up. "Which is why they scrubbed her corpse before they dumped it. They didn't want to set off any alarms."

"And since Carter Damon's van had both Nicole Bernardin's blood and traces of lab cleaning solvent," continued Raley, "I think it's a good bet that van got used to transport her body from where she was stabbed and scrubbed to where she got left in the suitcase. So our thinking is, if we can figure out where Damon's van traveled the night of her murder—"

"—We might just find the bioterror lab she discovered," said Heat. She added a "might" but liked this feeling, the little spark that could possibly kindle a break.

"But how could you ever learn where the van traveled?" asked Rook.

Detective Feller chimed in from his desk. "Doesn't

Homeland Security have cameras that scan license plates at key intersections and toll plazas so they can track suspicious vehicles that enter and drive around the city?"

"They do. They'd have video archives," Raley said. "So would NYPD."

Heat thought about the experience she'd just had in the bunker and said to Roach, "Start with NYPD."

"Your task force meeting was that good?" said Rook as Raley and Ochoa moved off to work the new lead.

"Shut up," she said, hiding her smile in her yogurt. "Let a gal enjoy her lunch."

"Sure. And while you do, let me share some thinking I tossed around with my partner. I'll admit it's an imaginary partner, which is why I'm so glad you're back."

"Rook, are you having a reality break, or does this have a point?"

"My point," he said, "is that if Tyler Wynn had so many foreign connections, why didn't he get out of Dodge instead of hanging around a month after you put the APB out on his traitorous ass?"

"Simple. To see the plot through."

"That's where I bump. What was the first thing Wynn said to you after the blast?"

"He asked me if Salena Kaye did it."

"No, exact quote, please, Detective."

Heat pictured the old man down on the kitchen floor. It all replayed like a movie. "He said, 'Was it Salena? Did Kaye find me?' "

Rook said, "See, now that's not just big, that's an XL."

"He's right." Randall Feller couldn't resist joining the spitball and came over. "The 'find me' part sounds like Wynn was hiding out from his own accomplice."

Rook continued, "And if Salena Kaye turned on him, and he was still hiding in New York, it suggests that his own organization cut him off and he lost the resources to flee these borders undetected. I've seen this before with my European spy friends. One day you're center car of the motorcade, the next you're hiding in Dumpsters, afraid to show your face and unable to board an airplane."

"The question is, why did they all of a sudden want him dead?" asked Feller.

"I hope to find that out," said Heat. "Maybe because I compromised him by surviving. When I came out of that subway alive, Uncle Tyler got on somebody's hit list because if we captured him, he might give up his co-conspirators."

"Good a reason as any," said Rook. "It also tells you why Salena hung around. To finish him off."

"And me," said Nikki.

"There she goes." Rook winked at Feller, then turned to Nikki. "It's all about you, isn't it?"

"Do you think Salena Kaye killed him?" asked Sharon Hinesburg. Randall Feller wasn't the only detective unable to resist joining the brainstorming session. But such engagement was rare for Hinesburg. Maybe she was trying to turn it around, after all.

"Kaye would certainly top the list," said Heat.

Feller crinkled his brow. "But isn't poison her MO of choice?"

Nikki said, "Best choice is the one that's effective."

"And we're sure he wasn't building a bomb and it went off on him?" asked Feller.

Heat shook no. "There weren't any bomb-making materials in his apartment."

"Please," said Rook in mock indignation. "This is Sutton Place we're talking about. The condo board wouldn't have it."

"Concierge records indicate a package delivered to his apartment," Heat explained. "Local messenger service, no trace. Probably bogus."

"So if he wasn't right beside the blast," said Rook, "the package probably wasn't rigged for opening."

"That leaves a timer or a remote detonation." Heat did another e-mail scan. "I'm still waiting to hear that determination. Forensics and Bomb Squad are both on that."

"You've got a lot on your plate," said Detective Hinesburg. "How about if I follow up and see what gives?" Nikki approved of the weak link trying to redeem herself and said sure.

Whether it was old-fashioned Heat Guilt or just to prove to herself that she could juggle it all, Nikki spent the rest of the day chipping away at the Rainbow case. She had finally surrendered to calling it that, which, hours later, constituted the only movement in the entire investigation. Satisfied that her squad remained diligent and engaged in the hunt for Rainbow, Heat allowed herself an indulgence. Like scratching poison ivy, she couldn't restrain herself, even though she knew the act would likely do more harm than good.

"Hallo, this is Vaja," said the man on the other end, whose soft voice and Eurasian inflections made her picture him in a Tbilisi coffee house reciting poetry.

"Dr. Nikoladze," said Heat in a cheery tone, keeping it casual, "Nikki Heat. How's dog business?" She could hear the breeze off the Hudson against his mouthpiece and the distant kennel sounds of his Georgian shepherds. "Am I going to be seeing you this winter at Westminster?"

"We had this conversation already, Detective. Good evening." The phone rustled, a dog barked, and the line went dead. "Call Ended."

She looked up from the blank glass of her iPhone screen, shaken out of her preoccupation by Rook, who had pulled on his sport coat and slung his Coach messenger bag over his shoulder. "I've got at least another hour or two to go here," she said.

"Yeah, I figured." He adjusted the wide strap of his bag to lie against the soft of his neck at the collar. "I got a call and have a meeting. Cocktails, and it'll probably turn into dinner." Nikki's solar plexus tweaked. In an irrational flash, she envisioned him and Yardley Bell in one of their spots. Boulud, Balthazar, or Nobu. Or, worse, one of the old Jamie Yardley haunts from when they were a couple. "It's more magazine business," he said.

"Good stuff, I hope."

"We'll see. My agent has set me up with some movie execs from Castle Rock. Just exploratory, but they want to talk about optioning the Heat pieces for film."

Nikki would almost have rather it were candlelight and mutually fed strawberries with Yardley. Well, maybe not, but close. "Are you kidding me? A movie? Based on my . . .

pieces?" She spat the word. The bull pen had mostly cleared for the night, but she kept her voice down anyway.

"Come on, this is nothing. You meet, you discuss. It's a dance. Nothing is set—or will be—without talking it over with you. You have my word as a member of the press." He laughed, trying to lighten the load with that.

She dismissed it with a hand wave, just to have it go away for now. The whole notion still chapped her, but Nikki made a tactical surrender because she couldn't bear the strain of one more ounce of conflict in her life. But she knew this tin can was only getting kicked down the road. "I get it. Fine, really." She stood and hugged him. "After spending a night on the couch here, I'm going home to turn in early, so why don't I see you in the morning?"

He leaned in. She gave him an office-appropriate kiss, watched him go out, and sat five minutes just to meditate herself calm.

Nikki came home with a to-go bag from Duke's around the block. During a comfort supper of Ma's Macaroni and KC Sloppy Ribs, Heat caught some baseball on TV. After her bath, the fans were just getting to "Take Me Out to the Ballgame," and she cocooned on the couch wrapped in a throw blanket while she battled sleep trying to stay awake for the late innings. Sleep won.

The phone woke her. She muted the postgame report and picked up her cell. The ID said "Unknown Caller."

"You had to know you'd be next," said the Darth Vader voice.

Rainbow.

Jolted, her heart pounded. She stood, pulling her bathrobe around herself, a primal reflex. "You're calling after office hours," she said, trying to mask the vulnerability she felt with some edge. The home call to her personal cell had done its job. He'd spooked her.

"Maximizing time," he said. "Who knows how many hours you have left? Well . . ." He chuckled. "Actually, I do."

"You're going to be disappointed."

"Could be," he said. Even through the electronic scramble, she could hear the earnestness of his admission. "You're a challenge, Heat. Like I said, you're smarter than the others." He paused slightly, then added, "But know what? It makes me wonder."

"What do you mean?"

"That you still don't know. That's what I mean." Then he hung up.

Heat felt like she should do something, but what? If she called to report this to Irons, he'd smother her with a protection detail or, worse, sideline her entirely, as he had a month ago with the enforced psych leave. Calling Detective Feller came to mind, as did Raley and Ochoa—all of whom had shown at one time or another what it meant for one cop to have another's back. But she didn't want to set off alarm bells or distract them from their work chasing leads. Same with calling her local precinct. The Thirteenth had covered her front door before with a blue-and-white, but once again, that could send ripples back to Captain Irons. Rook? She checked her watch. Almost 11 p.m.

She speed-dialed him, knowing he'd be more company than protection, but company would do nicely. He picked up on the third ring. "Hey, what's going on?" Rook spoke in a low voice, subdued, the way she had seen him take calls when he was somewhere he couldn't really talk.

"This a bad time?"

"No, not at all." She could hear silver clanging and table conversation, something like "Nathan would be perfect casting, if he's available." Nikki sensed his palm cupped around the mouthpiece. He said, "Just doing some spitballing with the Castle Rock folks. Can I call you in ten or fifteen? You gonna be up?"

"That's OK, stay on your meeting. I just wanted to say good night."

"Good night to you, too." She could hear the way he tried not to sound stilted—and his disappointment that he did nonetheless.

"See you in the pen in the a.m.," she said. Just hearing his voice had soothed her nerves. She made a double-check of her front door and all the windows, then went to bed with her Sig Sauer unholstered on the floor by the nightstand.

Sweet exhaustion took her, and she floated in a luxurious descent into the rabbit hole. An e-mail ping on her phone woke her at seven. Nikki twisted up on one elbow to check it. Agent Callan requested a conference call that morning. She tapped in a yes, then flopped back and stretched, drawing in a long, refreshing chestful, wishing she had asked Rook to come over. She turned to look at his pillow and sat up, quaking in alarm at what she saw resting there.

A coil of orange string.

TWELVE

"Tell me this really didn't happen," said Rook. "You let a serial killer touch my pillow?"

Heat laughed for the first time in days. When her laughter choked in her throat and she stifled tears, he held her, and Nikki let herself fold into him, wrapping her long arms around his back and pressing a cheek against his chest just for the grace of hearing a loving heart.

A throat cleared behind them. Benigno DeJesus, from the evidence collection team, stood in her open apartment doorway. Behind him waited his crew, also suited up in lab coveralls, footies, gloves, scrub hats, and masks. Rook said, "Love the costumes, kids, but the last trick-or-treaters got all the gummy bears."

DeJesus hadn't pulled his mask up yet, but even that wouldn't hide the grimness he exuded because of the nature of this visit. He greeted Nikki warmly, although they didn't even attempt to shake, each being an old pro at the contamination drill. "I'm glad it's you," Heat said, and not for the first time. She'd never worked with a better forensics detective than Benigno, and had requested him when she put in the call.

"Let's start by hearing about your night." He hauled a

grid-ruled pad out and made a quick, expert sketch of the hall, living room, and kitchen. "Tell me everywhere you went and anything you touched, however trivial, from when you got home until now."

She gave Detective DeJesus the narrated tour, awkward about having the witness shoe on her foot for a change. He made occasional marks on the pad, and when they had finished with the bedroom, including reference photos of the string, which still topped the pillowcase, he asked her if she noticed anything out of place. "That includes before or after you arrived."

"Before?" asked Rook. Then it sunk in. "Holy shit . . ." The possibility dawned on him, as it had on Nikki upon discovery of the string, that Rainbow might have been in the apartment, hiding, when she got home with her Duke's takeout and waited for her to go to bed, even placing his call from a closet or the bathroom.

"Nothing caught my attention before," she said. "And this morning, except for my security cam being disabled—which was the first thing I checked on—nothing. Absolutely no disturbances."

"If there's anything to be found, we'll find it." And they both knew that was bankable. Heat and Rook left for the precinct while the evidence techs got to work. Nikki paused in the hall for a parting glance into her apartment, imagining the serial killer roaming those floors while she slept. When they got on the elevator, she told Rook now she knew what people meant when they said they felt as if someone had walked across their grave.

Rook pushed the lobby button. "Let's walk on his instead."

Some wiseasses must have raided the precinct's emergency supply closet, because when Heat and Rook stepped into the bull pen, every detective sat hunched over a desk with a head on a pillow. Their gallows humor felt warmer than any hug they could have given Nikki. It called for a like response.

"Just as I thought. Killers are out there roaming free because you're all sleeping on the job." To signal the transition from play to work, she brought her latte up front without bothering to stop at her desk, and they all gathered for the morning debrief. Joke enjoyed; joke over.

"Obviously we have some Rainbow discussion on our agenda," she began while they slid their chairs around the Murder Boards. "But first, a follow-up about the bomb at Tyler Wynn's. Detective Hinesburg, did you connect with the bomb squad and Forensics?"

The detective's face blanched. "Uh . . ."

"Not filling me with confidence, Sharon."

"No, no, I did talk to them," she said, reaching to the floor and into her enormous purse. "You just caught me off guard and I wasn't sure I had my notes."

Heat waited for her to come up with her spiral pad. "And you were going to ask whether the trigger for the device was a timer or remote."

"Timer," she said without opening her notebook after all.

"Thank you." Nikki posted that on the Tyler Wynn section, then rolled that board aside. As Raley and Rhymer wheeled the serial killer boards in to replace it, Heat gave her squad the details of the call from Rainbow and of the creeping of her bedroom. "The hard drive connected to the lipstick cam above my front door is gone, and my building super did not let anyone in."

"Dude's putting it in your face," said Ochoa.

Detective Feller made a pistol of his fingers. "I'd like to put one in his."

Moving things forward, Nikki said, "In case anyone hasn't noticed, he didn't kill me when he had ample opportunity. I say Rainbow is strongly motivated by his head games."

"He's competing. Wants to prove he's smarter than the famous Detective Heat." When Malcolm said that, alluding to her celebrity, Heat exchanged a short glance with Rook. "Probably gets off on it. If he outsmarts you . . ." The detective realized where that thought led and stopped there, finishing with a "Sorry."

"No worries, Mal," said Heat. "I think we all know the stakes."

"And look how he's just taunting you," Detective Reynolds said, arching an indignant brow. "I mean even those mismatched socks on Joe Flynn? The odd socks?"

"Yeah, we all sort of got that. The price of having your life appear in print." Nikki didn't peek to Rook that time. She turned to Feller. "Randall, any idea yet how he managed to find out Joe Flynn had a connection to me?"

"Not yet. Working it, though."

Raley said, "This Rainbow must be some kind of evil genius. I mean what sort of brainiac could make all those links from Conklin all the way to you?"

"I don't think he did," answered Rook.

"Uh, Mr. Pulitzer?" said Malcolm. "I believe the strings say otherwise."

"It depends on what end you're looking at, doesn't it?" Rook moved to the Murder Boards. "Sometimes when I played Six Degrees of Marsha Mason, I'd cheat. I'm not proud of that, but I did. And when I cheated, know how I did? I didn't pick a celebrity and work my way up to Marsha Mason. I started with Marsha Mason and worked backwards." He paused and could see they were starting to follow. "Rainbow knew he wanted to match wits with Detective Heat all along, so he started with her and drew his links the other way." To illustrate, he pointed at Nikki, then to each victim, but in reverse this time. "From Heat to Flynn to Bedbug Doug to Berkowitz and Conklin . . . it gets easier when you work backwards. By the time you get to Conklin, he's almost a random choice."

Rhymer said, "But not so random. Take a look. From Conklin to Flynn, every person on that board, without exception, is some kind of investigator. Restaurants, consumer watchdog, art recovery . . . This guy has a thing for targeting inspectors. Maybe to show he's smarter."

"That makes sense, homes, it does," said Ochoa. "But I don't care how smart he thinks he is. We keep digging, we're going to find out where he fucked up and nail his ass."

"I'll tell you where he messed up," said Heat. "Coming after me."

After the squad broke up to jump on its assignments, Nikki quietly put in two calls: one to Bridgeport, Connecticut, the other to Providence, Rhode Island. The lead detectives in each department had the same reaction when she spoke to them. Chagrin that they had never put it together that the serial killer's victims had been inspectors of various types. From insurance claims adjustors to an HR administrator who did background checks, they all fit the profile. The homicide detective in Providence said, "What's this guy trying to do? Prove he can outsmart Sherlock Holmes?"

Captain Irons rolled in mid-morning from his weekly CompStat meeting down at 1PP. The CompStat sessions were an accountability ritual during which the city's precinct commanders presented their crime statistics to NYPD commissioners, then got publicly maligned, cajoled, and scoffed at before their peers. As harrowing a process as it could be, the Iron Man came from administration, not the street, so Wally generally survived the Police Plaza gauntlet, because the game played to his only strength, looking good on paper.

Nikki watched him drop his briefcase and doff his coat, knowing it would be a matter of minutes before he saw the report of her night visit from Rainbow. She found Rook fridge surfing in the kitchenette and asked, "Want to take a ride to the coroner's?"

He turned and grinned. "Shotgun."

They crossed Central Park on the 81st Street transverse, only to endure the cross-town crunch. "Where are we with Puzzle Man?" she asked.

"Haven't heard."

"Shouldn't you check in?"

"You don't push Puzzle Man."

"Why not?"

"I don't want to find out," said Rook. "Puzzle Man . . . he's such an enigma."

Shortly after Nikki cranked the turn south on Second Avenue, her phone rang and she popped in her earbud. "My DHS conference call," she told Rook. "Be quiet and don't make me laugh."

"Heat? Bart Callan. We're patching in Agent Bell."

"I'm on," said Yardley, sounding crisp, even for her.

Callan began, "This will be brief. Consider it a gentle heads-up for you about team protocol."

Nikki felt her pulse elevate and wondered if she should pull over for this. "OK . . ."

"Vaja Nikoladze," said Bell. "You were explicitly embargoed from contact and yet, what did you do? Made contact."

"He called to complain. Now, we can call this a mulligan," said Agent Callan, either trying to keep things from boiling over or to play Good Agent to her Bad Agent, who could tell? "Maybe you're used to a structure that's a little more elastic—"

"Oh, grow a pair and cut the shit, Bart," snapped Yardley. "Heat, you are not, repeat not, to fly against a directive again. Once more, and we freeze you out like January in Adak. Clear? Good. I'm off this call."

"Awkward," said Agent Callan. "But don't invest personally. Let's just stay in step moving forward, all right?"

But Heat had already hung up. She flung her earpiece at the dashboard and seethed.

"Problem, Detective?" said Rook.

Nikki whipped her head to him. "Your girlfriend, Writer Boy."

"Do I have to sit in your hallway with a shotgun all night?" asked Lauren Parry when Heat entered the little side office outside the autopsy room. "Because if you won't get yourself a protection detail, that's what I'm going to do."

"I keep telling her, Doc," added Rook as he slipped in.

Nikki said, "You talked to Miguel, didn't you?"

"Damn straight I talked to Miguel. And the handsome and tasteful Detective Ochoa and I agree you are crazy for not getting some firepower on your back, girl. That's because we have, what? Common sense." Heat wondered if there existed a single space in all of Manhattan where she could find peace that morning. Dr. Parry must have read her stress level because she notched back the pitch. "All right then, I've had my say. Now let's move on to a more pleasant subject, the new autopsy I did on Ari Weiss." She pointed through the window into B-23, the basement autopsy room.

"He's here?" asked Rook. "I've never seen an exhumed body. Can I see?" He didn't wait for permission but rushed up to the glass.

Lauren smiled. "I've seen four-year-olds do this at the car wash, but that's a first here."

The supine corpse of a man occupied the nearest table. Rook turned back to the ME. "I was hoping for something more gross."

"Then come back in fifty years. A body that's been hermetically sealed in a good casket in a dry environment will be well preserved."

"Even after eleven years?"

"Even after eleven years."

"You're no fun," said Rook.

In contemplative silence Nikki stared through the window at the body of Tyler Wynn's former associate. The man her mother had been grooming as an informant and who—much too coincidentally to suit Heat—died shortly after she did. "Have you got a confirmation of Weiss's blood disorder?" she asked Lauren.

"The babesiosis? We could wait for the lab or I could tell you my guess right now. Let me show you why I asked you to come down."

They suited up and followed the medical examiner into the big room. As they got closer, they could see that, although it had begun to skeletonize in places and showed a bit of tissue decomposition, the body remained remarkably intact. "You know me," said Lauren, "I'm never one to go out on a limb without test results."

Heat said, "Yes, but you do love to milk every bit of suspense you can out of something."

Even behind her mask, they could tell the ME was smiling. "It's people. I just love live people."

"Consider us sufficiently tantalized," said Heat.

"Fine. I predict the lab report will say Ari Weiss did not die of blood disease, but from blood . . . loss." With a flourish, Parry snapped the sheet covering Weiss's torso. When Nikki saw the large stab wound, it took her back to her mother's own knifing, and the implications hit her with a rush.

They hit Rook, too, but he was slightly more demonstrative. "Best. Exhumation. Ever."

The Caller ID on Nikki's cell phone displayed "WHNY TV." She slid into the driver's seat outside OCME and held the phone up to Rook. "Not sure I want this."

"I'd take it. I believe Channel 3 does its Dialing for Dollars contest about now between *Grace Under Fire* reruns. You could win cash and valuable prizes from their proud sponsors."

Figuring she'd have to deal with the interview request sooner or later, Heat pressed Accept. "Detective, it's George Putnam," said the Channel 3 news director. "You know that little stunt you pulled the other night, hijacking Greer Baxter's segment?"

"Listen, Mr. Putnam," said Nikki, as she keyed the ignition and gestured for Rook to buckle up, "I'm not going to apologize for using the media to aid an investigation."

"I'm not looking for an apology. I'm calling because someone responded to your plea. He doesn't sound like a crank, and he says it's urgent. Hold on, I'm conferencing him in." After the briefest pause, Putnam said, "You're on with Detective Heat. Tell her what you told me."

The man's voice sounded subdued, just above a whisper. "Hey, I can't talk too loud. She's here."

"Who?" asked Heat, unconsciously lowering her tone to match his.

"The lady whose picture you showed on TV. I'm manager at Surety Rent-a-Car on Fulton. She's at the counter now."

Heat checked over her shoulder and gunned the car out into traffic. "You sure it's her?"

"No. But it sure looks like her."

"What's she doing?"

"Asking to rent a truck."

In spite of the gymnastics required to access on- and off-ramps, the FDR won the toss for fastest route from Kips Bay to Lower Manhattan. Heat figured whatever time she lost in backtracking to get on and off the highway, she more than made up for by circumventing the one-ways and surface snarls.

She pushed it, racing there Code Three, to the delight of her ride-along journalist. When they passed the South Street Seaport to turn up Fulton, Heat killed the siren so—if the woman really was Salena Kaye—they wouldn't tip her off to their arrival. While Nikki concentrated on her wheel work, she handed Rook the phone to speed-dial Bart Callan at Homeland Security, who put out the call to his agents to meet and intercept.

Rook spotted the Surety Rent-a-Car sign ahead on the right, adjacent to an underground parking garage. "I'm serious," said Heat, "stay with the car." With that she notched it in park and hopped out right in the middle of the street, leaving the engine running and the gumball flashing as she jogged two doors up the sidewalk and into the garage entrance with her hand on her hip.

An Asian man in a long-sleeved shirt and a tie pushed open the glass door to the rental office as Heat approached. "Detective, that way. She saw you." He pointed urgently into an alcove of putty-colored cinder block in the corner of the garage, where a motorized overhead wheel spun, feeding a bright yellow upright conveyor belt down a three-foot hole in the concrete floor. Heat paused.

A man lift.

She had seen these things before; man lifts were in use all over the city at construction sites and parking garages. She'd never been on one and had never hoped to be. Not since she was a uniform and had to guard the remains of the parking attendant who fell off one. What she really remembered was the poor guy's elongated blood smear circulating on the continuous-loop belt until somebody turned it off.

Nikki checked the street, hoping to see some DHS backup. Then she addressed the man lift. The next toe-step fed by. She grabbed the guard handle, and got on.

Falling didn't worry her as much as the vulnerability. Disappearing down a hole in the floor was one thing. Riding feet first through a hole in the ceiling to the level below with your back exposed to an open garage made you a sitting—or hanging—duck. So Heat flouted OSHA safety rules and one-handed the grip, turned out from the belt instead of facing it, and held her Sig in the free hand. Heat hopped off on Level 2, found cover behind a metal trash can, and scanned the line of parked rentals under the humming fluorescents.

Out on Fulton, horns blasted. Rook accepted car horns as just the brass section of the New York soundtrack, but when he turned and saw the long line jammed by Heat's hasty parking job, he got out, waved to the queue as he came around the trunk, and got in the open driver's side door. "Technically, I am still in the car." He put the transmission in drive and eased the Crown Victoria to the side, still double-parked, but leaving sufficient room for others to pass.

Before Heat made a move, she looked up. The last time she'd found herself in a parking structure with Salena Kaye, she'd dropped on Nikki from above. Know your enemy, she thought, then crept forward, easing the soles of her shoes on the concrete, both to hear better and not to be heard as she ducked down to see under the cars.

A sound.

One tiny piece of grit, cracking under a shoe.

Heat rotated her head toward it. The instant she moved, a muzzle flashed across the hood of a Jetta and the air sizzled beside her ear. The slug hit the wall behind her, and concrete dust and paint fragments stung her cheek. She called, "NYPD, drop it," then rolled away from that spot for cover, coming up beside the engine block of an SUV.

The next shot punctured the Escape's hood. This time Heat returned two rounds from her Sig Sauer, aimed behind the flare. And waited.

She listened through heavy earwash as the gun echoes withered. She heard nothing. No movement, no moans. What to do?

A good cop is always thinking tactics and cover.

With ample cover and the anticipation of backup, Nikki decided to hold position.

But the game changed. Headlights blazed and an engine turned. A white Japanese compact squealed out of a parking slot and fishtailed away from Heat toward the exit ramp. Heat rose, braced on the hood of the SUV, and squeezed off another 9. The back window of the Versa spider-veined, but the driver turned the hairpin corner and disappeared up the ramp toward ground level.

Heat raced for the stairwell.

The Nissan's horn sounded a long and constant bleat, even frying the air outside the parking garage as it zoomed up the incline from below. Pedestrians heard it and scattered on the sidewalk to either side of the entrance as it flew out of the mouth of the structure and crossed the driveway out onto Fulton.

Jameson Rook floored the Crown Victoria Police Interceptor and T-boned the Nissan Versa, broadsiding the compact when it hit the street. The impact lifted the two nearest tires half a foot off the pavement and pushed the small car sideways into the rear of a cement truck, deploying the airbag in Salena Kaye's face.

It only took seconds for Heat to rush onto the driveway, but by then Kaye had already climbed out the broken windshield. Nikki searched the block and spotted her jogging away with a limp down Fulton Street. Heat knew she could take her down at that distance, but she wouldn't put bystanders at risk to prove it.

"Pearl Street. I've got her," said Heat, running past Rook as he got out of her Crown Vic.

He called out, "Hey! I stayed with the car!" Rook

couldn't be sure she heard him. Nikki had already rounded the corner. Improvising his own tactics, Rook briefed the rent-a-car manager to tell the backup which way Heat had gone, and then he ran off to take Cliff Street, the road that ran parallel to Nikki's.

"Vehicles, two minutes away," said Callan to Heat. "You should be hearing the chopper any second."

"I've lost her," she said into her cell phone. "How the hell could I have lost her in fifteen seconds?" She gave the DHS agent Salena Kaye's clothing description and pinpointed her position on Pearl Street, scanning storefronts and nail salons, as she walked and talked. "Just get here. Get here with everything now." Then she hung up.

Rook knew the neighborhood, and his plan was to follow Cliff until it intersected with John Street, where he would, theoretically, complete a pincer movement and meet up with Nikki in the middle of the block, closing off Kaye's escape. But before he reached John Street, he glanced inside a deli window and saw her—saw Salena Kaye at the steam table trying to blend in with the crowd.

And Salena saw him clock her. She started reaching inside her jacket.

"Bomb!" shouted Rook as he rushed in. "Everybody out, now!"

Amid the screams of panic and the stampede that jostled Salena Kaye, her draw got slowed enough for him to lunge for her. Rook's momentum slammed them into the steam table and her Glock came loose, sliding across the linoleum toward the back of the deli.

Rook was more a boxer than a combat fighter, and she easily broke free of his clinch, shoved him onto the floor, and started for her weapon. But as a proud college slacker, Rook possessed a talent more formidable than jujitsu: Frisbee. From a one-kneed kneel, he picked up a plastic dinner plate and executed a perfectly flung scoober that caught Kaye behind the ear. She didn't go down, but the plate edge stunned her enough to slow her.

She turned in disbelief only to be met by a barrage of salad-bar ice he shoveled at her frantically with both hands. Salena gave him a dismissive look, turned to get her gun, but her feet shot out from under her, slipping on the ice cubes. She landed hard. With no time to run to her, Rook hurled himself on his chest, slid across the floor on a bed of cubes, grabbed her gun, and stood, holding it on her. "Citizen's arrest," he said.

Heat appeared, making her way through the crowd outside, and stood in the front doorway. "Hey, Detective," he said. "Look what I caught."

As he finished the words, Salena Kaye yanked the legs out from under him by the pant cuffs, and he toppled backward onto the floor. In a flash, she scrambled through the vertical strips of hanging vinyl leading to the kitchen. Once more, Heat couldn't chance a shot that might take out a cook or a clerk. Slowly, she picked her way through the ice cubes and followed into the kitchen. The back door stood open. Nikki brought her gun up and rolled out into the alley—and found it empty.

Heat sprinted to the end of the passage where it opened

onto Pearl Street and looked both ways. She even looked up. How did that happen?

Salena Kaye had simply vanished.

Fulton Street had become a shining river of black vehicles when Heat and Rook walked back to Surety Rent-a-Car. SUVs and sedans with muscular engines and white US government plates filled the block, which had been sealed off. Air support and TV news copters circled overhead. Forensics technicians in coveralls dusted the mangled Nissan and took photos from all angles. More of the same went on one garage level below, with the added feature of the NYPD shooting team down there to rule on Heat's judgment under fire.

Heat and Rook found Agent Callan sitting in the backseat of his Suburban with the door open and his feet on the outside running boards, talking on a secure sat-phone. The boyish quarterback look seemed to have gained some weathering. He flicked a brow greeting to them, but pulled the door closed to finish his call.

A minute later, he stepped out, pocketing his phone. "Detective Heat, we have just kicked into a new era of heartache."

Heat shook her head. "How could she have vanished off the sidewalk? I was right behind her. There's no way she could have disappeared into thin air like that."

"Yeah, well a bigger whale just hit the fry pan. I'm sure you've been kind of busy the last half hour, but have you done any of the math on this?"

"Sure I have," Nikki said.

"Come on, Callan, we all have." Rook made a perimeter check to make sure they were out of earshot of press or civilians. "Salena Kaye's part of a bioterror plot, and she comes to rent a truck."

"We can all reach the same bottom line on that," said Heat.

"Well now we have a new figure to add to the equation." The agent side-nodded to the rental office. "Manager says she wanted to rent an E-350 cargo truck for this weekend." Nikki felt herself go weak. Rook let out a low whistle. Callan continued, "That's right. I just briefed the president's national security advisor that we have a high probability of a bioterror attack in New York City. And it's as soon as three or four days away."

THIRTEEN

Special Agent in Charge Callan didn't make it optional for Heat to join him in the Homeland Situation Room for a meeting of his Bioterror Task Force. He drew her away from Rook and said, "Listen, you will be there. And if there's some personality conflict between you and Agent Bell—"

"I think you know I'm more professional than that," she said, interrupting him. "I know what's at stake, and I would never let personal feelings interfere." And then, for his benefit, she added, "Personal feelings on any level, about anyone."

A hint of a smile, the first lightness Nikki had seen in him since his arrival on-scene, creased the corners of his mouth. "Guess we're all pros here, then."

"And given the very big clock that's counting down, I need to put my energy where it can do its best: working the street. Do I have time to button up my loose ends here?"

Callan slid the cuff off his aviator-style watch as he led her back to his Suburban. "I'm jumping on this now, but if you think you can make better use of time in the field, do it. I've got people en route from the Pentagon and CDC, and they'll be joining the meeting in-progress, also."

Rook heard that and cleared his throat. Nikki said,

"He can come, right?"

"I'm her wall. She bounces things off me." He raised his hand in oath. "And it's all off the record."

The agent scrutinized him. "Yes, Mr. Rook can join us, if that means you'll actually show up, Detective Heat."

"Oh, we will," said Rook.

"Parting orders?" said Agent Callan as he got in his vehicle. "Not a word about this. Not just press, Rook." He addressed them both. "Not to anyone. No mentions to sweethearts, family, friends, anybody. In this era of social media, we don't want word to spread and start a panic."

"Right," said Rook. "Who needs a viral threat to go, well, viral?"

"On second thought, Heat, leave him in the car." He slammed the door and roared off to Varick Street with the hidden emergency lights strobing in the grill of his SUV.

"You look just like on TV," said Alan Lew, manager of the Surety Rent-a-Car location. "Nothing like a police officer. You're beautiful like a model. Or Bond girl."

"Thank you, Mr. Lew. And thank you for calling in your tip. It was brave and extremely helpful."

"The picture on that Web site, *FirstPress*? Didn't do you justice."

"Oh, you saw the article," said Rook with a sly wink to Nikki.

"Yeah, it was OK. Good story. But the writing . . . not exactly Shakespeare, you know?"

Rook's smile vanished. "I think the detective has some questions for you, sir."

"We're going to keep the rental agreement she filled out, if that's all right."

"Absolutely."

"This photocopy you made is obviously of a fake ID and an alias."

"I pretended the copy machine was slow so I could stall her until you got here."

"Very resourceful. Can you tell me what she was doing during that time?"

He came around the counter and stood where Salena Kaye had been. Heat made a little sketch, out of habit, and marked the spot. Sometimes these interviews were perfunctory; sometimes they yielded clues. In her experience, motivated people like Lew made good witnesses, so Nikki paid close attention. "She was mostly right here the whole time. Looking around a lot. Watching me in the back when I called you. It took two tries to reach you, and I didn't want her to get away."

"May I?" asked Heat. Mr. Lew stepped aside, and she stood where he had and rotated. "Looked around like this?"

He nodded eagerly. "Except she was doing this." He repeated her move, but mimed holding a cell phone to his ear.

"She was on her phone. Did you hear anything she said? A name?"

The manager said, "She didn't say anything, she was just holding it."

She turned to Rook. "Go to the entrance where I came in, so I can see you coming." He trotted out to the sidewalk and walked in the garage driveway, as Nikki had. As soon as Heat saw him, she ran to the glass door and retraced Salena

Kaye's route to the man lift, timing herself. She walked back to the office, looking thoughtful.

A patrol officer came in. "Excuse me, Detective? Got an eyewit."

Outside the deli on Cliff Street, a bicycle messenger said he saw Salena Kaye race off in a silver minivan. "Did you get a plate?" asked Nikki.

The eyewitness shook his head. "It didn't have any plates."

"Was she driving?"

"Some dude." He didn't get a description of the driver. "I was too focused on staying alive. Van almost creamed me, booking ass out of there."

A technician from ECU had found Salena Kaye's shoulder bag under the deli steam table. Rook said, for the benefit of all in earshot, "She must have dropped it—when I took her down." Heat was too busy placing the bag's contents out on a table to pay attention.

She laid out a slim Eagle Creek travel wallet with the fake ID, a credit card in the same alias, a few hundred in cash, a popular lipstick and compact available from any drugstore, and a hotel room key with the identification tag removed. Heat also found a clip of 9mm ammunition. "A gal always needs a spare," said Nikki as she set it beside the other items. To her gloved touch, the outer pocket of the bag felt like it held another clip, but it turned out to be a cell phone. Nikki opened Recents and saw the last call received. It matched the time Kaye had been in the rental office. Using her own cell, Heat called the squad. Hinesburg picked up.

"Hey, Nikki," she said, the only one in the house who used her first name, a trait residing about midpoint on her list of annoying qualities, "did that tipster guy ever reach you?"

"You heard about him?"

"Yeah, some guy called and said he spotted Salena Kaye and wanted to talk to you. I started quizzing him to make sure he wasn't a crackpot, and he got all cranked and said he couldn't waste time and hung up on me."

Heat recalled the rental car manager saying he made two tries to reach her. "Detective, how come you didn't tell me?"

"I am." And then Hinesburg actually giggled.

"Detective."

"You mean before? I didn't bother you earlier 'cause I thought he was a nut job."

As she had so many times dealing with Sharon Hinesburg, Heat made a silent three-count before she continued. "You have a pen? Write this down." Nikki recited the Recents number from Salena Kaye's phone and asked her to run it. "And Sharon? Do call me immediately when you get the trace."

After she hung up, Heat furrowed her brow, considered the screwup potential, then pressed the speed dial for Detective Ochoa's cell. When he answered, she gave him the phone number and asked him to trace it. "And Miguel, don't let Hinesburg know you're doing this. I asked her to run it, and I'm having second thoughts about her follow-through."

"You mean just now?" He laughed and hung up.

"You think someone called and tipped Kaye off, don't you?" said Rook.

Heat continued to go through the shoulder bag. "Could be. Why do you ask?"

"Because back at the rent-a-car, when you asked me to go out and reenact walking in—playing the part of you—there's no way Salena Kaye could have spotted you without you spotting her, too."

"Not unless she has X-ray vision and saw me coming through the wall when I was on the sidewalk." She glanced up from her bag search and gave him a smile. "That's good deduction, Writer Boy."

"I walked a mile in your shoes, Nikki Heat."

"You can stop now."

"Stopping," he said.

"OK, here we go . . ." From a fold at the bottom of the shoulder bag she pulled out a small plastic card, about the size of a supermarket rewards chip. "Somebody joined a gym." She held up the membership card with the bar code on it so he could see. "Coney Island Workout."

Macka, the owner of the gym, paused his chore of rolling towels and stacking them in cubbies to scan the bar code on the infrared gun at Reception. "She bought a month-to-month. This who you're looking for?" He spun the computer flat-screen toward them. Salena Kaye's unsmiling ID photo, taken right there against the powder blue wall, stared out. But the name matched the fake credit card and license, not her real one.

"That's her," said Heat. "Do you have an address?"

"Sure do," he said and brought that file up for them to see. "It's in Fairfax, Virginia." No surprise to Heat. She turned away to scan the gym, hoping to find someone Salena worked out with—also a long shot; Kaye would be a loner and just use the facility to keep up her battle strength. Then Macka said, "But I know where she lives. You know, she's kind of a looker. I was waiting for my bus one night and saw her go in the Coney Crest on Surf Ave."

On their way there, Rook said, "Excuse me, you're not going to check in with our cousins at Homeland Security?"

Heat knew she should, but answered, "It'll slow us down," speaking the perfect brand of truth: the one that also functioned as camouflage for a deeper truth. Someone may have tipped off Salena Kaye about Heat's visit to the rent-a-car. Nikki simply would not take the chance that it could happen again, and made a field decision that this raid would be lightning-quick, minimal in size, and known solely by the actual participants. She only made two calls. One to Benigno DeJesus, whose evidence collection team had finished scouring Heat's apartment, and the other to the Sixtieth Precinct to request some uniformed officers to establish a perimeter around the motel and provide backup. Detective Heat never said for what, and nobody asked her to. Everyone just assumed it was all about the Rainbow case.

The Coney Crest fell into that subcategory of lodging known as the SRO, or single residence occupancy—a weekly transitional rental for the increasing number of unfortunate souls who'd lost their homes in a bad economy. In police shorthand, SROs also functioned as flophouses for the marginally legal and folks hiding out: shitheads, robbers, and offenders. The thing most of these places had in common was few questions asked, bad smells in the halls, and names that sounded classier than the joint.

As Heat walked the second-floor breezeway toward Room 210, a trio of uniforms crept up the far stairs to converge with her in the open hallway. She paused to look over the rail at the cloudy swimming pool where Rook waited beside the broken diving board. The Coney Crest's manager, no constitutional scholar, never asked for a warrant. The weary man with pouched eyes simply gave Nikki his passkey, even though he pointed out that the one Heat had brought from Salena's bag would fit 210 and about a half dozen other doors in the place.

Detective Heat and the officers behind her took positions on opposite sides of the door. Using the silent signals and the plan they had worked out in the parking lot, Nikki knelt, slid the key in the lock, called, "Salena Kaye, NYPD, open up," and unlocked the door. The nearest uniform booted it open and they all rolled in, covering one another and shouting don't-move commands.

In fifteen seconds, it was over. They had cleared the bedroom, the closet, the bathroom, even searched the modest array of cabinets in the kitchenette.

"You didn't really expect her to be in here, did you?" asked Rook when she allowed him in.

"Not really. Kaye's a trained agent. She'd been burned, we had her key; she'll never come here again." She smiled at him. "But let a girl have her fantasies."

"Every wish begins with Kaye," he said.

Benigno DeJesus had no trouble finding the place. He had been to the Coney Crest so many times over the years that he'd joked to his forensics team about renting one of the rooms to keep as storage for his gear. While Heat's go-to ECU detective snapped open his rolling case out on the breezeway and prepared to examine Room 210, he filled Nikki in on the results of his run of her apartment.

The report didn't take long. The intruder had gotten in through a closet window. The busted latch had been invisible to her eye when she'd made her check of the place, but DeJesus's inspection of the window from the outside revealed jimmy scratches and brass shavings on the sill from chiseling and prying. He found no sign of the missing hard drive from her lipstick cam or any evidence of DNA—translated as excrement (not uncommon) or results of sexual gratification—same with inconsistent hairs, fibers, or shoe scuffs. The orange string matched the same lot found on Joe Flynn's boat. The lab had it, but as with the other strings they'd tested, the prospect of finding anything useful on it seemed bleak. "We did lift some prints, but it will surprise me if they aren't yours, Mr. Rook's, and your building super's." He put on his scrub cap and added, "I know it won't make you rest any easier, but it's like a ghost came to visit you."

Instead of feeling spooked, Heat processed his comment dispassionately, as an investigator. She made a mental note to run cat burglars through the RTCC database downtown, then led him into Salena Kaye's motel room.

The forensics detective stood quietly in the center of the

room and simply looked around. After a few Zen-like moments of stillness, he asked, "Your raid team, how much did they disturb?"

"Minimal. Once they opened doors and cabinets to clear the room, I sent them out."

"Good." Finished with his overview, he continued, "Fingerprints will be tricky due to volume of room traffic in a place like this. But if she had visitors, you'll want to know who, so I'll do my best. We have some partials of Salena Kaye's from your Starbucks cup, and I assume we'll get more out of the shoulder bag you found."

"Actually, I got it away from her," said Rook. And, for a little extra hot sauce, he added, "During our fight." Benigno regarded him a moment, said nothing, and got to work.

He began in the kitchenette because he'd spotted several plastic bags from a hardware store on the countertop—rather inconsistent with food preparation. "See here?" he said, holding one of the bags open with his gloved hands. "Ball bearings, bulk purchased nails, screws and nuts . . . I'm betting these are her shrapnel leftovers from the Tyler Wynn bomb. It'll match, mark my words." He opened and closed cabinets. When he got to the one beneath the sink, he knelt and shined a work light inside. Then he turned to Heat, speaking casually. "I'm going to stand down until you have the motel evacuated and call the bomb squad. Just a precaution, but take a peek." She bent to look over his shoulder as he pointed to a plastic dish tub filled with cellophane bags, and an array of electronic parts. "None of it seems hooked up, but I see gunpowder, C4 . . . even a backup remote control device. See that tan garage door clicker next to those firing switches and wires? That's the same sort of radio controller that was used to detonate the package in Wynn's apartment."

Heat said, "I was told that got set off by a timer."

"Not by me," said the forensics man. "I know a timer from a radio controller."

Heat turned to Rook, who had not only read her mind, but already had his scoff on. "Another thorough job by the Queen of Detail, Sharon Hinesburg."

On the drive back to Manhattan, Heat put in a call to Detective Hinesburg—or, as Rook had christened her, Defective Hinesburg. "Oh, I was just about to call you." Somehow Sharon always managed to sound as if she'd gotten caught playing Angry Birds and was covering. It occurred to Nikki that that may have been more than merely an impression. "You know that number you gave me to check out? Burner cell."

"You're sure." Heat let her testiness come through.

"Yep. A prepaid phone, probably bought at a CVS or Best Buy. Not traceable."

"The reason I'm asking if you're sure is that you also said the trigger for Tyler Wynn's bomb was a timer, and I just learned it was a remote. Maybe not the end of the world, but my main concern—Detective—is that I can count on you to actually complete an assignment when I give you one." Nikki side-glanced to Rook, who was nodding feverishly and throwing shadow punches in the passenger seat.

"But I did." The whine did nothing to endear her.

"Then why did you say it was a timer?"

"Because when you called on me, I got all flustered. I

forgot which it was and said the first thing I thought of. I feel a lot of pressure in those Murder Board meetings." Hinesburg paused, and Nikki could hear her swallow hard. "I feel like you hate me, and that makes it harder. I'm trying to do better."

Heat felt like she was dealing with a preadolescent rather than a homicide detective, and cut her losses. "Here's where you can start, Sharon. Do what you're asked, and if you don't know an answer, don't make one up, OK?"

"See, you do hate me."

After the call, Nikki growled in frustration and said to Rook, "Last thing I need in the middle of two monster cases is Sharon Hinesburg's . . ."

". . . Bullshit?"

". . . Crap."

"You go, Nikki."

"I can deal with weakness. I can even handle a certain degree of incompetence. Sort of. But what I can't have is a lack of confidence. And there aren't enough make-work assignments just to keep her out of the way."

Rook said, "You should just bag her."

"I can't, and you know why."

Rook smiled as they entered the Midtown Tunnel. "Which is why I'd never sleep with someone I work with."

On the sidewalk outside the Department of Homeland Security, Heat made a quick call to Detective Raley before she and Rook went in. "You're still my King of All Surveillance Media, right?"

"I'm also clairvoyant," Raley said. "I predict my future holds canceled dinner plans."

"Uncanny. From now on, I'm calling you the Great Ralini. I just left Salena Kaye's SRO in Coney Island. The motel has some actual working surveillance cams, and the manager is holding the tapes from the last few weeks. I'd like you to scrub them to log her comings and goings and pull video of any visitors she might have had."

"On it," he said, and jotted down the address of the Coney Crest.

"And Sean, keep this between us, but that's one of the dives I asked Detective Hinesburg to check out a few days ago. She said she did."

Raley didn't need much prompting. "And you want me to make sure she actually showed up?"

"Wow," said Heat. "The Great Ralini sees all."

"Building a paper trail?" asked Rook when she hung up.

"He's scrubbing the video anyway." Nikki didn't know what felt worse, sneaking a check on one of her own detectives or having to because that's what happened when you lost confidence in a team member.

A whispered intensity crackled in the DHS basement bunker as Detective Heat and Jameson Rook stepped off the elevator and were met by their uniformed escort. Clearly the mode had shifted down there from serious to urgent. More personnel filled the darkly lit cavern than before, some squeezed double in the cubicles, scanning e-mail traffic, tracking suspects on the Watch List, and networking informants. Others monitored JumboTron displays of the power grid, reservoirs, and nuclear plants, as well as live cams of bridges, tunnels, airports, and harbor ship traffic.

Rook said, "If I ever buy a house in the burbs, I'm going to have a man cave just like this in my basem—"

A screeching, pulsing alarm broke the hush of the control center and a blinding light strobed above the two of them. Glass doors automatically slid shut in the offices lining the perimeter. A rolling metal shudder descended, sealing the door to the Situation Room. Inside its window, Nikki could see Agents Callan, Bell, and other members of the task force get up from the conference table and stare out. A squad of four personnel in moon suits and gas masks rushed out of nowhere, grabbed Heat and Rook, and scrambled them to a small room beside the elevator. Two of the moon suits waited outside; the other pair stayed in with them. One pressed a button that created a vacuum around the door seals they could feel in their ears, as if the room were an airliner gaining altitude.

"What's happening?" asked Nikki. They didn't answer, just separated her from Rook and began scanning both of them with sensors that resembled microphones on the ends of yellow garden hoses attached to whirring filter machinery.

"Nikki," said Rook. He tilted his head to a sign on the door that she had to read backward: "Contamination Quarantine."

Then one of the machines began to chirp and blink an array of yellow lights. The word "POSITIVE" flashed on the monitor.

The positive reading came from the machine testing Heat.

FOURTEEN

"You set off our sniffer." Agent Callan held open the door to Quarantine, and Nikki emerged in a borrowed DHS hoodie and mismatched sweatpants. As he walked her to the Situation Room, he said, "But I like the style. You can keep that while we test your clothes and find out exactly what bioagent you had on them." He gestured to the robotlike air sampling machine she had set off. "This here's the li'l guy that busted you." Heat had seen versions of these bioaerosol monitors throughout Manhattan, part of the city's—and Homeland's—attempt to get early warning of a dirty bomb or bio strike. "You aren't, by chance, moonlighting in a terror cell, are you?"

"Right. In all my spare time."

While Nikki changed, Rook had found a seat at the conference table—right beside Yardley Bell, who was deep in conversation with him until Callan and Heat came in and all eyes turned their way. "Prelim from the lab is some kind of trace material on her blazer," announced Callan as he took his spot at the head of the table. "Whatever set it off, it's not in sufficient quantity to be harmful, but at least we know the air sampler works."

"Great. Maybe we can wheel it person-to-person around

New York City during the next few days and find out who's planning the attack," said the professorial man in the bow tie. His crack was no joke, but an acerbic snarl of frustration. "I would be curious to know where you picked up this virus or bacteria, Detective."

Callan asked, "You didn't have any physical contact with Salena Kaye, did you?"

"No. Not today, anyway."

"Tough one," said Yardley Bell, sounding baldly condescending. "Don't feel too bad. Sometimes they just get away from you."

"Even the good ones." Nikki didn't need to toss a glance at Rook. Yardley was smart enough to get it. Heat chided herself for stooping to soap opera—even though it felt good on a primal level; oh-snaps were a trashy seduction. She redirected herself to the bow tie man.

"I could have picked something up at the place I just came from. The motel room where Salena Kaye has been hiding out." Nikki felt that announcing her rogue mission would be an unpopular bit of information, and she wasn't wrong. Throats cleared, butts shifted, faces grew taut.

"You mounted a raid on our suspect without notifying us?" asked Callan.

Rook jumped in, blurting, "There wasn't time," then shrank back in his chair after the looks he got.

Nikki explained the course of events, from finding Kaye's shoulder bag, to tracking down her gym, to the lead on her SRO and the bomb materials she discovered there. "Sometimes you have to make a command decision in the field. Given the fluidity of this situation, mine was to act with all speed rather than stop and wait for protocols." McMains, the NYPD counterterrorism unit commander, caught her eye; his alone twinkled in unspoken agreement. Callan asked her the name of the place then picked up his Bat Phone to dispatch a DHS swab team to the Coney Crest.

In this most uncomfortable moment, while Bart Callan made his call and Nikki felt the judgmental stares of the task force, a curious sense of ease cloaked her. Because even with all the tension and scrutiny coming her way, at least she felt a respite from the two killers hunting her. Down in that stress-filled bunker, Nikki felt safer than she did on the streets of New York. Then she wondered, What does that say about my life?

Her reflection got interrupted by a text from Lauren Parry at OCME. "I suppose there's one other possible source of my contamination," Heat said after Callan hung up. "I just learned the body we exhumed—Ari Weiss, the man who was my mother's informant in the terror cell—contained residue of a biological toxin. Ricin."

Agent Callan pressed another line and told someone on the other end to test Heat's blazer for ricin first. Putting the phone back in the cradle, he asked, "Is there anything else you're not telling us?"

Instead of rising to his bait, Heat stayed on point. "The significance of the new autopsy on Weiss is that his COD wasn't a blood disease, but a knife wound."

"Same as your . . ." Callan didn't finish, and took the silent interval to switch gears. "We can discuss protocols and team sharing later. Let's move forward. Dr. Donald Rose is here from CDC in Atlanta to brief us. Don?"

The expert from the Centers for Disease Control, a tall, lean support system for a walrus mustache, appeared more like an aging rodeo cowboy than a research chemist. He poured a glass of ice water from the pitcher in the middle of the table. "Thanks, Bart, appreciate it." Nikki wondered if the drink would wash the gravel out of his voice, or if he'd just down it and say, "Beef. It's what's for dinner."

"I'm here to bring you up to speed on what's out there in terms of biological agents," he began. "Down in Atlanta, I coordinate prevention and preparedness in the event of a bioterror strike." He smiled. "I tell my wife, If I do the first part right, the second part's a breeze." Not one chuckle. Instead of soothing, his laconic approach made his content all the more frightening. "Through our syndromic surveillance unit, we collect data on patients and symptoms at hospitals and walk-in clinics nationwide. We survey the size, spread, and tempo of viral and bacterial outbreaks. The idea of this is to track risks so we stay on top of them. Think of it like the Doppler radar you see on your TV news, except instead of sniffing out storms, we search for signs of an outbreak.

"What are we looking for? Lots. Let's start with anthrax. We all remember the anthrax incidents of 2001. It's on our danger list but—not to minimize it—anthrax is statistically inefficient for widespread dissemination in a big event scenario. We do stockpile ciprofloxacin, doxycycline, and amoxicillin to treat it, though.

"One potential weaponized bioagent is ricin. Others out

there, the filoviruses like Ebola and Marburg, as well as arenaviruses, can cause viral hemorrhagic fevers. Their classification is Biosafety Level-4 pathogens, or BSL-4s. A spread among the general public would be swift and difficult to contain. These viruses cause massive simultaneous organ shutdown and hypovolemic shock. Field medics treating hot zones in the Third World called it hell on earth, and that's using restraint. It's a messy, painful, gruesome death."

Rook turned to Nikki. "Personally, I'd lose that blazer." The laughter that followed was brief but welcome. Everyone needed to breathe.

The CDC expert paused and took another sip of water. Everyone waited, nobody moved. This was now *The Dr. Don Rose Show*. "Smallpox, if you don't know, was officially eradicated in 1979. Only two stores of *Variola major* and *Variola minor* exist in the world. In Russia and at the CDC in Atlanta. We watch for it, but unless someone manages to cook up a batch, smallpox is under lock and key. And for good reason. Smallpox is one of the bad boys. It has a thirty-five percent mortality rate."

"How would one of these bioagents likely be spread?" Agent Bell asked.

"Could be person-to-person. Could be food- or product-borne. But that would be a slower process, albeit unsettling. For your terror bang for the buck, I expect the release would likely be aerosol. Probably from a sealed metal container carrying it in liquid form with a propellant to help it get atomized."

Nikki asked, "What size container?"

"In a dense population center like this? We're talking

mere gallons." As the needle-in-a-haystack implications sunk in on all of them, he added, "Also, any part of New York City exposed to a mass release would be shut down and quarantined indefinitely."

"So we know the ugly," said Callan, turning to his DHS intelligence coordinator. "How bad's the bad?"

"Bad about says it," answered Agent Londell Washington. He looked to be in his late forties, but sleeplessness and stress had added ten years. You aged fast in this business. "We've ramped up surveillance since this landed in our laps. We're leaning hard on all our informants and undercover agents. Nothing. We've tracked movements of all known and suspected terror likelies on our Watch List to see who's gathering, who's become suddenly active, and who's gone underground. There's no anomalous behavior. We're monitoring phone calls, e-mails, chat rooms, Tweets, taxicab two-ways, even Love Line record dedications on the radio—I kid you not—nada. All the jihadists and ideologues are acting to pattern; there's no chatter like we usually get before an event, no spike in sick days among employees at the power plants, train stations, and so forth."

Rook said, "Maybe it's not ideological."

"Then what?" asked the bow tie, the professor not sounding so eager to hear theories from a hack with a visitor's badge.

Undaunted, Rook replied, "In my work I've met war criminals in The Hague, guerrilla fighters, cat burglars, even a former governor with a fetish for over-the-calf socks. People who go out of bounds do it for a lot of reasons.

Subtracting zealotry, their motives usually go to revenge, ego, or profit. My ex-KGB friend always says, 'First, follow the money.' Now, he stole that from Woodward and Bernstein, but you get the idea."

"With all due respect," said the professor, "I don't buy stateless terror. This has to be a government-sponsored plot. With all the logistics and expensive players like Tyler Wynn and his crew, who else would have the financial wherewithal to fund it? My intel points to the Syrians."

Callan tossed his pen on his blotter. "So after all this, we're still three, maybe four days out, and have nothing to go on."

"Perhaps we can go at this a different way," said Yardley Bell, addressing Cooper McMains, the head of the NYPD counterterrorism unit. "Commander, can you run down your top targets of opportunity?"

"Certainly. For this type of strike, the high-value targets are population-rich, symbolic venues. So, in no particular order: Times Square, the Empire State Building, Grand Central, Penn Station, Union Square, SoHo . . . and, of course the ballparks. And, since we're talking about Saturday or Sunday, I'd add Central Park. Weather's supposed to be good, it's going to be packed."

"Thank you," said Bell. She got up and went to the LED board at the head of the table and stood beside the list of targets, which had been bulleted on the screen as Commander McMains spoke.

"Detective Heat, you have a special connection to this case, we all know that. And this includes some persons of interest you developed from subjects your mother had under surveillance years ago." An odd sensation passed through Nikki. The acknowledgment of her efforts felt supportive, yet laced with a mild wariness that the recognition came from Yardley Bell. "Maybe instead of sitting here dead in the water, listening to the clock tick, we could examine some leads you developed. Tell us about a Jamaican immigrant by the name of Algernon Barrett."

"Barrett was on my short list of murder suspects before I determined who my mother's real killer was. However, I've revisited him in the past few days and he doesn't add up for me as part of this terror plot."

"Interesting." Agent Bell strolled back to her place at the table, walking the room like a TV lawyer making a summary to the jury. She put a hand on Rook's forearm and said, " 'Scuse me, would you?" and she tugged a gray file from under his elbow. "He's in the food business, right?"

"Jamaican jerk chicken. He retails spices and has some food trucks."

"Right, Do the Jerk, I've seen them. But our foreigner is making some changes to his business model all of a sudden." Bell opened the gray file and cited notes as she prowled back to the head of the room. "He told you about his—what are they called now?—'pop-up' stores?" Nikki's mild wariness had gone full-bore, and it must have shown. "Don't worry, I haven't been tapping you. Rook told me."

Heat turned to him. His expression resembled that of a dog who'd just dookied the new rug.

"You zeroing in on something, here, Agent Bell?" asked Callan, growing impatient.

"I am. For those who don't know what they are—they probably don't have a lot of pop-up stores in Atlanta . . ."

"Mom-and-pop's about it," said Dr. Rose.

". . . Pop-up stores are short-term retail or food spots that 'pop up' overnight, in vacant store fronts, do business with groovy, social media–connected millennials for about a week, and then move on. Very hip, very happening, and maybe, very deadly.

"Here's the list of where Algernon Barrett's jerk chicken stores are popping up this weekend." She positioned herself to stand beside the bulleted list of Targets of Opportunity on the LED, and recited from the file, "Times Square. Across from the Empire State Building. Grand Central's Eastern Passage. Penn Station. Next to Barnes & Noble in Union Square." She scanned the target list with her forefinger. "Huh. Seems we covered most of them, except for SoHo and the parks."

Heat said it felt like conjecture, but her words couldn't fight the hard silence that filled the Situation Room as Yardley Bell returned to her seat. At last, Agent Callan scanned the faces of his task force and said, "Sounds to me like we should pop up at Algernon Barrett's."

From there things happened quickly. The search warrant. The plan. The unchaining of the hounds. Homeland drilled for moments like this, and in Domino's delivery time, Heat found herself riding shotgun in Special Agent Callan's black SUV in a siren-and-lights convoy smoking uptown. He heard something he liked in his silicone earpiece and said to Nikki, "Bell says her advance team is in place and confirm Barrett at the location." She didn't reply, just sat chewing on her misgivings about this operation and how it had steamrolled so rapidly from a speculative mention in the Situation Room.

Bart Callan concentrated on keeping pace as the motorcade snaked a turn onto First Avenue. Once he rotated the wheel into the straightaway, he flicked a glance in the rearview to Rook in the backseat. "Never thought I'd say this, but glad you're around, after all."

"Yeah?" muttered Rook. His response came muted, not just from the backhanded compliment, but he'd been maintaining a low profile in the aftermath of Yardley Bell naming him as the source of her intel on the Jamaican. He knew this would be a discussion later with Nikki, and hunkering became his defensive strategy. But the man behind the wheel seemed to have a different agenda—and worked it—masking his digs inside praise, all for Nikki's ears.

"I'm serious. Without your special relationship with Yardley Bell, we'd never have this lead." Separately, Heat and Rook reacted with discomfort. They both wanted out of that car, but doing fifty in a Code Three wouldn't be the place. And Bart continued, sounding innocent even as he made one last pick at the scab. "You and Yardley must be good friends to have ended a romance and still be this close." Rook didn't answer that. Heat wanted to turn in her seat and eyeball him; wished for one moment of privacy so she could unload. That would wait.

"Know what this bridge is?" asked Callan as they crossed the Harlem River on the Willis Avenue span. "The twenty-mile-mark of the New York City Marathon. Know what we call this bridge? The Wall."

"Because this is where you hit it?" asked Rook.

"No." Callan scoffed. "Because this is where the lesser runners do."

An officer in black fatigues waved them into the staging area, the parking lot of the US Postal Service's Bronx sorting facility off Brown Place, around the corner and out of sight of Barrett's Do the Jerk warehouse. Callan scoped the blacktop, which was filled with hazmat vans, FDNY trucks, ambulances, and a pair of daunting, black military-style armored personnel carriers with battering rams. In a far corner, a portable hazardous materials scrub-shower area was being set up beside a medical DRASH tent. "Handy to have this USPS property here in the neighborhood," said Heat.

The agent nodded. "This is federal synergy at its finest." He sounded tongue-in-cheek, but his face meant every word. When they heard the click of Rook unbuckling his seat belt, Callan found him in the rearview mirror. He spoke softly but with the tone of a drill instructor. "You *will* remain in the vehicle." Rook folded his hands in his lap to wait.

Yardley Bell met them mid-block on 132nd, on their walk-up to the deployment zone, and recited the briefing. "Streets are cordoned, all exits blocked, neighboring properties . . . a shipping fulfillment center and a scaffolding business . . . have been cleared out. Quarantine team's ready and we have air support." She twisted to the sky. "We also attracted a couple of TV news choppers. I had FAA push them back one mile, and our public information officer is calling the stations to inform them of the readiness exercises we are conducting this week." Nikki listened to Yardley, so in-charge. She heard the competency and the confidence, and felt a little bad she couldn't admire her.

"Got your warrant, Agent Bell." Callan handed her the paper.

She gave it a quick glance and said, "Let's light the fuse."

They approached the front gate using one of the box trucks borrowed from the US Mail, the driver announcing a delivery for Algernon Barrett. The fence rolled back, admitting Mr. Barrett's delivery: a dozen armed federal agents Trojan Horsed in the cargo hold. The personnel carriers, Crown Vics, and half a dozen white vans marked with the blue vertical Homeland Security stripe drafted in behind it.

Bell went in first with a SWAT team, her badge and the warrant lofted above her head. She announced herself and ordered everyone to stay as they were, showing their hands. Detective Heat entered in the second wave, along with cooperating law enforcement and a platoon of biotechnicians lugging portable aerosol sniffers and other sensory gear. Once past Reception and the front offices, the rest of the facility appeared laid out, open plan, in one story under a corrugated roof. With no resistance and nobody fleeing, agents easily corralled the thirty startled employees near the loading dock while the DHS techies dispersed to sample air and inspect equipment and storage containers.

Because of her firsthand knowledge of the layout, Heat led Bell to Algernon Barrett's office. The Jamaican was gone, but the betting line for the upcoming Kentucky Derby blared from his big-screen TV and a pungent wisp curled up from a fatty in the ashtray. Both of them poised their hands on their holsters and cleared the private bathroom. The other door in the office gave onto a back hallway leading to the warehouse. Outside a door marked as the spice supply room, they took ready positions and entered. "Looky here," said Yardley Bell as Barrett emerged from between stacked cartons of Scotch bonnets and cloves with his hands up. "I found the secret jerk ingredient."

They searched him and took him back up the hall to his office. Nikki had warned them before they left Varick Street about Barrett's lawyer, so they were eager to get some interrogation happening before Helen Miksit complicated matters.

"Why did you hide?"

"Who are you?"

"Bart Callan, special agent in charge, Department of Homeland Security. Just one of the people in this room who can make your life hell. Now, answer my question. Why did you hide from us?"

"Habit, I guess. Doors get busted, man's got to run."

"You expect us to believe that?"

"Believe what you like, mon." Algernon turned from him and surveyed Nikki, who stood off in the corner, still wearing her Homeland hoodie. "So, Detective, this is what I get for cooperating?"

Nikki said, "Mr. Barrett, this will all go more smoothly if you continue to do so."

"Yeah?" He folded his arms and leaned back on the couch. "I'm not saying anything. I want my lawyer."

An hour later, after Callan and Bell did their best to brace him both head-on and sideways about his participation in a terror plot, they lost him to the Bulldog, who advised her client to say absolutely nothing. Her statement, she said, would suffice. "My client is a United States citizen and taxpayer. He operates a successful, legitimate business purveying spice rubs and chicken dishes to a loyal public. Any inference that he is involved in some sort of diabolical plot based on his foreign origin is wild speculation, offensive, and slanderous."

"What about his sudden expansion at key targets of opportunity?" asked Bell.

"They are targets of opportunity," said Helen Miksit. "For profit. So unless you have evidence or a charge to file, why don't you suck it?" If nothing else came out of this raid, Nikki thought that, just maybe, she could get to like Helen Miksit after all.

Out in the warehouse, while the forensic technicians continued their search for evidence of viral or bacterial agents in marination canisters, drums of spices, and refrigerators, Heat took Callan aside. "If it's all the same to you, I'm going to bag this and get back to my precinct."

"I so was hopeful this would give us traction." He

surveyed the activity, ending with a head shake. "Heat, we need a break."

"We do. I just never felt like it was here."

"Is that an I-told-you-so?" Yardley Bell, from ten feet away, handed the company's shipments manifest back to an agent and came over to join them. "See, Detective, here is the fundamental difference between us: You're ready to bag it because it didn't just land in our laps; I am ready to double down." She turned to Callan. "Pull me some more warrants, Agent. I want to toss Barrett's house, I want to toss the houses of his friends, his dealers, his hookers, his fucking pastor. I am ready to rattle some cages." She walked away backward, saying to Nikki, "And then, if we survive to Monday, I can be an I-told-you-so."

Callan arranged for an agent to shuttle Heat and Rook back to the Twentieth, which only further postponed the conversation looming over them about Rook's loose lips. He filled the trip mostly by complaining about his Callan-forced SUV time-out. "I hated that. I felt like I was sitting in the penalty box, having to watch a power play. Anyway, I made use of the hour and a half getting my mother out of the city."

"Rook."

"Don't worry, I didn't tell her why. I'm much sneakier than that."

"I know."

He sidestepped that and explained, "I called in an IOU from a colleague of mine at the State University of New York and arranged for Margaret Rook, Broadway's diva's diva, to receive the first annual Stage Door Prize at the SUNY Oswego

Drama Festival. It's short notice, but Mom's thrilled."

"What is the Stage Door Prize?"

"Haven't figured that out yet. All I know is it's going to cost me ten grand plus luxury accommodations. But it gets Mom out of harm's way. Just in case . . . you know."

She turned away and stared out the window as they turned off Lenox Avenue, remembering for a moment when she caught a glimpse of foliage at the north end of Central Park that it was spring. Her brief interlude with nature got interrupted by a text. "Weird," she said after reading it. "From Callan. Test results of the bioagent traces on my blazer came back. It wasn't ricin." She held out her phone to Rook.

"Smallpox?" His face turned ashen. "Didn't Dr. Doom from CDC call that one of the bad boys?" She nodded. "And all you can say is, 'weird'? Oh, excuse me, just a spot of bother. I seem to have picked up a bit of smallpox on my coat sleeve. No biggie."

"It is a biggie, I know it's a biggie. Apparently it's a marker, not enough to cause worry, but a medic is coming to give me a shot." She finished reading and said, "What's weird to me is that it's not ricin, so that means I didn't pick it up from Ari Weiss's corpse."

"So where?"

"I don't know."

There was a silence. Then the driver lowered his window. "Don't blame you, buddy," said Rook. "Stick your head out and breathe, if you like."

As soon as the DHS car dropped them on 82nd, Rook smiled and said, "So. We good?"

"That's it? That's what you call dealing with this? Shrug it off and say 'We good'?" She mocked him by brushing her palms as if dusting them clean. "God, you are such a boy."

"I am not . . ." He mimicked her palm brushing. "I just think we should be good because you know very well that I would never compromise you by sharing secrets."

"Then what do you call it?"

Sharon Hinesburg passed by with a take-out bag, and they held their conversation. When she went inside the precinct, Rook said, "First of all, before I can keep a secret, I have to know it's a secret. I thought we were all kind of working on the same team here, trying to stop the bad guys from unleashing a plague."

"Being on the same team is one thing, Rook, but that doesn't mean you can go reporting to other people. Especially Yardley Bell."

"You don't like her."

"It's not about liking her."

"You're still jealous because we have a history."

"It's not that, either. I just don't trust her."

"Why not?"

"Nothing I can pinpoint. It's an instinct."

"Hey, I'm the one with hunches and instincts, and you hate that."

"Well now it's my turn. And as irrational as it may seem, I want you to respect that." They regarded each other a moment, and in spite of the argument, all the good feelings held fast. Maybe that's what a relationship was, she thought. She reached out and he took her hand. "Look, you know what I'm juggling. All I'm saying is, with everything else I have to look over my shoulder about, I don't want you to be another one."

He reached out his other hand and she took that, and they faced each other. He smiled. "So. We good?"

Heat regarded him and knew that, above all else, Jameson Rook was a good man she could trust. Nothing else mattered. "We are good." She squeezed both his hands and they walked in together.

While Nikki received her shot of an antiviral, she thought through her day for any clue where she might have picked up that smallpox marker. A disturbing notion came to her. After quick calls to Benigno DeJesus and Bart Callan, the orange string Rainbow left on the pillow got priority-messengered to the DHS lab for testing. A certain conspiracy-hungry boyfriend would be quite proud of her.

One thing Heat did know for certain: There was no way in hell she would spend another minute in sweats at the cop shop. She opened her bottom file drawer where she kept what she called her emergency wear: backup apparel for those days she spilled coffee or got blood on her clothes.

After a quick change and a review of the Murder Boards, she decided it was time to hit the phones again. That was how an investigation worked. You got a new scrap of information and followed it up by talking to someone about it. Sometimes you got another scrap that moved you forward, sometimes not. But you kept making rounds, occasionally feeling like a tethered pony walking a circle at a kids' zoo, but you just continued plodding until something shook loose.

First call went to Carey Maggs at Brewery Boz. He came on the line sounding extra-Brit, which was to say deliciously cranky and jovial about it. "Catching you at a busy time?"

He chuckled, "Is there any other kind? You know, just running a business and saving the world in a failing economy. I'm like your Clark Kent, only not slim enough for the tights, I suppose."

She thought of the peace march he was sponsoring that weekend, and her heart ached wanting to warn him about the looming terror possibility, but where did something like that stop? There were hundreds of public events, conventions, bike-a-thons, and street fairs on the weekend calendar. Maybe if Rook optioned her article to Hollywood, he'd have enough money to give everyone in New York City an award at SUNY and get them all out of town. Putting that aside, she broke the news to Maggs about Ari Weiss: that his old friend had not died of a blood disease at all, but had been murdered.

"Christ in heaven," he sighed.

Weiss's murder was not only new information, the stabbing matched her mother's so closely that Nikki texted Maggs a picture of her killer, Petar Matic. She heard the chime on his cell phone as it arrived, then a deep exhale and some tongue clicking from Maggs's end as he studied it. "Know what? I have seen this guy."

"You're sure?"

"No doubt. It's the greasy long hair and the slacker eyes. Who is he?"

"He was my boyfriend."

"Uh-oh, low bridge, sorry."

". . . Who killed my mother." She heard a whispered curse and continued, "It's likely he stabbed Ari as well. Do you recall when you saw him, and where?"

"I do very well because I called the police about him. He was hanging about in the front of my apartment building a number of times and I wanted him dealt with."

"When was this?"

"Good lord, Detective, it was near Thanksgiving. Same week as Ari was staying with us. And same week as . . ."

"It's all right, Carey, I know what else happened that week."

Heat could hear the strain in Maggs as he absorbed the startling news she'd dropped on him about his old friend. But she pressed forward. He could recover later. Right now, she needed a new lead. "Carey, I want your help with something, if you're up for it." He sounded emotional but croaked out a yes, so she asked, "You mentioned Ari wasn't real social or political. Do you recall if he had any colleagues in the science world with whom he was close? Was there anyone in particular he talked about, or teamed with on any special projects?"

After some thought, Maggs said, "None that stuck in my brain. Sure, I'd cross paths with his crowd for a beer or to watch football at Slattery's, but to me they were, basically, this blur of boffins."

She didn't want to lead him with a name, so she asked, "Do you recall any foreigners?"

He laughed. "You're joking, right? That was most of them."

And then she said it. But Maggs didn't recall any Vaja Nikoladze by name, so she texted him his photo, too, and waited for him to look at it. "Sorry. He meets the boffin test, but I don't remember him hanging out with Ari."

Nikki chalked up another disappointment, but at least she'd gotten her ID of Petar, firming up his connection to Ari Weiss's murder.

Rook convinced her to step out with him for a quick bite at the new Shake Shack that had just opened on Columbus, but they didn't get that far. In fact, Detective Raley called them to a stop in the precinct lobby. "What's up, Sean? You spot something on the Coney Crest tapes?"

"No, still screening them. But Miguel and I just got a hit on something else. Trust me, you will want to see this."

"I think the Shake Shack will have to manage without us," said Rook.

When Heat came back into the bull pen, Ochoa had the results up on his monitor at Roach Central, which is what the pair had dubbed the corner where they had pushed their desks. "OK," he said as Heat sat in his chair, "we've been scouring the NYPD license plate surveillance cams from last month for any sign of that van that was hauling around the body of your mom's spy partner. We track the van, we find the lab, right?"

"We do," said Rook.

"We hope," said Heat.

"We scored," said Ochoa. "Big-time. Here's the first hit. And yes, it's from the night she was killed. " He clicked the mouse and a blurry image of the plate came up. The location read, "E-ZPass Lane 2, Henry Hudson Bridge."

"Is this right?" asked Heat. "All the way up there?"

Roach nodded in unison. "It's correct," said Raley.

"But we wondered the same thing," added Ochoa. "We asked ourselves, What's the van—and the body—doing coming down into the city from way up there? So we ran some further checks."

"I love you, Roach," said Heat.

Raley continued, "We combed a net of traffic cams at on-ramps in Westchester County and north."

"It wasn't as hard as it seems, since we knew the general time and exact date." Ochoa clicked again and the screen filled with four shots of the same plate at different locations. "So, backtracking, here's where we see the first appearance of the van on its drive south toward New York City." He double-clicked the top image. When it opened, the location stamp made Heat gasp.

FIFTEEN

That maroon van could have been coming from any number of places when it got photographed getting on the Saw Mill River Parkway at Hastings-on-Hudson, but Nikki Heat could only think of one. Rook said it out loud. "Vaja." In a single mouse click all the reasons—all the instincts—she'd had about holding on to the biochemist as a person of interest seemed to be borne out. Heat only prayed it wasn't too late.

"Roach, saddle up." She turned to the other detectives in the bull pen. "Feller. Rhymer. You, too. We're taking a ride to Westchester."

"What about me?" Detective Hinesburg came in from the kitchenette holding a plate of deli salad scoops. Suddenly it was PE class, all the teams had been chosen, and everyone started getting very busy avoiding eye contact. Heat simply didn't want Sharon there. And she sure didn't want to ride with her. She wasn't about to foist her on Roach or Feller and Rhymer, either.

"I need you here to hold the fort." Nikki felt bad for that, but in a way she knew she'd get over it in a hurry. In truth, Hinesburg could take care of a few things that would get Heat on the road faster. "Start by calling the State Police,

Troop K. Tell them we are en route for a seal and seize at a place off Warburton Avenue in Hastings and need an assist. Give the Troop K lead my cell. I'll coordinate logistics from the car."

"Got it," said Hinesburg, seeming content to be relevant. "What about town police?"

By then Heat and the others had reached the door. "I know the locals and have them in my contacts. I'll handle them myself after I notify DHS."

"What's this guy done, anyway?" she asked.

"I hope nothing yet." And then Heat rolled.

They took up observation positions where the Old Croton Trailway ran along a wooded hill above Vaja Nikoladze's property. "Got just about one more hour of daylight," said Ochoa. He turned to his left to indicate the low sun's reflection kicking off the glass skin of the Manhattan skyline twenty-two miles downriver. From that distance, it could have been Oz.

Heat didn't bother to look. Her focus remained through her binoculars, studying the secluded acreage below. She scanned Nikoladze's metallic blue hybrid, which sat empty, nosed against the weathered rail where the gravel drive met the pasture beside his house. The freshly painted Victorian showed no sign of life from her vantage point. All the curtains were open but to no movement, no passing forms or shadows. And no lights inside. A breeze rustled the pink blossoms of the stand of rhododendrons near the kennel on the right side of the pasture. Nikki had never seen all the dogs he kept in there, but on her first visit the month before, she met the Georgian shepherd Vaja had anointed to reclaim the glory of his beloved show dog that had suddenly died. It crossed her mind at that moment to wonder what unexpected tragedy befell the biochemist's dog, and if what she had read on Nikoladze's face as grief had actually been self-reproach. Heat listened for the dogs but only heard the stir of wind mixing with the clatter of a northbound train behind the trees at the back of the meadow as it traveled along the Hudson River.

"Callan's landing now," said Heat, adjusting the volume in her earpiece.

Rook turned to her. "Why couldn't we take a chopper?"

"Dude," said Feller. "We got here in like a half hour. In case you didn't notice, we are waiting for the slicks with their f-ing chopper."

"Maybe it's not so much wanting to ride in one. I was sort of hoping for once in my life I could turn to someone and say, 'Prepare the chopper.' "

Raley said, "Go ahead man, hit me one time."

"No, I couldn't."

"Really, here's your chance, go ahead."

Rook considered a beat and said, "Prepare the chopper."

"Eat shit," said Raley. Ochoa held out a fist and the partners bumped.

"Boys," said Heat.

"That's fine," said Rook. "I know you're just ripping me because you see me almost as a brother cop."

"Hey, if that works for you, bro," said Ochoa.

They met Agents Callan and Bell down on the road, around a bend that concealed them from being seen from Vaja's property. Callan greeted Heat's team and said, "Sorry for the delay—we had to set down in some nature preserve."

"Mayberry doesn't have a copter pad," said Yardley Bell.

Nikki spread a map on the hood of her car. "No sweat. Gave us time to set up logistics. We own the area, basically. State Police have closed this road to traffic between Odell Avenue and Yonkers Yacht Club. To the west, it's just railroad tracks and river. East is woods and the trail up the hill, where we had our OP. Detective Feller is up there maintaining surveillance."

"Any sign?" asked Callan.

"Nothing. Car's there, but that's not definitive."

Agent Bell asked, "What about his workplace?"

"Checked on that. I have excellent cooperation from local law enforcement," Nikki said, trying to push back on her Mayberry dig. "They drove my Detective Rhymer to the institute, and he confirms Nikoladze is not there. They are remaining on-scene in case he shows, and to make sure no calls go to him."

Special Agent Callan nodded approval. "Very thorough—for a local." He snuck Heat a wink and asked, "How we going in?"

Heat opened up a sketch she had drawn of the compound on a blank sheet of printer paper. Just as she pulled out her red Sharpie to mark arrows for the raid, Yardley Bell interrupted. "Here, maybe this will be more helpful." She unfolded a large, color satellite photo of the property. "This was taken just after noon today."

Rook tried to take the brittleness out of the air. "Noon, huh? Well, maybe we should use Nikki's since it was drawn ten minutes ago, so it's more current."

They took their positions on the road, behind bushes at the end of the driveway, and at key locations in the woods flanking the land to the north and south. Another contingent of State and Hastings police covered the railroad tracks behind the grove of hardwoods, to close the back door. Detective Heat's plan had been to approach on foot in a platoon, using silence to provide surprise, with vehicles as backup to create a tight perimeter. She got overruled. But before that, she got undermined.

"First thing, Detective," said Bell, "too much exposure on foot. You may sadly discover the surprise is yours."

Callan became swayed. "Kinda ducks in a barrel, if he's got a rifle."

Before Heat could show where the cover would be and identify the house's blind spots she had located, Yardley rolled over her. "Shock and Awe. Ever hear of that? There's a reason . . . It works. Flip the plan, Detective. Roar in with the vehicles first, deploy the foot soldiers. Shock and Awe."

Much as Heat had seen all week, Callan let his subordinate steamroll him. "Shock and Awe it is," he said.

On Heat's go signal they swarmed the place. SUVs and Crown Victorias with hell's roaring fire under the hood thundered up the driveway, kicking up pea gravel and chewing lawn to the front door of the Victorian. Car doors flew open. Agents and cops rolled out. Using the vehicles for cover, Heat, Roach, Callan, and the others leapfrogged to the side of the house, squatting low as they moved along the latticework of the gallery porch.

Agent Bell executed the same tactic across the lawn. An SUV and two cars scrambled across the meadow to the kennel, depositing Bell and her team to hug the walls there. That's when things unraveled.

As soon as all the vehicles were in, the double doors to the kennel burst open and ten Georgian shepherds ran out, barking and dashing in circles all over the compound. In the instant of surprise and distraction, an engine howled to life and an all-terrain vehicle screamed out of the building behind the cars and agents and headed for the woods. Bell and the others raised their weapons, but by then Heat had run across the grass from the house shouting, "Hold fire! Hold fire!" They had discussed it going in: They needed Vaja alive.

Yardley Bell peeled herself off the kennel wall and ran for one of the cars as she holstered her weapon. "I got him," she yelled to Heat.

Still closing in at twenty yards, Nikki called, "We're sealed off, he won't get far." Just as Heat made it beside the Crown Vic, the DHS agent slammed the door and fishtailed off, leaving Nikki to watch helplessly as she gunned it up the driveway to the road.

Rook saw the whole thing. Relegated to the rear flank, relaxing on a gurney in the back of a waiting ambulance, he first heard the dogs, then Nikki's distant shouts. That got him out and upright on the pavement in time to hear the high-pitched engine of the ATV snapping twigs on its way through the woods to his left and the growl of the Police Interceptor flying up the road behind him.

Vaja's four-wheeler broke out of the thicket and onto Warburton. Rook's first impression was how small the Georgian seemed, looking like a kid joy-riding his dad's quad. Nikoladze whipped his head Rook's way, but was really looking past him at the oncoming car. He might have done better to keep crossing and try his chances in the woods across the lane. Instead, he gunned it and tried to make a run for it on the pavement.

In a swirl of wind and grit, the Crown Victoria blew past Rook and pulled beside Nikoladze, slowing slightly to pace him. Before reaching the curve where a hidden roadblock waited, Agent Bell brought the right quarter of her car to touch the rear of his quad and jerked the wheel, executing what every law enforcement officer and anyone who's seen a freeway chase knows as a PIT maneuver. If it had been a car instead of an ATV, it would have spun, lost control, and stopped, facing the opposite direction. But it was an ATV.

It rocked wildly, nearly flipping over sideways. Nikoladze frantically worked the handlebars, steering madly to compensate and balance. The quad corrected, then set down hard with a bounce on its fat tires that sent the front end up in a wheelie. But the front end never came back down. It continued its rise up and over the head of the driver—until the rear wheels came up, too, and the entire vehicle went airborne—upside-down, backward. Unable to hold on with his knees, Vaja Nikoladze lost his grip and fell to the pavement on his back.

The ATV not only landed on top of him, it continued to rev and spin at a crazy high speed, churning the wheels and grinding axles all over his face and body, shredding his clothes and skin until it thumped over him like he was some meaty speed bump, crashed in the woods, and left him bleeding, lacerated, and dying on the road from a split skull.

Nikki Heat shifted in the front seat of her car, stirred from her nap by a rhythmic plunking of dew drops from a tree branch onto her windshield.

It sounded like a ticking clock.

Not quite awake, and determined to stay adrift just a few more minutes, she squinted to orient herself. Three flashlights moving in a line away from Nikoladze's dog kennel swept the woods, forming shafts of light stabbing at the wooly fog that had woven through Hastings-on-Hudson after midnight. A forensic technician's camera strobe flared out of the Victorian country house's upstairs window. Amplified by the hanging mist, the flash took on the intensity of lightning without thunder.

In a few moments, Heat would resume her search of Vaja's property with the DHS team. She tapped the Home button of her phone to check the time. Nikki had budgeted forty minutes of sleep and still had twenty precious more left to recharge.

Out there in the middle of a dark Hudson Valley pasture, she felt an odd sense of relief from the Rainbow case.

Normally, the hunt for a serial killer constituted a race against time to prevent the murder of his next victim. Ironically, since Heat was his next victim, she'd bought herself a time-out. Also, what better way to feel safe than being surrounded by law enforcement at a crime scene? Nikki couldn't do this every night, but for now, not going home and adhering to her usual patterns offered her a measure of safety.

She closed her eyes and replayed the fight she'd had with Yardley Bell after the collision, and cursed herself for losing her cool. Heat could have chalked it up to fatigue; the hours, the stress, and the intense pull of two major cases certainly gave her license to be on the raw side. But no, Nikki blamed herself for not controlling her temper. Simply put, she slipped her chain when the paramedics gave up on Vaja and Yardley's response was to turn to Callan—and shrug.

People talked about seeing red. Heat saw a blaze of white, the way an electric spark touched off the magnesium powder in an old-time photographer's flash lamp. The anger and frustration that had been building up during the week since she met Yardley Bell exploded. Nikki's first words could have been more inspired, but shouting "How dare you?" right in the woman's face got her off to a pretty good start at releasing her caged fury. Hours later, Heat still could see Bell's expression and enjoyed the fact that she had brought her own dose of shock and awe to the day.

Rook and Roach must have feared Heat would hit her because they took hold of her shoulders and dragged her back a few feet from the agent, even as she continued to unload. It all came out: Bell's smug intervention; forbidding Nikki to return and talk to Vaja when he was a legitimate person of interest; wasting critical time busting Algernon Barrett when the real suspect—"a freaking biochemist"—sat right there, untouched. "And then," Nikki added, scolding her, "if that's not enough, you not only spiked my plan for the raid—"

"I told you," Bell shouted back, "it was a tactical clusterfuck to walk in."

"Then what do you call driving in with all the cars committed so there's no vehicle perimeter?"

"A fucking car wouldn't have done any good when he headed for the woods, Detective."

"And yours wasn't much good when it came to capturing him alive, Agent."

"Oh, please."

"You recklessly caused the death of the one person who might have told us how to stop this terror plot. Vaja was twenty yards from heading into our roadblock. Why the hell didn't you just let him go?"

"Because I am not going to—and never will—leave anything to chance. He dealt the play. I brought him down."

"You certainly did. And now where are we?"

"Easy to throw blame, huh? Especially when you start to believe your own press. You think you have the smarts to figure it all out, but you can't, so you disrespect me. Heat, you need to remember what every good investigator knows: You cannot get the whole picture—ever. There's always going to be something that surprises you. Something you never saw coming. Or believed possible. Better pray it doesn't kill you."

Heat shrugged herself loose from her protectors and walked away to cool off.

With their prime suspect too dead to interrogate, the investigation suffered a forced reboot into forensic mode. The best of the best from Homeland Security showed up in a caravan of unmarked white panel trucks. Callan shooed the Staties and locals out of the area, fearing they'd probably trample more evidence than they found. Heat cut her own detectives loose to head back to the Upper West Side and keep working the Rainbow case. Certainly the looming catastrophe of a mass bio attack had tacitly dwarfed the serial killer investigation, but it had not set it aside. Death goes on.

"You don't need to stay, either," she told Rook.

"You going to be all right?"

"I already am. I just lost it. Past history," she said. "Done."

Rook studied her as only he knew how, searching Nikki's eyes with a tender, caring appraisal that made her feel more human just for his closeness. Satisfied enough with what he saw, he said, "Truth is, I can stay here and be told to wait in a car, or spend the evening in my own office pulling together research for a new article I'm going to pitch Monday morning." He smoothed a lock off her forehead with his fingertips. "And take that as a vote of confidence, Detective Heat, that there will, indeed, be a Monday morning."

As he walked off, though, he couldn't resist a parting Rook-shot. "That is, if you live upwind of New York. I hear Edmonton is lovely this time of year."

A troop of cyber and bioforensics technicians joined their Homeland Security counterparts who distributed themselves throughout the house and kennel. They performed basic searches for material evidence, plus fingerprints, computer assessment, bioagent and chemical sampling, and photo-documentation. There was even an expert to blow the safe embedded in the floor of the master bedroom closet.

"By the way, safe's empty," Callan told Heat after the all clear. In the second bedroom, which Nikoladze had set up as a home office, he pointed to the overflowing wire basket under the shredder. "Motor on that thing is still warm. It appears the good doctor had a bit of a confetti party before we arrived."

"Vaja knew we were coming," said Nikki.

"He sure knew enough to hide in the kennel," said Bell. She had been keeping her distance since their altercation, but professionals had a way of clearing air—or at least setting personal ugliness aside—in favor of a mission. "That could be because he spotted us, maybe caught a reflection of binoculars from the hill, you never know."

"And it is possible he was a compulsive shredder," offered Callan.

Heat said, "But put both together, and what do you think?"

"I think we keep looking," said Bell.

The kennel disturbed Heat in a way that caught her by surprise. The Georgian shepherds all had been rounded up and taken to a local shelter for care and examination, so the long, vacant barracks with the pea green walls lit by harsh fluorescents gave off an eerie morgue vibe. It could have been Room B-23 at OCME, except it was above ground. There was only one cage, in the near corner. The dogs slept in a series of individual open pens that ran the length of the east wall; each had a waist-high enclosure that had been left open to give them freedom to roam.

As Heat walked the length of the outbuilding with Callan and Bell, she had the morose sense that she was retracing the steps of Nicole Bernardin the way she had only theorized in the bull pen with her squad. On that night a month before, Nicole would have been alone, snooping for evidence of Tyler Wynn's deadly plot. It cost the agent her life. At the far end, they reached a wall of supply shelves full of dog food, vitamins, and grooming supplies. Beside it sat a bulkhead door. It didn't exist in the zoning blueprints they had acquired, and it looked like it led to a basement. "Sorry, sir . . . ladies," said the man in the white biohazard coveralls and gas mask. "No entry without a moon suit."

"You guys love your drama," said Callan. "This what you call an abundance of caution?"

"Sir, this is what we call saving your life. Our crew down in the basement has encountered evidence of bioagents."

"I don't know about you," said Heat, "but I'm all for the moon suit."

A few minutes later, after donning protective suits, including gas masks attached to metal air tanks on backpacks, they descended the aluminum steps to the basement in which Dr. Vaja Nikoladze, internationally acclaimed biochemist,

Soviet defector, and peace activist, had built his laboratory to culture biological agents for terror. Nikki thought, This is a James Bond villain's lair with bad lighting.

In size, it equaled the footprint of the building above and housed a fully stocked scientific lab, complete with test tubes and beakers, a centrifuge, and thermo-glass isolation chambers with safety glove sets built into the front panels. Four high-tech refrigeration units had labels stuck to the doors, but instead of the Little League pictures or dental appointment reminders found on most reefer doors, the labels were in Latin—some of the names Heat recognized from the CDC research she'd been reading: *Bacillus anthracis; Vibrio cholerae; Ricinus communis; Filoviridae Ebola; Filoviridae Marburg; Variola major.* Like sentries along a countertop stood numerous hermetically sealed, cylindrical stainless steel containers, each slapped with a bright orange sticker displaying the universal symbol for biohazard. "Love the stickers," said Bell, her voice muffled by the mask. "As if he didn't know what he was handling."

"The question remains," said Nikki. "Who was he handling it for? We still need to find them."

Heat and the DHS agents left the basement to the technicians and their sampling equipment, ascending the steps burdened by the worst piece of news: There was a gap in the row of sealed canisters, and the space was marked with a circular ring left on the counter. It appeared that one of the twenty-gallon containers had been removed and was unaccounted for.

Topside, a forensic specialist on his knees inside the cage

called them over. She indicated the drain in the floor and said, "This cage has been hosed and scoured with a laboratory grade solvent. It's going to make DNA sampling a bear." Then she rose and beckoned them to a spot on the inside cage wall where she held up an instrument that appeared to be an oversized cell phone. The plasma screen filled with an extreme close-up of the grating with a video-enhanced quality. "See what I'm picking up here?"

"That blood?"

"It is. And, unless one of those dogs is this tall, it's probably human. I'll swab and test."

"Nicole Bernardin would have been the right height," said Heat. "And she had a stab wound that would have been in her back about there."

"I could see someone backing into that and leaving a smear," said the forensic tech. "I'm also picking up fibers. Do you have the clothing from your victim?"

"I do."

"Get it to me. I'll be able to give you an answer in the morning."

In her dream state, Nikki assumed that the tempo of the dew plink on her windshield had picked up until she opened her eyes to find one of the DHS agents softly rapping his knuckle on her side window. "Sorry, Detective, I tried not to startle you," he said when she got out and stretched an unappeasable back cramp. "We finally found his cell phone."

The evidence bag with the phone inside it sat on the galley

table between Agents Callan and Bell in the RV command center. After walking more than four hours of grids in the woods, the flashlight team Heat had squinted at in her doze had located it not far from Nikoladze's ATV escape path. "Mind if I see it?" asked Heat.

Yardley Bell pinched a corner of the plastic bag and handed it over to Nikki. While Heat unsealed the pouch, Bell said, "Oh, we ran a Customs check on the nutty professor. Vaja Nikoladze made three trips to Russia this year."

"Probably accessed the smallpox culture there somehow and smuggled it out to grow here." Nikki held up the phone. "Anybody got a stylus? I don't want to touch the screen." The communications geek at the console whipped his out with fast-draw speed and seemed quite pleased with himself. Holding the phone in her gloved hand, Heat opened the window for Recents.

"We're way ahead of you," said Bell. "Vaja got a call about forty-five minutes before the raid. We're running the number now."

Nikki looked at it and slipped the phone back into the bag. "You don't need to. I know this number. It's a burner. The same one somebody used to call Salena Kaye at the rent-a-car." Heat zip-sealed the evidence bag then gave voice to what she had suspected ever since Tyler Wynn's bomb went off. "Someone is tipping off our perps."

SIXTEEN

Rook surprised Nikki in the Homicide Squad Room with a change of clothes when she rolled in just before six. "I fantasized about you in these butt-cupping jeans and your brown leather jacket to fight crime today," said Rook. "I couldn't find your Wonder Woman bulletproof bracelets at my place, though, so if you encounter any automatic weapons fire, you're going to have to rely on your lightning reflexes."

"Thanks, Rook, that's sweet."

"I just figured after a night in the field you'd want to tidy up. Oh, I also brought you a latte. Just how you like it. Sugar-free, two pumps of strychnine."

After she changed, Nikki filled him in on the discoveries up in Hastings-on-Hudson, ending with the phone tip-off. Even though they had the bull pen to themselves, he lowered his voice. "So that pretty much sucks. How do you think the information is getting out to all our suspects?"

"Not so much a how, Rook, as a who." Then, she said, "I was thinking on my drive down. Would I be too pushy to ask, where the hell is Puzzle Man?"

"Probably still working it."

"Probably?"

"Right. I'll see if I can encourage him."

Nikki met with each detective over the next few hours to get an update on case progress. It felt like anything but. Salena Kaye had gone underground and Rainbow had gone strangely silent. "At least he hasn't killed anyone else," said Detective Malcolm.

"Considering Heat's next, I think we can call this a win, so far," added Reynolds.

Rook caught her eye and they met up in the kitchen. "Puzzle Man gave me the old 'I was just about to call you' BS. No matter. He says he may be close to something."

"Really . . ." Nikki had been disappointed enough recently that her skepticism overshadowed her optimism. "Any hints?"

"No spoilers. And that's a quote. But I twisted his arm, and he says he can meet us tonight. Café Gretchen at seven-thirty."

"Great."

"Although for him that could be nine. The one thing Puzzle Man can't seem to figure out is how to read a clock."

"You leave me brimming with confidence," she said, and left him to microwave his container of instant oatmeal.

On her return to the bull pen Heat hesitated in the doorway, taken aback to find the visitor sitting beside her desk. "Agent Bell?"

"Good morning. Although, it sort of feels like the days and nights have melded, doesn't it?" Her smile seemed genuine enough, but Nikki approached Yardley Bell with healthy caution.

"Kinda." Heat allowed a neutral smile; no harm being civil to see where this was going. "What's up?"

"Brought you a peace offering." She indicated the coat rack behind Nikki, where the blazer she had left for testing at DHS hung on a hanger. "And relax, our lab has certified it as non-lethal."

"Thank you."

"As is that piece of orange string you sent over. It came back negative for smallpox." Which left Heat still wondering where she could have picked it up. "I also have some news for you. Is this a good place?"

Heat surveyed her bull pen full of cops working phones and computers, and sat in her task chair. "Works for me."

"First, forensics. We not only put our lab on priority turnaround, we have the capability of starting some of this process in the vans, on-scene and in-transit." Agent Bell didn't take out a file, a pad, or even an iPad. She did, however, elevate her gaze slightly above Nikki's hairline occasionally, as if reading bullet points in the air. "Fingerprints. In addition to Nikoladze's, we scored several lifts from Tyler Wynn down in the lab. Also one from Agent Bernardin." A sense of tainted relief enveloped Nikki. Putting the three people together in that basement tied the elements, albeit in disquieting affirmation. Bell moved on to her next bullet. "The cage. More prints there. Bernardin. Salena Kaye. That crooked cop."

"Carter Damon?"

"Yes. And Petar Matic. These IDs came quickly since they're all in the database." Out of habit, Heat made notes.

Bell waited for her to catch up. "That dried blood on the cage does match type for Nicole Bernardin. We can't get an exact match for her yet due to the sabotage of her toxicity lab work at OCME. But there's also a fiber match to her clothing, so we'll be able to run a DNA on that just to close all the loops." She paused and looked up. "Oh. We also have a positive match for the lab solvent that was used to disinfect Bernardin's skin."

Nikki reflected on the cage, the drain in the floor, and Nicole Bernardin's awful fate after discovery—caged, killed, and then baptized in a cleanser by Satan's own. Heat said, "So we have confirmed she was murdered there. That's good to know. Unfortunately that doesn't move us forward with new info."

"This does. We got the same reading from her clothes as your blazer. Smallpox. Consider yourself up to the moment on the forensics."

"Good. And I do appreciate this new sense of cooperation."

Agent Bell shrugged. "You and I got off on the wrong foot from day one. Last night's little . . . confrontation . . . got me thinking about that. This is me just wanting to see if we can stay close and avoid any more conflict. Especially considering my last piece of intel." She made a perimeter check and lowered her voice. "One of our deep-cover informants from one of the jihadist terror cells in New Jersey says he was contacted earlier this week by Salena Kaye."

"So you're calling this a Muslim extremist terror plan?"

"Not necessarily. He confirms from his other undercover

sources that Ms. Kaye has been making the rounds of numerous affiliations. She's basically shopping for a martyr she can recruit to deliver the punch."

"Has she found anyone?"

"Don't know. We only know one thing. We know it's happening Saturday."

Nikki felt a chilliness blow through her at the narrowing of the strike window. What had been two or three days to stop this calamity had been given a haircut to two. Heat and Bell held eye contact, one absorbing the alarming implications the other had already processed.

"Excuse me, ladies." Captain Irons appeared, standing over them. "Heat? My office?"

Irons closed the door and said, "Do you know what it's like to sit and watch everything going on around you and not be part of it?" Her answer, especially in that moment, would not have been terribly empathic, so Heat didn't reply. She just waited for Wally to get to his point, so she could get back to work. "I sit here sometimes and I look out there and . . . Well, it's hard to sit on the sidelines. Anyhoo, I was thinking, maybe there was something you could give me to help you with."

She thought a few seconds. "Cat burglars. Whoever crept into my apartment the other night knew how to get in and out without a trace."

"You want me to run cat burglars through the database?"

"Yes. See who's out of prison, any recent activities, especially around the areas the victims lived or were found." When she said it, his face lit up. Heat would have felt better about this bolstering if he weren't her precinct commander.

"On it," he said as she left.

When Heat returned, she didn't find Yardley Bell at her desk anymore. But she saw the agent across the bull pen, standing in front of her Tyler Wynn–Salena Kaye Murder Board, studying it. Rook came up behind Nikki wrapped in a smog of artificial cinnamon, stirring his oatmeal. "Hey, look who's here." Then his brow creased. "You two aren't going to have a duel or anything, I hope."

"No, we've sort of buried that hatchet. But still, I am not too crazy about her hanging out, surfing our board, looking over our shoulders, you know."

"You still hate her."

"Not at all—Much—A little. She's just sort of an uncomfortable presence. In here. Right now. Think you could—?"

"Done." He took a few steps and circled back. "You sure you don't mind that I—?"

"Go."

With mixed feelings, Nikki went to her desk, watching Rook chat up his ex: Why, Agent Bell, can I interest you in a hearty breakfast? I can zap one of these for you. Mm. Now, instant oatmeal may not be as memorable as *pain perdu* at Charbon Rouge, but it's a damn sight better than those mutton-fat pies we gagged down in Chechnya.

As they walked out, chuckling, Yardley asked, "So how's it going with the new article? I saw on your Twitter page you're getting offers from Hollywood . . ."

Heat made a survey of the Murder Board to see if

anything was up there she hadn't shared with DHS, so she wouldn't be accused of withholding. Satisfied, she decided to check in with Ochoa. Earlier she'd instructed him to call the bank that held the credit card Salena Kaye tried to use at Surety Rent-a-car. Ever since, he had been studying Kaye's account, tracking her spending for tips to her whereabouts or anything else that would shake loose a much needed clue as the terror deadline closed in.

Detective Ochoa handed Heat a printout he had made of Salena Kaye's credit card history. "I heard Rook and that DHS babe. Man, what's wrong with my life? Eight years of dog hours, a joke paycheck, deadheads either barfing on my shoes or shooting at me . . . Writer dips his toe in for a couple months, and George Clooney's sending him fruit baskets."

"You realize you are talking about my boyfriend."

"Awkward. Sorry. Just thinking out loud."

Heat started to open the file and then closed it. "George Clooney sent Rook a fruit basket?"

"He didn't tell you?"

Nikki dove into the file again, changing the subject. "What did you hear from Salena Kaye's bank?"

"She opened the credit card account two months ago under her alias with a cash wire transfer to fund it as a pay-as-you-go. Banker told me, in this economy a lot of lenders are offering those for new cardholders or folks rebuilding damaged credit. You can see that the only charge on it was for the attempted truck rental. I checked out the Virginia billing address for the card. It's for an accountant. I use the term loosely. It's basically a skeevy mail drop."

"Dead end?" said Heat, closing the file.

"On to the next," he said as he moved back to Roach Central.

Pushing forward was all a detective could do. Especially when confronted by brick walls, you kept moving until you broke through. In that spirit Heat picked up her phone and called Benigno DeJesus. "Detective," he said cheerfully, "how are you this morning?"

"I am in a forensics state of mind." Nikki asked him to summarize the work he had done on Salena Kaye's hideout. She had to force herself to recall that all that had happened less than twenty-four hours before. Such was the toll of a blended day after a lost night in Hastings.

The ECU detective said, "I just now got my confirmation from the laboratory. We have positive matches on the bomb materials that took out Tyler Wynn in his Sutton Place apartment. And I guess you've heard by now that there was no bioagent evidence in her room."

"Yeah, I got that from DHS. The reason I'm calling is I have my fingers crossed you found something that might put me on her trail again."

He chuckled. "You mean like a bus ticket with an address written on it in lipstick? Maybe a USPS mail-forwarding request?"

"No, huh?"

"Sorry to disappoint, Detective. She lived monastically and left no paper trail. Not even a receipt for a diner. From her garbage, it looks like she survived on microwave meals and power shakes from the gym. And you know me, I checked. We even Dumpster dived to locate her trash bags in the alley bins."

"Yes, Benigno, I know you," she said, unable to mask her disappointment. "Thanks, anyway."

"No problem. Say, did you find your iPad? I left it on your kitchen counter."

"My iPad?"

"Right. When my crew investigated your apartment yesterday, I found the tablet under your bed. Forgot to mention I left it on your counter so you'd see it."

"I haven't been home yet," Nikki said. She spotted Rook coming back into the bull pen and asked DeJesus to hold. "Rook, did you leave your iPad at my place?" He opened his courier bag and fished his out. Heat uncovered the mouthpiece. "Benigno, I don't own an iPad, and it's not Rook's."

Less than an hour later it arrived at Heat's desk, delivered in a sealed pouch by a runner from ECU, after Nikki's super had let Benigno into her apartment to retrieve it. Detective DeJesus told her he had already dusted the iPad, so she didn't need to worry about gloves. When she powered it up, the lock screen opened to a wallpaper photo of Joe Flynn smiling at the helm of his sailboat, with the Statue of Liberty in the background. Rook and the squad gathered around her let out a collective sigh at the chilling notion that Rainbow had also left this behind on his nocturnal visit to Gramercy Park.

"Well," said Randall Feller, "that's some progress. We found Flynn's missing iPad."

Heat managed her uneasiness by remaining analytical, her cop sense telling her this piece of intimidation could be turned into a lead if she kept her head and followed it through. "Why? What do you suppose the message is of this?" She turned to her crew as they drew seats around for an impromptu meeting. Or maybe to form a circle around her. "The string on the pillowcase made his point about my vulnerability and his power. No joke intended, but isn't leaving this sort of overkill?"

"A control freak's a control freak," said Malcolm. "Simple as that."

His partner, Reynolds, chafed at that. "Is that kind of thinking moving us forward? I don't think so. Let's stay curious."

"I know what makes me curious," said Raley. "I'm always wondering what somebody's into. What they've been surfing. May I?" Heat handed him the iPad. He opened the Google app and found a string of searches for Jameson Rook.

Ochoa turned to him and said, "This Joe Flynn guy a fan, or just stalking you?"

Raley tapped the glass a few times and said, "Neither. All these searches were made after Flynn disappeared and/or died."

"What's the search history?" asked Rook.

"Mostly to *FirstPress*, your Twitter account, and . . . let's see the most recent. Your Facebook page." A few taps later, he brought up a photo. "Recognize this?"

The group leaned in for a look followed by a mix of moans, wolf whistles, and cat calls. Heat said, "I do. That is our own celebrity writer posing for selfies with the hot messes he insists on calling his fan base."

"Don't hate me because I'm popular, all right?" said Rook, pretending to be hurt.

Nikki smirked at the woman with her heaving leopard print vest strategically thrust against Rook's upper arm. "I was there for that shot. That was taken outside the pizza place where we worked Roy Conklin's crime scene."

"AKA Rainbow victim number one," Malcolm observed. Then, with some friendly push-back on his partner, he added, "In the interest of staying curious, if Rainbow had this iPad, why would he search that picture?"

Detective Ochoa saw something and pulled the tablet away from Raley for a closer look. "Whoa, whoa, check this out." Ochoa zoomed in, resized the photo, then held the screen up to Heat. He had blown up the shot and centered it on a face in the crowd. The one any analyst would say belonged to a moody loner. The only person not cheering or waving for the picture. Instead, Glen Windsor stared right at the lens, boring into it with a look of amused contempt. Heat felt like the locksmith was looking right at her.

Because he was.

The busy squad room kicked up to a new level of activity. Heat sent Malcolm and Reynolds to round up some patrol officers and stake out Windsor's Locks, a surveillance task that did double duty since Glen Windsor also lived in an apartment above his shop. Their orders were to keep him under a lid until Heat got a warrant.

She wondered how this had slipped through the cracks. It was standard procedure in a homicide investigation for the police to take crowd photos and then study them for suspicious persons or known faces. Before Nikki berated herself too much for not spotting Windsor—whom she certainly would have recognized as Rainbow's sole survivor—she told Rhymer and Feller to pull up the CSU crowd pics from the four Rainbow victims: Roy Conklin, Maxine Berkowitz, Douglas Sandmann, and Joe Flynn. Heat and Rook joined in with the squad, divvying up the CSU shots and poring over them again on their monitors.

After careful scrutiny of all four crime scene crowds, face by face, the squad reached the same conclusion: Glen Windsor was nowhere to be seen in any of those photos.

"I don't get it," said Rook. "Why is he in my picture and none of the others?"

"Because the dude's savvy," said Feller. "He knew when to duck the official police photographer."

"You're right," said Heat. "We didn't spot him when we looked before because he didn't want us to." She held up the iPad with the picture taken by Rook, with Glen Windsor's photo bomb. "He didn't want us to find this until *he* wanted us to find this."

Detective Rhymer studied the Rainbow shot again and declared it freaky. "It's like arsonists who stand in the crowd because they get off sexually watching the blaze."

"Except he doesn't look turned on," said Ochoa. "He looks . . ."

"Defiant," said Heat.

"Windsor is definitely taunting you with this," agreed Raley.

Rook said, "Just like he taunted you at Joe Flynn's boat."

"With the orange string leading to my picture? Yuh, I kinda got that."

"No, I mean the odd sock." Rook paced off his nervous energy. "Remember we all said Rainbow was mocking you for your quote in my article by putting odd socks on Joe Flynn? This guy wasn't just mocking you, Nikki, he was handing you a clue."

"Holy crap, of course," said Raley. "Of all Rainbow's victims, what's the odd sock?"

Heat kicked herself for not seeing it herself, and sooner. "The odd sock—is the only one who didn't die."

"Dude set us up," said Ochoa. "He turned on just enough gas in that building to make it look like Rainbow attacked him. Probably left the back door open so he wouldn't suffocate. And to make it look like Rainbow got away."

Rhymer asked, "How do you account for the string and the clue on the rooftop. Pre-plant?"

"Count on it," said Heat, rising and adjusting her holster. "We probably can't get a warrant based on the fact that we saw him standing in a crowd, but let's bring Glen Windsor in. Maybe he'll let us take a picture with him."

Malcolm and Reynolds had the neighborhood around 77th and Amsterdam buttoned down by the time Detective Heat and the others arrived. Surveillance teams and extra manpower for pursuit covered all front and back access, including both ends of the alley. They had alerted School Police, who put nearby PS 87 on precautionary lockdown and cleared

Tecumseh Park on the corner of nannies and their charges, as well as a few day sleepers and one pair of trysters. Uniformed officers patrolled the rooftop of Windsor's building; others waited in the stairwell near his second-floor apartment and on the fire escape outside his bedroom window. For good measure, an NYPD sharpshooter had taken position atop the Equinox gym building across the avenue.

An ESU truck pulled up at 78th, behind Heat and her group, dispersing a black-suited SWAT unit. Nikki reflected that she had been seeing a lot of those brave folks lately.

A surveillance team with high-powered scopes, hidden across Amsterdam, reported no movement or activity in the locksmith shop. The plywood sheeting over one of the storefront windows Heat and Ochoa had busted out in their faux rescue of Windsor limited the field of view, but after thirty minutes, nothing had moved and nobody had gone in or out. The apartment building super, territorial and nosy, said he had seen Windsor leave his place first thing that morning and he had not come back. Just for drill, Heat asked Rhymer to dial the number of the shop. It rang out and dumped to voice mail.

"What's the play, Coach?" asked Malcolm.

Heat put on her bulletproof vest. "Roach, take Rhymer and Feller upstairs with you and hit the apartment on my green. The rest of you follow me. We're taking the store."

They took ready positions and when Heat radioed the green light, they moved on the double to the front door. Flanked by a pair of ESU tactical officers, Nikki took the lead. With about five critical seconds of window exposure, she raced to the glass door and pulled it open.

And her heart stopped.

A hand grenade dropped from the inside door handle and rolled on the linoleum at her feet.

Heat shouted, "Grenade!" and dove backward onto the sidewalk, where her two armored SWAT companions threw themselves over her body. In the eternity she waited for the blast, Heat replayed the heavy metal clonk on the floor and pictured the green thatched oval spinning before her in slow motion. While it spun, Nikki processed the deaths of Rainbow's prior detective victims, all of whom had been lured and ambushed. The iPad suddenly made sense.

Time started moving again without a detonation.

The emergency services unit quickly deployed handheld blast shields, and Heat and the others retreated behind them.

Still no explosion.

The bomb squad arrived with men in heavy suits and an armored disposal truck. They sent in a robot to retrieve the grenade. After much examination it was deemed a souvenir prop, the kind you'd see in a joke shop or on a type-A manager's desk as a paperweight.

The Roach team had cleared Glen Windsor's apartment with no drama and no Glen Windsor. After the bomb squad had swept the locksmith shop with dogs and sensors, Heat and her crew went in, with the obvious knowledge that they'd not find Rainbow in there, either.

Heat did find something left for her on the glass display

counter beside the cash register: the hard drive to her apartment's disabled lipstick cam. It was tied in a bow of string with all the colors of the rainbow.

Of all the pictures Heat had looked at that day, the one she would have loved to have taken was of Captain Irons when she told him that she had put out an APB on Rainbow. Wally's elation at the news of a break in the case made a hairpin turn when he learned that the prime suspect was Glen Windsor—the same Glen Windsor whom the precinct commander had photo-opped himself with at his Roosevelt Hospital news conference. The *New York Ledger*'s full-page photo of the grinning Iron Man with his arm around the rescued victim's shoulder still sat faceup on his desk, accidentally-strategically placed for the stray office visitor to notice and inquire about.

The tabloid hit the captain's trash can with a *shunk* that was audible in the bull pen as Heat left the briefing.

Rook stopped by her desk. "Congratulations," he said. "You broke it. You ID'd Rainbow."

"Congratulations? Rook, I only ID'd him because he wanted me to. And let's not forget he's still out there somewhere and he still wants to kill me. Personally? I'd hold off on the champagne until we catch him."

Rook said, "On the plus side, you just saved me three hundred bucks on a bottle of Cristal."

"Maybe to bathe in. I was thinking more along the lines of a magnum of the 2005. That's going to set you back fifteen hundred."

"Where does a cop learn about luxuries like that?"

"Hey, I've been doing a ride-along, too, you know."

"Do I ever." He grinned his dopey grin then noticed on her desk the hard copy of Glen Windsor's picture from the iPad. "I've been thinking about this guy. Perfect job for access, huh? A locksmith—I'll bet that's how he really got into your place. That jimmied window was just to throw you off. Plus he installs security systems. Which is probably why none of the surveillance cams were operating anywhere he struck."

"Yeah, trust me, I've been thinking about that, too."

"It makes perfect sense, in hindsight."

"Hindsight." Nikki dropped her head and moaned. "The shoe every detective kicks herself with."

"Hey, I didn't see it, either. But then, I'm just a writer boy, not a trained homicide investigator."

"Ass." She poked the Coach bag hanging from his shoulder and made it swivel. "Where you headed?"

"Magazine stuff. OK, a lunch about another option offer. I'm trying not to put it in your face." He reacted to her sniffing the air. "What."

"Is that pineapple I smell? And chocolate-dipped strawberries? Tell me, Rook, does George Clooney's fruit basket taste more vibrant than the ones I get from Whole Foods?"

"In fact," he said, "it not only tastes more vibrant, there's something about a Clooney kiwi. One bite, and I feel like I can make a difference in this world. And look damn fine doing it." He flicked his eyebrows at her and left.

Detective Feller swiveled his chair toward her and said, "Glen Windsor update. Traffic Department just located his locksmith truck parked a block from his shop. Forensics is going to scrub it."

"Good, thanks." Then, remembering Rainbow's history, she said, "Randall, run a check for other vehicles registered to him, out of state. Check Connecticut and Rhode Island first."

"This is your King of All Surveillance Media calling," said Detective Raley.

Heat smiled into her phone at the sound of his voice. "Is that why I don't see you at your desk? Are you in your realm?"

"Come hither," he said and hung up.

Detective Feller snagged her on her way to Raley's makeshift studio. "You were right. Got a DMV hit from Connecticut on a vehicle still registered there to Glen Windsor." He handed her the DMV fax. She read it and frowned. "What?" he asked.

"Not sure." Something about it nagged at her, but with so much on her mind, she couldn't bring it home. Heat handed the registration back to Feller and told him to get it out with Windsor's APB.

Nikki entered Raley's video screening booth, pointed to the cardboard hat propped on his monitor, and said, "If you want to hold on to that Burger King crown I got especially for you, this better be good."

"It'll be worth it. I finally got a chance to scan through the surveillance video from the Coney Crest. Man, you see a lot of freaks go through there." He shivered theatrically, and she laughed. "A couple of things of note. No hits on any of our usual suspects going in, other than Salena Kaye at check-in, and then up and down the stairs a number of times. It's basically, a lot of this." He clicked the mouse, and grainy video rolled—a split-screen: overhead of the manager's office on the right side; on the left, the exterior view of a metal staircase with pebbled steps that led from the second floor to ground level behind the lobby. Soon a pair of legs descended the stairs. When Kaye's face came into frame at the landing beside the ice machine, Raley paused the video on her. "Got about a bazillion of those shots, including the reverse trips. She comes, she goes—it's not award material."

"This the only cam, other than the manager's office?"

"Yes. And, as you see, the framing isn't wide enough to show the second floor or the door to two-ten. It's really set up so the manager can clock comings and goings between hits off his bong."

"Got it. Thanks, Sean."

"One more thing. You asked me to surf for Detective Hinesburg to verify that she actually showed up to interview the manager. She did." He clicked his mouse, and a second monitor awoke, loaded with a new split-screen video file ready to play. "If you don't mind," he said, "it's been a long session, and a gallon of coffee."

"Roll it, King, I'm good." Detective Raley double-clicked the icon to start the fresh video, and he hurried out. His task chair wasn't the most comfortable, but after the morning and night she'd experienced, Nikki melted back into it and lounged as Detective Hinesburg entered the motel lobby and spoke to the manager. The cam position was behind the registration counter with no audio, of course, so Heat had to satisfy herself watching across the back of the manager's head listening to Hinesburg's silent talking. What Heat really wanted to see was his face, for any tells when he lied about Salena Kaye's presence there.

Nikki wondered how Raley endured the tedium. Satisfied her defective detective had actually done as she had been told, Nikki let that video roll, in case the manager ever turned to the camera, and clicked the video on the other monitor to see more of Salena Kaye's comings and goings throughout her week there. She found the icon that increased the scan rate to maximum, and soon people were zapping up and down those stairs as if they were in a Charlie Chaplin movie. She decided goofiness like this was how Raley dealt with the monotony.

Then something caught Heat's eye that made her bolt upright in her seat. She scrambled for the mouse to stop the video and watched it again, riveted to every frame.

When Raley came back from the restroom a minute later, she had clicked all the video files closed. All the screens sat dark. "Find what you needed?" he asked.

"And then some." She stopped at the door and said, "Rales, save all that video, understand? No deleting, it goes nowhere else."

"Uh . . . sure. Everything OK?"

"And remember. This was just between us. We never screened this, clear?"

"Sure thing, but—" He never finished his question. She had already moved on.

Heat's brain raced. She bolted outside just to move her body. She didn't go anywhere, just paced a manic rectangle on 82nd Street outside the precinct, dodging the sidewalk smokers while she sought fresh air and clear thoughts. What she had just seen on that security video might have only been circumstantial, but for the jury in Nikki's head, it was enough. But she would need more.

Now Heat had another deadly secret to keep. And, with time running out, she needed to come up with a plan.

Sharon Hinesburg broke her concentration. "Nikki?" She sounded tense. Heat made a slow blink to clear her mind and turned to her in the open lobby doorway. "Phone call. Woman says she's Salena Kaye."

SEVENTEEN

Heat started at a speed-walk through the lobby, past the duty sergeant, but something about the jolt of the buzz lock made the armored door feel like a starting gate. She punched the push bar, flung it open, and broke into a jog. Hinesburg chattered at her heels all the way, trying to keep up with Nikki's pace on the way to the squad room.

"I'm not absolutely sure it's her."

"What did she say to you, exactly?"

"I didn't talk to her," said Sharon. The switchboard transferred it. But remember that tipster who called me the other day—"

"I do."

"After I messed up with him, I didn't want to blow this."

"Good."

"So I went and got you."

"Are you running a trace?"

"Switchboard is on it already." She read something in Heat's glance and insisted, "They are. Why are you looking at me that way?"

The bull pen was empty; all the other detectives were out on assignment. Hinesburg pointed to Nikki's desk. "It's the blinking line."

Heat reached for the phone, then hesitated. She took a few seconds to calm her pulse and fasten herself to the moment. Be present, Nikki, she thought. No time to get sloppy. Ready, she turned to Hinesburg. "Is this call set to record?"

"It should be."

" 'Should be'? Really?"

"It's set." Hinesburg bent over the small tan junction box coupled between Heat's phone and a hard drive. She flipped the toggle switch to On and a green mini-lamp lit. "Now it is."

"Maybe you should go grab Raley."

"I'm telling you it's set. The call will record, just pick up."

Nikki flipped to a clean sheet in her notebook and pressed the line. "Detective Heat."

"It's me," said the woman. And then, after a short pause, "Salena." The voice sounded like hers, only grittier and more subdued. Nikki tried to compare it to the one she had heard a month before when Salena Kaye insinuated herself into her life masquerading as Rook's physical therapist. Back when the two of them laughingly nicknamed her his Naughty Nurse and Heat had written her off as an airhead with a massage table. So much for profiling.

Nikki said, "You're going to have to prove it."

"I expected that. Do you want me to tell you about the twin freckles on your boyfriend's ass or how the shit Vaja Nikoladze cooked up is going to kill a couple thousand people?"

Heat ignored the personal bait. Instead her eye flicked to verify the green record lamp. She said, "Let's talk about what Vaja cooked up."

"You first," said Salena, who then chuckled derisively.

But lurking behind her contempt, Nikki heard something off in Salena Kaye's voice, something tight, like her bluster was fake. She sounded drunk. Or . . . afraid? Over years of interrogation Nikki had learned that shifts in demeanor were huge tells. Of what, she'd listen carefully for. "You called me. What do you want?"

After some throat clearing from the other end, a sigh. "Protection," she said. "I want to turn myself in, but I want protection."

"Like you gave Petar?"

"Can you give it to me?" Her voice rasped, sounding throaty and dry. Definitely scared. What was going on here?

Whatever it was, Heat didn't let up. "What's the problem, Salena? Running low on people to kill?" There was a long pause and Kaye muttered something. "Speak up, I can't hear you."

"They turned on me." Another pause. The fear mixed with something else. Remoteness, defeat. "They are going to find me and kill me just like Tyler Wynn."

"Excuse me, but I believe that was you."

"They have others. They can do it."

"Who are they, Salena? Names." While Kaye breathed heavily across the mouthpiece Heat signaled to Hinesburg, swirling the hurry up circle with her forefinger. Sharon dialed the switchboard and checked on the trace. "Start with one name, I can wait."

"You'll never trace this call, so don't bother trying to stall me."

"I think you're the one wasting *my* time."

"No, don't go," she shouted. "I do have names. I know

everything. I'm just not giving it up. Not until I'm in." She slurped saliva. "And safe. Then I'll tell you everything." Heat had heard thousands of plea deal offers. Kaye was saying all the right words, but there was something about the way she said them that didn't sell. To Nikki, they had to pass the Valentine's Test. "I love you" has to feel like it. No tingle, no deal.

Over at her desk, Hinesburg waved for attention and gave the thumbs-down.

With no trace coming, Nikki moved things to the next round. "Tell you what, Salena. You come in, and I'll do my best for witness protection. But no promises unless you deliver."

"Agreed!" Jumping at that a bit quickly, Heat thought, for a cold-blooded assassin.

"Good. Do you know where the Twentieth Precinct is located? West Eighty-second off Columbus?"

"Nice try. No way."

"Oh, I get it," said Heat, pushing the sarcasm. "You want us to come to you."

"If you were me, wouldn't you?" Nikki had to admit, she had a point. After more rustling and throat clearing, Kaye said, "Remember the East River Heliport?"

"Hard to forget."

"Yeah, you lost me there after I spiked your coffee at Dunkin' Donuts." But it had been Starbucks, not Dunkin'. Odd. Would Salena forget a detail like that? Nikki wondered if maybe she really was drunk. Or something else . . . "Eight-thirty tonight. Come alone. I trust only you."

Heat jotted down the place and time but said, "No, Salena, you come here."

Kaye held her ground. "Take it or leave it. And if you bring anyone else, deal's off. And you can thank yourself when this city turns into a fucking hot zone."

The line went dead.

"She gone?" asked Hinesburg. Heat simply nodded, deep in thought, pondering the strange call and the drastic change she read in the bold killer. "What did she want?"

"To turn herself in."

"Holy fuck." Then Hinesburg said, "Fuck, sorry about the 'fuck.' I heard you mention the precinct. Is she coming here?" Nikki didn't answer. "Hello?"

Heat looked up. "Sorry, just thinking something through." Nikki tapped her notepad then shoved it aside. "I need some air. If she calls back, you know where to find me."

Out on the sidewalk Nikki felt a new vulnerability. Not just from recognizing her exposure on the streets of New York these days, but something more intimate. That phone call represented critical movement in the terror investigation—not to mention her mother's case—but at the same time, something inside her—Nikki's innate wariness—struggled for attention. So many things about that outreach did not add up: its unexpectedness; the treasure of information it offered so easily, like a dangling carrot; the strained quality of Salena Kaye's demeanor.

Nikki pondered all that as she sidestepped the ancient discs of dried chewing gum that had blackened the concrete. Her self-talk balanced the allure of capturing Salena Kaye with the bigger picture of her experience the past week.

And with what she had just seen in her video screening.

Detective Heat's innate wariness whispered in one ear, but a louder voice spoke in the other and filled her with the butterfly sensation that she may have arrived at the hinge point of two big cases. That voice shouted to her, telling Nikki to act—calling for her not just to seize the opportunity but make the most of it.

After ten more laps around the chewing gum obstacle course, she began forming an idea of just how to go about that.

Rook picked up a nanosecond before the voice mail dump. "Sorry, couldn't hear the ringer, it's so noisy here." It sounded like a saloon in the background for a good reason. "My Hollywood lunch segued into Manhattan happy hour."

"How's that going?"

The long squeak of a heavy door filled Heat's earpiece. The background din on Rook's end quieted and his voice echoed in a vestibule. "It's too bad you're not a media whore, Nikki. Between the two of us, we'd clean up."

"Help yourself. I'm calling because I won't be able to make seven-thirty with Puzzle Man tonight." Heat told him about the unexpected call from Salena Kaye and the proposed surrender meeting.

When she finished, Rook said, "Of course you told Kaye you wouldn't show."

"I did."

"And yet, you're informing me you can't make our

meeting. What the hell are you doing?"

"I've been thinking it over, and I have an excellent hunch why Salena reached out. I need to see this through."

"A hunch? Flaky hunches and wack theories are my department. Are we going to be one of those old couples with matching track suits and his-and-hers aluminum foil hats?"

"As long as we don't start to look alike."

"And I can't talk you out of this?"

"No more than you can convince me to let you come. She said alone, and this woman's got experience and a secret agent's radar. She'll know if I've got backup." Nikki chuckled. "And besides, what are you going to do, squirt her with one of your fountain pens?"

He paused. "You should at least call Callan."

"No."

"He not only has a stake in this, too, he'll know how to back you up, undetected. Did you hear him talk about his surveillance dome over Tyler Wynn the other night?"

"And how did that work out?" She let that sink in and continued, "Rook, listen to me. There are too many leaks screwing everything up at every turn. I'm not telling anyone."

"You sure?"

"And neither are you. I mean it."

"Fine. What do I tell Puzzle Man?"

"Tell him to figure it out."

"Zinggg. Do you at least have a plan?"

"I do." Then she said, "And I've got until eight-thirty to come up with it."

According to the Web site for the East River Heliport, New York City ordinances closed them for air traffic at 8 p.m. daily. Heat made a check of the time. Almost six. She didn't stop to close the window on her monitor. She rolled her chair away from her desk, made a holster check, grabbed her jacket, and hurried to the door. She got to the hall, stopped, and made a U-turn and came back into the bull pen.

"You all right?" asked Hinesburg.

"Uh, yeah, just a little hassled for time." Heat unlocked a drawer and took out an extra clip for her Sig Sauer. "Oh, Sharon?" she mimed a phone with her thumb and pinkie. "Check the hard drive, will you? Make sure that phone call recorded? And nobody else goes near it." Then she left. She didn't look back. She didn't even take the sheet from her pad on which she'd written the time and place of her meeting.

Somehow Nikki didn't think she'd forget.

She got there early and flashed her badge so the attendant would let her park in the rehab center lot at East 34th Street. He even moved a cone to open a spot for her where she could sit in her Crown Victoria and observe the entrance to the heliport across the service road that ran underneath the elevation of the FDR Drive.

One hour to go. The sun wasn't due to set for about fifteen minutes; however a storm front pushing in from the Ohio Valley had cast a high curtain of black thunderheads against the western sky—enough to cause the cyclists using the esplanade's bike path between her and the heliport to switch on their helmet lamps. The air thrummed, trash swirled, and the last Sikorsky of the day ascended over the East River, rotated, and banked a graceful turn east toward Long Island. Ten minutes later the fluorescents switched off in the mobile office trailer that served as the headquarters and boarding area for the helicopter facility. Two cars exited, the last one stopping as the driver, who wore a white shirt with epaulettes, got out and padlocked a chain through the gate before he left, too.

She waited, watching everything closely now. The number of joggers and cyclists dwindled, and cars became sparse, with only an occasional taxi passing by on its way somewhere else at that hour. Then the lights around the helipad all cut off, all at once: the orange floodlights, even the red aviation lamps that ran along the edge of the pier. Strange. Could they be on a timer, or had they been doused deliberately?

A truck from a paper shredding company blasted its horn at an ambulette servicing one of the nearby hospitals. While the drivers exchanged shouts and fingers in front of the heliport, she momentarily lost sight of the area. When they cleared away, everything seemed as before.

Five minutes away, close enough. She reached up to switch off the dome light before she opened the car door and got out.

As a precaution, she walked half a block down the road to cross over beyond the heliport's line of sight. Keeping to the shadows, she arrived at the one-story modular office-trailer for the helicopter operation. The building just fit beneath the underbelly of the FDR, with about five feet of headroom to spare. The side facing the road had no doors, only four unlit windows. She lowered her head as she passed them and came to the north end of the structure, near the gate. Her vision had adjusted enough to the darkness when she got there to see that the chain around the gate now hung free. It had been popped, and the heavy-duty padlock swung at the end of it, tapping lightly against steel pipe. She drew her gun and squeezed through the opening.

The knob of the entrance door inside the gate wouldn't turn, and a serious deadbolt above it was likely engaged. There wasn't enough light for her to see in the crack if the brass tongue had been thrown. She moved on, inching forward, pressing herself against the corrugated steel siding toward the landing area. She brought her service weapon up to an isosceles brace and peered around that corner.

A fresh wind rolling down from Hell Gate blew across the blacktop helipad before her. The only other sound to compete with Manhattan's ubiquitous white noise of traffic came from the lapping of the East River against the pilings. The area was empty but for a single, parked helicopter occupying the space designed for five choppers. Nylon tie-down straps held its rotors in place, although they rocked slightly in the night air. The Sikorsky remained as it had landed, nose-in toward the building, with its tail above the red and white striped curb that marked the edge of the pier as a guide for pilots as they approached over the river. The craft appeared every bit like a stealth bomber's cousin at that moment: an ominous form, pitch-black except for a faint glow coming from inside. Curiously, that glow was the most foreboding thing on the pier. Because it beckoned to her in the darkness.

She waited with her back against the steel, measuring risk. Twenty feet of exposure stretched between her and the helicopter. To her right, at the south end of the tarmac, a vacant parking lot—minimal worry there. To her left, a parking lot full of double-decker stacked cars bordered the north end of the blacktop. Lots of cover. That's where trouble would come from.

Her eyes became attracted to that light, and she made a decision. She broke across the open space, a crouching silhouette cleaving to the shadow of the helicopter when she got there. She panted, listening. A dinner yacht churned by, a charter spilling party sounds and light. Only when it left did she dare to move and peek inside the cockpit window.

It was empty. She ducked quickly to stay in the shadows and ran a memory recap. The glow had come from the rear compartment. Duckwalking a little over a yard, she used the body of the chopper for cover. Then she rose up and peered in the window of the rear door.

What she saw stopped her heart.

Salena Kaye stared back at her from the passenger seat through dead eyes. Her mouth hung open in a frozen scream, exposing smashed and missing teeth. Welts and cigarette burns marked her face. A picklock protruded from the nearest ear canal, above a dried flow of blood and plasma that had streamed down the side of her neck, staining the shoulder of her white T-shirt. The handle of a large, military-style knife jutted out of her sternum above an oval blotch of red. And around the knife's knuckle grip, someone had tied a string. An orange string.

Attached to a dangling bullet.

At that moment, lying prone atop the flat roof of the heliport's office, Rainbow watched her silhouette through the sight scope of his rifle. She had come to him like all the others had. Inducing her had taken more doing than with the rest of them; Salena Kaye had required an extraordinary amount of persuasion to make that phone call. But her torture opened a surprising new door to his enjoyment. And the result of it had succeeded in luring her to him. None of them could resist the seduction of a great clue. Not even the famous Detective Heat.

Rainbow took his time, waiting for the moment. He wanted to witness the juncture of horror's full absorption—the lightning-crack realization when all the tumblers fell into place, when all the strings connected. The months of planning and the weeks of execution came down to this, and it would not be rushed. The taking of Nikki Heat's life had to come right at the instant he saw the revelation break across her face.

To rush made it cheap. To wait made her his.

Patience. He settled the rifle stock on the sandbag and held the back of her head center-scope so the crosshairs would track across her ear to her temple to her brow to her forehead when she came around.

At last she began to turn.

EIGHTEEN

Rainbow wished he could see more of her face. Too much silhouette and shadow, he thought. Maybe he shouldn't have killed so many lights, after all. But the glow inside the Sikorsky's cabin should be enough. If she would only favor him just a bit more. He tensed his jaw and muttered to himself, "Come on, Nikki, let me see you."

"You'd have to turn around," said Detective Heat, "but I wouldn't advise it."

He lifted his head up from the rifle scope and cocked his head slightly to the side. In his periphery he made her out. Heat, not ten feet away, hidden behind the rooftop air-conditioning box with her elbows braced and her Sig aimed right at his head. She spoke quietly, in total control. "NYPD. Move your hands away from that rifle, or I'm going to get your brains all over my favorite jacket."

Windsor complied. "How long have you been there?"

"Well before you," said Detective Heat, the poster cop for tactics and cover. "Now crawl backward toward me, slowly." He got up on all fours, creeping in reverse, moving out of reach of the rifle. "Good. Now, facedown, nose to the deck. Spread your arms wide and turn your palms up." As soon as he parked himself, Heat came around, patted him down for weapons, and stood over him, bending slightly so her head wouldn't bump the steel girders on the underside of the FDR. "You even scratch, I'll shoot." He said nothing, just kept his face to the tar.

Nikki half-turned to the helipad and called out, "Detective Hinesburg."

Below, the silhouette near the helicopter spun her way. In the dim light, Heat could barely make out Sharon Hinesburg's arms coming up in a combat stance, but then, back-lit by the window of the helicopter, Heat saw her pointing locked hands toward the rooftop of the modular building and sweeping them frantically back and forth. "Hold your fire, Detective," she shouted. "I've got Glen Windsor in custody. Get over here and cover him while I get him down."

Hinesburg repositioned the fire safety ladder Heat had used, carrying it to the front of the building where they could take advantage of more ambient light from across the river. From the rooftop, Nikki trained a bright Mag-Tac LED in Glen Windsor's eyes to glare him out as he descended to Hinesburg. Both detectives held weapons on him. "Kiss the deck again," said Heat when he reached the bottom. Nikki waited for the other detective to cuff his hands behind his back before she descended.

"How the fuck?" asked Rainbow, twisting his head to the side.

"Rule one of an ambush," said Heat. "Show up first."

"But how did you know?" asked Hinesburg. "I didn't know."

Heat didn't have time for the list of things Hinesburg didn't know—that would be coming, and soon—so she kept it brief. "Salena Kaye sounded drugged on that call. Tortured, too, it turns out. She even tried to give me a signal by mixing up Dunkin' Donuts with Starbucks. Those raised my suspicion.

"But then I got the DMV hit on the minivan you have registered in Connecticut," she said to Rainbow. "The silver minivan. Same color and model seen taking Salena Kaye away when I chased her. But you didn't rescue her, did you, Glen? You'd been stalking me and kidnapped her. What did you do, chloroform her?"

"Chloroform," he said. "They always go quietly."

And then Heat made it all formal. "Glen Windsor, you are under arrest for the murders of Roy Conklin, Maxine Berkowitz, Douglas Sandmann, and Joseph Flynn." With a glance to the helicopter, she added, "And Salena Kaye."

His only response was to ask if he could get up now. Heat had more to accomplish and said no.

"Want me to get my car?" asked Hinesburg.

"No. I want you to give me your gun."

Sharon chuckled nervously. "Excuse m—?" In a quick, unexpected move, Heat jerked the Smith & Wesson from her hand and slipped it in her jacket pocket. She held on to her Sig Sauer, covering both of them now.

"Nikki . . . What was that for?"

Heat popped her Mag on again and shined it down on Windsor so there'd be some light without blinding her. "This will help them spot us. I texted for backup while you moved the ladder. I'd like you on the ground, Sharon."

"What is going on here?"

In the new light, Nikki could see the widening of her eyes. And the fear. Heat said, "Glen beat you to it."

"To what? What the hell are you talking about?"

"You came to kill Salena Kaye before she could give up the terror plot. Or you came to kill me. Or both."

"I . . . Wha . . . Seriously?"

"I knew you would listen to the recording of Salena's phone call. It's how you knew to come here. But just in case, I left the pad on my desk with the time and place of our meeting."

"You baited me?"

"It's only bait if you take it. Right, Glen?"

"Fuck yourself."

Hinesburg said, "This is nuts. I came here to back you up."

"Sure, you did. Very proactive of you for a change, Sharon."

"OK, know what I think? You need to stop. It's one thing not to like me, but—"

"This isn't because I don't like you."

"Then why?"

"It's because you're the mole." Hinesburg's mouth opened to protest some more, but nothing came out. Nikki leveled her gaze at her and said, "I saw you on video at the Coney Crest, Sharon. Salena's hideout."

"Yuh. Because you told me to go there." Hinesburg sounded worse than unconvincing. She sounded chin-deep in quicksand.

"I watched the security video from that place. Know what got my antenna up first? When you talked to the manager, you never flashed tin and you never showed him the picture of Salena Kaye." Hinesburg started to talk, but Nikki pressed forward, cutting her off. "That got my attention, but I could even dismiss that as part of your sloppy work habits. Trust me, the least of your worries. But I let the video roll and I saw you on the other cam. Sharon, you went up to the second floor."

"That does not mean anything."

"No, but then I kept watching. And when you came down you were putting something in your bag. It looked just like a garage door opener. But it wasn't, was it, Sharon? It was the remote control for the bomb that killed Tyler Wynn, wasn't it? That's why you showed up uninvited for that raid, to get close enough to trigger it."

Hinesburg didn't reply. Her eyes began to fill. She stared into nothingness. Heat waved her gun toward the blacktop. "Assume the position. Don't make this worse for yourself than it is."

Not so much defiant as immobile, Hinesburg stayed put. Her lip began to quiver. "They came to me one day and asked me to stay close to you."

"And do what? Screw up my investigation?"

"No, just to keep track. Let them know what you were doing. And when. That was all." Even in the dim light Nikki could see Hinesburg's features draw slack under shame's gravity. Heat wondered, was Sharon's incompetence real or, as the playwright said, was she just being wise enough to play the fool? "I never knew it would go this far. When people started dying, I freaked. Nikki, do you have any idea how much pressure I've been under?"

At that point Heat went with fool.

"Then they started asking me to do more than just inform. When I saw what happened to other people, I didn't dare say no. They had me slow down the investigation wherever I could. And then warn them when you were coming on a raid. And what did I get for all my stress? A few thousand extra and the joy of fucking Wally Irons to keep my job." She wiped away a clear string of snot. "They'll try to kill me, too, you know." Wheels started turning. "I want protection."

Heat had heard those very words a few hours before. From the corpse staring out at them from the rear seat of the chopper.

"Sharon, the bomb you triggered killed a man."

"I'll deal. I know stuff."

"Start now. When and where's the bioterror event?"

"That, I don't know. Honest."

"Who's running it? Who's running you?" Sirens grew in the near distance. "Now would look better for you, Sharon."

Glen Windsor's play came so suddenly she found herself halfway to the ground before she realized he'd made his move. She didn't see it, but figured later that it must have been some kind of break-dancer's body pop. He bounced his chest off the tarmac and flung his calves at the back of Heat's knees, taking her down. She dropped the flashlight, but held on to her gun. When she came up, he was running toward the river full speed with his hands cuffed behind him.

Nikki made a fast check of Hinesburg. She stood nearby but had the rabbit look in her eyes. Torn, Heat turned back to Windsor, approaching the tail of the Sikorsky, steps from diving into the water. She braced, called, "Stop, or I'll shoot," then fired low, planting one in his calf. He crumpled, moaning on the tarmac against the red and white safety curb at the river's edge.

A voice behind her shouted, "Heat, gun!" Nikki hit the deck at the same time she heard the distinctive crack of a .40-caliber. She rolled, presenting the smallest target to the shot direction, and braced to fire. But she held.

In the shadows, she recognized Special Agent Callan standing over Sharon Hinesburg, who was sprawled on the blacktop under the nose of the copter. "Clear," he called. Strobing lights from police cruisers and plain wraps flashed outside the gate and reflected off the badges of unis rushing toward them. Heat got up, dragged Glen Windsor away from the river's edge, and dropped him hard. Then she ran to Callan, getting there just as he kicked a pistol away from Hinesburg's hand. In his own he held his P226 Elite. Nikki could still smell gunpowder.

"She was going to back-shoot you," he said. "You're fucking lucky I made it."

Heat told the uniforms, "Get paramedics, two down. Hurry." She knelt beside Hinesburg. She had a fat hole in her temple.

Her eyes looked just like Salena Kaye's.

Dry lightning sparked to the north when Heat finished her debrief with the shooting team. Lauren Parry had wrapped up her exams of Salena Kaye and Sharon Hinesburg, preliminarily finding both causes of death obvious, but worthy of follow-up. The ME told Nikki she'd pull an all-nighter and perform the postmortems so she could have the findings first thing in the morning.

She found Bart Callan sitting with his elbows on his knees on the short wooden ramp that led from the tarmac to the boarding area of the modular. He stared blankly at the sheet over Hinesburg's body and the numbered yellow marker the shooting team had placed beside his ejected casing. He didn't acknowledge Heat. She stood beside him and followed his gaze, then said, "Tough to take someone out. Especially a cop."

He held up the evidence bag with the pistol inside it. "Hinesburg's backup piece. Mini Glock Twenty-six. Nine millimeters to spoil your day." He set the bag down on the ramp between his shoes. "I can live with the kill. Lose a cop, save a cop."

She put a hand on his shoulder. "Thank you."

He gave the shortest nod and said, "Guess you had your hands too full to pat her down."

"You could say my attention became somewhat divided by his escape attempt." She realized her palm still rested on him and drew it away. "You got here fast, thank God. I'd barely put out the ten-thirteen."

"I was already en route." When he saw her reaction, he said, "Soon as I heard about your meet, I thought I'd better get over here and cover your idiotic butt. Any complaints?"

"None." Then she asked, "Heard about it how?"

"Yardley Bell told me."

"Agent Bell? How did she know?"

He picked up the evidence bag and stood. "Didn't ask. I just assumed she heard it from your boyfriend."

Rook spun through the revolving door at the entrance to Bellevue Hospital and shouted her name as the door spit him out into the lobby. "Nikki!" echoed in the cavernous atrium renovators had built five years before, encasing the old stone hospital in glass like a living museum display. When he reached her, Rook grabbed Heat in his arms, clinging tight, whispering in her ear, "Holy shit, Nik, sometimes you scare the hell out of me." When they kissed, he sensed her reserve and studied her. "You OK?"

She considered a moment and let it go at "Been a hell of a night. Glen Windsor is upstairs getting his calf sewn up. Soon as he's out, he's mine to interrogate."

They found a couch to wait on in the Hospital PD Squad Room near the ER, and she bulleted the sequence of events, first going back to how she knew from the sound of Salena Kaye's phone call something was up; how she sounded either drugged or under duress, and how she'd even slipped Heat a hidden message.

"But what gave you the idea to connect her to Rainbow?"

"That by itself would have been a Jameson-esque leap, but it's been bugging me how quickly Kaye just vanished off the street when I chased her out of that deli."

"After my Jameson-esque takedown?"

"What have I started?" She pressed her forefinger on his lips and continued, explaining the DMV trace on the silver minivan that made Glen Windsor a probable. "I couldn't be certain, but I figured, if he was setting me up, I could get there early enough and get in position to take him."

"And if it hadn't been a setup by Rainbow?"

"Then, worst-case scenario, I could still apprehend Salena Kaye."

He processed it and said, "Well done. Very Nikki-esque."

"Don't even."

"Hinesburg, though . . . Man."

"I have to admit, I feel sort of blindsided, too. I guess I started to have inklings that I must have denied—I mean she was a flake—but that security video from Coney Crest was the big domino, knocking down all the others. Every one of her cute little screwups and oversights started looking more like sabotage: telling me Wynn's bomb was a timer when it was a remote . . ."

"Because she triggered it . . ."

"Screwing up the tipster call from the rent-a-car guy who spotted Salena Kaye . . ."

"So she could warn her . . ."

"And on and on."

"It's ingenious. Incompetence masking subterfuge. And there she was, hiding in plain sight in the middle of your bull pen." He reflected and said, "One good thing. You flushed out the mole. No more looking over your shoulder before you say something."

"I sure hope not." She shaded that thought and got his attention.

"What?"

"Know how Callan got to the heliport so fast? Yardley Bell told him about my meet."

He thought about that. "How would Yardley know?"

Nikki gave him an appraising look. "You tell me."

"Wait, you don't think I—Nikki, seriously?" She said nothing, one part interrogation technique, the other not wanting to think it was so. "Hey, I will admit to a lot of things. Yes, I went to Nice with her. Yes, I told her when I was trying to track down Tyler Wynn through his . . . through his wine and custom shoe purchases."

"And about the jerk chicken pop-up stores."

"Yes. But when you tell me something is between us, it stays between us."

"Then how did Yardley know?"

"No clue. But I can look you square in the eye and tell you it wasn't me?"

They held each other's stare. After a few seconds her phone buzzed with a text.

"Is that my lie detector result?" he asked.

"Don't need one. Lucky for you, pal, I trust you." She held up the phone. "Glen Windsor's out of surgery. Want to come?"

"You bet." Rook stood up and got out his cell. He gave Heat a sly grin and said, "Let me call Yardley first."

The uniform stationed outside Glen Windsor's private room on the second floor gave Rook an appraising once-over as they arrived just before midnight. "It's all right, she's with me, Officer," Rook said. The cop actually laughed and, following Heat's nod, gestured them both to pass.

They found the prisoner with his bandaged leg up on a pillow, watching NY1 news on the overhead. He didn't seem surprised by Heat's visit but said, "Wow, Jameson Rook, too. Am I going to be featured in your next article?"

"Absolutely. I'm doing one on excrement."

"You'll pardon me if I don't get up." He tugged at the manacle that cuffed him to the bed rail. "But I can still wave hello." He gave Rook the finger and laughed. Nikki switched off the TV. "Hey, come on, I'm the lead story. I want to see it again."

"You'll be hearing about it for some time, Windsor," she said.

Rook added, "Like the rest of your life."

"Hey, why the disrespect, Rook? It's not like you're the one I was trying to kill." He grinned. "Allegedly."

As Heat drew over a chair she eye-signaled Rook to ease up, and he took a spot leaning his shoulder against the doorjamb. "How's the leg?" she asked Windsor.

"You need some time on the range to requalify, Detective."

"I put it right where I wanted it, believe me. If I'd killed you, we never could have had this chance to chat." She took a seat and gave him some silence in an attempt to claim the meeting. Detective Rhymer had e-mailed Windsor's file to her and Nikki opened the printout she'd made downstairs at Hospital PD. "Our detectives turned up some interesting things at your apartment."

"Yeah?"

"Let's start with the electronic box that alters voice pitch over the phone."

Windsor scoffed. "I only use that to order pizzas. You'd be surprised how fast they deliver when Darth Vader places the call."

Nikki decided to ignore the glib distractions and continued. "In your desk they found numerous files of clippings about me. Not just that cover story from last fall's magazine—heavily underlined and highlighted. Also articles about cases I've worked over the past few years and photos of me—and not clipped. We checked your camera. They were taken by you without my knowledge. Pictures of me in the supermarket, pictures of me jogging, pictures of me taken through windows into my apartment."

"What can I say? I'm a fan."

"Your computer history shows a ton of searches for me, for Rook, and others in my life, including my parents, coworkers, even criminals I have arrested."

"Detective, everybody clips articles and searches shit that interests them on their computers. It's not like I have this secret closet with your pictures plastered all over it."

"No, that would be nutty," said Rook. Nikki flattened him with a glower, and he stared at the floor.

When Heat turned back to Windsor, he said, "He doesn't get it. Calling it nutty."

"What do you call it?" she asked.

"Preparation." He held her gaze a moment, letting that settle before he continued. "I learned about you in his first article. You know, *Crime Wave Meets Heat Wave*? I read it over and over and thought, This one . . . this detective . . . is different. A challenge." The words twisted Heat's solar plexus as she recalled the other detectives Windsor had engaged over the years. And killed. Now she was designated as "this one." He watched her from his pillow and must have known exactly what she was processing because he said, "I decided last fall I would test myself with you, but it wasn't until I saw the online teases for Rook's new article about you that I said I'd better get moving."

He stopped there, leaving Nikki time to reflect on a psychopath's classic need to share—or even claim—the limelight of his fixation. "Tell me what you mean by that, to get moving."

"I wanted to test you when the article came out. When you had everyone's attention. When there'd be heat around Nikki." He grinned. "Tell me I don't have a poet's touch."

Heat's temper sat one inch from breaking the surface, and she struggled not to lose it with this guy. But her objective—even more immediate than building a case against a serial killer—was only one thing: Nikki needed to learn whatever information he had tortured out of Salena Kaye so she could stop the bioterror plot. "Tell me about the conversation you had with the dead lady in the helicopter."

"Now? I really wanted to see Ferguson's monologue tonight."

Letting her rage explode wouldn't get her anywhere. She decided the time had come to get under his skin for a change. And Heat believed she knew the soft spot where the knife would go in.

As soon as Glen Windsor came on the radar as a suspect,

she had unleashed Malcolm and Reynolds to do a biographical search on him. Heat held the results in her lap. She picked up the single page she hoped would tip the balance her way. "You like being a locksmith, Glen?"

"What's that supposed to mean? It's a job. It pays my way."

"Yeah, but you? A . . . locksmith?" Nikki had respect for every trade, but for this purpose, she put a shit stank on the job title. He shifted slightly on the hospital bed and examined his fat bandage. "Not what you had in mind, was it?" His eyes flicked over when she played with the page in her hand. Nikki waited to milk the moment and said, "We did some research—yeah, we do computer searches, too—and know what popped up? You were dismissed from the NYPD Police Academy."

"That's ancient history," he blurted, not sounding like it was archive material, at all.

"Maybe so, but it's kind of interesting. According to records, you got bounced because you failed the psychological evaluation."

"That's a fucking rigged test." His breathing became more rapid. Wilding flashed in his eyes. "You ever seen that test?"

"I have," she answered quietly. "I took it myself. Passed." She delivered that with a smile and let it sit there. "The thing about the psych eval? The deficient ones never think it's valid."

His manacles clanged against the stainless bar as he tried to sit up. "Hey, fuck you. Deficient, my ass. I was too smart for those losers at the Academy. They were threatened by my special gifts and set me up to get bounced. Jealous shits."

"Bet you would have made a great detective, otherwise."

"Fuckin'-A right."

"Except I see the NYPD wasn't the only place you failed. I don't have all of them here, Glen, but there's a short list of you washing out as an investigator at several top security firms and then a sort of descending curve of gigs until you landed at . . . locksmith." Then she added, "Oh, and security systems. So you did have that going to keep the dream alive."

"This is bullshit. I know what I can do. I know who I am. I know my destiny. I am smarter than all those assholes, and I've proved it."

Rook chimed in. "By ambushing Bedbug Doug?"

"Hey, fuck you, too."

Heat didn't mind the gang pile this time. "Rook's got a point."

"The fuck he does."

"Is that what your destiny's all about?" she continued. "Sneaking up on innocent people pretending you're better than they are?"

"And smarter. Don't tell me you don't know that. I had to practically draw you a picture to keep you in the game."

"Oh, so you think I'm a loser, too."

His demeanor snap-shifted from defensive to pure manic. "No, no, no, Detective. You made it all . . . come to, I dunno . . . life. You brought my game to the next level."

"Well, game over, Glen," said Heat.

"Like hell it is."

Nikki reached out and clattered his chains with her thumb and forefinger. Then she closed the file, slid her chair away, and started for the door. When she got there, Windsor shouted, "You want to talk about Salena Kaye?" Nikki stopped, and he said, "I know stuff. I learned shit about this bioterror plot."

Heat turned to Rook. "And Detective Windsor cracks his case."

When she turned away, Windsor called, "I got it all out of that bitch when I worked on her. And trust me, Heat, you'll want all of it."

She stayed by the door but said, "I'm listening."

"No. I want a deal first."

"Don't make me laugh, you're a serial killer."

"It's not supposed to end like this." He yelled and jerked at the wrist chains hard enough for the uniform to come in and make a check. After the uni left, Rainbow said, "You should have killed me, Heat. I deserve to go down in a blaze." Destiny again, she thought. He became contemplative. Then he said, "You know where the deals are. Come up with something. Like doing life in a shitty prison versus a nice one out of state, maybe in warm weather, for starters. California. Arizona."

"Clock's running, Windsor. You want to talk deal, you'd better give up something you learned about this terror plot."

He thought a short while, then calmly beckoned her over. When she stood beside him, he smiled and said, "When I'm ready. Come back tomorrow, I've had a hard day." Then he closed his eyes and rolled his face away as if going to sleep.

On the way downstairs, Heat turned to Rook. "Don't say it."

"You mean, 'Game not over'? 'Do not proceed to the exit'?"

"I hate you."

When Rook postponed their meeting with Puzzle Man, he had instructed him to hang loose. Now, as he and Nikki crossed the Bellevue lobby, he got out his cell to call him. Heat looked at her watch and said, "Now? These are drug dealer hours, he's not going to—"

Rook held up a palm to her. "Keith. Rook. Hey, puzzle me this. You still good to go?" He grinned and gave her a thumbs-up.

Heat's eyes burned from fatigue, and she felt so hungry that she was no longer hungry. But sleep would have to wait. "Can he meet us someplace they serve food?" she asked.

Tavern 29, walking distance for them, served all night, and Nikki craved one of their bacon burgers, which she ordered before she even sat down. A beer would have been perfect to go with it, but she didn't want to lose her edge, and so went for a seltzer. They were both finishing their meals by the time Keith Tahoma strolled in, gray ponytail swaying, yakking from the door to their table about the awesome energy of New York freakin' City at night. Heat was more interested in what he held in his hands than his speed-talk. He carried a tan cardboard tube from an empty roll of paper towels.

He ordered a coffee, and when it came, he repeated his ritual of six sugars and an OCD paddle stir. Heat asked him if that was going to keep him awake, and he laughed, saying, "So far, so good."

Rook said, "Keith, I hate to put the squeeze on, but it's been a long one, and we're kind of eager to hear whatcha got."

"Oh, yeah. For sure." Nikki's energy level perked up as Puzzle Man brought the cardboard tube up from his lap and set it on the table. "Apologies for the delay, this was one tough nut."

"But you cracked it," said Heat, not really asking so much as hoping. Or willing.

His answer was to pat the tube gently and wink. "Now, just so you don't feel bad about not solving it yourselves, those little lines and squiggles were totally meaningless. I ran every cipher I could without success. And I know 'em all. Even invented a couple over the years. Then this morning, I'm sitting in the park, working my chess games, waiting for the other dopes to realize they're six moves from losing. I look up and see this bird flapping along. And I saw a jet, probably coming around to land at JFK, five thousand feet higher than the bird. But to me, it looked just like the two were going to collide. You see?"

They both shook their heads.

"You will. It was a visual trick. The optical overlay created a message in my brain." He stacked his hands flat before his eyes like pancakes.

Heat started to get there. "So you thought maybe all the pages could be overlaid, and this would be revealed."

"No," he said, then slapped the table and smiled. "Not all, but a few of the pages could be. After a fair amount of trial and error, I managed to find four pages of your mother's sheet music that, if I stacked them and held them up to a lightbulb like a shadow box, I got a message. It wasn't even in a cipher, it was right there in front of my eyes in the King's English. Hot damn, I felt smart."

"Do you, um . . ." Nikki gestured to the cardboard tube.

" 'Deed I do." He presented it to her with a flourish.

Nikki took it from him, made a privacy survey of the tavern, and pulled the furled sheets of paper out of the tube. She unrolled them, squared the edges on her place mat, and then, with her heart pounding, held the four stacked sheets to the candle. In her mother's clean handwriting it read: *Unlock the Dragon.*

Her eyes went to the code breaker and then back to the message. Heat moved the pages, scanning them in front of the candle, hoping for more. "This is all it says?"

"That's all she wrote, pardon my French."

"May I?" asked Rook. She gave the sheets over to him, and he did the same thing, trying to scan for more text. While he held the pages to the light, Nikki thought about the Dragon. The word—obviously a code name—had first come into this case only days ago when the skyjacked helicopter passenger heard Salena Kaye call someone by that name on her cell phone. What had she said? "Dragon, it's me." So Dragon was Salena Kaye's controller. Also Tyler Wynn's, by his dying declaration. But now, in this code from the past, her mother mentioned him, too. All of which told Heat that the Dragon was as alive today as he had been eleven years ago.

Her mother had no way of knowing it would take so long for her daughter to get this message. But the code still left Nikki confused. And she sure didn't have another eleven years to figure it out.

She didn't even have eleven days.

Puzzle Man said, "You two seem a little less excited than I'd hoped you'd be."

"No, no," said Heat. "You did great, it's just . . ."

Rook finished the thought. "We don't know what it means."

"Well, that's an entirely different task," said Puzzle Man. "Times like these, I go back to the wisdom shared by my *shi'nali*, the Windtalker. My grandfather used to tell me there's one code you can never break."

"What's that?" asked Nikki, holding the words to the light again.

"The one that's only known by two people. The sender and the receiver."

Cynthia Heat spoke to her daughter in the nonsensical way apparitions do in sleep. Nikki saw her as she had countless times over the last eleven years, mostly in the middle of the night, although sometimes at unbidden daytime moments as mundane as when she reached for her MetroCard on her way down to the subway or smiled at a *New Yorker* cartoon. Her mother usually spoke to her from her own pool of blood on the kitchen floor. Over the years she'd said many things to her, mostly as much non sequiturs as the appearances themselves. This time, from the leaden depths only Nikki's mattress seemed to possess, her mom sat playing her piano—the one in the room right up the hall—and spoke the same two words again and again like a video loop on an online avatar. Cindy Heat kept telling her daughter, "You know. You know. You know . . ."

A hand on Heat's shoulder nudged her awake. She blinked. Still dark. Rook sat beside her, holding out her ringing cell phone. Heat cleared her throat and said her name into it. Listened, then moaned.

"What?" asked Rook.

"He's out. Rainbow escaped."

Heat got to Bellevue in record time because she didn't have to get dressed. In her exhaustion at 2 a.m., Nikki had collapsed onto her bed still dressed. Four short hours later, she and Rook strode into Glen Windsor's room on the second floor of the hospital, both wearing the same clothes as the night before. She looked at the empty bed and said, "Somebody explain this to me." An NYPD uniformed officer standing with a pair of unis from Hospital Police lowered his eyes to the floor. She went to him. "What's your name?"

"Slaughter."

"Your first name."

"Nate."

She canted her head to put herself in his field of view. "Listen to me, Nate. I know this feels awful. But you've got to put it in your back pocket. This guy's very resourceful, so hold off on the blame. Just tell me how it came down."

Officer Slaughter said, "About one-thirty, the night nurse came in to take his temp. She didn't realize it till later, but she had a pair of reading glasses in her front pocket he must have boosted when she leaned over to check his dressing." The uniform indicated the eyeglasses on the counter.

Rook bent over them. "Temple's been snapped off the frame."

"Yeah, we figure he used the metal end to pick his cuffs."

Rook said, "He didn't tear off somebody's face to use as a mask to get out, I hope." The three cops stared at him. "Spoiler alert: *Silence of the Lambs*?" Then he said, "Continue, Officer Slaughter."

"He overpowered an orderly when he came in, put on his scrubs, and waited for shift change so he could walk out past me." The cop appealed to her, "I never saw him come in, so how could I know what he looked like?"

Alone in the elevator, Rook said to Nikki, "I'm sorry, but if your name's Slaughter, you ought to have a little more swing in your dick. Just sayin'."

"Glad you're having such a good time," she said. "I've got twenty-four hours to stop a bioterror plot, we still have nothing to go on, and my best hope to get a lead is my damned locksmith serial killer who just escaped. And you want to joke?"

He paused and said, "I mean, if your name was Slaughter, wouldn't you at least hit the gym?"

Bellevue Hospital turfed to the Seventeenth Precinct, so on the cab ride uptown, Heat called Feller and assigned him to become best friends with the One-Seven detectives and to make sure Glen Windsor's renewed APB extended to Amtrak, the airports, and the cut-rate buses in Chinatown. When she hung up, Rook said, "I've been doing some thinking."

"More gags for your stand-up?"

"No, about the case. Jeez, what do I have to do to get you to focus?" Then he became sober and continued, "I don't think you need this APB."

"Why not?"

"Because Rainbow is going to come to you."

"Right."

"Nikki, look at his pattern—and the evidence. Think of what you saw in your interrogation last night. Windsor is not just obsessed with you, he's a full-goose borderline personality. Narcissistic, for sure, and I'll bet grandiose. Clinically, that's an ego that feeds on being the center of everything."

"So you're saying I should just call off the search?"

"No, I'm saying he's going to reach out again like he did before. He has to. This is his moment, and he needs to engage you to claim it."

"Engage me, like when he said I brought his game to the next level?"

"Exactly. Maybe I'm wrong. Maybe he won't make contact. But, in case he does, I'd be thinking how to play him."

Heat said, "This is the thing I hate most. Playing games."

"You not only have to play this one, Nikki, somehow you have to figure out how to beat him at his own game."

This was the essence of Rook, she thought. Sometimes he wore the clown paint. Sometimes he brought the goods. "If you're so smart," she said, "why don't you tell me how to do that?"

He stared out his window a moment and then said words that echoed from a dream. He said, "You know."

Heat and Rook walked into a bull pen blanketed by a quiet as toxic as doomsday ashfall. The palpable tautness radiated from a single empty desk—the one with the "Detective S. Hinesburg" nameplate. Everyone continued his or her work, but with a hollow look, not so much from mourning as from disillusionment. Somehow one of their own had gone bad. It felt different than corruption; cops on the take were still as much a reality in New York as anywhere. This was different. This was treason inside the Blue Line.

The lights were off inside the precinct commander's glass office. Rhymer reported that Captain Irons had e-mailed saying he would be at One Police Plaza for an indefinite period that morning. The squad speculated whether he would ever be back, following his nightmare double-whammy. "Not a good day to be the Man of Iron," said Detective Malcolm, with typically mordant understatement. "Bad enough he holds a press conference embracing a dude who turns out to be a serial killer. Now his office punch gets outed as a bioterror spy."

"Fail," said Reynolds.

"Epic fail," added Feller.

Raley and Ochoa came in from their all-nighter at Hinesburg's apartment. Benigno DeJesus followed them in his navy evidence collection unit windbreaker carrying two cardboard boxes of items he and his crew had collected there. He said they were headed to the lab and then to Internal Affairs. But since he also had to bag and tag Hinesburg's desk, he'd brought along the apartment boxes to give Heat a chance to look them over before they went downtown. "Just wear gloves," he said.

Rook and the squad gathered around as Nikki lifted the

lids and carefully picked through the contents, replacing each in its carton following examination. She scanned the stack of open mail and bills, finding nothing useful. Underneath a toiletry kit of noncontroversial prescription meds, she found an evidence-bagged pocket pistol and held it up. "A Smith & Wesson M&P9 Shield," said Detective DeJesus in his precise, curator's manner.

Through the cellophane bag, Heat examined the 9mm, a favorite for deep undercover work because of its subcompact size. Feller scoffed. "Hinesburg had backups for her backups—for all the good they did her." Nikki pondered that thought then returned the pistol to the box.

"Anybody check this computer?" she asked, holding up a brand-new laptop.

Detective Raley hinged it open and, while it booted, said, "Spent a couple hours on it. Nothing juicy saved on the drive, that I could find. No maps, no calendar entries for Saturday. But she had a link to a cloud e-mail service with the 'keep me logged in' box checked, so I was able to access it. Mostly Web shopping receipts, but there was one sent e-mail Hinesburg must have forgotten to delete." He paused while it loaded. "Check it out."

He turned the screen to Nikki, and she read it twice out of disbelief. The recipient's e-mail address was some alphanumeric scramble, not a proper name, but the Web domain ended in .fr, signifying France. The subject line read: "Heat." And the message itself said: "Arrives today. Hotel Opera, Rue de Richelieu."

Rook said, "That was our hotel. And the date she sent

this is the day before you and I went to Paris last month. Where we met Tyler Wynn."

"Ready for the real smoking gun?" said Detective Ochoa, who excused himself and reached past Heat into the second box. He came out with a vanilla cell phone and held it up.

"Is this what I think it is?"

Ochoa handed it to her. "Can you believe it? Genius actually kept the burner cell. Slipshod and half-assed to the end."

While Heat opened the Outgoing Calls list, Raley pulled a slip of paper from his vest pocket. "The last two outgoings match these phone numbers I pulled. They fit the times for the warning calls that went out to both Salena Kaye and Vaja Nikoladze. You'll see there's two other numbers in Recents. One was Tyler Wynn's apartment. The other, I tried calling to see what it was but got a disconnect."

Heat said, "I recognize this number . . . At least it looks familiar." With a furrowed brow she took out her own cell phone and scrolled a few seconds until she found what she was looking for. She grabbed her keys and raced to the door, calling out, "Roach, Feller. Get your cars and follow me—*now.*"

NINETEEN

Overhead space heaters recessed into the apartment canopy took the chill out of the morning air on the Upper East Side. Heat and Roach waited behind the potted firs that flanked both sides of the lobby entrance. A black luxury town car sat poised in the circular cut-stone drive with the engine shut off. Detective Feller had replaced the car service driver and the motor block ticked as it cooled. "Lobby now," he whispered into his walkie-talkie. "Doorman first, suspect behind."

Raley and Ochoa nodded an acknowledgment to Heat from behind their cypress. She heard the automatic inner door of the vestibule slide open and put her hand on her holster. Then the outer doors parted at the shiny brass frame. The uniformed doorman led the way, waving the town car up for his tenant. As soon as the second man passed by, the detectives stepped in from both sides, bracing and cuffing him.

"Hey! What the bloody hell is this?"

Heat said, "You'll be riding with us today, Mr. Maggs."

Carey Maggs sat with his hands clasped before him in a relaxed fashion on the table of Interrogation One. "You can't simply detain me without cause. I may not be a United States citizen, but I am afforded due process." He may have possessed the cultured air of Oxford and worn the bespoke threads of a millionaire businessman, but when Nikki responded to his protest with stone silence, the Brit reacted the way they all did when they were dirty, from gang bangers to sous chefs. His eyes roved to the magic mirror, either to wonder who lurked behind it, watching, or to check himself out to see how he was doing—or both. Maggs didn't appear as uncomfortable with her silence as she would have liked, and he brought it back to her, sounding anything but fazed. "I've heard about these sort of bully-boy tactics on the news, but I must say, Detective Heat, I never expected this sort of grot from you."

"Well, I guess we all hold a few surprises."

"Perhaps you could end the suspense a bit and tell me why you snatched me up like some common criminal and brought me here."

Heat held her cards. Experience had taught her not to get ahead of things, to let this interview build, in spite of the crushing time pressure she felt. If she jumped right to the information she needed—the when and where of the bioterror event—Maggs would smell her desperation, and the power balance would tip to him. If she kept him worried about how much she already knew, he might give up more, and sooner. So Nikki didn't answer his question. Instead, she adopted a detached mode to match his.

A moment passed. She withdrew a photo of Petar Matic from the file in front of her. "When we last spoke on the telephone, and I asked if you could identify the man in this picture, you stated that you didn't know his name but that you had seen him lurking near your apartment the week Ari Weiss stayed with you. The week my mother was murdered."

He didn't bother to look at the picture. "That's correct."

"You also said you were suspicious of him and called the police to report it." He flicked his brows and shrugged, showing agreement. "We've run a computer check of records at your neighborhood's precinct, the Nineteenth. There's no record of any call, any complaint, any visit to your building."

"Maybe the police didn't log it. Or, who knows . . . ?" At last she could see the slightest fissure in the façade of calm as he improvised. "Maybe I didn't actually call it in myself. I may have left it to the doorman, yes."

"Which is it, Mr. Maggs?"

He shrugged. "Eleven years is a long time, love."

Heat smiled at the man across the table she believed had ordered her mother killed after she uncovered his terror plan. "You don't need to tell me."

Her smile unsettled Carey Maggs. Heat liked that. But just as she was about to move to her next question, the door burst open and Bart Callan strode in followed by Yardley Bell. "Heat, we're tagging in," said Callan.

"Excuse me," said Nikki, rising. She opened her arms, gesturing them out.

Carey's eyes widened. "Who the hell are they?"

Nobody left. Anything but. "I'm Special Agent Callan and this is Agent Bell, Department of Homeland Security. We have some questions for you about your terror plot."

As the words were spoken, she saw the look on Maggs, saw her carefully built sandcastle kicked over, and cursed to herself. "Agents?" she said. "Maybe we should take a moment?"

Bell stood with her arms folded and glowered at Heat. Callan jerked Nikki's chair over by its back so he could plant one foot on it and lean on his knee, looming over the table. "Let's start by finding out what your number was doing on the cell phone of a spy we busted in a bioterror plot."

"Am I to understand you are accusing me of terrorism because someone happened to have my number in a phone?" He turned to Heat. "Fuck this, I want my lawyer."

Nikki called a time-out. They left Maggs to stew at the table and adjourned to the Observation Room. The shouting began as soon as the air lock closed.

"How about a courtesy heads-up before you barge in on my interrogation?"

Bell said, "You're talking courtesy? Seriously?"

"I looped you in about the arrest."

"An e-mail after the bust is not looping in," said Callan.

"Not looping in is what screwed the pooch at the helipad last night," added Agent Bell. "We should have been there for the takedown. Not playing catch-up."

Heat pointed through the glass at Maggs. "His phone number was in Recents on Sharon Hinesburg's burner cell. I didn't want to lose him."

Yardley Bell moved nose-to-nose with Heat. "Bullshit. You made another unilateral decision to cut us from this process. From our own fucking case. Why?"

"Because," said Nikki, "there are too many moving parts."

"What's that mean? You don't trust us?"

Heat didn't answer. Just refused to blink. Callan finally spoke, in a more civil tone this time. "Let's hash all this out later. We have a mission. What have you gotten from him so far?"

Nikki stepped away from Bell. "Feigned innocence. I was just starting to piece him off when you came in."

Yardley stepped away muttering, "Jesus . . ."

"All right, let's be pragmatic," Callan said. "First, he gets no lawyer."

"I guess I could invoke an Article Nine and hold him for a psych evaluation," suggested Nikki. "I'd like to buy some time for my detectives to report back. I've got crews tossing his home and business, and Rook's doing some financial digging."

"What kind of financial?" asked Callan.

Before Nikki could respond, Bell jumped in. "Why are you farting around with a bogus psych hold, Heat? The National Defense Authorization Act allows federal officers to detain any terror suspect for an indefinite period, period." She brandished the federal DHS badge hanging around her neck. "*Now* are we a team?"

In their rekindled, albeit fragile, spirit of cooperation, Special Agent Callan dispatched his top forensic specialists to join Heat's detectives at Carey Maggs's apartment atop the Upper East Side high-rise, as well as at his brewery gastropub at the South Street Seaport. Much as in the searches that had been made at Salena Kaye's SRO in Coney Island, Vaja Nikoladze's compound upstate, and Sharon Hinesburg's one-bedroom, they'd hunt for material evidence like computers, mail, and receipts, as well as sniff-sweep for bioagents.

Saying he felt his "asshole puckering by the minute" as noon arrived one day before the bioterror target date, Callan also activated military resources to stop and search every truck coming into Manhattan, augmenting the spot checks NYPD had already initiated at key zones around the island. He also triggered the army and National Guard roll-out of the disaster medical apparatus they had discussed in the bunker at Homeland headquarters. The Fort Washington Armory uptown in Washington Heights plus the two armories at opposite ends of Lexington Avenue were being converted to vast indoor medical triage centers. Underneath the RFK Triboro Bridge, the soccer fields of Randall's Island would quietly overnight become a military tent city for mass casualties.

Higher-ups held to their decision not to announce the coming threat. "Without specifics, all it would cause is panic." At that moment, everyone in that precinct knew what that felt like.

They decided to let Detective Heat continue as lead in the interrogation. Unfortunately Carey Maggs decided to continue his pose of indignant innocence. Several hours into his genteel stonewall Detective Rhymer slipped into Interrogation One and passed Heat a file of research he had pulled from his bank canvasses. She perused it and gave Maggs a look of significance. "Let's talk about Salena Kaye. You recall Salena Kaye, right?"

"By name I do. But only because you've been flogging on

about her as if we should be mates. Wouldn't know her if I tripped on her, as I've made clear."

"We know that Salena Kaye was busy lately contacting radical jihadists, searching for volunteers to martyr themselves. I called it volunteering, but she has been offering a hundred thousand dollars to the families of whoever signs up."

"If you say. I still don't see how this has bugger all to do with me."

"One hundred thousand dollars. Where would a registered physical therapist like Salena Kaye get her hands on a spare hundred grand or two?"

"Ask her."

"She's dead. And you know it, don't you?" Maggs kept his eyes passive during the silence that followed. His expression gave away nothing. "I want you to tell me. Whom did she hire and where are they?"

"I guess we're stumped" was all he said.

Accustomed to the denials, she pressed on and held up a scanned page from the file Rhymer had brought her. "Just got some interesting information here. Salena Kaye's personal account received a wire transfer for two hundred thousand dollars this week from a bank named Clune Worldwide Holdings." She set that page down and took out the next sheet. "This is a copy of the receipt from the credit card Salena Kaye used at Surety Rent-a-Car the other day when she tried to rent a box truck. We ran a search and the line of credit was funded through Clune Worldwide Holdings." She paused. No response, so she produced another page. "The personal bank statement of Sharon Hinesburg."

"Another name you insist I should know."

"See these yellow highlights?" She held the statement up; he barely gave it a glance. "These are one-thousand-dollar payments wired electronically into Hinesburg's account from Clune Worldwide Holdings."

"And?"

"And," she echoed, turning another page, "Clune Worldwide Holdings, an offshore bank located in the Cayman Islands—aka Switzerland with palm trees, when it comes to money laundering—is the same bank that happens to maintain the account for Mercator Watch, the charitable organization you fund."

"Means nothing," he said. "The bank I use also happens to pay those other people? Lots of banks pay other people. One bank in those TV adverts seems to pay Vikings. Does that make their other customers Vikings, too?" He chuckled.

They allowed Maggs a supervised bathroom break, and when he came back into Interrogation to find Rook seated beside Heat, it took him off balance, if only slightly. He covered with more nonchalance. "Glad, actually, to have an investigative journalist join the proceedings. If they sod me off to Gitmo, I'll need someone to record the injustice."

"Full disclosure, I'm not here to chronicle the Free Carey campaign. I'm helping Detective Heat stop you from killing innocent people."

"Well, at least we understand each other."

"More and more," said Heat.

Rook continued, "You might even say that I understand everything, Carey. All of it." Maggs's eyes darted to the papers the writer had brought with him. "See, one of the perks of being an investigative journalist is I have this cool list of high-level sources. It's an interesting relationship. Sometimes I owe them payback for favors, sometimes they owe me. I have a high-level guy at the Securities and Exchange Commission, and, hoo-rah, it was his turn to put out.

"There's an old Watergate catchphrase. 'Follow the money.' It was sort of the 'What's in your wallet?' of its day." Rook winked. "Now, with my SEC friend's help, it only took me a couple of hours to follow yours and gather your investment portfolio. I know the entire distribution of your wealth. Well, at least the part you don't stuff in your shoes when you fly to the Caymans."

Maggs strained to read the pages upside down as Rook arranged them in the order he wanted before he continued. "Mercator Watch. Your foundation that monitors international child labor abuse. Actually more a fund. Let's set that aside and look at your investments. All profitable, congratulations." He turned a page. "Pranco Corporation, European government contracts to build low-cost housing in Third World villages decimated by war. Nevwar Enterprises, multimillion-dollar, multinational manufacturing company employing ex-prisoners of conscience from totalitarian regimes." He looked up from the page. "It goes on and on like this, Carey. One company after another turning a solid profit on radical ideals and causes."

"None of that makes me a fucking terrorist, does it?"

"On the contrary, it's like Brewery Boz being founded on the Charles Dickens principle of exposing social injustice."

"And corporate greed," said Maggs in a blurt of anger. "My portfolio is all ethical capitalism, beating the fucking one-percenters at their own game. There's no crime in that." It was the first time Heat had seen him worked up.

Rook nodded agnostically and turned to the last page. "All fine. But this one here. This stands out as, I dare say . . ." He turned to Heat.

"An odd sock?" she asked.

"Let's see. You are the principal shareholder in a BeniPharm Corporation." They watched Carey Maggs's blink rate double. "Now, the odd-sock part is that BeniPharm's the only investment in your jacket that is not in the radical scheme." Rook returned to the SEC data. "It says here the company was formed in 1998 with your cash and a token buy-in by minor partner, Ari Weiss, MD . . . now deceased. The company rolled along and along, operating solely on paper, for all intents, until two years ago when it branded itself with a signature product. Do you want to say what it is, or shall I?"

Maggs cleared his throat and said in a tattered voice, "Smallpox medicine."

"Interesting," said Heat.

"BeniPharm's prospectus says it's uniquely positioned itself as the world's leading source for the smallpox antiviral remedy. I didn't realize it until Detective Heat got hers, but if you get this medicine within five days of exposure, you won't get smallpox."

"That's right," said Maggs.

Heat asked, "Why throw all that effort into a medicine for an extinct disease?"

"Paranoia," said Rook. "We live in an era where nuts can unleash bioterror. In fact, according to this, BeniPharm has a contract from the United States government for half a billion dollars' worth of your company's smallpox medicine."

"Nothing wrong with that. I . . . we . . . perform a public service."

Heat said, "And what would happen to your profits if there were a smallpox outbreak?"

"You're reaching—"

"Or if smallpox were weaponized and released in a terror event? In a major metro area?"

"This is a frame."

"What would it do?" Nikki asked. "Would your profits double? Triple? Would other countries buy in? Tell me, what would you gain? Ten times the profit?" Heat rose, shouting, slapping a palm on the table. "Is that worth killing thousands of innocent people? Was that the cost of my mother's life, you son of a bitch?"

Spent, Heat stood there panting. The room grew still.

At last, calmer, she spoke. "Do one right thing, Maggs. Tell me when and where."

He rocked his head. "I'll tell you this." And when he had their attention, he said, "You're all still guessing."

Heat flung the door with both hands, and it smacked the wall in the Observation Room. "I can't break him."

"You did great," said Callan.

Bell said to Rook, "You both did great. Couldn't have played it better."

Through the window, they saw Maggs slouched in his chair with his head tilted back, eyes closed. He could have been a commuter dozing on the train to Connecticut instead of the prime suspect in a mass terror plot. "He's got balls," said Rook. "He comes just to the point you think he's going to crack, and he sucks 'em up."

"What's he got to lose?" said Bell. "You laid it out yourself. An upside of billions, if he keeps his mouth shut; life in prison if he suddenly gets a conscience."

"After five o'clock," said Callan. "I say we move off traditional means and take him for a ride to the Black Barn."

Rook's face lit up. "You guys really have a Black Barn?"

Callan frowned and looked at Nikki. "Is he for real?"

"Well," insisted Rook, "do you?"

Nikki said, "He's not going anywhere. We don't do that."

Behind her, Yardley Bell chuckled softly. Agent Callan said to Rook, "She's right. Sadly, this is US soil. Much as I wouldn't mind doing a little tenderizing, we're going to have to keep working him constitutionally." He walked to the window and said, "Let's take five. When we come back, I get my shot at this prick."

Heat found her voice mail stacked with messages when she got back into the bull pen. Lauren Parry had left word she had some interesting postmortem news to share. Nikki saved that one in order to first return Detective Ochoa's call.

"Where are you guys?"

"Team Roach is currently inside Brewery Boz at South Street. How's it going with Maggs, anything?"

"Nothing yet. He just keeps acting like he's going to put me on some Amnesty International list just below North Korea."

Ochoa said, "Unfortunately we're not going to be any help. And, trust me, we swarmed his apartment and the brewery like an Indy pit crew. Forensics, too. That includes NYPD and the DHS geeks with their R2-D2 vacuum sniffer things."

"Everything's clean?"

"Not just clean. Antiseptic."

After they hung up, she'd just started to fill Rook in when one of the precinct aides rushed in and interrupted. All she said was, "Rainbow."

Nikki reached out to grab the phone. Rook surprised her by clamping his hand over hers, holding down the receiver. "Rook."

"Take your time. Let him wait."

"I might get something out of him about the attack, I can't wait."

"Same as Maggs, if he smells that, you're dead." He gave her hand a gentle squeeze and released his. "Remember what I said. You played his game; make him play yours."

Heat pondered that, and even though it ran counter to everything she felt—to everything she so desperately needed at the eleventh hour—she agreed. If Rainbow smelled desperation, Rainbow ran the table. She waited a full thirty agonizing seconds before she picked up. "Heat."

"What? Are you keeping me on hold to run a trace?" She recognized Glen Windsor's voice and gave Rook a nod to affirm. "I'm not an idiot. I know how to set up a phone so it can't be pinged." And then an inspiration struck Nikki that scared the hell out of her. She didn't examine it, she didn't weigh it, she simply acted on her impulse.

She hung up on him.

"God damn," said Rook.

Just as she felt nausea's burn greeting her with the notion she might have just made a fatal mistake, the line purred again. Heat snapped the record switch on the junction box and let one more ring pass before she answered. Windsor jumped in before she even spoke. "What the fuck was that about?" His voice cracked with agitation. The power of the game, she thought.

"Glen, I'm busy." It took all her effort to sound detached.

"Fuck you busy. We need to talk."

"Hang on a sec." She covered the mouthpiece loosely and called off to nobody, "Just wait for me, OK? Be there in ten seconds. Ten seconds." Rook clench-pumped both his fists to give her encouragement. Committed to the strategy, she waded in. "Listen, if you want to talk to me, why don't you come in? Otherwise, you'll have to wait."

"Have you lost it?"

"No, in fact, I kind of have a clear head for a change. See, I just don't have time for you now. I have something bigger to deal with."

"Bigger?" She could hear his breathing accelerate. "What, that bio plot?"

"You'll have to wait, Glen. Your moment has passed."

"You're a fucking idiot, you know that?"

The more he went over the top, the more flat she made her voice. "You know, I really can't deal with this now."

"You don't know shit. You don't even know where this stuff's going to be released."

She waited, just in case he offered. When he didn't, she said, "No, but I will. I'm going to be there to stop this madness, and when I do, you're going to be no more than an asterisk."

"Bull. Shit."

"It's not you, Glen, it's just the way it goes. A bigger fish came along."

"No, I fucking own this now. At nine tomorrow morning, I'll be gone, but everyone will know I did it. I'll make history, and you can live with it."

"Got to see that. Want to tell me where?"

But he'd hung up.

Heat raced out of the squad room, saying, "Nine a.m. Let's tell Callan."

Rook kept pace with her down the hall and said, "Considering that you're someone who hates to play games, remind me never to cross you."

Nikki hurried into Observation One and found it empty. A creeping certainty weakened her limbs. She rushed to the glass to look into Interrogation.

The room was empty.

"Maggs is gone," she said to Rook as she ran back out the door. "And so are Callan and Bell."

The desk sergeant had seen them lead Maggs out through the lobby but thought nothing of it. Why should he? They were federal agents escorting a prisoner. In a knowing act of futility, Heat and Rook trotted out through the glass doors onto 82nd. All they found was the air-conditioning puddle where Callan had parked his SUV and an empty street between them and Columbus.

"Looks like we have one additional moving part," said Rook.

Heat spent the next hour working to reach them. The obvious calls came first: to Callan's cell phone, then to Yardley Bell's. Heat left voice mails that she knew in her heart would be ignored, if they even were listened to. Rook followed up with e-mails and texts to Bell—even posting a heavily masked Tweet about getting in touch.

The hour stretched into a full night of fruitless outreach. Nikki called every number she had at Homeland Security, her gut telling her that she was hollering down a black hole. She tried NYPD Counterterrorism and managed to get connected to her colleague on the DHS counterterrorism unit at his home. Commander McMains said he'd look into it, which she took as code for letting the feds have at Maggs all they wanted. "We are coming to the brink, Heat, in case you hadn't noticed."

In desperation, Rook even called Paris and woke up his

Russian spy pal, Anatoly Kijé, just to try to shake loose any private numbers or e-mail addresses he might have. The secret agent cursed in Russian and told Rook to get real; his Rolodex of American spooks was slightly limited.

When they had exhausted their options, they made the same rounds again with nothing in the end to show for it all but lost energy and time. "Know what the hell of this is?" said Heat. "The effort we're putting into chasing our own people is pulling us away from heading off that event tomorrow."

Rook checked his watch. "You mean today. It's after midnight."

"Excellent."

"But the other side of the coin is they may do better at heading this off than we will. I mean ethical questions aside."

Heat snapped at him, "We don't put ethics aside, Rook. It's not who we are. It's not who I am, anyway. Don't you think I would love ten minutes alone in a locked room with Carey Maggs?"

"You mean to work out your mom stuff, or to stop the smallpox attack?"

She thought about that and said, "I guess I have the luxury of not having to know the answer." A moment passed and she asked, "What about your mom? Did Margaret get out of town?"

"Oh, yes, Oswego-bound, hours ago. I have a feeling that, at this very moment, Broadway's 'Grand Damn' is in the lounge, on her third Sidecar, and the Drama Festival committee is wondering what they got themselves into."

"You know, Rook, we've done our best. No points off if

you want to leave. You have your place in the Hamptons."

He took both her hands in his, looked into her eyes, and said, "Yeah, I'm outta here." And after they both laughed at that, they kissed.

Since they were all alone, they made it count.

In the overnight Heat didn't dare leave her desk. She dozed in ten-minute intervals in her chair and left her cell phone on ring instead of vibrate so she'd be sure to get any calls. Raley and Ochoa checked in just after four when they wrapped Brewery Boz. For the hell of it, she asked them to swing by Varick Street and door-knock the Homeland HQ to see if they could create some movement. They called back an hour later with no joy.

At sunup the commander of NYPD's counterterrorism unit called from his staging area at the 69th Regiment Armory near Gramercy Park. He didn't want Heat to think he had dismissed her, and reassured her that he had put calls out through all his sources to learn what he could about the whereabouts and status of the DHS agents and Maggs. Heat told McMains he was a good man and asked him to keep her posted. "And God help us all," he said.

After too many days and nights in the same clothes, Nikki budgeted herself five minutes for a quick shower in the locker room, which did a world to make her feel sharper for the day ahead. After she toweled off, she smiled, amused that she was actually resorting to changing into her backup bag of backup clothes, and wondered if she should have a backup for that, too. The brown leather jacket she'd been wearing seemed a little warm for the forecast, so when Heat returned to the bull pen, she hung it on the coat rack and got down the blazer Yardley Bell had returned to her after its DHS bioagent sweep.

When she slipped it off the rack, she noticed a clear plastic evidence bag had been looped over the hook of the hanger. Thoughtfully, the Homeland Security scientists had emptied her blazer pockets and returned all their contents with an inventory slip. Nikki looked inside. She found a lipstick, her sunglasses, a notepad and golf pencil, and an open package of Reese's peanut butter cups. She doubted she would want the remaining candy and took it out to throw away. Her hand froze above the trash can.

"Rook," she called.

Couch springs groaned from the break room, and he appeared in the door with bed hair and one shirttail out. "What?"

She held up the blazer. "Now I know where I picked up my contamination. Come on."

TWENTY

Detective Heat's Crown Victoria ripped across West 79th Street rolling Code Three, full lights and siren. She had Rook speed-dial her phone for her so she could keep her hands on the wheel while she called the dispatcher to rally her crew and the counterterrorism unit downtown at the protest march Carey Maggs had helped sponsor. Rook held her cell with one hand and gripped the door handle with the other as she wove around slow cars or braked, then g-force accelerated through stoplights. At that hour on Saturday morning, traffic was light, and in record time she steered them around the rotary onto the Henry Hudson Parkway heading downtown.

In her call to Dispatch, she described what to be on the lookout for: a red 1870s London Fire Brigade wagon with a large copper boiler kettle on the back. "I believe that's the container holding the bioagent, so proceed with extreme caution."

Seeing clear lanes of straight highway ahead, Rook spoke to her, elevating his voice above the siren. "What was your lightbulb? What made you connect it?"

"The peanut butter cup," she said. "I remembered I ate the peanut butter cup the morning I visited Maggs at his brewery."

"You are amazing. How the hell did you remember something as trivial as that?"

"Because it wasn't trivial. I was pissed at you when you called from Nice. With Yardley."

"And the candy fits in because . . . ?"

"Because I ate it in a rage binge. I was furious at you for being so goddamned stupid and completely insensitive." She paused to make a quick maneuver around a sanitation truck. "Hey, some people kick trash cans, I break out the Reese's."

They rode in silence. At last, Rook said, "Glad I could play a role."

It only took Heat and Rook fourteen minutes to get to Battery Park on the southern tip of Manhattan, but when they arrived, Emergency Services, the Hercules team, and the counterterrorism unit had already gathered at their staging area on State Street and Bowling Green in the plaza near the old Customs House. Nikki wove between riot cops and bright rows of pink tulips in full spring bloom until she found Commander McMains marking up deployment maps. "Hard to think of a worse scenario, Detective."

They surveyed the situation across the street in Battery Park, where several thousand protestors had gathered behind the giant banner stretching across the Hope Garden declaring the Walk Against Global Oppression. Heat spotted the logo for Brewery Boz as corporate sponsor. "This is the event Carey Maggs has spent all year promoting. Doing all he could to draw a big crowd—so he can release the smallpox on them."

"Sunny skies, gentle breeze, unfortunately a perfect day for it," said the commander. "Latest guesstimate from the airship puts them at four thousand marchers. That includes kids and toddlers in strollers." He shook his head. "And they're still streaming in."

"Why can't you stop them?" asked Rook. "Just move them out."

"Great idea, here you go." The commander held a bullhorn out to Rook, then pulled it back. "Sorry for the smart-ass, but I'm going to guess you have limited experience breaking up a protest mob. They tend to fight you on that, and this group's no different." McMains shifted his attention to Heat. "When I got here, I got clearance to announce the bioterror danger to the organizers. They think we're lying, just trying to disrupt their march."

Nikki scanned the area and saw several hundred riot control officers adding gas masks to their preparations. "Any sign of Homeland Security?"

"Right here," said Agent Callan. They turned as he and Yardley Bell stepped in to join them.

"What happened to my prisoner?" demanded Heat.

Callan gave an oblique reply. "Congratulations. Looks like you did better than us, after all."

"I asked you, what happened to Maggs?"

"He's not a concern right now, Detective. Let's do the job first, all right?" He didn't wait for a response but answered for her. "All right. Now describe this fire truck we're looking for."

Once more Heat swallowed her anger for the sake of the mission. "It's a vintage London fire wagon Maggs restored as a promotion for this event."

"And, apparently, refitted with a container to spray the

crowd," added Rook. He finished tapping his iPhone screen and held it up. "Here's a promo picture of it from the Brewery Boz Web site."

"Text that to me," said Agent Bell. "I'll get it circulated to everyone here."

Someone with a bullhorn in the park called out, "No justice, no business! No justice, no business!" The crowd picked it up and chanted it back. "Crap," said Callan. "What time are they scheduled to move?"

Commander McMains said, "In thirty minutes, at nine o'clock." Hearing the time nudged Heat to make a scan of the area, wondering if Glen Windsor lurked out there and, if he did, what he had in mind. They gathered around a map as McMains unfurled it on the hood of a nearby patrol car. "Their permit calls for a parade from where they are now, proceeding up Broadway, and terminating at City Hall Park."

"Side streets?" asked the special agent.

"All closed. And we have pipe barricades to keep them off the sidewalks. I've also closed the Four and Five subway station to cut off new arrivals." McMains took a ballpoint from his uniform chest pocket and drew brackets mid-route. "Most of our assets are set up here to keep them from getting any ideas about taking over Wall Street or Exchange Place." Just as the commander voiced the notion, the "No justice, no business! No justice, no business!" chant punctuated it.

Callan closed his eyes as if having a conversation with himself. Then he clapped his hands together once and said, "That's where we put everything. Wall Street is the vulnerable part of the whole circus. If that virus gets released up there, we're not only talking mass casualties, a quarantine would shut down the New York Stock Exchange, maybe even the Federal Reserve Bank. Can you imagine the ripple effects of that?"

"Let's not," said Agent Bell.

Since nobody had spotted the Boz Brigade fire wagon, not even the choppers, Callan and McMains formed a plan to hustle agents and uniforms up the route of the march and throughout the Wall Street financial blocks to check parking lots and garages for the vehicle. All the detectives from Heat's squad had arrived and would join her on the search, as well.

"And do not tell me I have to wait in the car," said Rook.

Heat replied, "I won't. Because you're going to stay here."

"You really think I'm going to be in the way?"

"Not really. But I don't want you up there if something bad comes down. We have it covered, end of discussion."

"I'll be fine, I have this." He held a gas mask over his face and breathed loudly. "Luke, I am your fa—"

She pulled the mask away. "You're staying here." Then she left with the others.

Rook stood off moping to the side of the staging area and watched a contingent of uniforms in riot gear and gas masks attempt to form a containment barrier with orange plastic netting while a lieutenant addressed the crowd, asking them to stop the march and disperse for their own safety. They drowned him in boos.

At nine sharp, an organizer raised an air horn and gave it a long blast. Cheers erupted and the mob moved forward, slowly pushing past the lines of police for the march up Broadway.

Some of the protestors, schooled in civil disobedience tactics, threw themselves down and linked arms on the ground to form a barrier between the passing crowd and the police who were attempting to contain them. As the cops advanced to deal with the human chain, Rook decided he didn't like his proximity to the flailing and shouting and drifted across the street into the park, circling around the mob toward the rear of the action.

He passed a Statue of Liberty street mime, a "living statue" in turquoise greasepaint. In a Chinese accent Lady Liberty hawked a souvenir pose with him for only ten dollars. As he walked on, the asphalt path Rook followed curved through the park to Castle Clinton, the sandstone fort built as a cannon battery to protect Manhattan from the British in the War of 1812. Port-a-johns set up for the protest lined the castle's north wall near overflowing trash cans and about two dozen stragglers who had decided sharing some choice weed held more allure than a long walk. He came upon some plastic tubs filled with melted ice and a few unclaimed bottled waters floating between the cubes. His tongue still felt furry after the long night, so he helped himself to one while he leaned against the castle and watched the rear flank of the march shuffle uptown.

About four blocks away, two NYPD helicopters hovered at different altitudes over the skyscrapers of the Financial District. He felt the sun on his face and listened to their engine hums mix in with the bullhorn shouts and the chorus of chants. Off to his right, he heard a sound like a large flag fluttering. But when he turned, he saw it was just someone pulling the white fabric flap aside to open the covered first aid tent. He watched the choppers some more, envisioning Heat and the others underneath them, sweeping those streets and checking garages, and wishing he could be part of the action. But then another noise coming from that tent drew his attention.

Rook heard a whinny.

Hoof clops came next, and a draft horse ambled out of the large white event tent. Rook dropped his bottle of water and already had his cell phone out by the time the red Boz Brigade cart rolled into view behind the horse and stopped. A man walked out of the tent on the far side, blocked by the carriage. But the limp visible under the chassis told Rook all he needed for confirmation.

Nikki answered her phone without a hello. "No, Writer Boy, you still have to stay put."

"He's here," he said in a whisper.

"Where?"

"Castle." And as soon as Rook said it, the serial killer climbed up, stood on the coachman's step, and made eye contact. "Rainbow."

Up on Whitehall Street, Nikki held her phone away from her ear, about to tell Agent Callan about Rook's sighting, when their radios came alive with calls from both choppers. "Red fire wagon in sight." And "Got it. Castle in the park."

Heat didn't wait. She sprinted to a blue-and-white idling at the curb, yanked open the passenger door, and said, "Hit it."

Glen Windsor's gunshot wound slowed him down getting both legs up and into the driver's box. He kept his eyes on Rook the whole way and even gained some time as the writer hesitated when he looked inside the tent. Sprawled on the ground there, the bodies of two jihadist volunteers bled out from neck slashes. They were martyrs, all right, thought Rook. Just for a different cause—a cause that was not their own. He turned away from the pair of dead men and ran toward the fire wagon. Windsor dismissed him until he saw Rook make the smart move, angling for the horse, not him, so he quickly snatched up the reins, gave them a snap, and the big animal started off.

The sergeant at the wheel knew which back streets had been cleared as emergency lanes, so he and Nikki flew until they got to the entrance of Battery Park. A band of protestors locked arms and blocked the car, laughing and hurling insults. Heat bolted out and ran, leaving the door open as she wove through the crowd.

Rainbow clucked to get the horse moving so he could catch up with the marchers. He twisted in the coachman's seat to do a shoulder-check for Rook, and was surprised when he couldn't locate him back near the white tent. Then the carriage jolted and the suspension iron groaned under a sudden weight. Windsor pivoted more. As the wagon rolled across the meadow, he peered around the copper boiler full of virus behind his seat, and saw a hand come up over the boot. Then he glimpsed Jameson Rook, hoisting himself up on the back of the carriage and crawling toward him.

He jerked the reins and pulled the brake handle, trying to lurch Rook off with a sudden stop. But it only thrust him closer to Windsor as he held on. Then Rainbow went to the whip, and Rook almost fell backward as the horse reacted and yanked the fire wagon forward toward the great lawn, scattering panicked stragglers as it thundered ahead.

The wide belly of the boiler presented the greatest obstacle. As the carriage bounced and swayed, Rook had to climb slightly outboard to get around it. At his most vulnerable spot, Windsor lashed him with the whip. But Rook grabbed it on one of his wild thrashes, pulling it away.

Galloping across the pasture, closing in on the rear field of marchers, Windsor reached for an orange electrical cable draped over the dash rail in front of him. Rook's heart sank when he saw the grip device dangling at the end of it. He knew that would be The Switch: the release button for the spray. He visually traced the wire to where it came out of the seat back and snaked up between the copper steam tubing to the valves on the boiler vat, then to the modern set of plastic aerosol nozzles beside his head on the chimney.

Rook yanked at it. The cord wouldn't budge from the mechanism.

He glanced up front. Windsor had hold of the cable. The switch was nearly in his hand.

Nikki Heat fought her way out of the back of the crowd, drew her Sig, planted her left knee on the grass, and combat-braced on her right, drawing aim at the fire wagon charging toward her. She had to be careful not to hit the horse. The animal was not only an innocent, but if it dropped, it could topple the carriage and spill the virus. The same caution held for the vat. She had to wait for an angle of fire that wouldn't risk puncturing the copper boiler if she missed Windsor or if the slug went through him.

She saw him going for the switch on the orange cable and wondered if she should just take the shot. That's when Rook pounced on top of Windsor and clawed over his shoulders for the button. Heat holstered up and sprinted for the carriage.

Rook's lunge knocked the cable out of Windsor's hand. He let go of the reins and bent down into the well of the coachman's box to retrieve it. While the undriven horse began to run a circle in the meadow, with screaming protestors diving for safety, Rook clambered to drape himself over Rainbow, reaching down past him to get the switch out of play. When Windsor came inches from getting to the end of the cable, Rook switched tactics. He balled a fist and started pounding the fresh gunshot wound. Rainbow shrieked in pain but held fast to the wire. Rook punched his calf again and again. Windsor twisted to punch Rook, and when he did, Rook snatched the cable from him and tossed the deadly end of it over the back of the seat, where it dangled out of reach.

Rainbow removed his hands from his bleeding calf and elbow-smacked Rook's nose. As Rook fell to the side, Windsor pulled his knife from a belt sheath. Through watering eyes, Rook caught the glint of the blade and swung his forearm up. Just as he made contact with Rainbow's wrist, the carriage double-bumped over the stone curbing of the park path and the combination flung the knife out of the killer's hands and onto the passing ground. Unarmed and desperate, Windsor hurled himself up, bending over the back of the seat rail, groping to reach the swaying cable. But the fire carriage lurched again as Heat caught up and leaped aboard. She snatched Windsor by the back of his belt and shoved him headfirst right over the seat. He fell into the gap of air between the coachman's box and the boiler, landing hard on the ground speeding underneath. The wagon shuddered as the rear wheels rolled over him. Nikki jumped off.

Sniffing back blood, Rook grabbed the cable and drew it safely into the coach. He called a soft "Whoa" and tugged the reins. The horse came to a docile stop amid hundreds of marchers. Across the lawn he could hear Rainbow, facedown in the grass, pleading to Heat who stood above him. "Shoot me! Aw, fuck, please, just fucking do it!"

But not all destinies are fulfilled. Nikki ended the killing right there. She cuffed him, holstered her gun, and waited for the rest of the crew to catch up while Rook neatly coiled the orange cord.

And then under the thrum of hovering airships and the urgent wail of sirens, a strange and graceful quiet enveloped her, as if mayhem's shadow had been carried away on the spring breeze off the harbor. In her soundless world cushioned by deliverance, Nikki looked around at all the faces in the crowd, at all the people who were going to live. And looking down at Rainbow, she knew she was going to live, too.

Ten years, twenty-three weeks, and four days of agony,

apprehension, and dread—all over in a single moment. She reflected on that decade-plus. Her entire adult life had been honed by loss, faith, preparation, sacrifice, and tenacity. But also by fortune. A deadly plot might have been fulfilled if it hadn't been for a serial killer getting himself involved.

And if Detective Heat hadn't been juggling both cases.

Monday evening Nikki came home from the federal arraignment of Carey Maggs feeling relief and agony. When Rook called from his suite at the SLS in Beverly Hills to check in on her, she said, "You know, everyone says there's no such thing as closure. But I'm starting to learn I'm not so much interested in that as I am in a finish. I expect it's natural that I'll carry this hurt about my mom all my life, but I sure wouldn't mind having the work of it end."

"And Maggs pleading not guilty keeps it in your face."

"Absolutely. Months and more of trial and delays. I want to be done, Rook."

"At least the investigation part is."

"There's that," she said. "You should have seen him today with his Dream Team of legal heavyweights. It looked like he was sitting there with Mount Rushmore."

"The feds are still going to nail him, you know that."

"But it won't be without a long fight. His team already has petitioned to throw out the corroborative testimony from Glen Windsor's confession. They're calling it fruit from a tainted tree."

"I hate that," said Rook. "What has this country come to

when you can't trust the word of a serial killer?"

"I'd laugh if it weren't true. I've been involved in enough cases to know how this will work, too. The prosecutor will trade that away if the defense doesn't pursue DHS taking Maggs off for his extracurricular interrogation."

"They do have a Black Barn, I know it."

"So tell me about your meetings. Is your head swimming with fruit-basket love?"

"Truthfully, Nik, it all feels sort of empty. I mean, after single-handedly saving the world as I did."

She chuckled. "Yeah, maybe you, Batman, and Lone Vengeance should form a support group."

"Sure, we could call it . . . I dunno . . . Cape-Anon. Although, superheroes are generally anonymous already, so it would have to be Cape-Anon-Anon."

"Good night, Rook."

"Good night? But you got my Spidey sense all tingly."

"Hold that thought."

Home alone with no obligations after a harrowing few weeks, and a deep fatigue she thought she would never sleep off, Nikki contemplated an evening of scented candles, bubble bath, and soulful divas on the boom box. But that felt like distraction; more superficial than the inner healing she craved.

Besides, she knew she could never relax with missing pieces or loose ends.

She brought out the cardboard tube and set it on the coffee table. Puzzle Man, however unnerving a partner, had proved his worth and managed to crack the code. The message felt incomplete, but with the arrest of Carey Maggs as the leader of the conspiracy, Heat told herself to let it go.

But she couldn't.

Back to her mom. Back to lack of closure.

Why, she wondered, would someone work so hard to construct a coded message that, essentially, didn't reveal information? Her mother was more practical than that. No wasted effort, everything for a purpose. The apple didn't fall far.

Nikki slid the papers out of the tube and laid them out before her. Then she stacked them and held them to the light, getting the same message as before: *Unlock the Dragon*.

As she had done, ad nauseam, she considered the significance of each word. Nikki focused on "Unlock" because that felt like a call to action—one she hadn't taken. That's what kept her persevering. Nikki had not unlocked anything.

She had spent eleven years going around that apartment searching for locks or secret boxes. Her father had let her go through some of their things that he had brought to his condo in Scarsdale, and she had found nothing there. So no more house searches.

Heat stared at the message until her eyes glazed. Then she spread the four pages apart, kicking herself for going back to square one like that. But she did.

Why was this so difficult? What had Puzzle Man said? That the hardest code to crack was the one that's only known by two people? The sender and the receiver.

If Nikki were the intended receiver, she wondered, why choose her? When her mother was murdered, Heat was a theater student at Northeastern, not a cop, and with no hint of becoming one. Or maybe her mom knew more about her nature than she did. Or simply trusted her completely.

"So, Mom," she said aloud, "what's just between us here?"

She tried not to picture the mother of her nightmares sprawled on the kitchen floor. Her gaze fell across the room, and the ghost of her recent dream came to her: Cynthia playing the piano in the corner, saying, "You know . . ."

It began to seep through as she laid her eyes on the four pages again. Nikki removed her focus from the coded marks themselves and contemplated the sheet music they had been written on. A recollection drifted to her on a trail of time's smoke.

Those four pieces comprised one of Nikki's piano recitals when she was sixteen. She rushed to the piano bench and dug out the old program. There they were on the list. Those four songs, and no others.

Why choose them for the code?

That recital lived clearly in her memory. She recalled her stage fright, and making only one mistake in her fingering, which (for the first time) she had not let shake her confidence. And what else? Oh, yes! Her mother was so proud of her that night she celebrated by taking Nikki out for dinner—and letting her have her very first drink. They'd gone to the Players, where her mom was a member. The club sat only a few doors from their place but carried a grand history and specialness to Nikki. Her mother asked the bartender to go in back and unlock her private wine locker for a special bottle. When he uncorked it and left, Cynthia drank down the water from Nikki's glass then poured her daughter some of the celebration wine. Her mom only allowed the sixteen-year-old a half glass. To Nikki, it was brimming.

Heat checked her watch and stood. The new warmth that flowed through her came from something more than revelation, more than closure. She felt a connection.

Nikki put on her coat and stepped out.

The bartender's hair had gone white over the years but he still remembered Miss Heat, same as he recalled everyone who ever had been a member or honored guest at the Players. If George had been working the Grill Room when Samuel Clemens knocked cue balls around the billiard table that still lived there, he would have memorized every shot, quip, and bawdy curse from Mr. Twain.

He got his keys off the hook above the bar sink, and as he led Nikki to the back, he said, "I still see your dad come in from time to time. Although not so much since . . ." George's brow fell. He left it there.

In the back of the room, past cases of hard liquor and house wines, built-in cabinets filled a wall. "Here we go," said George, "the private stock." Each cupboard, the size of a small gym locker, was marked by an oval brass plaque etched with the member's name. Nikki recognized a lot of them; most belonged to famous actors, but a few to composers, journalists, and novelists. They weren't arranged alphabetically, but the barkeeper knew where each stash resided, by heart. He fit the key into the door of the locker labeled "Cynthia Heat" and stepped back. Discreet to a fault, George smiled and said, "I'll leave you to do the honors," then melted away to the Grill Room.

Heat opened the door and found no wine. All the locker housed was a solitary bottle of beer: Durdles' Finest Pale Ale. A banner on the label read, "Now crafted in America at Brewery Boz, South Street Seaport." Nikki lifted the bottle and saw her name on the envelope it had been resting on.

She ran the pad of her forefinger over her mother's handwriting and opened the envelope flap, which Cynthia Heat had left folded but not sealed.

The note to Nikki was short. She absorbed it with surprise, at what it said and at the unexpected sense of closure she'd always believed could never come. The words under the signature at the end of the note made her eyes cloud with tears: "Always remember Mom loves you."

She left the beer, took the note, and departed with one fewer loose end, and then some.

Nikki's quad protested as she stretched on the mat at her gym early the next morning. The soreness from the physical ordeal of the past weeks, coupled with skipping workouts and sleep, made her feel like an out-of-shape slug. Heat smiled through her grimace, thankful she belonged to the only gym in Manhattan without mirrors.

When Bart Callan came in, he was grinning, too. "You weren't kidding, Heat. This facility is bare-bones. I expect to see Rocky Balboa working a side of beef."

"I like it this way. No frou-frou, no posers. It's come to work, or stay out."

"Is that why we have it all to ourselves?" He dropped his gym bag in a corner then stripped off his sweats down to his basketball shorts and a Homeland T-shirt with the sleeves hacked off, revealing seriously ripped upper arms. She wondered if he had altered his tee just for her.

Heat and Callan double fist-bumped in the center of the mat to signal readiness. Nikki shifted her weight back and forth on the balls of her feet to get a read of him, and in an instant, she got her assessment. He made a feint left and a lunge right, grabbing her waist and sending her to the mat. "Finally," he said. "Contact."

"Man." She got up and said, "Rusty."

This time she went for him. As she came forward, he dropped to a knee and flipped her over his back, and she came down with a thud on the mat. "Remember, you called me," he said. "You sure you're up for this?"

"We'll see. I didn't sleep much last night."

"The arraignment?" He waved the air dismissively. "Don't sweat that."

They circled each other, throwing decoys and fakes, nobody committing yet. "I'm fine with the arraignment. I was awake because I finally broke a coded message my mom left me." She threw a low shoulder, straight to his waist. He didn't react in time and he went down. This time, she helped him to his feet. "She definitely busted Carey Maggs."

"A little late now that we closed the case, but congrats."

Heat shook her arms to keep limber. "Bart, when I asked

you to check Maggs out, didn't you send me an e-mail clearing him?" He must have thought she had her guard down. He suddenly dropped to his seat and made a leg sweep toward the backs of her knees. But Nikki jumped his move like a double-Dutch, landed on her feet, then danced in place, letting him haul himself up this time.

"Can't believe I just whiffed." He got on his feet, and shook his head at getting skunked.

"Didn't you say Maggs was clean?"

He forearmed some sweat off his brow. "Database doesn't catch everything."

"Guess not," she said. He tried to shoulder-tackle her at the waist, but she rolled with it and landed on top of him. She hopped to her feet. While he bounced to his, she said, "Got a question for you about the helipad, the other night."

"Heat, are we here to spar or talk?"

"How did you know to get there first?"

"I told you, Yardley Bell told me." He moved for her right side. She expected a fake, but he committed and clotheslined her down.

She said, "Rook said he never told her."

"How else would I know?"

"Hinesburg, maybe?" She got to her feet, watching him closely.

"Hinesburg? Why would I be talking with Hinesburg?" They came at each other at the same time, locking up their arms. Standing at a stalemate. They broke apart and danced a circle sideways, facing each other.

"Weird thing," said Heat. "When we searched

Hinesburg's stuff, we found her backup gun. At home."

He side-danced some more. "So she had another. What the hell is this?"

"And my friend, the ME, caught up with me over the weekend. She found trace metals and powder burns on Hinesburg's entry wound."

"What can I say? My cannon barks." He made a move for her, but pulled back when she got ready to counter. Then, when she let down, he rolled her across his hip onto the mat. He put out a hand and pulled her up.

"Another thing in that message of my mother's? In addition to nailing Maggs, she also had something interesting to say . . . About the Dragon." She paused. "How much was Carey Maggs paying you?" Callan's fist lashed out so rapidly, it stunned her. With no time to block it, he clocked Nikki's jaw so hard that she flew off the mat and landed sideways on the hardwood. Before Heat could clear her head, he turned and raced to the corner where he'd left his stuff. He reached down into his gym bag and brought out his service weapon.

But Heat had speed he didn't count on. Before Callan could come around with it, she dropped him from behind with a tackle that whipped his face into the cinder blocks just above the floorboards. He twisted around, blood streaming from his nose, and locked her head between his knees. She felt his arm coming down toward her with the gun. She reached up, flailing blindly, caught hold of his wrist, then kicked hard onto the floor with her heels and kipped her body up. Her momentum carried her feet in an arc up and over her head so that her kneecaps came down, pile-driving his torso. He cried out and his leglock slackened. Nikki sprung to all fours and flipped him over facedown, her one hand still clamped onto his right wrist to hold the gun up and away.

The man was strong and struggled hard against her grip, but Heat held fast. At last Nikki felt him start to give in. But then, in a sudden move, Callan thrust his head upward. The back of his skull smacked her sharply on the chin. Her head rang and her vision darkened at the edges. Then she blacked out.

It couldn't have been for more than a second or two, but when her brain cleared and she jumped to her feet, Callan was on his, too, bringing the Sig Elite up on her.

She braced herself for the shot, but he hesitated. "I didn't want this," he said. It sounded like an appeal. "When you accidentally ended up at the heart of this thing, I kept steering you away. And the deeper you dug, I tried to steer you away again and again." Callan swiped the flow of blood from his nose with the back of a wrist while his other held the gun steady. "Nikki, I cared about you. I did everything I could . . . But now I have to kill you."

"You don't." But they both knew he did. She measured distance. Close but risky. To Heat, the muzzle of the pistol looked as wide as a tunnel.

"Don't even," he said.

"At least tell me why." She looked into his eyes and saw conflict. Even sadness. So she held the gaze and made an appeal of her own. She used his first name. "Bart, if there was ever anything between us, at least let me go to my grave knowing why." Nikki could see him considering. "Bart, please? I know who. Don't I deserve a why?"

He wristed his nosebleed again, thinking about it. His eye went to the door. Then back to her. "You figured it out already. The bioterror plot funded by Maggs."

"He paid you?"

"Yes."

"And Tyler Wynn? How did Maggs turn him?"

"I turned him. He was ripe. Classic profile. An obsolete agent with expensive needs."

"But why Wynn?"

"European recruiting. After Ari Weiss became a problem, he did a search for a biochemist with workable morals."

"Tyler found Vaja?" Callan didn't answer her. Didn't need to. "And that's why this plot went to sleep for eleven years? Just to find one biochemist?"

"Not just. Maggs also needed to set up his pharma company. Then get the government contract. Distribution capability. That took time. Years. The promise of a couple billion buys a lot of patience."

A motorbike *ying-ying*ed on the street and it spooked him. Before he changed his mind, Heat fired another question. "Why kill Nicole Bernardin?"

"Vaja lit up her radar when he started making trips to Russia recently to get the smallpox strain. That's what we were waiting for. The last piece of the puzzle. Getting the virus so he could brew it and weaponize it. Nicole got too good at her job, and . . ." He let it hang there. The sentence carried deadly implications for Nikki.

Callan didn't seem eager for the next step, either. "Bart," Nikki said, personalizing again. Trying to sound sensible instead of pleading. "Have you thought this through? If you kill me, you still have to run. You can also choose to *not* kill me and still run."

He shook his head. "Not in the cards."

"Or you could cut a deal. Turn evidence on Maggs. Come on, we do it for perps all the time. You've done it, I've done—"

Heat thought the loud bang was the gunshot, but it was the metal door slamming open against the gym wall. Nikki turned and saw Yardley Bell holding a pistol. Callan spun toward Bell with his Sig Elite. Nikki lunged for him, clamped a hand around his gun wrist, and pointed the weapon to the ceiling. The pistol shot thundered and paint flurried down on them as Heat jerked his left arm behind his back until she heard a nauseating gristle snap inside his shoulder. Callan's scream echoed through the gym, and his Sig Elite clattered onto the floor.

Nikki dropped him on his face and put a knee in his back as Agent Bell rushed over to cuff him.

Heat turned to her and said, "You're late."

Nikki Heat and Yardley Bell stood together on the sidewalk outside the gym while the paramedics in the back of the ambulance braced Callan's dislocated shoulder and cleaned the blood off his nose and chin. Heat said, "Think he'll give up Maggs for a deal?"

"He's already laying track." Bell studied Nikki. "You

don't mind hanging it out there, do you?" asked Bell.

"I had to. My mother's note only said she suspected Callan was the Dragon, but couldn't prove it. I wanted to smoke him out and see how he reacted."

"And?" They both chuckled at that. Then Bell said, "I always had concerns Callan might be dirty. All the way back when he was FBI and running your mother's case, but they were too flimsy to justify, and I was just a rookie."

Heat remembered Algernon Barrett telling her how he eavesdropped through the peephole on her mother and the lady who looked like a cop, and now she figured that must have been Bell. "Nice of you to tell me, Agent."

"You mean like you told me about your mother's code, Detective?"

Nikki had to give her that and said, "Fair enough."

Bell continued, "After Nicole Bernardin got killed on Callan's watch, I called in a chit with the director to send me up here to collaborate on the case. But really, it was so I could get inside and stay close to him."

"Callan thought you were there to Bigfoot him."

"And you thought I was the Dragon. Or at least the mole. Come on, you did." And when Nikki didn't answer, she said, "Or maybe you just hoped I was."

Nikki smiled. "Let's say that I consider all options viable until proven otherwise."

Callan cried out as the EMT tried to maneuver his arm into a brace, and both women turned to watch. Bell said, "What put you onto him?"

"You know how it goes, things accumulate. Initially, I

suppose, it was his interference in my case. Like you—no offense—Callan was very disruptive. But the major giveaway for me was the helipad. All the inconsistencies. And Hinesburg, shot in the temple like that."

"Close range."

Heat looked again in the ambulance. "Sharon probably thought he was going to rescue her. But she was working for him and he had to shut her mouth."

"You do know he wanted you."

"You mean to join the team so he could keep me on a leash?"

"Come on, Heat, I saw the way he looked at you. You didn't pick up on it?"

Nikki had done enough interrogations to smell bait being cast in the pond. She played it down. "I never bought it. I mean, none of what he said ever really felt romantic."

Yardley said, "Maybe you just weren't receptive."

Heat paused then looked Rook's ex in the eyes. "Count on it."

Rook unlocked the door to Heat's apartment and dropped his carry-on by the umbrella stand. And he waited. "Hello? Back from the coast. No greeting?"

"In here," she called.

He draped his jacket on a chair back and made his way to the living room, where he found Nikki reclining on the floor atop a tropical-patterned beach blanket. She held a rum punch in one hand, and in the other a copy of *Sizzling*

Sixteen. "So, this what you had in mind?"

"Sort of." He sat on the blanket beside her. "You're naked."

"As can be."

"I see." He looked around the room. "Just what kind of island is this?"

"Fantasy."

She set the drink and book down and reached her arms out to him. Rook got on his knees, hovering over her, and they kissed softly. He lowered himself to her and she drew him close, feeling his weight drape over her skin, the warmth of their bodies melting them into each other, even through his clothes. Soon the heat of their connection filled them with an urgency that grew into a powerful need. They teased and touched each other, and they joined each other deeply. The release from responsibility, the closeness of their bodies, and the hunger each brought to that moment cast them aswirl, into the heart-pounding, frenzied dimension created by their passion.

Later, enfolded in a lazy tangle of limbs in her bed, they dozed, skin to soul. Nikki's fingers caressed his two-day beard, and her breast rose and fell in rhythm with his placid breathing. Her cell phone double-pulsed and she dutifully checked the text, then put the phone back on the nightstand.

Without opening his eyes, Rook said, "Please, not another murder."

"Worse. Yardley Bell wants to have lunch tomorrow."

He blinked open. "You going to go?"

"I don't need a new best friend."

"You should go."

"I don't like her."

"You don't know her."

"I know all I want," said Heat. "And I know what I like."

"So do I."

"Show me."

And he did.

RICHARD CASTLE is the author of numerous bestsellers, including the critically acclaimed Derrick Storm series. His first novel, *In a Hail of Bullets,* published while he was still in college, received the Nom DePlume Society's prestigious Tom Straw Award for Mystery Literature. Castle currently lives in Manhattan with his daughter and mother, both of whom infuse his life with humor and inspiration.

ALSO AVAILABLE FROM TITAN BOOKS

MURDOCH MYSTERIES

BY MAUREEN JENNINGS

Except the Dying
Under the Dragon's Tail
Poor Tom Is Cold
Let Loose the Dogs
Night's Child
Vices of My Blood
A Journeyman to Grief